By JOEL SKELTON

Dress Up
Jolly Old St. Barts
Aunt Dee Dee's Holiday Check

BENEATH THE PALISADE
Beneath the Palisade: Reliance
Beneath the Palisade: Courage
Beneath the Palisade: Justice

Published by DREAMSPINNER PRESS
http://www.dreamspinnerpress.com

BENEATH THE PALISADE

# Justice

**Joel Skelton**

Published by
DREAMSPINNER PRESS

5032 Capital Circle SW, Suite 2, PMB# 279, Tallahassee, FL 32305-7886 USA

http://www.dreamspinnerpress.com/
This is a work of fiction. Names, characters, places, and incidents either are the product of author imagination or are used fictitiously, and any resemblance to actual persons, living or dead, business establishments, events, or locales is entirely coincidental.



ISBN: 978-1-63216-843-6
Digital ISBN: 978-1-63216-844-3
Library of Congress Control Number: 2014922889
First Edition April 2015

Printed in the United States of America
∞
This paper meets the requirements of
ANSI/NISO Z39.48-1992 (Permanence of Paper).

This story is dedicated to straight women, men, and children everywhere who have helped, and continue to help their gay brothers and sisters in the quest for equality. Many of you have worked tirelessly in your church, your communities, and even within your families and for your efforts, I am forever grateful.

# Acknowledgment

Thank you to Ann Hinnenkamp, Carol Moss, and Jennifer Hutchins for taking the time out of their busy schedules to beta read this manuscript. Their comments and suggestions were invaluable, and this story has benefited greatly from their input. Although not appropriate for this story, thanks to Kristopher Krentz for sharing his considerable knowledge regarding Cretaceous-Paleogene extinction events.

# CHAPTER One

OWEN GRADY stood on the pedals of his mountain bike and coasted along the shoulder of busy County Road 3. Twenty miles from home, his butt ached from the longest ride of the season. He had pushed hard, and his legs tingled from the effort. The weather, iffy at the start of the week, had turned in his favor. It was a beautiful morning for bird-watching.

Passing clusters of trillium, he left the shoulder and zoomed down the ditch onto a dirt snowmobile trail. A stream, lively from the spring melt, bubbled alongside, and the air, noticeably cooler in the forest, refreshed his warmed body. He pumped his way up a sharp incline and onto a sun-drenched meadow. April rains combined with early May warmth to produce a wildflower explosion. Bees buzzed, and butterflies danced as he peddled.

*Whoa!* His pulse raced as he applied the brakes, coming to a stop near a fallen birch. He hopped off and stared into the trees. *No way... a dickcissel? Impossible*!

After swatting a hornet from his face, he removed his water bottle from its holder and took a healthy swig. He cocked his head to one side and listened intently. A split second later he was treated to the distinctive, incessant song from the sparrow-like male of the *Spiza americana*—the dickcissel. A common inhabitant of the Midwestern plains, a dickcissel this far north, away from its preferred breeding ground, the grasslands, caught him by surprise. Although he was confident of his ability to identify this bird by its call, if he got lucky, he'd have a visual sighting before the end of the day.

He released the bungee cord securing his pack to the back rack, removed his binoculars, tossed the strap around his neck, and fished out his birding journal. He opened the small notebook, thumbed to a new page, and wrote *June 4th, followed by—male dickcissel—Trail off County Road 3, and finally—Happy Birthday Owen!!*

He took a moment to visually mark his location. Satisfied he would be able to find it on his return, he wheeled his bike to a clump of sumac and laid it on its side. Just to be safe, he strolled past from both directions to ensure it was properly hidden. *Perfect.* He stashed the bottled water in his pack and headed down the trail.

He'd been walking, blissfully content, for only a few minutes when the sound of tires on gravel caught him by surprise.

*What the hell?*

The slap back to civilization was jarring. Entering a clearing, he was disappointed by the sight of a small parking lot. And then it dawned on him—*ah, this must be the infamous Connor's Point.*

Connor's Point, a sight for keg parties several years earlier, had lost its appeal when, shortly after beginning his senior year at Jefferson High, popular and extremely drunk Kenneth Milton had been killed when he drove his truck into a ravine after partying all night. The town was devastated by the tragic loss, and local law enforcement began making it a regular stop on their patrol.

Owen spotted a black SUV through the trees. He focused on the path ahead until he passed it. This remote entrance to the park was so out of the way, the majority of the visitors to the area didn't know it existed. Most likely anyone here was doing what he was doing, enjoying one of the most stunning spots on the North Shore. Huge, stately pines created a canopy of green overhead. Lush ferns framed the spongy path—he was walking over decades of fallen needles. Humbled by the surrounding beauty, he barely missed stepping on a mound of bear scat.

He continued in this almost trancelike state until he was halted by a noisy woodpecker. Once he identified the direction of the sound, he moved with stealthy grace toward the chipping. He hiked up a small slope and spotted a diligent yellow-shafted flicker carving out a new home high overhead. *Look at you. Aren't you a handsome one.* He made a note to enter the sighting later in his journal.

His fascination with the bird was terminated by the sound of a snapped branch. He spun around, more out of curiosity than fear, and stared down the trail in an attempt to identify the source. Nothing. Looking deeper into the woods, he hoped to see a deer or perhaps a bear, but after watching for several minutes, he gave up.

Inhaling a hefty breath of rich, forest air, he continued until another, much louder snap stopped him in his tracks. The invasion into his privacy frustrated him. It silenced the flicker. He canvassed the woods in the direction of the noise, the uncertainty making him anxious. Seconds ticked by until, to his relief, a man appeared from around the bend. He stopped just shy of where Owen had first heard the woodpecker. For a second, he confused him for Simon Pollard, one of his best friends from college, but quickly realized his mistake.

Frustrated, he looked around for a diversion to occupy his attention until the hiker passed by. He preferred not to be followed, but had he used the park entrance closer to home, no doubt it would have been much busier.

He surveyed the forest floor and was delighted to discover one of his favorites—Indian pipe. Surreal due to their lack of chlorophyll, the white, plastic-like pipes sprouting from the base of a rotting tree never failed to delight him. He squatted down for a closer look and at the same time, glanced down the trail.

*Why isn't he passing me?*

The intruder appeared to be watching him. Annoyed, Owen stood up, this time opting to turn and face the man.

*What's your deal, buddy?*

Smiling, the dude slowly advanced. He thought about returning the smile but decided against it. As he was becoming more pissed off by the second, a smile at this point would take considerable effort. And if at all possible, he wanted to avoid conversation. This was prime birding time. As midday approached, many of the species would become inactive, and the chances of spotting them more difficult as they kept to their perch.

When the man had walked to within fifty feet, he stopped. Unsure of how to react, Owen was forced to turn away. More intimidating, the guy, who appeared to be close to his own age, was handsome. Extremely—in a way that couldn't be ignored. Tall and broad shouldered, the hiker had jet black hair and dark eyes. He was wearing shorts, and Owen had no problem seeing the fine dusting of dark fuzz on his legs and arms. The face, even from a distance, had just the right amount of chisel to get the juices flowing. Braced for a confrontation, Owen looked back. When he did, the guy flashed a wicked grin and then brought his hand down to his crotch and began massaging himself.

Stunned, Owen once again turned away. His mind raced. His heart pounded against his chest. Nothing like this had ever happened to him before. He'd heard about men meeting up in remote locations for casual sex, but to actually be involved in something this crazy was a first.

Staring into the woods, he was surprised to discover he was becoming aroused. There was nothing he could do to stop it. His brain told him to run. At the same time, his body expressed an undeniable interest. A whistle caused him to turn. He watched, incredulous, as the hiker lowered his zipper and inserted his hand into his shorts.

Before he could wrap his mind around what was happening, the man turned and gestured several times with his head toward a spot off the trail, as if to indicate he should follow.

Inspired by one of the finest butts he had seen in a very long time, Owen reached down and touched himself. When the man looked over his shoulder to confirm he was being followed, Owen quickly removed his hand and shoved it deep into his pocket, embarrassed he'd been caught in the act.

*I can't believe I just did that. This is crazy.*

Inexplicably, he was unable to resist the temptation to follow. Absolutely unsure of what to expect, he timidly advanced. At the same time, he engaged in a wild debate as to whether he should continue. The not-so-subtle seduction was steadily gaining ground over his trepidation. *That's one fine ass.* Not to mention the combination of a sexy, casual swagger and bulging calves. He felt helpless to ignore the strong, pulsating dispatches his body was sending.

*Nobody's around. The woods aren't going to tell anyone.*

Confident he could abort at any time, he walked toward the spot where the man had exited the trail. The host of this impromptu adventure had moved a dozen or more feet into the forest by the time he arrived. Peering through the branches, the guy gestured for him to keep coming, and then stepped behind a cluster of dogwood.

Astonished by the absurdity of it all, Owen followed. When he came around the brush, he discovered the hiker posed with his back against the trunk of a tree. "Wow," he said under his breath.

"Hey," the guy greeted with a tempting smirk.

"Hey," Owen answered with a nervous chuckle. "Beautiful day," he tacked on and then wished he hadn't, because it sounded so out of place.

"Sure is. And it just got a whole lot more beautiful, stud. You're one hot surprise. I sure as hell have to say that."

The compliment was as much encouraging as unsettling. Owen took a few more steps and closed the gap between them.

"You from around here?" the good-looking guy asked, while either adjusting himself or taking inventory.

"Yep," Owen answered, unable to resist a glance at the man's crotch. The zipper of his khaki shorts was down, and the outline of his impressive hard-on answered many questions. "I… I—" Momentarily distracted, he blinked and finished. "—came here this morning to bird-watch."

Acknowledging his obvious interest, the man shoved his hands behind his back, pushed his waist out from the tree, and gave his lips an alluring circle with his tongue.

This was it. It was clearly his move again. Trembling, he stepped to within a couple of feet of the stranger. A gust of wind rustled the leaves high above. Owen's eyes darted up, and when he brought his focus down to the attractive face staring back, he was clobbered by reality. He was making a mistake. Probably not a big one, but it didn't matter. Suddenly, nothing about where this encounter was headed felt okay.

"I'm sorry," Owen admitted, "I'm just not comfortable doing this here… in the woods."

"All you need to do," the guy said as he grasped his dick through his shorts, "is get down on those knees of yours, and I guarantee, those pesky little worries of yours will be a million miles away in no time."

During this last exchange, the expression on the man's face changed radically. The once playful, teasing smile was gone. His dark inviting eyes now seemed to penetrate right through Owen.

"Maybe we could meet in town for a drink—"

The man lunged at him before he could finish. Startled, Owen dropped his pack. Before he knew what was happening, his right hand was forced behind his back, and his head slammed face-first into the tree trunk. His knees buckled, but the man pressed his powerful body against his shoulders and back and prevented him from going down. Pain radiated from his forehead all the way down to his chin. He was sure his skin had been torn by the rough surface of the tree.

"An uppity pretty boy?" His attacker hissed into his ear with breath both warm and sour. "Are you too good for me?"

Gasping, Owen blinked in an attempt to clear his vision. He felt the man's hard dick rub seductively across his butt. His cheek and left eye throbbed against the bark. He knew he had to make a move. Summoning all his energy, he twisted his body and surged forward, using his head to ram his assailant in the stomach, pushing them both several feet away from the tree. His effort was rewarded with a painful punch to his side and a debilitating knee to the crotch, which drove him to his knees. Owen clutched himself between his legs for protection, and the man kicked him several times in the thigh—hard. "Please stop," he pleaded.

"You know what you are? You're a fuckin' prick tease."

Owen was shoved all the way to the ground, and in the process, had his mouth filled with a hefty portion of the forest floor. Sputtering, he shuddered when a tongue licked behind his ear before journeying down his neck. A knee kept him pinned. "What's your name? Tell me," the man ordered, using his free hand to hold his face down.

"Owen," he cried. It was clear he was physically no match for this monster. "Please stop. You're hurting me." Fear and pain battled for attention. What was happening? Was he about to be raped?

"I'm hurting *you*? You hurt me, *Owen*. You did."

The attacker sat down on the small of his back. The hand forcing his face into the ground relaxed. He heard a clanking sound. Seconds later, his hands were brought together behind him. He whimpered as handcuffs were snapped into place.

Scared into silence, he listened as the labored breathing behind his head slowed. "You have to be punished. You get that, right?" the man snarled.

Something shiny flashed in front of his eyes. *No!* Fearing his throat was about to be cut, he made another attempt to free himself. Anchoring the toes of his boots in the ground, he heaved his body up in an endeavor to buck the enemy off him. He felt the weight momentarily ease, but before he could scramble out from under, what felt like a ton of rock came crashing back down, forcing the wind out of him.

"Nice try, faggot. You're fucked. Here's why."

The shiny thing reappeared in Owen's line of vision. This time he was able to recognize the shape. It wasn't a knife. It was a badge.

"You *will* be punished. Punished for leading me on, but I'll have to spin it a little differently back at the station. I'll come up with something by the time we get there. Didn't see that one coming, eh prick tease?"

Owen began to sob.

"Who's going to believe who, I wonder? Such a shame too. We could have had so much fun out here. Anyway—" The man grabbed him by the arm and jerked him to his knees. "—stand up, asshole."

Shaking, he stumbled to his feet.

Out of the corner of his eye, Owen watched the man bend down, pick up his pack, and throw it over his shoulder. "Let's go, *birdy*. Hey, that was a good one, don't you think? Birdy? I'm Officer Daniels by the way. Officer Luke Daniels."

BRENT BURNS walked out of his freshly painted office carrying a stack of boxes he'd just unpacked. Still apprehensive about his color choice, he looked back for about the hundredth time to confirm that he'd made the right selection. He'd agonized for days over the darker, more dramatic Mocha Mayhem before eventually choosing the lighter Lemon Meringue.

*Screw it. I like it.*

He returned from the dumpster and he joined his law partner, Harper Callahan, and the cofounder of the Men's Center, Alex Stevens, in the newly remodeled conference room that had recently received a fresh coat of September's Mist. Aqua Passion was Brent's choice, but he was overruled when Harper commented that it would feel like he was sitting inside a rubber glove.

"What's up?" Brent asked, taking a seat.

"I know how busy everyone is, so I won't take up much of your time," Harper promised. "Ian called this morning to let me know he finally had to give our perpetually inebriated resort manager the boot. Apparently the dude came in smelling like a vodka stinger, and Ian, who you both know is a good and forgiving soul, up to a point, clearly had reached the point of no return."

"I know what's coming." Alex looked to Brent.

"I know you do." Brent resented how connected Alex and Harper were and then hated himself for it. *Shithead.* "I'm not receiving on as many bars as you."

Next to Ian, his husband, nobody knew Harper as well as Alex. The three men had lived together for over a year, and nothing comes close to offering insight into a person's personality like cohabitation.

"Most times I wish I couldn't read him. My life would be so much simpler," Alex confided with a heartfelt nod and looked across the table at Harper.

"You'll think differently when you eventually mature," Harper shot back.

"Whoa." Brent pushed his chair back a few inches from the table. "Ouch."

"There's the pain and suffering too." Alex sighed and wiped an imaginary tear from his face. "It's unbearable most days."

"Always with the drama. Here's the situation," Harper resumed, apparently finished jesting. "Ian needs our help. Actually, strike that. He needs *your* help.

"I got mornings." Alex, minus the attitude, playfully slapped the table with his palm.

Clueless, Brent experienced an urgent need to connect. "Anything. I'll take anything. Throw me the tiniest nugget, and by God I'm there. I'll be right with you. Play fair. This has something to do with the resort and the drunk dude getting the axe…." And then he had it. He and Alex were being asked to act as replacement staff until something more permanent could be arranged. Brent knew when he signed on to partner with Harper at the Men's Center's new law firm that the resort would be part of the deal. He was surprised to find his involvement with it would start so soon. "I guess I could do afternoons."

The Palisade Beach Resort, successful right from the start, enabled Harper, along with Alex, to open up the Men's Center after Alex was discovered using a convenience store to meet guys to satisfy his sexual needs. Conceived to provide a variety of services to the entire LGBT community, the addition of a law office within the Center had been a dream of Harper's from the beginning.

"Thanks." Harper sipped his coffee and then added, "Ian's so busy this time of year with maintaining the grounds and coordinating all the weddings and special events, there's not enough hours in his day to wedge the office in too."

"What are you doing tonight?" Alex asked Brent.

"Tonight? Oh, tonight's kind of special. I'm going to stop on the way home and pick up a frozen pizza to enjoy while I continue to unpack my worldly possessions into my luxurious five-hundred-and-fifty-square-foot apartment." Brent looked away and bit his lip as he waited for one or both of the smartasses at the table to respond.

"Hmm…." Alex sat up in his chair. "Worldly possessions. Would you be talking about the impressive, black vibrating cock you've nicknamed *Denzel*?"

"Denzel? Ha." Harper threw his head back and roared.

"Bitch," Brent shot back.

"Feel like cooking?" Alex asked Harper after he stopped laughing.

"Sure. A nice pasta perhaps?"

"Perfect." Alex reached over and gave Brent's shoulder a slap. "Let's meet up at the office tonight, and I'll show you the ropes. Denzel could probably use a break."

Feeling defensive, Brent lamented, "There was no need for Denzel when I had—"

"Okeydokey." Harper leapt out of his chair. "Put together a schedule for the next, oh, you'd better make it two weeks. If you run into any conflicts you can't work out, let me know, and I'll cover for you. Seriously, I knew I could count on—"

Harper was interrupted by the phone console buzzing in the middle of the table.

"I'll get that." Brent moved to accept the call but was stopped by Harper.

"Sit. We have a receptionist, remember?" Leaning back in his chair, Harper tilted his head toward the open door. "Check this out."

From down the hall, a few paces away in the reception area, came a loud gasp and the sound of something hitting the floor. "Sugar shoot. I knew I was going to spill that," an exasperated voice remarked.

"Oatmeal bowl," Harper enlightened them with a knowing nod. "She's had a bowl of oatmeal at her desk every morning since she started."

While the phone continued to ring, they heard papers being shuffled and "Crap! Which button did he say? Oh my… crap, *crap*."

The frantic grunts and various other noises caused the audience in the conference room to abandon all form of eye contact.

"Gosh a Moses. I think it's this one."

Hoping the trauma surrounding the incoming call had finally ended, Brent inhaled cautiously.

"Hello, you've reached the law offices of… Callahan… crap, Burns and Callahan," the flustered, raspy receptionist announced. A herd of elephants could have lazily strolled by before she added with a rush, "A very pleasant good morning. My name is Fern. Fern Smuckler. How may I help you?"

Harper glanced wildly back and forth between Alex and Brent, his eyes begging them to appreciate how funny this was.

"Hello? Is anyone there?" she inquired with palpable despair. Fern made two more attempts to identify the caller before the technology-challenged assistant unleashed one last, large sigh, followed by what certainly must be her catchphrase: "Crap."

The first to crumble, Brent smacked his hand to his lips in a hopeless attempt to block a laugh.

"Oh shit," Harper barely eked out while he closed the door.

"We have to work on delivery. She sucks," Brent added between snorts once the door was closed.

"Yeah, that's not good," Alex agreed, wiping his eyes with his shirt sleeve.

"I'm going to create some scripts for her," Harper explained while still struggling to compose himself. "But crap, I just haven't had the time."

The inclusion of "crap" was all it took to launch another round of hysteria.

"So, I have to ask." Brent leaned back in his chair. "Why her? Were the pickings really *that* slim?" Harper had hired Fern the week before Brent arrived.

"Just you wait, smarty. She worked at the Duluth courthouse in the filing department for over thirty years. Fern Smuckler knows how to create every pleading imaginable. You can't find that kind of experience anywhere these days."

Brent shared a skeptical glance with Alex, which prompted Harper to add, "Besides, she can type the hairs right off your fanny."

"Excuse me?" Brent asked feigning disbelief after a moment of silence. "Type the hairs right off my fanny? That's a tad… *inappropriate*, don't you think?" He looked at Alex for confirmation.

Alex sat up in his chair. "I've *never* brought up how hairy your ass is to anyone. Pinky swear." He leaned over and offered his finger.

"I do *not* have a hairy ass," Brent voiced in exasperation, confident he had a fine, smooth, sculpted ass, which he took great pride in and which had been complimented many times over. The fact that his ass was the subject of slander troubled him greatly.

"I can see I've touched upon a sensitive subject." Harper displayed an ample supply of sincerity before adding, "My apologies. There's absolutely nothing wrong with a hairy, manly ass."

The phone in the center of the conference table buzzed again. Before another round of hysterics launched, it was answered.

"I don't have a *hairy ass.*" Defiant to the end, Brent shot his best "kill" look to Alex, who continued to offer up his little finger.

A soft knocking brought their exchange to a halt. Harper got up from his chair and opened the door. "Oh… hi, Fern."

Brent bit his lip. Fern, a spinsterish woman in her sixties, stood obediently in the hallway. Even though it was the holier-than-thou Harper Callahan who had called their attention to Fern's unpolished phone skills, Brent, as he did so often, instinctively felt guilty at the sight of her innocent, earnest face peering into the room. A room filled with jackals. *I'm a shithead!*

"I'm terribly sorry to interrupt your meeting, Mr. Callahan," she whispered. "A Theodore Engdahl is on the phone for you."

"Theo?" Alex asked surprised.

As much as he tried to not go there, the very mention of Theo's name unleashed a wave of sadness that Brent valiantly fought to quash.

Attractive in an athletic way that sneaks up on you, the blond, mop-haired Theo had swept Alex off his feet when Theo came to the Center for help coming to terms with his sexuality. Working with one of the Center's counselors, Theo soon accepted himself as a gay man, opening the door for his romance with Alex.

Before Alex had Theo, the man of Alex's dreams had been Brent. Boyishly handsome, Alex had legs that wouldn't quit, and hands down it was the best sex Brent had ever experienced. And there had been no shortage of sex prior to Alex. They shared a casual, intimate relationship. Brent would come up to the resort for the weekend, or Alex would head down to the Cities. Separated by a two-and-a-half-hour drive, they managed to make it work. But Brent never saw Theo coming, and by the time he had a chance to make a play for Alex, it was too late.

Brent forced himself to smile and look unaffected. In his heart, he knew Theo and Alex were meant for each other, but it still was a tough pill to swallow.

"Thanks, Fern. Call me Harper, and please tell Theo I'll be with him in just a minute."

"Of course, Mr.... Harper."

They watched Fern leave.

"What's Theo calling you about?" Alex appeared surprised.

"Relax, snoopy." Harper patted him on the back as he led them all out the door. "You'll know soon enough."

OWEN GLANCED out the back window of Officer Daniels' SUV as his bike, after being partially dismantled, was crammed into the compartment behind him. In the brief period of time they had been on, the cuffs were starting to irritate his skin.

Overwhelmed by the enormity of his predicament, he struggled to stay composed. Bursts of anger, intermingled with raw emotion, churned his stomach until it ached. This thing, this officer who had lured him into the woods, was frightening. He guessed any attempt to talk his way out, or to reason with this despicable beast would not have a favorable outcome. In the short time they had spent together, he had seen enough to understand his opponent wasn't playing fair. He had an agenda. *Don't provoke this psychopath.* A tremor of fear gnawed at his core. What would it take for someone like this freak to drive him farther into the woods and—*No! Don't go there.* He jumped when the hatch slammed shut.

"Okay. Off to the station," Daniels announced as he climbed into the driver's seat. "How's the temperature back there? Want me to kick up the air?"

Cold, dark eyes peered back from the rearview mirror. Knowing he was being watched, Owen shook his head and stared out the window.

"Suit yourself. It's not far."

As they pulled out of the park, Owen spotted the dickcissel hop from a fallen log up onto the lower branch of a birch tree at the same time his door was automatically locked. He fought back tears.

*What is happening to me? Is this guy really a cop? Why did he attack me?*

He surveyed his surroundings for clues that would indicate this asshole was really law enforcement. With his options limited, verifying it would be a comfort. The cream-colored interior of the car was spotless—probably new. It still smelled new. He caught a glimpse of the dashboard and his fear nudged up several notches. Other than a GPS, which anyone could have, nothing distinguished this vehicle from his next door neighbor's—no special radio, radar, or anything else official-looking. *God, please don't let this nut job be impersonating a cop.* If only this were a bad dream—a ghoulish nightmare. He trembled as reality began to sink in. This could be his last day on earth.

They traveled in silence. Every inch of his body screamed in agony from his altercation back in the woods. Daniels had kicked and punched him hard several times. He could tell he was developing a black eye. It throbbed from its encounter with the tree. At least for now, there were no signs his vision had been compromised.

He was frantic to come up with an escape plan. If this was it, the end, he wasn't going down without a fight. There wasn't much he could do handcuffed in the backseat of a locked car, but he could try to make his move once they stopped. With his hands restrained, his only weapons were his feet, his head, and combined, the force of his entire body. He would have to time it exactly right to be successful.

*Never show your cards.*

Why that phrase chose that moment to surface was a mystery. It was the voice of his grandfather. A thought began to take shape and morph into something he might be able to build on. Strategically, it would be to his benefit not to divulge anything this creep could use to his advantage later.

"Hey, birdy."

He looked up. The beady eyes were back.

"Be honest with me. You wanted my dick didn't you? Before you went all freaky and hurt me. I saw you looking at it. It's an awesome dick. Come on, admit it."

"Yes," Owen answered, hoping he had chosen the safest response.

"One of the best! Thick, long, and this is going to make you crazy."

*Look up and acknowledge this fucker.* Owen forced himself to make eye contact.

"Just between me and you, I've seen a few dicks in my travels, and there have only been a handful—"

Owen closed his eyes until Daniels stopped laughing.

"A handful. Can you believe that? I should write comedy," Daniels bragged.

Attempting to stay calm, Owen stared at the road ahead in hope of coming up with a plan. He needed to eliminate the fearful "what-ifs" flooding his thoughts. It would be a mistake to be caught off guard. Every second mattered.

"Here's what's going to make you as sad as I am right now," Daniels said, looking at him in the mirror. "I *love* plowing this big dick of mine up a tight ass. And birdy, something tells me you're going to regret for the rest of your life not having the opportunity to experience… me—my big, fucking dick."

Repulsed at the thought, Owen leaned forward to ease the pressure of the cuffs that dug into the small of his back.

"It's a fucking shame." Daniels sighed and added, "A great big fucking shame."

More silence. The car slowed as it entered the city limits.

*Maybe he's bringing me to his house so he can tie me up in the basement and torture me.*

He felt a sense of relief when they turned off Main Street, into the police station.

*He's a cop. He's a fucking cop.*

Owen passed that building practically every day on his way to and from work, and had never received a parking or speeding ticket. There weren't more than a few dozen parking meters in town, and he'd never lost a pet. It was inconceivable that his first visit to the station would be under arrest.

*This is better than having your ass split wide open and your throat cut.*

Daniels opened Owen's door and said, "Step out of the car, please."

Humiliated to the point of being ill, he stepped out and stood with his head bowed in shame. Taking him by the forearm, Daniels led him across the lot and through the front entrance.

He spotted a woman and a small boy seated in front of a desk. Neither one of them looked familiar. *Thank God.* An officer was writing as the woman talked in excited bursts. He recognized him from football games at the high school. He always appeared to be in a jovial mood, laughing, and joking with the spectators as they passed through the ticket gate, into the stands.

Daniels brought him through the main area, past the desk, and into the inner sanctum of the station. "Hey, Chief," he greeted another cop who bore a slight resemblance to Owen's uncle, Walter.

"Need any help?" the man asked.

"Nope. I'll tell you about birdy after he's processed and placed in the holding cell."

"I'm running out for a quick bite. I'll be over at the Lip Smacker if you need me. I have my phone."

"Will do. See you in a few."

Owen watched the chief slide a card through the locked door and exit.

"Let's take a walk over to Miss Darlene." Daniels gestured to a young woman. "She'll help us out with your guest registration."

It was obvious by the way Darlene came to life when Daniels stepped up to the counter, he was one of her favorites.

"Howdy there, Luke. I was wondering if I'd see your smiling face around here today."

"Took a drive out to Connor's Point this morning. Haven't been there for a couple of weeks. I wanted to see if there's been any recent party activity, and I came back with this one. Give him the full-meal-deal while I change into my uniform and start on his report."

Daniels stepped behind Owen and unlocked the cuffs. "Give Darlene any trouble and trust me, you'll regret it. Is that understood?"

Devastated, his face on fire, Owen stared at the floor.

"I believe I asked you a question."

Darlene was probably enjoying the show. "Yes," he answered.

"Glad to hear it." Daniels placed the cuffs on the counter. "You have the right to remain silent. Anything you say can and will be used against you in a court of law. You have the right to speak to an attorney and to have an attorney present during any questioning. If you cannot afford an attorney, one will be provided for you at government expense. Do you understand your rights?"

"Yes." Owen was shaking and found it a challenge to stay on his feet.

"Anything you want to say before we make it official?" Daniels hooked his thumb on the waist of his shorts, directly above his zipper. There was no doubt about it, Owen was being teased. Even here, with someone else present.

"I'll take your silence as a no. You're allowed one call. Darlene will help you place it. He's all yours, Dar." Daniels walked to a small office on the right and closed the door.

"Did you have someone you'd like to call?" she asked, holding a phone receiver in her hand. Her voice seemed kind, almost sympathetic.

"No." He was finally able to look up and make eye contact. Who the hell was he going to call, his parents? The less anyone knew about this the better. Thinking Darlene might be a good source for more information, he asked, "How long will I be here?"

"I don't know any of the particulars. You can ask Luke… Officer Daniels when he comes back."

Dazed and feeling totally helpless, he obediently followed directions while he was fingerprinted and photographed. When Darlene finished, she hollered to Daniels, who came out of his office dressed in his uniform. He grabbed Owen by the arm again and walked him down a short hallway to an area containing three empty cells.

"Put your hands way up here on the bars and spread your legs." Daniels pointed to where he wanted Owen's hands.

As instructed, he reached up and grabbed a bar in each hand before spreading his legs apart.

"Almost there, birdy. Back up about six inches and put another six inches between those shoes."

After Owen made the adjustment, Daniel caressed his ass cheeks. He thrust his other hand between Owen's legs. He gasped when he came into contact with his cock and balls.

"Nice," Daniels whispered after a soft moan. "What a fucking shame."

He moved his hands up to Owen's chest, where they continued to explore. Owen winced when Daniels pinched his nipples through his T-shirt.

Panting, Daniels pressed his body against him. Owen closed his eyes, not sure what to expect next. There wasn't a camera in sight to catch this assault. He wanted to vomit.

"You passed," the cop announced with a snort. "Bring your hands down to your side." He opened the door with a key card he extracted from his pockets shoved him inside, and then stepped out and shut the door.

The tiny room was similar to those he had seen on television. It contained a simple cot-like bed, a small sink, and a toilet. All open to anyone who might wander by.

"You'll be here at least overnight. We'll chauffeur you to the courthouse in the morning where you'll be arraigned."

Stunned, Owen felt his lip quiver.

"One of us will be by with dinner later. Any questions?"

There was one very big question he needed answered. Summoning every ounce of courage he could find, he asked, "Is there a way to be released now and return to the courthouse on my own tomorrow?"

"Not that I know of, birdy. Indecent exposure and evading arrest are very serious charges."

To Owen's horror, Daniels cupped his junk through his uniform pants and tugged up and down. "Here's a little something for your dreams tonight, prick tease. Relax and enjoy your stay."

Overwhelmed with emotion, Owen lowered himself onto the bed and buried his head in his hands. *I'm so fucked.*

When Daniels arrived with dinner a few hours later, turkey and gravy over mashed potatoes with a blob of canned green beans, Owen could do no more than look at it. His stomach ached from the tension his arrest had caused.

"Suit yourself, birdy," Daniels sneered when he returned for the tray. "This is no place to be finicky. There's no twenty-four-hour room service or midnight raids on the refrigerator. You might get a donut in the morning if I'm feeling particularly generous. I wouldn't count on it, though."

Owen stretched out on his cot and tried to make sense of what had happened. He quickly determined that he couldn't. Officer Daniels had big problems, and apparently he was the only one who knew this.

As he tried to fall asleep on the hard cot, he caught bits and pieces of a discussion between Daniels and the chief of police, whose coarse voice he recognized from his earlier encounter, prior to being booked. He wanted to scream from his cell when he heard Daniels refer to him as "birdy," over and over. The laughter the name elicited from the men deepened Owen's despair. Sleep never came.

Midmorning, he was placed back in cuffs and transported to the county courthouse. A man who identified himself as the prosecuting attorney handed him the complaint listing the charges brought against him—indecent exposure and evading arrest.

Several others were arraigned before he was asked to stand. The first thing the judge did was confirm if he was in receipt of the complaint, knew the charges against him, and that he understood his rights. He tried to stay in the moment, but his mind raced frantically from one thought to another. It was all happening so fast. A hearing date was set for six weeks out, and he was encouraged to find a lawyer. The judge's final action—he was to be held on $1,000 bail. Owen paid this with a credit card, and Daniels drove him back to the station.

With a smile, Darlene handed him his pack. Daniels then led him out through the front door, where his reassembled bike stood waiting.

"Have a nice ride home, birdy. See you in court," the cop tacked on with a sadistic smirk.

Feeling shamed and dirty, Owen hopped on his bike and sped out of the parking lot. A block from home, tears streamed down his face. Where could he turn for help?

# CHAPTER Two

*WHERE AM I?*

Every inch of his body ached. Owen couldn't tell if his eyes were open or closed. Darkness was all around. What seemed like hours passed before he felt confident he wasn't having a horrible nightmare, or experiencing what it might be like to be in a coma.

Each time he attempted to move his head, he found it impossible. The pounding was like nothing he had ever experienced. His mouth was bone dry.

Bouts of nausea intensified and with them, a renewed sense of fear. What if he lost the contents of his stomach and was unable to breathe. He would surely suffocate. And his body, it was… whacked out of shape. It felt displaced and awkward. Eventually he was able to confirm it was his own arm, the left, that lay limp over his ear. This revelation allowed him to change focus to his right arm, which rested on top of a hiking boot. The rest of the puzzle fell quickly into place.

*Help me.*

He began to cry as he lay helpless on the floor of the living room, sick from an attempt to deaden his pain and suffering by consuming more alcohol than he would typically imbibe in a year. The enormity of his foolish mistake in the woods was too hideous to comprehend without the aid of drink.

He managed to slide his left arm off his head and down onto the floor, where it made contact with an overturned bottle and its spilled contents. In the process, he splattered his face and neck with the pungent liquid. His stomach reacted to the stench by hurling its bitter contents up into his throat. It took enormous concentration to make the bile retreat.

He slowly brought himself up onto his hands and knees, only to be forced down again to stop the room from spinning. Sunshine flooded in from the large picture window. He winced as he crawled slowly across the floor to the stairs. The journey up seemed to take forever, but eventually he made contact with the cold, tile floor of the bathroom. He kept going until his chin hit the side of the toilet. Raising his head slightly higher, and without a second to spare, he surrendered, and released the contents of his stomach into the bowl.

At some point he fell asleep. When he opened his eyes again, he was surprised to see a blue saxophone, one of the many musical instruments that adorned his shower curtain. The side of his face still rested where he last remembered putting it, on the edge of the toilet seat.

Summoning every ounce of strength available, he picked himself up off the floor and plopped onto the seat. Wobbly, he extended his hand to the nearby sink to steady himself.

*I want to die.*

Starting with his stained T-shirt, he removed his clothes. He eased his butt off the stool and yanked down his shorts and boxers at the same time. Naked, he dropped back onto the floor and crawled into the shower. Reaching above his head, he turned on the water. The cold spray made him gasp. Just when he thought he wouldn't be able to withstand the chill, the spray warmed and then rapidly turned hot. Frantic to avoid scalding himself, he reached back up and gave the dial a hard turn. The tepid compromise was tolerable, and Owen felt his body begin to relax. Once the water began to cool again, he forced himself to stand and shut the shower off.

He closed his eyes to help stabilize himself and systematically toweled his body dry. When he reached his face, he winced as the coarse fabric brushed against the bruises. Chancing a glance in the mirror, he confirmed what he had suspected—his left eye was black and the surrounding skin scraped raw all the way to his neck. With hands shaky from his abusive night of drinking, he removed his toothbrush from the shaving mug on the side of the sink. Remembering he had used the last of the toothpaste, he lowered himself onto his knees and searched through a drawer. He eventually located a small, half-empty travel tube he had discarded ages ago. More than the shower, cleansing his mouth went a long way to quell his nausea.

Moving like a zombie, he entered the bedroom and stopped. His mind had gone blank. Seconds passed before he was able to rejoin his earlier train of thought. He stepped to his closet, nabbed a pair of sweat pants off a shelf, and sat on the bed. Bending, he inserted one leg and then the other. Then he stood and hauled them over his hips. For a brief moment, he thought about crawling into bed, but a loud rumbling from his stomach encouraged him to make the effort to reach the kitchen.

He opened a cupboard and stared blankly at its contents. Nothing appealed to him. After eliminating several choices, he opened the refrigerator and took out a plastic bottle and poured himself a tall glass of lemon soda. He spotted half of a loaf of bread on the lower shelf, he took it out, and went back to the cupboard for a jar of peanut butter. Mindlessly he slathered two slices and carried them across the kitchen. What little appetite he had vanished when he plopped onto the bench of the breakfast nook and spotted the documents staring back. In bold print he read, "The State of Minnesota v. Grady, Owen Nathaniel." Below it, in large print, was the word, COMPLAINT.

He shoved it to the side of the table and stared at his food. He knew he had to get something into his stomach. Biting off a small piece of crust, he reached for the glass of soda and quickly washed it down. He repeated these little nibbles until he was interrupted by his phone playing Beethoven's Fifth. He pawed it off the table, identified the caller—his mother— and placed his head in his hands.

*Oh God, I have to answer. She'll be worried.*

Propping his head up with his hand, he accepted the call. "Hello."

"Finally," a familiar, boisterous voice responded. "I've been trying to reach you for days, *birthday boy*."

Owen closed his eyes and held the phone away from his ear while his mother sang one entire round of the traditional celebration song ending with a chipper, "Many mooooore."

He was at a loss for words and fought off the urge to hang up.

"So, I hope you were out having fun. You don't turn twenty-eight every day, you know. Tell me, what did you do? Wait. Hang on. Your dad wants to say something."

Static on the line was soon replaced by the voice of his father. "Happy birthday, son."

"Thanks, Dad."

"Well, come home when you can. Here's your mom back."

"So tell me, did you have a hot date?" his mother asked. "Go out with friends? Owen, you didn't stay home by yourself, did you?"

They were miles apart, but Owen had little trouble envisioning the hopeful bite of her lip, a familiar expression she used in situations such as this. One of her missions since his childhood had been to encourage her son to be more outgoing. It had extended itself into his adult life. It was likely she would never give up hope. *Please not now.*

He needed to end the call. If he didn't, she would mine for details, and he'd be on the phone with her all day. Sitting up in his chair in an attempt to channel another much-needed burst of energy, he announced, "Mom, someone's at the door. I'll have to call you back. I'm super busy right now."

"Okay, brush me off like a breadcrumb even though I brought you into this world. I'll survive. I love you, honey. Happy birthday."

"I love you too, Mom. Bye."

He ended the call. Exhausted, he rested his face on the table. He spent the next several minutes trying to make the throbbing in his head subside. When he felt he'd made progress, he sat up. Loath to have the arrest papers displayed as a reminder of what deep shit he was in, he gathered them into a pile and set a ceramic bowl filled with apples on top. *Go away.*

He needed sleep, but he shuffled into the living room and nabbed a short stack of newspapers off the coffee table. He thought he remembered seeing an ad for a new law office in Two Harbors. *Will anyone believe me?* A whiff of the spilled liquor was all it took to send him stumbling out of the room. The mess he made would have to stay until he had more energy and a steady stomach. With great effort, he climbed the stairs to his bedroom and collapsed face-first onto his bed.

"SORRY I'M late." Brent opened the screen door and reluctantly entered the resort office. He wasn't really sorry he was late, but he couldn't share that with Alex. "I got tied up with some things at the Center." Another untruth. *Shithead.*

Helping out at the resort office seemed like an effortless task until the night before, when Alex had explained his extensive duties and the common inquiries he could expect from guests. Apprehension turned to panic on the drive home from the training session. The intricate reservation system, which, according to Alex, was one of the simplest and best, coupled with the credit card process, made his head spin. He hadn't been this tense since the bar exam. He was sure something unthinkable would occur on his watch, and he would be labeled a putz for life.

"No worries. I'm trying to write an ad for the newspaper. I want to make the job attractive. You know, fun sounding. Even though it's…." Alex laughed. "You know, I used to think it *was* fun. I was so proud of how smoothly I ran this place."

"What do you have so far?" Brent walked behind the large front counter.

Alex read, "Wanted—Office Manager at Popular Resort."

"Sounds right. What comes next?" Brent waited while Alex stared at the computer screen. When nothing was forthcoming, he sidled up to his friend and patted him on the back. "Why don't I take this one on? It will give me something to do while I'm waiting around to give someone directions to the Lip Smacker. Last night I was kind of edgy, so I made s'more kits."

"Dude. Don't make another s'more kit. I'm totally serious. We have enough to last two seasons."

Harper and Ian had come up with the idea the first season. They gave a complimentary s'more kit to each party that checked in. The gift bags were tied up with a ribbon with the resort's business card attached. They were a huge hit. Alex made the comment the night before that if he got bored, he could make a few. Out of nervousness, he burned through the supplies in back until he eventually ran out of crackers. "Once you get going with those," Brent reported with pride, "they're a snap to put together."

"Work on the ad. I have to run home." Alex pocketed the keys to his truck. "Theo and Ian have been on my case for not painting. I promised I'd make the effort. It's not easy. I can't seem to motivate unless I've got a special request or a deadline to meet. So many more important things always come up."

"Yeah, that's usually the way it works." He was glad to hear painting was on his friend's mind. For his birthday last year, Alex gave him an amazing watercolor of a storm barreling off the big lake. He prominently displayed it in his new office at the Center, alongside his law degree. "You're a gifted painter. It's something you have that hardly anyone else has. Nothing's more important than that. Trust me."

"I'd have more time to paint if I didn't have to sit here mornings. Maybe you…." Alex smiled as he reached for the door.

"Nice try, Van Gogh. I'll have the ad done tonight, and then I'll personally drive it over to the paper in the morning. Enough of this team-player bullshit. Oh, wait."

"What?" Alex turned around.

"We were talking about painting, and I can't believe it didn't remind me. Okay, after I ran out of s'more fillings last night, I was looking around."

"Snooping?" Alex accused, shaking his finger."

"Yeah, pretty much. Anyway, I had this idea." Riding a wave of enthusiasm, Brent came around the corner into the room. "This little apartment the office manager usually lives in back here? I'm thinking it's a liability. Not too appealing unless you're eighteen years old and this is your first job. I mean, you would have to find exactly the right person. You… and Petra last year, with you guys, it worked. But for someone just looking for a job, maybe not so much."

Brent smacked his hands together to announce the beginning of his pitch. "So, what would happen if we said good-bye to the apartment and turned the space into…." He couldn't contain his excitement. "What would you think if we turned the space behind the office into a kind of hybrid gift shop—maybe even a gallery—so you would have a place on-site to sell your paintings?" Jazzed by its clear brilliance, he nodded, encouraging Alex to agree. "Not bad, huh?"

"Hmm. I need to think about that one." Alex wore a funny look.

It took a few seconds for its origin to register. *This place holds a special meaning for him, shithead. It was his home for over a year.* "I'm sorry. I didn't mean to—It's a nice space the way it is. You know me, Mr. Sensitivity."

"No. You're right. That was part of the reason I was struggling with the ad. I still think of this as a home for the person who manages the office. I need to move on. We aren't the small, little resort that could any longer. The business has expanded so much."

"Speaking of business, do we have anyone checking in this afternoon?" Brent crossed his fingers behind his back. *Please say no.*

"Let's take a look." Alex strolled to the computer and entered a burst of key strokes. "Oh goody." He threw his arms in the air and waved them back and forth. "The Lingles from Majestic Pines are coming in tonight," he sang out.

"Did you just say *oh goody*? Seriously?" Brent couldn't believe the level of dweeb his friend displayed.

"I *love* the Lingles." Alex clapped his hands together like a child. "They're regulars who stay with us at least once, maybe twice a season. You'll love them too. Bernadette, the wife, is a real trip." Giggling, Alex stepped toward the door. "Last year—this is so funny…."

Brent waited while Alex waved his hand in the air, an apparent attempt to gain some control over his elation.

"Last year," Alex said, laughing and talking at the same time, "Harper was on his morning run and…."

"Alex, you're scaring me. I'm not kidding." Brent folded his arms across his chest, unable to find even the slightest thing funny.

"Harper," Alex continued unfazed, "discovered Bernadette passed out on a bench down by the lake with an empty bottle of pinot grigio at her side." Laughing, he clenched his sides, and continued in bursts. "She'd stuffed her shoes with acorns." Laughs turned into a roar. "Harper discovered them when he tried to help her get herself together." Doubled over, Alex slapped the wall, devastated by the memory.

Brent felt like faking sick. Not only was someone checking in tonight, it was Alex's favorite guests, the Lingles, who probably knew how the place ran better than he did. "I can't wait to meet them." *How'd I get so lucky?* "I'll make sure to say a great big howdy doody to Bernie from you."

"Bernadette. Oh do that," Alex begged when he could finally collect himself. "Tell them I'll stop by and say hi in the morning. If you run into any problems tonight, give me a call. We'll be around. Later."

Brent slumped onto the stool in front of the computer and stared at the screen. "Wanted—Office Manager at Popular Resort," he mumbled out of the corner of his mouth. It was going to be a long night. A long night, alone.

"THE SHOP, the house… it's all yours." Harper looked up from the documents and smiled at the young man seated on the other side of the large mahogany desk. "How's it feel to be rich? Theo? You there?"

Theo had journeyed to a place far, far away. Harper could hear the twenty-three-year-old tap his foot steadily on the Oriental rug that graced his floor. One of two things could be going on here, he thought as he watched Theo squirm in his seat, unable to look anywhere but the floor. Either Theo was still very much affected by the death of his boss, Artie Johnson, who was killed in a car accident two weeks before, or the news that he had inherited a sizeable estate contradicted plans already in place.

"Knock, knock. Anyone home?" When Theo didn't respond, Harper leaned forward and asked, "Something troubling you?"

Theo shifted his athletic young frame from side to side until it became clear he needed to be released from the confines of the chair. He leapt up and began to pace while running his hand through his moppy hair.

Harper sat back and watched with fascination as Theo made several tours of the space between the window and the door. Just as he was about to start another round, he slowed, his shoulders slumped, and finally he stopped. He turned to face Harper and asked in a tone overflowing with frustration, “Does Artie have a relative or close friend we can give all his stuff to?”

*Ah. So there is an issue. This should be good.* “He does. Hang on.” Harper reached into a folder and pulled out a piece of paper. Taking a sip of his diet soda, he read, “Sister—Eunice Johnson. Relationship—None. Comments—Even if she is penniless and dying on the street, she should not get a cent from me. No matter how much she begs.”

Theo began another circle between the desk and the office door.

“He hated her. Did you get that?” Harper asked.

Stopping just shy of the new floor-to-ceiling shelf unit Harper had recently installed for his law books, Theo teetered. Seconds later, wearing the face of defeat, he shuffled back to his chair and collapsed. “I should be grateful.”

He looked up long enough for Harper to catch a glimpse of the bizarre expression on his face. *This kid is absolutely suffering.* He had to do something. “Who says? Your mom? Your dad? It’s okay to be conflicted on this.”

“Does Alex know anything?” Theo asked in a sudden panic.

“Of course not. That would violate attorney-client privilege. True, Alex is like a son to me, which by the way makes you like a son-in-law. But ethically, I’m bound to Artie, my client.” Harper folded his hands on the desk. If he just waited, Theo would eventually reveal the source of his dilemma.

“Can we talk?” Theo appeared on the verge of an emotional breakdown. Although Theo was quiet by nature, Harper typically felt an undercurrent of unbridled energy radiating from him. Not now. It was nowhere in sight.

“Of course.” Harper moved his papers to the side of the desk. “I’ll help you with anything you need. You know that. Spill, buddy. I’m so intrigued by where this is going, I’m about to leak.”

Extending his feet, Theo gripped the arms of his chair. “Okay. But you have to promise not to give me shit, or… or laugh.”

“I….” Harper brought his hand up to cover his mouth. “I *promise* not to laugh.”

Theo sprang from his chair and resumed his well-traveled path around the office. "You'll probably think this is the stupidest thing ever, but I want to…."

"Tap dance across the big red states?" He couldn't resist. The atmosphere was ripe.

"You really suck sometimes, you know that?" Theo displayed the beginnings of a smile.

"What's on your mind?" Harper watched as Theo chanced sitting down for the third time. "We've been here for days now."

"I want to go to college and get my degree. I don't want to spend my life… working at Artie's, or even *owning* Artie's," Theo stated with considerable defiance.

A million retorts begged expression, but the sincerity and determination on Theo's face held him back. Harper pursed his lips and fought the urge to be snarky.

"I'm not sure in what yet…maybe business."

Before Harper could respond, Theo was back up and on the move, a clear signal there was more to follow. An internal struggle of some kind prohibited him from understanding, and accepting, the wonderful thing that had just happened. It was all good.

*Theo, what the hell is it that's got you so worked up?*

"I can't spend a minute more in Artie's shop," Theo blurted out to the room. "I get the creeps there. It's like he's watching me. Makes my skin crawl."

*Ah. So that's what this is all about.*

Disclosing his uneasiness with Artie's spirit obviously came with a price. As painful as it was to watch, Harper knew it was probably best to let Theo struggle through it.

"Everywhere I look," Theo said, punching the air. "I see Artie. I feel Artie. It's like he's right there beside me. Yesterday, I had a simple fucking engine the customer wanted to pick up at the end of the day, and I barely finished it in time. Artie's presence was so strong, I had to step outside the shop to get away. It took everything I had to go back in again. I can't take it anymore. My heart was beating so hard. I thought it was going to explode right out of my chest."

This admission seemed to drain the last of Theo's energy. Seconds ticked away. "I'm so *ashamed* of myself for feeling this way," he finally added in a barely audible voice. "Artie was so *good* to me. I can't help it, Harper. I just can't."

Harper rose from his chair, walked around, nabbed Theo by the arm, and sat him back down. He sat on the edge of his desk, ruffled Theo's hair, and said, "Listen. I can relate to what you're experiencing, and I'm sorry I was so flip with you earlier."

Theo unconsciously scratched his nuts. Harper chose to ignore it. "You have to trust me on this. The will—I've read it over *several* times and not once did I come across the paragraph which details how or what specifically you have to do to honor this inheritance. It's not there. Understand?" Harper paused, hoping Theo would make eye contact with him.

"Yeah."

The simple response sounded insincere. Theo either wasn't listening, or he was still too worked up to see the logic. Harper decided to call him on it. "Don't placate me, Theo. I'll try this again. You have no obligations to Artie or anyone concerning this will. Now for my own benefit, let me ask again, do you understand?"

"Yes. I wasn't…." Theo's face flushed. "I'm sorry."

"Okay. Now that we're on the same page, let me tell you I'm thrilled you're thinking about furthering your education. Even if you never end up with a degree, it's still a wonderful way to discover yourself. Albeit, an expensive way. But something tells me, once you get your feet in the door and get a taste of higher learning, you'll go all the way."

Theo looked up and grinned. *Ah. It appears we're making some headway here*. Harper couldn't stand to see anyone close to him in pain, especially if there was something he could do about it. It would take time, but Theo would sort it all out.

"A college degree is a pretty cool thing to have, but as important," Harper advised, "is what you do with it. I'm curious. Do you have any ideas?"

"Not really. I just know I don't want to stay at Artie's." Theo sat up in his chair, noticeably relieved. "Sorry I'm such a basket case. I freaked when you read the will. And then I felt like an ass for not being grateful."

"Second question." Harper had an idea. "Do you have funds saved up for tuition?" He sat down behind the desk.

"Yeah, but not enough, I'll bet. Living with Mom and Dad for all that time made it easy to save. This last year, I've been splitting the house payment with Alex, so I haven't been able to stash as much away."

"Here's a suggestion to think about. Sell Artie's house. Put the money into an interest bearing savings account. I can talk to my accountant and see if he has any ideas. But I'm thinking something you can draw on for tuition. I haven't seen Artie's house, but I can't imagine it's nicer than the home you guys already have." Harper scribbled a note to place a few calls on Theo's behalf.

"It's nice, but small. An older two story in town. There's no way we'd move from our house. We've worked so hard on it over the last year. It's going to be home for a long time. Maybe forever. So selling Artie's is a great idea."

"I have another thought." Harper rubbed his chin. "It might be a better idea to keep the house as an investment and rent it out. We'll look into that."

Now that he had a few options on the table, Harper could see the wheels turning. Theo was regaining his confidence.

"Here's another consideration." *I'm on a roll.* "I have no idea what the market would be for Artie's shop, but maybe you'll get lucky and a buyer will step up and you'll be able to unload the whole thing with a minimal amount of effort. I made a note to call Tiffany, our realtor friend. Maybe she can point us in the direction of someone reputable who deals with commercial real estate. Sound like a plan?"

"Harper, be honest with me. Do you think I'm an asshole for not wanting Artie's house and shop? I feel guilty even thinking about putting them on the market. Artie worked his butt off his whole life. He'd be so disappointed to find out I don't want his stuff."

This wasn't an easy decision for anyone. But being a realist, Harper saw the opportunities before he became emotionally chained to a set of circumstances. You could spend your whole life going around trying to please others. But why? Get your own ducks in a row and then tackle the other challenges life brings. *Thank you Lolly and Gramps.* Hardly a day passed he didn't say a prayer for having been raised by such sensible people.

"I know you feel guilty, and we'll work on that one later. Here's a thought that may help." Harper placed his hands behind his head and then sat back in his chair. "You're not Artie, so stop worrying about trying to do things like you imagine he would." That pesky, skeptical look Theo sported was holding on for dear life.

Tired of treading on eggs, he couldn't resist having a bit of fun. It was owed him as a reward for his sage advice. "Wait. Tilt your head to the side." He leaned forward in his chair and rested his elbows on the desk, staring intently at Theo.

"What?" Theo looked confused.

"Come on, tilt your head. Start by looking left." Harper pointed left and waved, urging Theo to comply. "Just what I thought," he said after a brief inspection. "Okay, now look to the right." Again, he pointed his finger in the direction he wanted Theo to look.

Once Theo had dutifully performed his required tasks, Harper leaned back and proclaimed with confidence, "Artie had long, curly hairs growing out of his ears. At least for now, you're clean."

The look on Theo's face was worth it. Under the guise of a serious discussion, and fearful of getting slapped down again, Harper had managed to slip in a silly that took Theo by complete surprise.

"Ha. You're so serious. I couldn't help myself. Lighten up, my friend. Artie just made your life a whole lot easier, a whole lot faster." Enjoying his own mindfuck, Harper laughed as he watched Theo stiffen in his seat. "No fair punching an old man," Harper cautioned. "Theo, you can spend time feeling guilty, or move on. Can you honestly sit across from me and say that, if you had come to Artie while he was still around, and you told him you needed to move on because you wanted to go to college, he would have disapproved?"

"No." Theo sat back.

Harper understood how effective the power of his reasoning could be. He was slowly winning the challenge of eliminating Theo's guilt. "And let's say, for shits and giggles, you didn't have the required funds to go to school. If you went to Artie for a loan, do you think he would have given it to you?"

"Yes."

"There you have it. A free ride to the college of your choice, courtesy of Mr. Artie Johnson. You see, Theo, as far as the inheritance is concerned, it's yours to do with however you choose. And like I said before, I'll help you navigate through all the hurdles along the way as best as I can. If you'll let me, I'd really like to help." Leaning forward to take a sip of his soda, he gave Theo a moment to let it all sink in. "So," Harper asked when it felt right to continue, "you've been talking this over with Alex? I bet he's happy for you."

"I haven't shared the school thing with anyone yet. I didn't want to bring it up until I had an idea of how I was going to go about it. Alex knows I'm looking for a change. That's it. I was being selfish, I guess. I didn't want to have to answer a whole bunch of questions I didn't know the answers to." Theo looked away as if disgusted with himself for not being more forthright with his partner. "He doesn't know I'm spooked at Artie's. I can't…."

"Theo, what the hell am I going to do with you?" Harper came to the rescue.

"What'd I do now?" On the verge of total exasperation, Theo sank farther into his chair.

"Damn. Those parents of yours sure heaped a hefty pile of nasty on you. Here's another Harper lesson. Listen to this closely. Your first and most important priority is yourself. I sort of touched on that earlier. You need to do what is best for you. You're a terrific guy. We love you and are so thankful you and Alex found each other. The idea you want to better yourself by going after an education is awesome. I guarantee this will make you a much stronger individual, because you'll have a healthier opinion of yourself. So take the breaks that come your way and stop—" Harper paused for effect. "—second guessing yourself and destroying what is good by letting those evil feelings of guilt beat you down. Do you hear what I'm saying?"

"Yes. You're right. Artie would approve. I know it. So what do I do from here, wait until we hear back from your realtor friend?" Theo sucked half the air in the room into his lungs and blew it out, causing the hair above his eyebrows to flutter. His mood had turned around considerably. The laid-back, friendly expression he wore so effortlessly had returned.

Harper was pleased his efforts had obviously been a success. *Precious moments.*

"Go tell Alex the good news. And remember, it's important to shop early to find the deals on school clothes. Looking your best is just as important as studying." Harper stood and walked around to Theo's side of his desk. "Ain't life fun?"

Theo chuckled. "Yeah. A barrel of laughs." He extended his hand.

"What's this? Come here, you little shit." Harper wrapped him tightly in his arms. "Think of it this way. It's the beginning of Theo, part two. Should be a smash at the box office."

# CHAPTER Three

"THANK YOU for returning my call, Ms. Dingman. Mr. Callahan asked I remind you to bring all your employment records for your meeting with him today. Yes, all of them. We will make copies for our file while you're here. You can take the originals back home with you."

Brent smiled at Fern while he waited for her to finish her call. He had to admit, she'd made great strides over the last week. Gone was the nervous fluster. Her tone was efficient and friendly.

"You know, I'm not sure if they will be of interest to him or not. If it's not too much trouble, bring them along. Mr. Callahan will look them over and decide." Fern looked up and rolled her eyes. Her personality was starting to emerge too. Brent liked what he saw.

"I understand. There is a lot to this. Well, any other questions? Right. Just like it says in our letter, 2:00 p.m." Fern looked hopeful she'd reached the end of the conversation. "Terrific. I'll look forward to seeing you this afternoon."

She hung up and blew a strand of hair away from her eye. "Ms. Dingbat, if you ask me. Crap. I don't think I've ever dealt with such a scatterbrain. It's a wonder the woman can find her way home on her own."

"Is this the new workers' comp case Harper took on last week?" Brent asked while fumbling through the mail.

"Sure is. Now you were asking about the pleadings going to Judge Mallory. You know, my dear boy, I don't think he's specified…."

Fern stopped midsentence. Brent followed her gaze and looked to the door. Through it walked a lanky young man who sported an impressive black eye that even his superhot designer glasses couldn't hide. He carried a manila folder. Despite the bruises and scrapes covering much of his handsome face, Brent recognized great potential. Over the years he had fine-tuned an image of someone he deemed highly fuckable. It was his very own benchmark by which all prospective players were measured. This unknowing contestant easily qualified for the championship round.

"Good afternoon. May I help you?" Fern asked with more than a hint of caution.

Brent pretended to look through a stack of folders. Curiosity kept him from heading back to his office. *Shithead.*

"I was wondering if I could talk to someone about… well, I…." Obviously distressed, the man paused and shifted from one foot to the other.

Intrigued and attracted in a strong way that usually led to arousal, Brent speculated, *bar fight.* Before he could think of anything professional to say, Fern came to the rescue.

"We're a law office. If you enter the building through the main door, you'll find materials on the other services the Center provides," she stated delicately and then asked, "Are you looking for legal assistance?"

"I need an attorney," the man said softly, while his eyes, meeting Brent's for the first time, screamed for help.

Understanding this was his cue, Brent stepped forward, extending his hand. "Hello, I'm Brent Burns. I'm an attorney."

Another panicked expression flashed across the man's face when he looked at Fern. That was enough for Brent to reevaluate his approach.

"Let's do this." Brent gestured over to the area across from the reception desk. "Have a seat, and I'll be back in a minute. We'll go into one of our conference rooms to discuss your matter. Will that work?" *We're making headway with the sensitivity thing.*

"That would be great." Obviously relieved, the man sat.

"Fern, please take a message if someone calls. Say I'll be back to them before the end of the day," he added as he turned to leave.

"Sure thing."

His pulse raced. He couldn't wait to find out what this was all about. "Would you care for a cup of coffee or a soda?" he heard Fern offer as he made a beeline to Harper's office.

"Hey." Brent knocked on his partner's doorframe.

Seated behind his desk, Harper looked up from a stack of documents. "Hey."

"Some guy just walked in all banged up. His face… black eye, cuts… ew. He's a mess." Brent took a few steps inside the office.

"Seriously?" Harper looked mildly interested.

"Yeah." Brent folded his arms across his chest. "He's kind of nervous too. Anyway, I have him waiting out front. I was going to bring him back to the conference room to chat. Care to join us? I know you have a client coming in soon."

Thinking this was one of those times where he needed to be assertive, he suggested, "I can take this if you'd like." Maybe too assertive. "Or, should I have him stop back? You know, make an appointment?" *God, you fucked that up.* Despite being made a partner, Brent couldn't shake the feeling of continually being evaluated. Bordering on paranoia, he scolded himself. *What's he going to do, fire me?*

"No." Harper bolted out of his chair. "Don't have him come back. That's one of the big-city, big-firm practices I think really sucks. I want us to be an open door. I've been meaning to have that discussion with you. Your instinct to bring him back was the right one."

"Part instinct and part I haven't got anything else to fucking do at the moment," Brent joked.

Harper led the way into the reception area. "Hello," he greeted the guy seated on their tastefully upholstered new sofa.

Startled, the man spilled the contents of the folder he was carrying onto the coffee table. Harper's dazzling looks and confident manner caused calamities like that all the time. Brent was used to them. "Hell… hello." Flustered, he bent down, collected his papers, and stood.

"Fern." Harper leaned over her desk. "We'll be in the conference room. Please let me know when my two o'clock arrives.

"Certainly."

"I'm Harper Callahan, the other half of Burns and Callahan. I trust you've met my partner?"

"Yes," the man answered, clutching his folder tight to his chest as he accepted Harper's hand for a shake.

"Care for something to drink?"

"We've covered that," Fern announced as she typed away.

"Of course." Harper winked at Brent. "Your name is…?

"Owen. Owen Grady."

"Owen Grady," Harper repeated, "how did you hear about us?"

"I saw your ad in the paper."

They reached the conference room, and Harper motioned for Owen to step inside. Brent pulled out a chair at the head of the table for Mr. Grady and gestured for him to sit. Harper preferred to have the client seated front and center for two reasons. In most cases, they would feel as if they were getting special treatment, but more importantly it made it easy to focus on what wasn't being said. Facial and body language were as important as language at this early stage—a little bit of strategy Brent remembered from his days as Harper's assistant. Harper closed the door and seated himself across from Brent.

"I have to ask, Owen," Harper said, smiling and upping a notch on the charm meter, "how did you come by the bruises on your face and that impressive black eye? It sure had to hurt."

Owen brought his hand up to his mouth and coughed. "It's part of the reason I'm here. A cop roughed me up."

"A cop?" Harper asked, incredulous. "One of our local guys?"

"Yes."

Brent sat captivated as Owen, in a soft, steady voice, detailed his arrest. His face reddened, and his speech became unsteady as he admitted to being intrigued enough by Daniels to follow him off the path. Confidence returned as he described how the situation turned ugly after he realized his mistake and attempted to disengage.

"Interesting." Harper locked eyes with Brent when Owen came to the end of his story. He recognized the look on his partner's face. Harper was processing. Analyzing, and creating his own mental file, which he would systematically add to as the case marched along.

Looking down at his legal pad, Brent freaked after he realized he hadn't written down a single word.

"Do you have any idea why a police officer would lunge at you like he did?" Harper asked.

Owen responded by shaking his head.

A knock on the door changed the energy in the room. Fern poked her head in. "Harper, your appointment is here."

"Thanks. I'll be right with her." Harper stood and took a step to Owen, extending his hand. "I'm sorry. I have a previously scheduled appointment."

"Oh, no problem." Owen attempted to stand, but Harper placed a hand on his shoulder, indicating he should stay seated.

"Brent, can I see you for a second?" Harper stepped into the hall.

"I'll be right back," Brent told Owen before dutifully closing the door behind him.

"Wow," Harper said. "What do you think of that?"

He wasn't sure what he thought. If what Owen was telling them was true, they had one hell of a case on their hands. Unwilling to expose his uncertainty, he asked, "What do you think?"

"Let's just say I'm skeptical. Do this—go back in there and get all of the background you can from him. Start with the basics, contact information. And then if you can, dig deeper until you can paint a clear picture of this guy. You okay with that?"

"Yeah, sure." Brent noticed the concerned look on Harper's face and added, "No, really. I'm fine."

"Look for holes in the story. They're there. I'm sure of it."

"Right. I understand." Brent wanted to ask Harper what he meant by "holes" but decided to wing it. The moment called for leadership. He would trust his own curiosity to lead him in the right direction.

"Great. We'll connect on this later." Harper turned and headed toward the reception area.

*Wow. Does Harper think he's lying?* Wishing he had more experience in these situations, Brent stepped back inside. "Do you need anything before we continue? Restrooms are right down the hall."

"No, I'm good." Owen had arranged the contents of his folder in front of him.

"What do you have there?" Brent asked, taking his seat.

"My complaint and some notes. Yesterday I wrote as much down as I could remember." Owen slid it over.

"Give me a few minutes to give this a look."

Brent began reading through the complaint. As he moved on to Owen's notes, he was surprised to discover he had already formed a bias—he believed this guy. Harper apparently had his doubts, which Brent trusted were well founded, but until he uncovered something to make him think otherwise, he was going to trust his instincts. The circumstances of the case made him angry. The cop was a monster.

"Wow." Brent turned the last page over before closing the folder. "What's happened to you is really hard to comprehend."

With a hint of a smile, Owen nodded back.

"You live in town?" Brent asked, backing his chair out from the table and crossing his legs.

"Yes. I own a home several blocks from the high school where I teach."

"You teach?" Brent uncrossed his leg and sat up. His heart sank. *You used to teach. There's not a chance in hell, no matter how successful we are at proving your innocence, you'll see the inside of a classroom again in this town.* He was reminded of the studies he'd read in law school. The stigma that permeated the lives of people who were accused of a sex crime. Regardless of being innocent or guilty, it stuck to them like glue. The only recourse was relocation, and even then, with social media on the rise everywhere, the accused wasn't entirely safe. "What do you teach?"

"I'm in the music department."

Brent had to look away. Owen's voice was tainted with gloom. *Does he know his teaching days here are over?* How awful. Everything about this guy seemed on the up and up. He had so much to lose over such a bizarre, evil event. Brent willed himself to look up and when he did, Owen continued.

"I teach primarily band with a little choir thrown into the mix. There used to be both a band and a choir instructor, but after budget cuts and a lack of student interest, the job was revamped. I'm the first hire the district made for the combined job." Owen coughed again into his fist.

"How long have you taught at Jefferson?" Thankful to have his legal pad as a prop, Brent positioned his pen to record the response.

"Fall will be the start of my third year. I was lucky to have landed this job fresh out of college."

His heart panged for the second time. The similarities in their career paths were hard to ignore. He had been fortunate that Harper snapped him up fresh out of school. Brent forced himself to focus. *Keep your emotions out of this.* He tapped his pen and assembled a brief mental list of what to cover. "I'm going to ask you some personal questions, if you don't mind." Hopefully the answers would prompt other information to surface.

"Sure." Owen, as if preparing himself for the unexpected, placed his palms flat on the table.

"Do you live alone?" Brent asked after writing Personal Info at the top of the page.

"Yes."

"Are you currently married or in a committed relationship?"

"No."

*Seriously?* Brent couldn't believe Owen wasn't already taken. *Okay. This shouldn't be weird. You have every right to ask.* "I don't want to assume—I have to ask—are you gay?"

"Yes." Owen coughed into his fist again, apparently a nervous tic, but appeared to relax into his chair for the first time since he sat down. "I'm out to my family and a few friends. I don't hide it at school, but I don't promote it either."

"I see. Well that's probably a good thing, given the nature of this situation." Brent loosened his tie. It had suddenly grown too tight. To his knowledge, this was the first conversation he'd ever had with a stranger that required he pry into their personal life. It felt awkward, but it was exactly what he needed to do.

"Gay here too," he offered and then realized it was a reckless mistake. There was a flirtatious lilt to his voice he recognized from those times when it was intentional. *Shithead.* "But you've probably already surmised that given I'm an attorney here at the Men's Center," he added because he felt something more had to be said.

"I hadn't given it much thought," Owen replied.

The response, absent any detectable malice, annihilated him. He felt as if he'd been stabbed. Owen was suffering in ways he could only imagine. Looking at his notes, Brent scolded himself. *Of course you haven't given it any thought. And the reason you haven't is because, unlike me, you're not a shithead. And you've got a monstrous obstacle to get over, so whether or not I'm registering on the dick-o-meter hasn't even crossed your mind.*

When Brent finally looked up, after who knows how long, Owen hadn't moved, but the smirk he wore was new. *He thinks I'm a prick.* Furious over his lapse in judgment, he adjusted his posture in the hope it would signal that he was a professional. The innocent eyes looking out from behind Owen's stylish glasses begged for help and understanding. Brent was momentarily humbled by the power he possessed. He represented Owen's only hope of salvation.

*That's it. Why didn't I think of it earlier?*

"Before I forget." Brent looked up from his notes. "When you were attacked, what happened to your glasses? Didn't they get messed up when your face was smashed into the tree?" Proud of himself, he sat back and tapped his pen on the table. *Harper will eat this up. This is exactly the kind of questioning he was talking about.*

"It was lucky I had my contacts in that morning. They're better with binoculars. My eye is still too swollen to wear them right now."

"Oh. Oh sure." He fought off a measure of disappointment. The answer rang true.

"Would you mind if I had a glass of water?" Owen asked.

"Of course not." For a second, he thought about using the newly installed phone system to contact Fern for the request. That's what important attorneys did. They had people bring things to them in meetings. But with his ego already in the crapper, he accepted the need for a break in questioning. The air and the walk would do him a world of good. "Are you okay with bottled water?" He moved to the door.

"That would be great. My throat is a little dry."

"The air is dry in this building. Be right back." Brent stepped out of the room and stood for a few seconds with his back against the wall. *My God. Will questioning a client like this ever get any easier? This sucks.* Running his hand through his hair, he walked into his office and pulled two waters out of the refrigerator. He placed one up against his forehead. When he felt he had collected himself, he puffed out his chest, strolled back into the room, and closed the door. He handed a water to Owen. Then he sat and made a completely random note, its only purpose to buy another minute to regroup. *You have every right to ask these questions.*

"Do you date? How do you meet men?" Brent sat rigid in his chair, poised to log the answer.

"It's hard finding guys around here to date. Sometimes I'll head over to the Main Club in Superior and, well not very often, I'll go home with someone. If it feels right, I'll invite them back to the house. I'm pretty cautious. Haven't met anyone yet I'm interested in developing a relationship with."

"Have you attended any events at the Men's Center?" The brief break seemed to do the trick. Maybe he could get through this after all.

"I can't believe I haven't been over here. I'm kind of a loner at heart."

The adorably shy expression that came with this admission made it all the more difficult to pry deeper into Owen's life and habits. It was hard to imagine a situation more challenging.

Understanding it was his turn after a brief lapse, Brent summoned the courage to forge ahead. "Not counting what happened last week, have you had any trouble with local law enforcement in the past?"

"No. This is the first time anything like this has *ever* happened. That's what has me so… so scared."

*Shy and scared?* It was a classic one-two punch. Rattled beyond repair, Brent had serious concerns about being able to get up off the mat after this last blow. The sheer honesty in his voice made Owen an odds-on favorite in this matchup.

"Do you have any hobbies besides bird-watching?" Brent eventually asked, unable to hide in his voice the impact the last few minutes had had on him. "Is that how you say it? Or it is birding? It seems to me I've heard both."

"Both work. I prefer to say birding because bird-watching always sounds so nerdy. But maybe that's more fitting, when I think of it," Owen joked.

"I think birding is great. I would love to get out and try it sometime." *You're such a liar, shithead.* "So, is there anything else you enjoy when you're not working?"

"My friend Ben, works at the radio station. He and I and a couple of other guys have a band. It's still in the garage phase, but we have hopes to branch out to the bars. We do mostly covers, and I've written a few songs with Ben. He's kind of a poet, and I put music to his words." Owen shrugged as if he'd just provided information that was unnecessary.

"Seriously?" Unable to even hold a tune, Brent had a great respect for those who could. "What instrument do you play?"

"Keyboards and trumpet. I minored in piano."

"I'd love to hear you guys." This time he wasn't lying. "What's the name of the band?"

"We really don't have one. Any ideas?" Owen cocked his head to the side and waited.

"I'll give it some thought."

There was only one topic Brent could think of that they hadn't covered. Secretly he hoped it wouldn't offer any further challenges. "Tell me a little about your family."

"My dad just retired. He worked in administration at the University of Minnesota. My mom's a nurse. She still works, but not as much as when I was growing up. I have a married sister, Karen. She has two kids. They live in Waseca." Owen folded his hands on the table and waited for him to ask another question.

Brent dropped his pen and smiled with considerable relief. "I think that's it for now. What's the best way to get ahold of you?"

Owen fired off his cell phone number. While Brent was in the process of writing it down, Owen removed his phone and placed it on the table with a frown. Someone had just attempted to contact him.

"Everything okay?" Brent asked.

"My boss just sent me a text. She's the principal at Jefferson," Owen added as he looked up. "She's asking if it would be okay to meet up for coffee."

“Do you get texts from her often?” This wasn’t a coincidence. Brent was positive he knew why.

“Not really. Occasionally to inform me of a meeting change. We have a good relationship, but nothing social.”

“My guess….” He thought about how he should approach this. He didn’t want to add to Owen’s fear, but it was important he prepare him for what could lie ahead. “My guess is, word has gotten out about your arrest. This is a small town, and your… what happened to you,” Brent corrected himself, “is probably the biggest news anyone’s heard in a long time.”

“Oh my.” Owen’s posture deflated. “What should I do?”

“I think it would be prudent to meet. What’s her name?”

“Deena Phelps,” Owen answered.

“This isn’t something you want to hide from.” He jotted the name down. “That might send out the wrong message. Meet and tell her you’re in the process of securing legal representation. Whatever you do, don’t get into the details of your arrest. If she asks, I think you can assure her you’re innocent. Ask her what she needs from you at this time and then come back to me with her answer before you commit to anything. Try as hard as you can to be yourself. Don’t give her an ounce of fuel for the fire. Does that make sense?”

“Yes. I know what you mean.” The color had completely left Owen’s face.

Unable to stop himself, Brent reached over and patted Owen’s hand. “Let’s head out to the front. If you don’t mind waiting for few minutes, I’m going to have Fern make copies of these documents.” He stood and walked to the door.

“That’s fine.” Owen joined Brent in the hall. “Does this mean you’re taking my case?”

“Personally, I’m very interested in representing you. I’m going to meet with my partner later this afternoon. After we’ve had a chance to discuss what we’ve talked about today, I’ll give you a call.”

What was he thinking? He stopped, forcing Owen to take a step back. There were at least two questions that still needed answering before he could bring his findings back to Harper. He’d almost forgotten the law school basics.

"Owen, if we do decide to represent you, can you assure me what you told me is the truth? This would be a good time to let me know if you've stretched the truth in anyway."

"It's the truth. I have no reason to lie about anything."

"Good." That's what I thought," Brent was impressed Owen wasn't offended by his frankness. "Is there anything I didn't ask back there you think I should know?"

Owen leaned against the wall. "I guess…." A pained expression washed over his face as he looked down the hall toward the room they had just left. "I came very close," he continued barely above a whisper, "to having a sexual experience in the woods that day." He made direct eye contact with Brent and added, "But I didn't. I stopped it. I need you to believe that."

Brent understood Owen's concern and gave him a reassuring pat on the shoulder. "I believe you. Let's get some copies made so you can be on your way." *I need a beer.*

"YOU WANT a beer?" Harper opened the built-in minifridge he recently had installed behind his desk. Secretly Brent wondered if it wasn't his partner's attempt at keeping up with the Joneses. *My fridge is better, and you know it.* It was a little thing, but because of Harper's godlike stature, he'd take what he could get.

"Maybe two." Brent, seated across the large wooden desk, organized his notes. Where to start? Meeting Owen and getting to know a little about him had been one of the most interesting experiences he'd had in a long time.

"Here." Harper handed him a cold bottle and then walked around and plopped down in his chair. "That's quite the story we heard this afternoon."

Brent shook his head. "Before we get into this, I want you to tell me why you don't believe him."

"What are you talking about?" Harper sipped. "I never said I didn't believe him."

"True. However, you're implying it. In that special way you do. Imply things."

"But I do have to pose the question—why do you think the cop reacted the way he did?" Harper asked.

"I don't know. Maybe he was humiliated at being turned down or something." Brent needed more time to think this detail over.

"Big stud cop not used to being refused? It's possible, I guess." A few quiet moments passed. Harper took another swig. "Trout Simmons, the chief of police, is a friend of mine. There's not a chance in hell, I can assure you, he would have someone working for him like this Grady described. Something doesn't add up here."

Brent thought about this. It did seem incredible. But like it or not, he believed Owen's story. "Does the something that doesn't add up—" Brent sipped. "—does that something have to be Owen Grady's something? I mean, there could be unknowns out there that caused this to happen. I'm just saying."

"Ah yes." Harper laughed. "Innocent until proven guilty. The golden rule. Look." He took another long pull and leaned back. "I know you're itchin' to take this case. And you're right. There's a chance, albeit a small one, this guy is telling the truth. We're not busy right now. You run with this. I'll step in here and there because I'm too nosey not to. But you have to promise me one thing."

Brent couldn't contain the smile that blossomed. "Absolutely. What?"

"It's taken me a few years to establish the relationship I have, not only with Trout, but with this community. I'm very protective of it. Before you get all revved up and go into attack mode, especially if it involves our local law enforcement—which I can't see how it wouldn't—we have to talk. This is very important, Brent. I'm not shitting you here."

"I get it. You don't have to worry. I'm not going to burn any of your bridges. Those bridges will probably become my bridges." And to top it off in a way Harper would find amusing, he added flatly, "A dog doesn't shit where it sleeps."

Harper laughed. "You're right about that. Typically it doesn't." He laughed again. "Ian had a dog growing up. Pickles or something like that. It used to shit on his bed if it felt neglected, but I think that's different." He slapped the top of his desk. "I'm so glad you came up here to do this… this thing with me. I'm sure we're going to disagree with each other from time to time, and I'm fine with that, provided you let me win."

Brent laughed, luckily *after* his sip of beer had made the journey down his throat.

"Seriously. Give this guy your, I mean *our* best shot," Harper revised midsentence. "Come to me for help when you need it."

"Thanks. I'll give the client a call and let him know we're on." Brent thought about how to say what was on his mind. He wanted to let Harper know, even though he had said it many times before, how thankful he was for his generosity. After a very brief analysis of his options, he decided to play it simple. "I'm glad I'm here too." And then he added, for what he hoped would be interpreted as comic relief, "I'm not having sex as often as I used to. I'm making do."

"Nor are half the gay men in the Cities now that you've moved up here. I'm surprised we haven't heard accounts of dudes rubbing themselves against doorknobs. Shocked in fact."

"Sure. Make fun of the single guy." Brent finished his beer and stood. "I've got to get over to the resort, or Alex will have a cat."

"Brent?"

"Yeah?" As he turned back, Harper stood. "There's nothing wrong with being single. I don't want you to feel pressured to go out and find someone. That is, unless that someone happens into your life. Ah fuck, you know what I mean."

"No worries. I'm good." Lately he'd had doubts, but as soon as he gave a relationship serious consideration, the obstacles and limitations he envisioned prevented him from going any further.

"WHAT'S WITH all the fidgeting?"

"Can't sleep." Harper turned onto his side and rubbed his nose on the sleeve of Ian's T-shirt. His husband had a special scent that was irresistible.

"I got that part. Maybe you should get up and do something. I have an early morning tomorrow and a game in the evening." Ian turned away, pulling the covers across his broad shoulders.

*That's right.* Harper stared up at the lazily twirling ceiling fan. Tomorrow the resort was hosting its first wedding of the season.

Weddings, anniversaries, and special events had become a very lucrative piece of their pie. Who would have thought, back in the early days, when the grounds were just beginning to take shape and all they had to worry about was ten little resort cabins, that this endeavor would get so big? Times certainly had changed. The state legalization of gay marriage was an unexpected boon to business.

"We have a new client," Harper said to himself but then realized he'd said it out loud.

"That's nice, hon," Ian mumbled in response.

"He claims one of Trout Simmons's officers lured him into the woods for a little 'I'll show you mine, if you show me yours.' And when our client refused, the officer bashed his head into a tree and arrested him for indecent exposure and evading arrest."

Ian slapped the side of the bed and turned onto his back. "This is important to me… why?"

Harper sat up in the dark and fluffed his pillow behind his back. Sleep seemed to be impossible. "It's not so important, hon. I'll work through it."

Ian, letting loose a massive sigh, sat up next to him. "Apparently we're talking about this."

So used to Ian's attentive nature, Harper blasted right into what was troubling him. "Something doesn't feel right about this guy's story. I think he might be lying." Harper raised his arms in the air and then brought them down to his sides.

"Maybe he is." Ian propped his head up with his hand and ran his finger across Harper's chest. "Is Brent involved?"

"He's taking the lead on this case."

"So, Brent will have to figure out if the dude's lying or not." Ian leaned over and kissed his arm. "There, did that help? Should I give law school a consideration?"

"Probably not." Frustrated, Harper took his turn at slapping the bed. "Here's what pisses me off so much about this—the Men's Center. Alex and I have worked our asses off, with help from you and a lot of people, to create an environment where gay men can come and meet other gay men. From there, they can go off and do whatever it is they're into. But the Center—one of its primary functions is to create a safe and legal place for people to meet."

"Oh. I get it." Ian put his head back on the pillow and moved his hand from Harper's chest down to his thigh, where it stopped. "Well, not everyone's going to play by the rules. It's reality."

"I know. But I can't help view the mess he's gotten himself into as an insult, or worse, a comment on the Center and how ineffective it might be. For Christ's sake, it's why we created it in the first place."

"You won't know the answer to that until you have all the facts. Maybe you'll be surprised." Ian's hand made a detour that ended when it cupped Harper's balls.

With a touch that had no equal, Ian worked his nuts, until, in a whisper, Harper managed to finish his thought. "I'm starving for signs that the Men's Center is a success. This is a big step backward."

There was only one way for Ian to get back to sleep. Thankfully, it was a process Harper never grew tired of. He watched as Ian's head disappeared under the comforter. Soft kisses in all the right places were soon replaced by an eager, wet mouth.

*That's what I'm talkin' about.*

Harper closed his eyes and savored Ian's efforts. When the time felt right, he pulled the blankets down, exposing his lover. After years of intimacy, this was their understood signal for the beginning of phase two.

Facing the opposite end of the bed, Harper straddled Ian. He enjoyed pleasuring Ian, who never seemed to take their lovemaking for granted. He was either in the game, or would let him know at the onset if it was a pass.

Conscious of soft, anxious kisses on his backside, Harper eagerly accepted the introduction of Ian's curious tongue. Moments of shared pleasure passed before Ian indicated that he was ready to begin phase three by administering a series of gentle spanks. Harper moved over and crawled back up to his pillow. He turned onto his side and felt Ian's powerful arms wrap around his chest and shoulder. He gasped as Ian pushed forward until Harper felt his powerful torso connect with his butt.

A nibble to the ear. A kiss to the neck. Of the many things Ian excelled at, making love was certainly near the top of the list. Harper couldn't dream of anyone making love better than Ian.

"Babe, I love you so much," Ian whispered in his ear. "I hate it when you're unhappy."

"I'm happy now. Almost all better, in fact," Harper reported enthusiastically.

They shared a chuckle.

"I love you so much too." Harper reached back and stroked the solid, muscular body wedged up next to him. "Nothing in life compares to how I feel when you're making love to me."

Ian increased his efforts and, at the same time, took hold of Harper with his hand and began to pet and then stroke. In response, Harper caressed as much of Ian as he could get his hands on. Slow, gentle motions fell away to urgent, powerful thrusts.

"Oh… I'm there," Harper panted. "Yes!" He was first to cross the finish line but not by much. Ian was relentless as he stroked him to the end, while he allowed his own body to release.

After they calmed, Ian separated and led the way to the bathroom. "Better than counting sheep, wouldn't you say?" He winked into the mirror.

"Oh, slugger," Harper said, slapping his partner's muscled ass, "that *never* gets old."

"Keeping it fresh." Back under the covers, Ian leaned forward and kissed Harper on the forehead. "I'm all over that. Now if you don't mind, can we try and get some sleep?"

Thanks to Ian, what seemed so important, so troubling, was a million miles away. He buried his head in his partner's armpit and drifted off into the night.

# Chapter Four

"HEY," THEO hollered out his window as he turned off the highway onto the road leading to the resort. "Looks awesome. Might even cause a few accidents."

"There's a goal worth working toward." Ian wiped the hair from his eyes and strolled to the truck. "Seriously? You don't think it's too much?"

"Nope. I think it's perfect. You know, a preview of what the guests will find down the road. It's the best-looking sign on the North Shore."

"Well, I don't know if I'd go that far. But, yeah. It is," Ian admitted with a laugh.

Theo marveled at Ian's landscape-design talent. He had created something amazing. On both sides of the narrow entrance, waterfalls cascaded down from huge boulders hauled from the lake. "Palisade Beach Resort" written in large raised lettering on the top stones advertised the resort from each side of the entrance. The entire sign concept was classy and eye-catching.

"Glad you like it. What finally motivated me to change it up was that tacky vacancy sign. Hell. We haven't had a vacancy for two seasons."

A pickup drove by and honked. Ian waved. "That's Marcus Freeman, the guy who just opened Greta's, the microbrewery in Silver Bay. Harper helped him with his business plan. Hey. We're going to the grand opening on Friday. You guys should join us."

To Alex, Ian and Harper were like family. They had rescued him from the throes of a shit existence. They cherished him like a son. Now they were Theo's friends too, and that made him feel wonderful. “Sure. I brought lunch for Alex, so if you need a hand later, I’d be happy to help.”

“Thanks, but I’m good. I’ve got the crew coming up here this afternoon to throw in some shrubs. Hopefully the electrician will be by too. I don’t need to be around for any of that. They can follow the designs. Hey.” Ian leaned into the truck. “Don’t tell anyone, but I’m going to take the afternoon off and park my butt down by the lake. I need to do some sketching for a few upcoming projects.”

“It sure looks nice.” Theo watched the rushing water tumble over the rocks.

“It looks pretty cool now, but at night it should really pop.” Ian used his shovel to point to a few spots. “Lights will be installed on both the top and bottom of each of the falls so the cascading water will be easy to see from the road. I saw some bronze deer that would look great. You know, like they’re drinking out of the catch ponds below. Harper saw how much they cost and pulled the plug on the idea. Maybe I’ll win the battle over the deer next year. They can always be added later.”

“How about—” Theo poked his head out of the window like he was sharing a secret. “—I make little comments here and there like, I love the sign the way it is, but what would make it really cool is to have deer or something on the edge, like they’re drinking.” Theo smiled and wiggled his eyebrows. “Whaddaya think?”

“Couldn’t hurt. Go for it, my friend. You guys coming to the game tonight?”

Ian, the star hitter for the Duluth Taconknights, loved it when his friends showed up to watch. The best part? The games were good, and Ian always played as if his life depended on it.

“That’s the plan. But the little mister’s been kind of crabby lately.” Theo felt a surge of guilt for venting his recent frustration with Alex. Ian, he had discovered over time, was a trusted ear. His whining wouldn’t go any further or be inflated into more than what it was—an opportunity to release.

Ian laughed. “Take him over your knee and whap his ass good and hard. Teach him life’s too short to be going around all bunched up and pissy.”

"Right." Theo chuckled. "If I ever tried that I'd wake up with my nuts cut off. He's a little stressed having to spend time at the resort office. At least that's what I think it is."

"Well boo-fucking-hoo. Maybe *I'll* whap his ass. Everyone's busy." Ian shook his head the way a parent does when they're struggling to understand their kids. "Listen, if it doesn't get to be too late, let's plan on grabbing a beer after the game. I'm buying."

"Perfect. Hit one out of the park for me." Theo waved and put his truck in gear.

"Will do. Later."

"Everyone's busy," Theo mumbled as he drove toward the lake. Ian's words stung. It was true, everyone *was* busy. *Everyone but me.* Now that he'd organized Artie's shop for a buyer, he didn't have much to do. Brent had agreed to rent Artie's house, even volunteered to help pack and organize his belongings for an estate sale to be held later in the summer. That news had come as a huge relief. He couldn't have spent time alone in his boss's home going through his belongings. Brent didn't know Artie, so the task wasn't as complicated or strange, he reasoned. Theo hated how easily spooked he had been, but there was nothing he could do about it.

He parked his truck behind the office and grabbed a bag of sandwiches from the Lip Smacker off the seat. Alex was nowhere to be found when he stepped inside. "Hey. You here?" he called out.

"Hey," Alex hollered from somewhere in the back. Seconds later the most important man in his life came through the door carrying a toilet brush and can of Ajax. "I hate cleaning toilets."

"I've been trying to think of ways to make it fun for you at home." Theo accepted the extended middle finger presented him without complaint.

Alex sat on the stool behind the counter and organized papers that were scattered about. "That reminds me. It's your turn at home."

"You sure?" Theo placed the bag of food on the counter, walked around the desk, and took his man into his arms. "How's my grumpy artist doing?"

"Mmmm. Much better now you're here."

"Show me you mean it." Theo cocked an eyebrow and held his ground.

Alex placed his hand behind Theo's head and pulled him forward for a kiss. He accepted Alex's tongue and at the same time, cupped his ass in both hands, pulling him in tighter. A stirring in his jeans had him wishing they were in the privacy of their home.

"You believe me, or do we need to take this into the back room?" Alex's smirk was challenging and inviting at the same time.

As tempting as the invitation was, Theo couldn't go there. Not in the resort office. Privacy was essential for optimum performance. The last thing he wanted was to have someone stop by and catch him with his bare ass in the air drilling into his hot lover. To show how satisfying the kiss had been, he brought Alex's hand down to his crotch, where a thin layer of material separated it from his pulsating dick. With a wink, he pried Alex's eager hand away before it coaxed him past the point of no return. This turned out to be a very good call. Only seconds later a guest came through the door.

"Hello, Alex. We're all packed and ready to head back to the city. Everything was so wonderful. Please thank the rest of the staff for making our stay here so memorable."

"Mrs. Preston, is the week up already?" Alex accepted the key from her. "I'm glad you enjoyed yourself. By the way, I don't think you've had a chance to meet my partner, Theo."

Dressed in lavender and wearing bright white tennis shoes, Mrs. Preston reminded Theo of his grandmother. She had a rosy face and smelled just like his Nettie. A potent, flowery scent entered the office with her.

"Theo. As in Theodore?" she asked.

"Yes, ma'am," he answered, glancing to Alex, who was smiling from ear to ear.

"I adore that name."

A single honk of the horn brought a frown to her face. "Fifty-nine years of marriage and you'd think I'd be able to teach that man a few manners. I'm not giving up hope. I'll tell you both as much."

They all shared a laugh.

"I'll have Bud call you. We'd like to come again next summer."

"Sounds good. Safe travels," Alex said as they watched her leave the office.

They brought their lunch to the little table by the front window. “I wonder what we’ll be like in fifty-nine years,” Alex said.

“I’m not sure.” He found the thought too enormous to contemplate. “I promise not to honk at you.” He bit into his chicken salad and asked, “What were you working on before I showed up?”

“This is on the down low, okay?” Alex waited for Theo to agree.

“Sure.” He shoved a handful of chips into his mouth. It felt odd to learn Alex had been doing something he wasn’t already aware of. In a flash he was reminded of how he’d protected his decisions about Artie and school until they were more thought out. He wondered if Alex felt the same way. It wasn’t his intention to pry, but he knew what it was like living with a secret. It was too much like his life had been a few years earlier, before he’d found the courage to come out.

“Brent and I were talking the other afternoon. This is butthead’s idea by the way—he thought the chances of finding someone who would get off on living back here *and* managing the office, weren’t very good. Shit. It worked for me, but I didn’t have a shekel to my name. This place was like my palace.” Alex waved his hand as if to shoo the thought away. “So anyway, Brent thought it would be cool to do away with the apartment and use the space for an upscale gift shop. Maybe even include a small gallery for my watercolors.” He took a sip of his Dew, which was never far away.

“I never thought of that, but you’re probably right.” He loved how down-to-earth Alex was, despite the airs and attitude he sometimes put on. “The remodel,” he agreed, “could bring in a lot of extra revenue for the resort. You could do some really cool T-shirts and other stuff. Not the cheap shit you see everywhere else, but expensive, classy things. Yeah. I really like that idea.” He finished the first half of his sandwich and asked, “Why is this so hush-hush?”

“It’s not, really.” Alex placed a single chip into his mouth and continued. “I want to have the idea worked up and in pretty good shape before I bring it to Harper and Ian.”

“Can I see what you’ve got?”

“Sure.” Alex got up from his chair and grabbed his work off the counter. “I tried to capture the area back there from a few different angles." He sat down and slid the drawings over, turning them around so Theo was viewing from the right direction.

Theo wiped his hands on a napkin and flipped through the designs. Alex had basically gutted the space, keeping only a portion of the already tiny bathroom and using the rest for storage. Shelves and display areas were strategically placed in a way that, at least on paper, seemed to make the entire area seem larger and more open.

"I don't think I did a good job showing this, but I also expanded the front office by three feet. It won't be so cramped behind the counter now."

Theo wanted to play a bigger role in the grand scheme of things. This was exactly the kind of project he could excel at.

Alex glanced at his watch. "Shit. I have to organize invoices for Brent before he gets here. He's got a case now and won't be able to spend as much time helping in the office as he thought." Alex grabbed what empty wrappers he could from the table, leaving the drawings with Theo.

*I wonder....* Theo grabbed the rest of his lunch, along with Alex's sketches, and walked to the counter. "I could work in the office. I mean, if you think that would help?"

Alex looked up from his work with an expression Theo had seen several other times—he was skeptical.

"I'm serious," Theo pledged. "I've got nothin' to do right now, until school starts up. I could learn the office stuff, and...." Realizing he was talking like a kid, he stopped.

"You could manage the remodel," Alex finished for him. "That would be so great." Still not fully trusting the offer, Alex gave a nervous laughed and asked, "Are you fucking with me?"

"That comes later—tonight after the game. You got me so riled up earlier that when we get home I'm going to...."

"Say it isn't so, Mr. Engdahl," Alex interrupted while furiously fanning himself. "I can't *imagine* what you're talkin' about." Appearing shocked, he stumbled several steps back.

"You'll have a good idea soon enough, I reckon." Theo tipped his imaginary hat and strolled toward the door. "You best do those stretchin' exercises if you know what's good for ya."

"I declare. I'm about to faint." Fluttering his eyelashes Alex placed his hand over his heart.

Theo laughed. They had watched part of an old western in bed the week before and had been talking like the characters from the movie ever since.

"Alex, this will be good for me." Theo stepped out of character. "I need a project. Everyone has projects but me." He walked back and leaned over the counter. "Your drawings are great. Bring them home, and I'll start making a list of what we need for building materials. From there, I'll make up a budget. Who approves stuff like this? Harper?"

"Ian is more into the design detail. And yeah, as far as the budget, that's Harper."

"Well, it's a great idea. Why don't I plan on hanging with you here tomorrow, and you can show me the ropes." He couldn't believe he hadn't thought to offer his services earlier.

"Tomorrow is perfect. I'll organize the notes I made for training Brent, and we'll go over everything. There's nothing to it." Alex frowned as if the offer were too good to be true. "You're sure about this, hon?"

"Alex?" Theo cautioned.

"Sorry." His partner smiled meekly. "I do trust you. Honest."

There'd been an issue early in their relationship where Alex seemed to request confirmation at almost every turn. Theo had lost his patience one time in a big way, and since then Alex had made the promise to take him at his word. There was an occasional slipup, but not often.

"See you at home. I'm heading over there now." Sticking his thumbs into the front of his jeans, he eased back into the role of marshal. "I reckon there's a bathroom or two that needs a good scrubbin'. Adios, amigo."

"Ooh, baby, that western thing really works for me. If you know what I mean." Alex winked and giggled.

"Oh yeah? That gives me a few *ideaers*," Theo teased, walking to the door. "You best get home a little early if you catch *my* meanin'. We might be a little late for the game."

"Well I declare, Marshal. How you do make a young man blush."

ANXIOUS TO get the legal process rolling, Owen showed up at the Center fifteen minutes before his appointment. His face lit up when Brent, dressed in charcoal gray pants, a bright white shirt, and an orange tie, entered the reception area. It wasn't clear who he would be meeting with. He hoped it would be Brent. The young attorney seemed genuinely interested in his case. Harper Callahan was too hard to read, and that made him uneasy.

"Hi, Owen."

"I'm here early. Sorry about that." Owen coughed into his hand, an attempt to gain control of his nerves.

"We like early. It's late that causes problems. Fern, any messages?"

"No, it's been pretty quiet this morning. Here's Mr. Grady's retainer agreement. I've marked where he should sign."

"Thanks." Brent collected a folder from the corner of the desk. "At the very least, we'll make our relationship official today, Owen. Come on back."

Owen followed down the hallway and unexpectedly found himself fixated on the handsome attorney's backside. The cut of his pants displayed his curvaceous rear in all its pert glory.

"Hey. If you don't mind, let's meet in my office," Brent suggested as they passed the conference room they had used for their last meeting. "It's more comfortable, I hope." A little farther down the hall, Brent pointed out, "This is Harper's cave. He's at a luncheon meeting."

Sneaking a quick glance inside as he passed, Owen observed the office was tastefully done in rich, masculine tones. By contrast, Brent's office, at the far corner of the building, was fun and cheerful. It was funky, he thought.

A contemporary, uncluttered blond wood desk anchored the room. An aquarium took up most of the space on a shelf to the right of a large window that looked out into a bank of majestic pines. A huge globe held by a wooden frame stood guard on the other end of the room. Various photographs and art shared the side walls. Clearly the standout piece in the office belonged to a full-size red and chrome refrigerator. Owen suspected it offered a strong hint to Brent's personality. It made him smile.

"You're probably wondering about the fridge. Once the practice really gets rolling, I'm prepared to spend a lot of my time here. I'll keep it well stocked with the essentials—beer, Snickers bars, peanut butter, and bread. Please, have a seat." Brent gestured to one of the quirky red leather chairs opposite the desk. "I hate to stop what I'm doing when I'm focused on a deadline."

Owen laughed and sat. Although the odd shape of the chair made it look uncomfortable, he was pleasantly surprised. Glancing around, he discovered another hint into Brent's character—a lime green lava lamp on a small table to his right. "I've always wanted one of those," he confessed.

Taking the seat next to him instead of sitting behind the desk, Brent explained, "A gift from my parents. Isn't it cool?" The attorney looked at it over his shoulder. "They were bitten hard by the sixties. It's the first thing I see when I look up from my desk."

An awkward moment of silence forced Owen to look toward the window. There were so many thoughts badgering for attention. It frustrated him that, after sharing so much of himself and his story, he didn't feel a greater sense of relief. This journey was just beginning. He badly wanted it to end.

After leafing through the document, Brent handed it to him. "This is our retainer agreement. It's a standard contract for our services. Take a minute and read it over. If everything's okay, I'll have you sign it, and Fern will prepare a copy for you to take home."

Owen read through it and found nothing to take issue with. "This is fine," he affirmed with a smile.

"Great. Here." Brent handed him a pen from his shirt pocket.

The pen took on a special meaning as he grasped it in his hand. It was a bond of sorts. He quickly signed where indicated and handed both the pen and the agreement back.

Brent placed the folder on the desk, adjusted the crease in his pants, and said, "I'd like to start this meeting by asking if you've had any new thoughts or memories from your encounter with Officer Daniels. Has anything surfaced since the last time we met up?"

Having replayed the scenes of his arrest over and over in his mind, each day, several times, Owen wished he could come up with something more, but there was nothing to add. “I can’t think of anything else. I’ve told you everything I can remember. At least, I think I have.”

“Okay. Well, please don’t hesitate to share with me what’s on your mind. You might think it trivial or maybe even embarrassing, but don’t let that limit what we talk about. I’m in your corner, Owen. Please trust that. I need all the tools I can get my hands on to do the best possible job for you on this case.”

Nodding he understood, Owen waited for Brent to continue.

“Have you had any conversations regarding this matter with anyone outside this office? Your parents? A trusted friend maybe?”

A trusted friend? *Is there such a thing*? Who in God’s name could he share this with? Eventually word of his arrest would get out. He understood that, and there was nothing that could be done to prevent it from happening. To initiate a conversation with someone regarding his troubles seemed an insurmountable task. It was tough enough rehashing what he’d been through with Brent.

“I haven’t left the house much,” he answered. His mouth had become so dry he could hardly talk.

“I’m going to grab a water. Would you like one?” Brent had apparently picked up on his discomfort.

“Yes. Please.” Not wanting to risk another unbearably tempting moment, he chose the aquarium for his focus until Brent handed him a chilled bottle.

“Don’t feel like you’re going to jeopardize your case if you venture out. If you behave like you’re guilty, a person could make that assumption. Besides, it would be good for you to be out in public. You might hear things. People can’t help themselves. If word’s gotten around you were arrested, and it most likely has by now, it’s possible someone will confront you. That reminds me, have you met up with your boss yet? Let’s see….” Brent flipped over a page of his notes. “Ms. Phelps?”

“Not yet.” Feeling the need to explain, he added, “This probably wasn’t the best idea, but I sent her a text saying I was out of town for a few days and would get ahold of her when I got back. Emotionally, I wasn't up for it. I think I am now, though."

Owen wasn't someone to ignore social responsibilities. The severity of his predicament held him captive. The anxiety and stress, which accompanied thoughts like those he was experiencing now, created a stomach cramp. *I hope I'm not developing an ulcer.* He reacted by clutching his midsection as discreetly as possible. As much as he wanted to cooperate by answering each of the attorney's questions as truthfully as possible, he loathed having to revisit the details connected with his arrest. The residual anxiety associated with what had happened was almost more than he could manage.

"Hey, you okay?"

It was time to trust Brent's concern. Nothing during their time together seemed suspect. "No. I'm not okay," he reluctantly reported.

"Is there anything I can do?" Brent leaned toward him.

"Please," he pleaded. "Make this all go away. I'm a good man." Embarrassed at showing weakness, Owen stared out the window. A blue jay hopped down a few branches on one of the giant pines.

"I know you are," Brent answered softly. "And I believe what you've told me."

The bird cocked its head and stared into the office, its vivid color striking in the afternoon light. When it flew off, Owen brought his hands up to this face. He wished he could just disappear.

The sensation of having a hand placed on his knee startled him. The hand didn't move. If he tried now to voice his frustration, he'd surely lose it. He shook his head sadly and fought to keep his emotions from getting the best of him. How quickly the tone of the meeting had changed.

"We're going to get you through this, and you *will* enjoy life again, my friend." Brent gave him a few gentle pats. "You will, Owen. I won't settle for anything less."

Despite Brent's comforting presence, Owen was devastated by the hopelessness of it all. It was so hard to believe his life would someday get back to the way it was before his arrest. How could he possibly get from here to the point where he woke up and trusted his day would be his, free from fear and anxiety? *Brent is here to help.*

His attempt at maintaining composure was failing miserably. Up until now, his anguish had been private. Powerless to hold it all back, he began to cry, and that infuriated him. He had shed enough tears over this mess and had hoped by now he was all cried out.

"Ah… come here." Brent stood and reached for Owen's hand, guiding him out of his chair. "Fuck it. This is about as wrong as it gets, but I don't care." Brent took him into his arms. "Sometimes a hug goes a long way. Besides, us gay folk play by different rules."

Unable to stop the tears, Owen wrapped his arms around his handsome defender as if they were beginning a slow dance, and wept. Being held was so comforting; he wished the embrace could last forever. It felt right in a way that was impossible to express.

Although their relationship was professional, there was something, a feeling he had for Brent Burns that he couldn't ignore. It was more than a mere physical attraction, although that aspect of the connection was as strong as anything. His body didn't lie. It was sending a strong signal of approval. He rested his chin on Brent's shoulder when he managed to rein in the tears. Brent's body had warmed, and his scent was intoxicating.

*Please don't let me go. I can't handle this on my own. I'm not strong enough.*

At the sound of a car pulling into the parking lot, Brent released him. Owen was surprised to see the attorney's boyish cheeks had colored. Wiping his face with his sleeve, Owen sat back down. He reached for his water, opened it, and sipped. "Thank you," he said softly, staring into the middle of the room.

"My whole family is huggie," Brent joked. "I'm going to have to try and resist moments like that if I expect to have a successful career in law."

Both men laughed, and then, as if they were old friends, sat together for a moment in silence.

"California," Owen voiced out loud. The thought came crashing down out of nowhere.

"What's that?" Brent gulped down the remainder of his water and placed the bottle on his desk.

It hadn't occurred to him before, but this could be an important piece of the puzzle. "Daniels. His voice… when he talks he sounds like my cousins." He remembered noticing the unmistakable accent before things went bad.

"You're saying he has a California accent?" Brent picked up his notepad from off the floor.

"It's weird, I know." He brought his hand up to cough and then stopped. "I remember resisting the urge to ask him if he was from California. I used to make fun of my cousins who live south of San Francisco. They would always tease me about my Midwestern accent. We would exaggerate the differences in the way we talked. I'd be surprised if I was wrong about it."

"Well, you never know if something like this will turn out to be important or not." Brent jotted down a note. "One thing leads to another. Right now we need leads."

Brent circled something else in his notes and then, after a moment, looked up. "Look, I know this isn't easy for you. Putting myself in your shoes, I'm pretty sure I would self-destruct. Hang in there. Please rely on me if the going gets tough. I want to be there for you. Okay?"

"I'm lucky to have met you." Owen wasn't sure how sharing this would be interpreted. Now wasn't the time to worry about such things. His life had changed so quickly, he couldn't trust any of his thoughts or feelings anymore. He was a good person with good intentions. Hopefully Brent truly believed that.

"HOW DO you feel about defending me in a murder case?"

Brent looked up from his work to see Harper charge through the door and plop down in a chair.

"Dingman. The… the thing… the brain dead *thing* I'm representing in that workers' comp case is the stupidest waste of human flesh I've *ever* come in contact with." Harper opened the top button of his shirt and then yanked his tie off in one, quick move. He tossed it high into the air, and it landed behind him.

Not having seen his partner this agitated since they worked together in the Twin Cities, Brent sat back and laughed. And even then he might not have been this stressed. The typically cool, even-keeled man sitting across from him was almost a stranger. Harper had come to the end of the road with Delores Dingman.

"What did she do this time?" He couldn't wait. There'd been rumblings about this client's stupidity since the day she first contacted them. Even Fern found it hard to mask her distaste.

"Oh, you're not going to believe this. Guess? Come on." Harper placed his hands on his knees and leered at him. "Just fucking guess."

"Hmm…." He thought about it for a second. "She entered you in the United Way's pie eating contest up at the mall without asking?"

"Oh, I'd do that. I'd do that naked if it meant I could be rid of this woman once and for all. First, she called and left a wandering voicemail that went on for—I fucking kid you not—seventeen minutes. She described in excruciating detail some walk she took near the lake. Like I give a shit? I mean, seriously?" Rubbing his five-o'clock shadow, which typically began making itself known to the world by midmorning, Harper emptied his lungs with a huge sigh. "And that's not the worst of it."

"It's not?" He found that hard to believe. "What else?"

"When I called her back, and I *had* to." Harper gave the side of his chair a good, hard whack. "If I don't call her back, she keeps calling until I do. I can't put Fern through that torture any longer. It's not her fault I didn't screen this imbecile before taking her case. Anyway, when I called back, she asked if there was any way I could go after the money her mother paid for a television she bought, secondhand, from someone two years ago on fucking eBay because the fucking remote doesn't work any longer." Obviously exasperated, Harper punched the air a couple of times.

Brent held back as long as he could before he slapped his hands on the desk and exploded in laughter. The look on Harper's face did nothing but fuel his hysterics. "Oh my God," he gasped. "It's so funny this is happening to *you*."

"I want to die. Truly, I want to die." Harper buried his head in his hands and massaged his scalp.

"So now tell me what she did that got you all worked up," Brent teased when he could finally talk.

"Huh?" Surprised by the question, Harper looked as if he were about to explode before he realized he'd just been fucked with. "Funny boy. Seriously, what am I going to do?"

"I think," he said, leaning forward and delighted Harper had asked for his opinion, "the first thing you should do is to tell her to stop calling. You could threaten to bill her for each call going forward regardless of its nature. Or do this. Tell her you'll formally terminate the relationship if she keeps it up."

"That's exactly what I'm going to do." Harper walked over to where his tie had landed and picked it up. Folding it into a neat ball, he stuffed it into the pocket of his dress shirt. "Enough is enough. Hey, I almost forgot. Did you see what I put in your fancy refrigerator?"

"What did you put in there?" Brent shot out of his chair. "I swear if you put dog shit or something gnarly in there, I'm going to be really pissed off."

"Easy. Easy, my friend. That's Ian's MO. I don't know how you could ever think such a thing of me. Honestly." Harper opened the fridge and nabbed two small pony bottles from the bottom shelf. "Here. Try your first Big Lake Ale and let me know what you think. It's one of the brews they have for sale at Stella's, the pub that just opened up in Silver Bay. Tasty stuff, me thinks."

Brent twisted the cap off the small bottle and gave it a try. "This *is* tasty," he agreed and smacked his lips together loudly.

"I thought you'd like it. The owner trained as a brewmaster in Europe before meeting the woman of his dreams in Brussels and bringing her back to the states to raise a family."

"Hope they make a go of it up here." Relieved his prized possession hadn't been sabotaged after all, Brent walked behind his desk and sat back down.

"Okay." Harper took his seat. "There're a few other things on my mind. First, I want to thank you for agreeing to rent Artie's house. That makes things a whole lot easier for Theo."

It was a win-win situation. "It's perfect for me." He fell in love with the little house the minute he laid eyes on it.

"You're not going to get stuck packing up all of Artie's stuff either. Ian and I have a plan. They'll be plenty of us to help on moving day too. There won't be much left for you to do."

"No problem. The price is right. I love the neighborhood, and it's certainly a step up from the cum stain I call my apartment."

"Can I ask you something personal?" Harper rubbed his chin.

Not that he would, but it wouldn't matter one gnat turd to his partner if he said no. "Sure. Fire away."

"I've always wondered about this. Actually, I gave it some thought prior to inviting you up here last fall but then thought it was silly. Is there any tension, or animosity, between you and Theo, given your history with Alex?"

Brent was prepared for just about anything, but Harper's question caught Brent off guard. He sipped. The answer was complicated. He hadn't really had a chance to establish a friendship with Alex's new man yet. "I don't know if I would call it tension," he answered carefully, knowing that Theo had moved into "family" status. "I don't feel any anger coming from him, but I do think he's careful or cautious when I'm around. Harper, you're not bringing this up because you think I've stirred the pot up now that I've relocated up here, are you?"

"Oh hell no." Harper sat up in his chair. "That was a reckless question, and I apologize. No, nothing like that. I want you to be happy here and not threatened. I want everyone to be happy. In that regard, I'm worse than Lollie. I was just wondering."

Sweet, Lollie. Brent fondly recalled his telephone conversations with Harper's grandmother back when he was Harper's assistant. At Christmas, she always sent a box of cookies just for him. Harper and Lollie had a strong bond. Raised by his grandparents after his folks were killed in a plane crash, Harper had been devoted to her. Her unexpected death from a stroke the previous summer had hit hard.

"Yes." Brent confessed. "Part of the reason I jumped at the chance to rent the house was because of Theo… and well, Alex too. There certainly aren't any hard feelings on my part, but if there was anything smoldering within Theo, I wanted to make sure he understood I was on his side. Agreeing to pack up Artie's belongings wasn't something I'd typically sign up for. I thought I might earn a few points."

"Oh, it did. Theo's not the best communicator. You can't believe how relieved he is to not have to spend time in that house. He had a hard enough experience readying the shop for sale. This doesn't leave the room." Harper picked something off his pants and flicked it into the air. "He's spooked by Artie's spirit. I don't think he's seen a ghost, but he's felt Artie's presence. He had a scary thing happen working at the shop alone. Poor kid. No amount of talking can make something like that go away."

"I had a friend growing up who suffered from the same thing." He felt the need to show empathy. "Part of me wanted to tease the crap out of him, but the fear was so intense, you felt bad. Well, I hope I answered your question. Now I've got a couple things for you. Is there another beer in there?"

"Absolutely. I wish I could get Ian to enjoy a good ale."

Brent drained his bottle and walked to the fridge.

"Me too, please." Harper drummed the side of his chair with his hands.

"We need to talk about Owen Grady," he announced after he delivered Harper's beer. The time seemed right to unload his most problematic issue.

"Sure. That was on my list too." Harper sat back and hauled one leg over the other.

"I know you have your doubts, but I don't." He had rehearsed this exchange several times. There wasn't much room for error. "Owen isn't lying. Now that doesn't mean we've uncovered the whole story—the truth—but I don't think what's missing has anything to do with our client. Daniels. We need to talk to him."

Harper didn't answer immediately. He scratched his ankle. "I trust you say this because you've explored all the suspect avenues with Grady, and you've come up with blanks."

"Yes." Adjusting his tie, he secretly snuck in a breath before continuing. *You've got this covered. Don't worry.* Using his law school texts for inspiration, he had assembled what he believed to be a complete list of questions. It was important he got this right, this being the first case he was taking the lead on. "I went over all the basics with him in our meetings. Work and personal stuff like relationships, his family. You name it, and we've been over it. When Owen seemed vague, I drilled him for clarification. He's not lying. It's just not possible."

"You asked him about his Internet use?" Harper sipped.

Brent felt his stomach tighten. He hadn't.

"Have there been any incidents at school that could be perceived in the wrong way? Our client has been charged with indecent exposure. This opens the door for just about any accusation you can think of."

Stunned by how efficiently Harper identified the holes in his questioning, Brent wanted to vomit. His inexperience couldn't have been more exposed.

"I'd also want to know if there was any criminal history in his family. Can you imagine if the jury found out Grady was abused as a kid? That would kill us."

Sickened by his shortcomings, Brent rose from his chair and walked to the window. Every ounce of confidence had been sucked out of him in a matter of seconds. Worse, he now understood his deficiencies as an effective questioner. *You're a disaster.* What was so different about this compared to law school? He routinely outsmarted, outperformed his contemporaries. Something was getting in the way of doing an effective job with this case, and it frustrated and disappointed him that he had failed so miserably. The shame this revelation created was so powerful he couldn't turn to face his partner. His inexperience had led him off the cliff.

"Brent?"

"What?" He watched a hawk circle in the sky above the tall pines.

"Take a seat."

The tone of Harper's voice had changed. The challenge it carried earlier was gone.

Destroyed, Brent turned and shuffled back to his chair.

Harper placed his beer on the floor, sat back up, and smiled. "This lawyering thing, it takes time. You can, like you did so impressively, blow the roof off of law school. But the world they create there has nothing on experience."

At this point, Brent didn't know what was worse, being exposed for being a crap lawyer or having to listen to Harper dance around the issue by trying to make him feel better. He felt like a kid who had just been scolded for something he knew was wrong.

"I know you're smarting right now. I know this from experience. Look at me, my friend."

When he finally found the nerve to look up from his prized Harvey Milk paperweight, Brent shook his head sadly, accepting defeat.

Harper chuckled. "I was knocked around and challenged by my senior colleagues. I always came away from those sessions with such a profound feeling of defeat it took me weeks to process it and move on. Don't make that mistake." Harper stood. "Okay, just one more, and then I have to run. They're small."

Harper strolled to the fridge, retrieved two more beers, dropped one in front of Brent, and plopped back in his chair. "The mistake we guys make early on is we go to the bad place. We wrongly deride ourselves, when we are actually guilty of nothing more than inexperience. Are you following me?" Harper crossed his legs again and opened his bottle.

As he was expected to do, Brent nodded. Sadly he understood in his case, it was more. He was emotionally involved, and that's what differentiated his experience from Harper's.

"Anyway, move on."

Harper held his gaze until he was forced to agree again. "Okay," he managed, correcting the slump his body had been beaten into.

"You're right. It's time to talk to Trout Simmons. Enough time has passed now so this Daniels guy, if he's the kind of psychotic mess you think he is, is probably starting to think he's gotten away with this one. This is good for us. I'll talk to his boss, who will undoubtedly go back and question the randy officer. And with any luck, Daniels will start to question his game. That's when mistakes are made."

Wow, Brent hadn't seen that one coming. The very best he had hoped was for Harper to allow him to go back to Owen to ask the questions he had missed. Maybe then, after Harper was satisfied they had covered everything thoroughly, he'd agree to meet with his buddy, the chief of police.

"Shit. I'm kind of buzzed." Harper laughed. "I'd better stick around and work for a few hours until it wears off."

"Harper?" Brent asked.

"Yes, sir?"

"Thank you." Brent knew he was exactly where he needed to be at exactly the right time. He would take Harper's advice and he would grow, not wither in defeat.

"Well, I don't know what I did to deserve that, but you're welcome. You go back to the client and fill in a few more of the blanks. I'll call Trout and set up a meeting for some time later in the week. I need to strategize and give this some thought."

Harper got up and collected the empty bottles.

"Just set them on the desk. I'll make a dumpster run before I leave." Brent stood and stretched his arms above his head.

"You wouldn't have time to take a worker's comp case off my hands would you?" Harper asked.

"Sure," Brent answered without hesitation. "I'd be glad—"

"I'm fucking kidding." Harper laughed as he walked out the door.

Brent lowered himself into his chair, buried his head in his arms, and closed his eyes. Harper was so right. *This is called a second chance, shithead.*

# CHAPTER Five

RAIN MIXED with hail pelted the windshield as Owen pulled into the parking lot of the Lip Smacker. He hauled his hood over his head and made a beeline from the car to the diner's entrance.

Inside the foyer, he removed his glasses and dried them on his sweatshirt. The lunch crowd was long gone. He spotted his boss, Deena Phelps, seated alone in a booth midway down the row. She waved.

Deena was in her fifties, and her city look seemed out of place for the homey diner. She was classy, kind, and likable, and he always left meetings wanting more time with her. Today she was dressed in a navy blazer over a bright white blouse. Her hair always looked perfect—short and cut in a way that accented her narrow but pleasant face. If she had a noticeable fault, he had thought on occasion, it was her beakish nose.

"Wow, it's really coming down out there." He slid into the booth.

"I was lucky. I got here before the worst of it hit. You look good." Deena patted his hand. "Are you enjoying the break from school?"

On the drive over, he had cautioned himself about being overly suspect of his boss's request to meet. Like Brent had speculated, the chances were better than good she had heard something regarding his arrest. 'Are you enjoying the break from school' seemed an odd opening if, in fact, she had heard of his arrest. *What does she mean by that?* "The weather this summer has been great," he replied, carefully sidestepping her inquiry.

"Hello, what can I get you?" a server in a melon and white uniform asked as she approached the table.

“Ice tea.” He handed back the menu. Nerves had successfully squashed his appetite.

“Comin’ right up. There’s sugar and sweetener on the table.”

“Order food, Owen, if you’re hungry. I had a little something at home.”

“I’m good. It’s nice to see you, Deena. How’s *your* summer been?”

“It’s been typical. These budget cuts are starting to really affect my ability to manage. Just when I think I’ve got a solution, there’s a new leak in the dam. But that’s what I’m paid to do, so I guess I’d better stop complaining.” She chuckled and added a few splashes of cream before gently stirring her coffee. “Have any summer trips planned?” she asked after the waitress had dropped off his tea.

“Not really. How about you?” *This isn’t a ping-pong match. You’ve got to give her something.* “I would love to head into the BWCA for a week. Other than that, nothing set in stone.”

“I’ve lived in the area for over thirty years and I’ve never been. I guess if I’m being honest with myself, I’ve never been the camping type. And Frank, my husband… well, you’d have to knock him cold before he’d find himself in a canoe, not to mention a tent. He’s a city boy who prefers to enjoy nature from the comforts of his La-Z-Boy.”

They shared a laugh. He watched their waitress push a Hoky back and forth at the rear of the restaurant.

“Owen, I’m glad you were able to meet me today. Situations like this are never easy, so I’m just going to come right out and ask, are you in some kind of trouble? I’ve had two calls in the last week from individuals who think you might be.”

*Here we go.* Owen took a second to organize his thoughts. He hoped the smile on his face would allow this process to go undetected. As ready as he’d ever be, he answered as Brent had instructed. “I’m fine. There was an incident, and I have secured legal assistance to deal with it.”

*Christ, you might as well not have even answered the question.* He owed her more. Not because he had to, but out of respect for a woman who had been nothing but his champion from the start.

"Deena, I can't talk much about this now. I'm not sure what exactly it is you've heard, but I can assure you I'm innocent, and I'm hoping that will be proved sooner rather than later."

"Owen, please believe me when I tell you that regardless of the situation, I'm here for you if you need help in any way. This is a small town, and things tend to get bent out of shape rather quickly. I'm going to trust you're handling whatever it is you're involved in professionally, and with respect to your position at Jefferson High."

The friendly smile that trailed the end of her sentence morphed into a look of concern.

"I can tell you nothing like this has ever happened to me before." What more could he say to make things better for her? "I'm acting on the advice of an attorney I'm working with."

"That's good enough for me. We benefit greatly by your teaching talents, and the students adore you."

Their waitress approached the table. "More coffee and tea?"

"No thank you. I'll fly out of here if I have any more coffee." Deena placed her hand over her cup even though the waitress had shown up empty-handed.

"I'm fine. Thank you." Owen was grateful for the interruption.

"I'll leave your bill. No rush. I ain't goin' anywhere. You can pay at the cash register when you're ready."

"Thank you." Deena snatched the check the instant it hit the table. "This is on me. I really appreciate you taking time out of your day to meet. Before I go, I have some news— well two things, actually. First, before we move off the subject, I have a board meeting coming up in two weeks. If people are talking about your situation, Owen, you can bet I'm going to hear about it. I don't want you to worry, but I also want you to understand, if you have any new developments you think would…." Deena stopped. It was clear by the look on her face she struggled with how to finish her thought.

"Deena, I love my job more than you'll ever know. I don't want to lose it. Especially not over something as unfortunate…." Like Deena, Owen decided it was better to leave it at that. "I'll be in contact with you."

"Perfect. Now the other thing I want to share is exciting. At least, I think it is. Gordon Flatterly, the principal at Region High in

Comstock, called me last week to discuss the possibility of establishing an area marching band. It would be open to students from both our schools, plus he was planning on approaching Mack Stenrud over in Tilden Falls to see if he had any interest. The reason he called me is due, in part, because of you and the fine job you're doing for us. As tough as it was for him to admit"—Deena shook her head with a snicker—"we have a stronger music program, and he thought maybe we should take the lead on this if the concept meets with a favorable response." She took a sip from her cup and asked, "Do you have any marching band experience? I don't think we've ever talked about that."

His heart soared. He could hardly believe what he had just heard. Membership in the award-winning University of Minnesota marching band was an accomplishment he would cherish forever—the absolute highlight of his college days. Unable to contain his excitement, he recounted his experience. "The commitment required to be in the band was on par with being on a sports team. We practiced before classes and after classes. It was a part of your life. But I wouldn't have given up a minute of it. It's one of the things in my life I'm most proud of."

"Well, we certainly have a shot at making this work, if it moves forward." Deena eased herself out of the booth. "It's been so nice to see you, Owen. We'll leave it this way. I'll contact you with any new news, and you do the same. Sound good?"

"You have my word."

The rain had stopped when he climbed back into his car. He waited to make sure Deena was safely on her way before he pulled out of the parking lot. She could not have handled their meeting more professionally. But the prospect of a marching band, *his* marching band, was an incredible development. He pictured himself in a uniform, marching at the side of his young legion. *Please let me be around to make this happen.*

THE MINUTE Harper set foot in Barney's Bar & Bottle, he felt he'd entered another world—the earthy, heavily plaid domain of the Northwoods hunter. Squinting, he paused at the door until his eyes adjusted to the intentionally dim light. It created a bizarre twilight world—a dependable and comforting home away from home. A few patrons seated at the bar stared at their beers as if they were magic balls on which a message would soon appear, pointing the way to salvation. What caused a person to settle for this lonely existence? If he dwelled on it too long, it would make him sad.

Most of the area watering holes looked so similar, you would be hard pressed to identify a distinguishing characteristic. The bottles and snacks behind the bar were arranged to follow a universal pattern. Harper was quick to spot a few of his favorites—like the requisite jar of pickled eggs. Gray white orbs floated in murky liquid like pods out of a science fiction movie. *Who the hell would eat one of those?* Next to it sat a container filled to the brim with jerky. Large dill pickles were wrapped individually in plastic bags and stapled to a cardboard sign tacked to the wall. Another bar staple, the toaster oven, which faithfully produced cardboard-crust frozen pizzas, sat quietly waiting to be fired up. Endless signs of all shapes and sizes, opining on life and its funny peculiarities, added a sense of whimsy to the decor.

Earlier in the day, Harper had set up a meeting with Trout Simmons, the chief of police, to discuss their new client's case. He frowned, and for a brief moment thought about fleeing, when he spotted Trout at the end of the bar talking to Tubby Heckler, a local character he despised. Tubby was a know-it-all. From what Harper could discern, he knew very little. Greasy hair, yellow, nicotine-stained teeth, and an obnoxious habit of repeating idiotic wise cracks only Tubby found amusing added to the repulsion. But a wave from Trout lay to rest any plan to retreat.

"Howdy, Harp." Trout patted him on the shoulder as he brushed past Tubby.

"Hello, Trout." For a brief second he thought about greeting Tubby but decided against it. He didn't care what the obnoxious bullhorn thought of him, and by the look on Trout's face, he was sure his lapse in manners was understood.

"A city-slick attorney sure as hell classes up the place, don't ya think?" Tubby looked around to see if anyone else was listening. "To what do we owe your presence, Harp? Get a little tired of chasing ambulances?" Signaling for another beer, he emptied the remainder of a bag of chips into his mouth.

"Something like that." To take issue with this asshole's comment would get him nowhere, fast. Harper had learned his lesson in past meetings. He ordered when the bartender showed up with Tubby's refill. "Tap beer please."

"Beers are on me, fellas," Trout announced, slapping cash on the bar when Harper's tall glass arrived. Excuse us, Tubby," the sheriff begged off with a slap to the dimwit's back. "We have some business to attend to. Let's take us a seat at one of the tables, Harp."

"Was it something I said?" Tubby laughed and waved them off.

*That and so much more, Tubby.*

Trout led the way to a table in the corner, underneath one of the largest mounted black bears he had ever seen. It reminded him of something else he and Ian enjoyed at these dives. Most bars had an area, usually near the entrance, devoted to pictures of local hunters with their prized kills posted for all to admire. It had become a regular event to do a little inconspicuous hunting of their own—a hot dude dressed from head to toe in neon orange was the trophy they were after.

"There's no trouble at the Center, is there?" Trout asked as they sat.

"No, nothing like that." He glanced at the large creature looming down at the table and offered a toast. "Whazzup, Yogi?"

"Good. One of my deputies thought they saw something fishy going on a week or so ago in the parking lot of the Men's Center, but it turned out to be a high school kid and his sweetheart getting familiar with the birds and the bees. After scaring the urge to merge right out of them with a warning, he sent them on their way."

Harper laughed at the image. "Thanks for keeping an eye on the Center, Trout. I really appreciate it."

"It's a small town. Doesn't take much effort to drive around and make sure all is well. So what's on your mind?"

Resting his elbows on the table, Harper said, "We had a guy stop in the firm the other day who claims he was falsely accused and roughed up by one of your deputies. Daniels was the officer's name."

"Luke Daniels?" Trout appeared caught off guard. It was clear the idea of one of his officers behaving in such a way was unthinkable to him. "That's one heck of an allegation."

"That's what I thought," he agreed.

"I think I know who you're talking about, now that you mention it. Luke hauled a guy in, oh it's got to be going on two weeks now, for exposing his tallywacker on the trail out near Connor's Point." Trout chuckled. "Birdy. That's what Luke called him. I guess the guy was there watching birds until he spotted my officer." Trout shook his head. "The minute it warms up around these parts, you get the crazies. They come from all over. But this guy was local, if I remember right."

"Yes," he confirmed. "That's him."

"So, he's claiming he's innocent?" Trout asked, bringing his glass up for a sip.

There wasn't any reason to sugarcoat this. "The guy says your Daniels smashed his head into a tree when he refused to engage in sexual activity," Harper reported with a grimace.

"Can't say I was expecting that." Trout sat back and tapped his glass with his finger.

By the look on the sheriff's face, Harper wasn't sure how to interpret his friend's reaction. Trout stared across the table with an amazed look before he threw his head back and laughed so hard he had to slap his knee several times to recover. "What's so damned funny about this?" he wheezed. "You just got to know Luke. Open the dictionary to ladies' man, and he's staring right back at you. He can sure get them riled up in next to no time. And I'll tell you something." Trout leaned forward and whispered, "The women are lining up around the block for an opportunity to date him. Makes me damn sad I'm not in his shoes."

He chuckled along with his friend. "Is that right?"

"I've had women stop in for safety brochures and the like in record numbers since bringing him on. He's a good sport. Got a solid head on his shoulders. Never disrespectful."

Trout was certainly proud of his hire. There was no doubt about it. His portrayal of Daniels was going to be a tough pill for Brent to swallow.

"How long has it been since you hired Daniels?"

"He came aboard last August. Best addition to the force in years. I took him fresh out of school, before anyone else had the opportunity to mess him up. Boy, did he ever come along at a good time."

"Why's that?" Harper couldn't place an event involving law enforcement to attach to Trout's comment.

"I wasn't sure what I was going to do. Bill Deeders, who'd been on the force before even *I* got here, retired a month earlier. So we were short a man. And my Ginny was going through chemotherapy down in the Cities at the same time."

Harper could still hear the concern in Trout's voice. Ginny was, and always would be, Trout's better half. He'd offer that without even being prompted. "I have to apologize." Harper tapped his glass on the table. "I can't believe I've sat here talking to you for all this time without asking you about Ginny. How's she doing?"

"She's doing fine. Her doctors feel confident they were able to get it all. I've faced a lot of tough times, but losing her would hardly leave a life worth living. Sorry. Don't mean to be dramatic, but I'm man enough to tell you I was pretty damned scared there for a while." Trout's frankness told the story best.

"Well, that's wonderful news. Make sure you greet her for me. It's been a while since we've crossed paths. I used to run into her at the supermarket all the time."

"Well, chances are you'll be running into her there soon enough. The woman's day doesn't seem to be complete unless she brings home a sack of groceries. Christ. We have enough food around the house to feed a hundred people for a week."

"I'm not sure I understand what you're complaining about," Harper joked. "You mind if I ask you a few more questions about Daniels?"

"Fire away." Trout downed half of his glass.

"How did you and Daniels find each other?" He'd have to bring more detail back to satisfy Brent.

"I e-mailed information regarding the position to a few postsecondary schools, and he was one of the folks who answered back. A few had previous law enforcement experience, but after he came up for an interview, I knew he was the one. Damned near the only benefit for getting up in years"—Trout shook his finger at Harper—"I can spot bullshit a mile away. I never spotted it with you, my friend, and not with Luke neither. Honestly, with Ginny as sick as she was back then, I didn't have the time to really recruit. It was truly a blessing he came along when he did."

"I can't imagine facing cancer, and I hope I never have to find out what that's like." He finished his beer. "Trout? You feel like one more?"

"Hell, I always feel like one more, but it's close to suppertime, and I don't want to ruin my appetite. You go ahead if you want. I've still got time before I have to run off."

"Nope. I'm good. Getting back to Daniels if you don't mind." Harper folded his arms across his chest. "Where is he from?"

"He's a Minnesota resident. What I can't recall is where he grew up. I think it was one of the suburbs in the Twin Cities if I remember right." Trout frowned. "Damned memory."

"Any problems at all with your guy? Performance issues of any kind?" Depending on Trout's answer, this would probably be his last question.

"Exceeds expectations." Trout laughed. "That's one of the choices on our employee evaluation forms we get from the state. Suits him perfect. This is just between you and me, okay?" Trout looked side to side as if, by chance, someone had snuck in and taken a seat at a nearby table.

"Sure."

"I'm going to hang up my hat for good in a few years. I'm hoping Luke will go after the job. He's got those leadership skills that can't be taught."

"Really?" He hated like hell to hear Trout talk retirement. The fact that Daniels was being considered as his successor took a backseat to this news. "I've got to be honest with you. The day you retire isn't one I'm looking forward to. I've told you this before. You've been a friend to me, to the Center, while others around here were still wondering if their property values were going to go down because a couple of gay guys bought up an old resort. Say what you want, but I'll never take for granted all you've done for us."

"You know, we might not be the most progressive group of folks up here. But for the most part, we aren't stupid. You and Ian have brought with you more than your share of value add. We're the lucky ones." Trout raised his empty glass in toast.

"Thank you," Harper toasted back. "Thanks for finding some time for me today."

"Pleasure was all mine. Say. What's going to happen now with this guy? Ah shoot. Listen to me." Trout shook his head. "I forgot all about attorney-client privilege. Well, if there *is* anything you can tell me, I'd sure appreciate it."

"We'll probably want to talk to Daniels, at some point. I'm going to try and avoid that, given what I've heard from you. But we may have to do it just to make sure all our i's are dotted and our t's are crossed." He pushed his chair back from the table.

"Just say the word. Luke can hold his own. He's got nothing to hide." Trout walked his glass back to the bar.

Thankfully Tubby was nowhere in sight. With the exception of a woman seated in the same spot where Trout had been earlier, there were no changes in clientele. Nobody was having fun, including the bartender, who stared like a zombie at a television.

"I'll give you a call once we sort this mess out," Harper said as they stepped into the daylight. "Say hi to Ginny."

"Greet Ian for me."

"Speaking of." Harper pulled out a pair of sunglasses from his pocket. "He's having a good start to the season. We should catch a game together."

"I'd like that. He's a hell of a ballplayer. One of the best." Trout gave him a wave before getting into the squad car.

*Something's got to give here, and based on what I just heard, I think it might have to be Brent*. He waited for a line of traffic to pass and then turned onto the highway. It had been a long day. Time to head home for a little snuggle with his slugger.

SLEEP DIDN'T come easy after his arrest. A restful night was a thing of the past. When Owen did manage to drift off, it was short-lived. At the first sign of daylight, he crawled out of bed and showered. Saturday mornings were devoted to housework. It felt good to be busy. For several hours he managed to forget the arrest and all the baggage connected with it. And then he'd catch himself enjoying life, and the whole shit-mess would come flooding back.

Except during sleep, today had easily been the longest period he had gone without remembering he was in trouble. With any luck, the good days would start to outnumber the bad. As Brent had told him, life would someday return to normal. Owen sighed. Even if it was true, those days were a long way off.

He wrapped the cord around the holder on the upright vacuum and used his bare foot to push it into the linen closet. He hated wearing socks and shoes. When he was a kid, the minute it was warm enough to escape a scolding from his mother, he was barefoot. By the end of the summer, the soles of his feet were so tough he could walk over glass. With the exception of winter, it was rare to catch him in the yard with anything on his feet other than a pair of flip-flops, if he remembered to throw them on.

He poured a cup of coffee from the second pot of the day, carried it into the living room, and placed it on top of a magazine, protecting the wood surface he had just oiled. *How about some music?*

He knelt in front of his entertainment center—a series of long, pressed-wood shelves he picked up on his last trip to IKEA—looked over his collection, and decided on one of his favorites, Miles Davis. He inserted the disc, waited for it to start, and then adjusted the volume. When he had it to his liking, he moved to the couch and plopped down for a well-deserved break.

Unclipping a pen attached to the crossword page from yesterday's newspaper, Owen lowered his head onto an accent pillow, stretched out his legs, and found the place where he'd left off. Because he was spending so much time at home recently, he had started doing the puzzle as a diversion and found it interesting enough to hold his attention. He was better at it than he thought he'd be. Nepotism, Gandhi, rejuvenation, and pimple were today's victories. Then he began to drift off.

He napped until men's voices and the sound of car doors slamming woke him. The puzzle he had been working was still on his chest, but the pen was nowhere in sight. A spirited hunt ensued before he eventually dug it out from under the sofa cushion.

He sat up and peered out the window. Parked directly across the street were two pickup trucks. A group of men had collected in Artie Johnson's yard. He missed Artie.

A few yard-to-yard chats with his neighbor had quickly developed into a valued friendship. He was delighted when Artie invited him over for a cocktail one summer evening. It turned out they both shared a love for jazz. Although he didn't have an extensive collection, Artie had assembled many of the classics. He seemed to favor female vocalists. Discussions that started out primarily about music, over time expanded to include personal matters.

A few generous tumblers of scotch, and halfway through the famed Ella—Montreux '75—recording, Artie announced, with great ceremony, that he was gay. With pride, he told of his coming out, which he owed to the Men's Center—where he frequently met with a group of guys who were in various stages of the process. Owen, sensitive to Artie's journey to self-acceptance, shared his desire to find a man he could finally settle down with. Artie joked it was another cruel twist of fate that Owen hadn't been born twenty years earlier. He made no secret of his attraction to his younger friend.

Owen didn't understand how important Artie had become to him until after it was too late. He hated himself for not attending the wake and funeral.

Careful not to be noticed, he pulled the curtain back just enough to get a better look at the activities across the street. To his surprise, he spotted Harper Callahan, the attorney who worked with Brent. *What the hell is he doing there?* He couldn't remember when he'd seen a better-looking group of men—every one well above average. Was Artie leading a secret life?

"Holy shit." Owen got up on his knees and backed away from the window. The man on his mind of late, Brent Burns, had walked into view from behind one of the trucks. His heart raced, and his pulse shot off the charts.

*I'm so sleep deprived, maybe I'm hallucinating. Why would both attorneys be at Artie's? The estate?*

Artie had never mentioned family, so it was anyone's guess who would claim the house. That had to be it. Owen sat breathless while he watched Brent carry a box up the stairs.

When he slept long enough to have them, his dreams were mostly unpleasant. Lately, a few had been erotic at the start, before turning scary. Brent—always the hero, always naked—starred in the early, good part of these dreams. Owen sat on his heels and rested his chin on the back of the couch, recalling as best he could how the good part of the dream usually went.

Beams of warm light found their way through the dense forest canopy, making the dew-covered plants glisten. Birds, all his favorites, flitted around like in a cartoon, landing on nearby branches as if to show off.

As he watched the men across the street huddle together, he thought about his favorite part of the dream. Brent pulled Owen's T-shirt over his head and then, with a smile, carefully placed it on the end of a branch. With plenty of kisses and licks, he slowly stripped him. It felt extraordinary to be naked in the woods. They laughed and inspected each other, delighted at how their bodies were responding to the attention. Taking him by the hand, Brent led them off the path and into a clump of fragrant lilac, to a bed of soft leaves. This was the spot where his dream took a turn for the worse.

A snapped twig warned of an intruder. Bending back branches, they watched as Officer Daniels stepped into view and turned toward them, his steely, piercing dark eyes probing the woods as if searching for prey. Thankfully this horrifying recollection ended abruptly when Brent stepped out of the house and walked to one of the trucks.

For the first time, he had the pleasure of viewing Brent in something other than his office attire. Camel-colored cargo shorts accentuated the same tantalizing curves of the ass he had admired in dress pants. His legs were a wonderful surprise. Well-defined calves, works of art, bulged and begged for closer examination. Owen savored every inch as he worked his way up to Brent's chest, emphasized in all its glory by a red muscle T. Owen sighed when the hot stud leapt up the stairs and went into the house.

Too wound up to stay put, Owen hopped off the couch and brought his cup of cold coffee into the kitchen. From there, he went downstairs and pulled the last load of clothes from the dryer. He returned to empty the laundry basket onto his bed and began organizing by group—the first step before folding. That's as far as he got before the urge to keep an eye on the action across the street got the best of him.

Back on the couch, he eased into the corner where he could view Artie's front door and one of the trucks. The more he watched, the more confused he became. *What the hell is going on over there?* Two of the guys who he had never seen before were carrying stuff inside the house, while Brent and Callahan carried boxes out and tossed them into the truck bed.

At the next lull in the action, he reluctantly pried himself away from the show to resume his chores. He replaced the Miles CD with an Art Tatum and went about pairing socks, smoothing out underwear, and hanging T-shirts until all were neatly folded and put away. *I've got to have just one more look.*

He raced back to the couch and watched the two men he didn't know haul out a small sofa, place it in the truck, and then go back inside. Owen sat back on his haunches and waited. He hoped Brent would reappear, but when that didn't happen, he grew frustrated and decided to give up the watch. *Spying like this is stupid. Go do something healthy.* It was probably better for him to be seen out and about than not, so he decided to go birding. The weather was too nice to spend the day inside.

Before he could act on his plan, voices from outside brought his attention back to the street. The entire group exited the house and got into their trucks, leaving Brent Burns standing alone at the top of the steps. They had an uncomfortable moment after the trucks pulled away. Brent was staring across the street, right into his front window.

Recoiling out of sight, Owen banged his head hard on the wall in back of him. Rubbing to make the pain dissipate, he carefully crawled forward and ventured one more glance. Brent, to his amazement, opened the door to Artie's house and walked inside.

Owen released the curtain and stared blankly into space. A leg cramp eventually brought him out of his stupor. He stumbled into the kitchen and poured a glass of water from a pitcher in the refrigerator. He downed it in only a few gulps, placed the glass in the sink, turned, and thrust his arms wildly into the air, dancing his way through the house. *Brent's my new neighbor. How lucky is that?*

"WHAT I like most about this"—Harper stood back from the rest who were huddled over a blueprint—"the design accentuates the rustic feel of the property and doesn't needlessly try to update."

He and Ian had vowed to keep the original look of the resort intact while modernizing as money and time permitted. In his mind, the resort office was the centerpiece. That it too would eventually need a makeover had crossed his mind on several occasions, but more important projects had always kept it on the back burner. "I can visualize it. Nice job, guys." He initiated high fives with both Theo and Alex.

"Is it hard for you to see the apartment go bye-bye?" Ian asked Alex. He stepped from behind Harper's desk and sat in one of the chairs facing them.

"No. Not really." Alex draped his arm around Theo. "It seems so long ago. Almost like a dream."

Harper caught Ian's eye, and they smiled. Theo blushed from Alex's impromptu sign of affection. "It does seem like a very long time ago." Harper wandered around his desk and sat next to Ian. "Makes me feel like a really old man if I dwell on it."

"You *are* a really old man," Ian quipped, making everyone except Harper snicker. "Thirty-five is a milestone, my dear. You best get your affairs in order. You could go any day."

"I can't tell you how much I hate that you're six months younger than I am." Harper swatted his husband's knee.

"I love that it bugs you." Ian reached out and tapped the blueprint. "Theo, how confident are you with your proposed budget? It will *really* bug the old man here if you're off. It's a little-known fact that he's the master of frugality. He taught Alex everything he knows on the subject."

They laughed together, knowing, as close friends often do, that there was more truth than fiction in Ian's dig.

Before Harper could go on the defensive, Theo piped up. "It won't run any higher than what I predicted. Wait. I just thought of something." He rolled up the design. "When I was driving into the resort the other morning, I had an idea about the new sign." He held the blueprint up and waited while Alex slid a rubber band over it. "It would be cool if there were animals, maybe deer or something, drinking from the pools under each of the waterfalls."

Harper knew the second Theo brought up deer, that he was being had. Turning to Ian, he said flatly, "That was highly unsportsmanlike conduct. I'm shocked you would go so far as to recruit others to do your dirty work."

"Deer would look awfully fine there, poopsie. You know, like in the picture I showed you the other day. That pair of *bronze deer*." Ian shot Harper his best "pretty please" face. Perfected over the years for maximum effect, it never failed to nab his heart and rip out any existing resolve. Today was no different. And although there wasn't a chance in hell he'd admit this to Ian or anyone else, the deer had been on his mind too. The front entrance was gorgeous, but the addition of Bambi and a friend would complete the setting.

At about the time he realized all eyes were on him to explain his reluctance to green-light the bronze deer, he had an idea.

Harper picked up a folder containing Theo's budget. "You guys don't play fair. I hope you know that. It's bullying, pure and simple."

Ian offered another look—an interesting mix of "you can't beat city hall" and "I had nothing to do with this."

Holding the folder out for all to see, Harper addressed the group. "Buckling under tremendous pressure from none other than my own people—the very ones whom I love dearly, *bronze* dearly, and up until a moment ago, trusted without question—I've come up with… well, a challenge, really."

"Brace yourselves, men," Ian cautioned. "This could either be a tactic designed to distract, or one of those situations where we think we've won, when in fact we've lost and we don't even know it."

"I have been guilty of pulling a fast one in the past," Harper admitted.

"What's the challenge?" Alex asked.

"Bring this project in on time *and* under budget, and I'll place the order for the deer myself. You guys game?"

"Deer for both sides of the entrance?" Ian, risking nothing, sought clarification.

"Yes," Harper confirmed.

"The nice *expensive* bronze deer in the picture?" Ian looked to the others for solidarity.

"For fuck sake, Ian. Yes. Honestly." In a display of mock frustration, he tossed the folder on the desk and folded his arms across his chest. Before anyone else could speak, someone knocked on the door. "Come in," he hollered.

Brent walked in with a folder of his own. He handed it to Harper, looked around the room, and asked, "Did they approve the remodel?"

"Yep," Theo and Alex announced at the same time.

"The original idea was mine," Brent announced.

"All the more special," Harper commented dryly. "Okay. One more piece of business, and then I have to get back to crafting a letter that effectively argues back pay for one of the world's leading dingbats. Theo, Brent? Would you please leave us for a minute? We need to check Alex's body for ticks, and that requires a certain degree of privacy."

Alex, sharing a look with both Theo and Brent, laughed nervously. "What are you guys up to? I want to know before I'm left alone with these two."

Walking to the door, Harper gestured for Theo and Brent to leave. "Out, please. We'll call you when we've completed our inspection."

Brent followed Theo out and closed the door.

"Take a seat, Alex." Harper pointed to the chair next to Ian. "And relax. You look like you're going to shit yourself."

Alex did as he was asked. Ian motioned Harper to hand him the folder. He opened it, glanced at the contents, and nodded his approval.

As much as Harper hated to see Alex made nervous, he was pleased that the earlier frivolity had been effectively replaced by a sense of formality. "Alex," he began as he sat on the corner of his desk. "Ian and I have something we need to discuss. You need to know and understand the decision is yours, not ours...." An unexpected wave of emotion attacked Harper out of the blue. Looking to Ian, whose eyes were already moist, he collected himself and continued. "Regardless of your decision, we want you to know how much we love you. You've become so important to us. I think you know that already. I hope you do."

"I do." Alex looked at them both. As happened so often when he was put on the spot, his feet began a steady dance on the carpet.

Harper sat back and smiled as Ian handed their young friend the folder containing a single-page document. This was one of those moments in life that he would remember forever.

A few moments passed in silence before Alex closed the folder and rested it on his lap. Harper realized by his posture that Ian was struggling to keep it together. The three of them had been through a lot together.

"Um...." Alex fidgeted in his chair. "Do I get to change my name?"

Ian grabbed Alex by the head and pulled him in for a hug, causing the folder to fall to the floor.

"Well." Harper fought to stay composed. "I guess that depends. Ian and I favor old world names, like Ingrid and Constance. We aren't too keen on Brandy or Heather. What did you have in mind?"

Ian released Alex, who picked the folder up off the floor. "You know, I used to dream about this happening, so often. Especially in that first year. And then, when I realized you guys weren't going to leave me...."

That's as far as Alex got before his lower lip began quivering as fast as a hummingbird's wings. Unable to keep his own eyes dry, Harper knelt next to Alex and explained, "Some things were just meant to be. Both Ian and I felt a powerful bond with you from the very beginning. You know that. The first time we talked about adoption was shortly after you lost your dad. We felt so bad we tried to come up with a way to make you feel loved and safe. Over time, it got to be the kind of thought that wouldn't go away. We decided once we were legally married and the firm was up and running, we would make the offer official."

"I want to own your ass, dude," Ian joked.

They all laughed through tears.

"Alexander Burke Callahan," their young man announced when he had regained his voice. "I love both of your last names way more than my own. Stevens. I mean it sounds so… suburban.

"Suburban? Interesting." Harper looked at Ian, who nodded his approval. "Done." He walked to his desk and grabbed a pen. "Sign on the dotted line before you get cold feet."

When he finished signing, Alex pointed to Harper and asked, "Does this make you my dad?"

"It could, if that's what you wish. I'd be honored."

"Great." Alex turned to Ian. "Mommy?" The word was barely out of his mouth before he bolted out of his chair and ran.

Ian was up and after him in a flash.

"Ah yes." Harper crossed the room, careful to stay clear of Ian as he chased Alex around the desk. "We'll enjoy years of bliss and togetherness."

Brent led Theo and Fern into the office. All three were cheering and wearing "It's a Boy!" party hats. Alex and Ian stopped in their tracks.

Harper pulled a bottle of champagne out of his minifridge and popped the cork. When everyone held a glass, he toasted, "Here's to proud parents and cherished friends. May we all enjoy long, healthy, and prosperous lives."

"LET ME staple the corner, and then you can let go of it." Theo reached above his head next to Alex, who held a clear plastic tarp against the ceiling. "There. Thanks for helping. The only thing I can't prevent from coming into the office is the noise from the power tools. We'll have to devise some sort of signal for when the phone rings or someone stops by."

"What about a flashing light? That would be pretty easy to rig." Alex folded the stepladder.

"Perfect. That would be supereasy to set up. The hard part is, I have to remember to pay attention to it." Theo moved behind Alex and wrapped his arms around his waist. "I love you so much."

"I know you do. I love you more."

"What those guys did yesterday—the adoption—was so cool. Not sure if this makes sense." Theo hugged Alex tighter. "It makes me feel even closer to everyone. Because you're mine."

"Jesus H. Christ. What the hell is going on in here?" Ian burst into the office and tossed his gloves on the counter. "At least your pants aren't bunched around your ankles."

"Hey, Mom. Time for lunch?" Alex joked.

"I'm warning you, keep up that mom shit, and you're going to be very sorry. Theo, do I look like I'm joking?"

"Not really. No, I guess." Theo was pretty sure Ian was serious. He was never 100 percent sure.

They separated. Alex went back to the computer. "What's happening?" he asked Ian when the silence went on for what seemed like a record amount of time.

"It's been a bad morning. Some critter got into the flower bed down by cabin six and tore the hell out of it. I salvaged most of the annuals, but I'll have to make a run into town to see if I can find some replacements. Sorry, guys. I'm a little cranky."

"I'd be glad to help," Theo offered.

"Thanks, dude. I'm okay. I came back here because I have a candidate coming in to interview for office manager. Anyone show up yet?"

"Nope," Alex confirmed. "Why don't you go back to what you were doing, and I'll run down and grab you when they show up."

Ian scratched his head and looked at the clock. "Thanks, but I'll hang here for a minute. I hope this woman isn't late. She said she knew right where we were."

"Wouldn't it be cool if we found someone like Petra again?" Alex sipped from his can of Dew.

"That would take a miracle," Ian agreed. "But then again, we had no idea what we were getting when we signed on Petra. She just blossomed into a great employee. Maybe lightning will strike in the same place twice. All I know is, I can't wake up every morning with this still on my plate. It's killing me."

The sound of tires on gravel signaled an arrival. Out of habit, Alex lifted his shirt and squeezed his nipples enthusiastically—an expression of silly he learned from Ian, the master.

A car door slammed, followed by footsteps on the pebbled path beside the office. Theo watched a shadow pass quickly by the window. Seconds later the screened door opened, and the person stepped into the tiny space.

In disbelief, Theo staggered backward, ripping down a section of the tarp. "Mother, what are you doing here?"

# CHAPTER Six

"GO TO the guest icon to the left." Theo shook his head in disgust when the cursor toured the entire computer screen twice before settling on the tiny trash can at the bottom. "That's the recycle bin. Point the arrow at the one that looks like a *person* and *click it*."

"This one?" his mother asked, making an adjustment to her already textbook-perfect posture.

"Yes. Like I said, it's the icon that looks like a *person*."

Years of anger and hurt boiled up from Theo's core. *Why me? I can't stand being near her. I should never have said yes to Ian.*

It wasn't only Ian who was spearheading this unwelcomed reunion. Harper was in on it too. And, although silent on the decision to bring her on as the new office manager, so was Alex. He could see it in his face. In the short time he and his mother had been working, Theo had watched each of them stroll past the window. He hated being spied on. It made him feel untrustworthy.

"This is so different from the computer program we have at the church." Darla Engdahl looked up and smiled.

*That's because it was designed by Jesus.*

"I click this person thingy first, right?"

"Yes."

It had been a little over a year since he had spent any time with his mother. The day he moved out from his parents and in with Alex was the last time he had seen her. Newly outed by the local paper, which had run a front-page photo of him and Alex kissing at the Pride festival, had made living under the same roof no longer an option. There had been a few lunches with his dad, but he never once felt a need to reconnect with his mother, who he thought wicked at best. The quicker he could get her trained in and back out of his life the better. This remodel was going to be completed in record time.

"Oh, honey, you are so *smart*. That worked just like you said it would," she announced in her all-too-familiar, sickening way.

Closing his eyes, he begged to be removed from this nightmare. "Follow the prompts on the screen," he forged on, trapped. "Choose the date, and if the guest party is already confirmed, a name will appear with their contact information. If no name is there, you enter what is missing from the reservation form." He could barely keep the tone of his voice civil. "You should be able to figure out the rest from there. I have to get back to work."

"Thank you, Theodore. I just hate not knowing how everything works." She removed her fingers from the keyboard and swung around to face him. "Can we talk for a minute before you leave me?"

*No.*

"What's up?" Theo folded his arms across his chest. She was pushing her luck. Testing him to see how far she could go before he snapped and showed weakness. Whatever she was up to, Theo vowed to keep one step ahead of her.

Darla rested her hands in her lap and stared up at him with a pained expression. "I know you don't like me, Theodore."

"Theo. I hate it when you call me Theodore," he shot back in anger and then wished he hadn't. *Careful of these traps.*

"I'm sorry. Theo."

The resentment in his voice caused his mother to break eye contact, which never would have happened before. She could bore a hole right through you before you were forced to look away and declare her the winner. And Darla was always right.

"What I meant to say," she clarified, resuming her focus on him, "is that I understand *why* you don't like me, and I'd like you to know that I was wrong."

It was his turn to look away. *Fuck me. Did she just admit to being wrong? I didn't see that one coming.* No. She was up to something. There was no doubt about it. He stared back at his mother. If he were patient, the words spewing out of her mouth would end on their own.

"I know it might be hard for you to believe, but for some time now, I've wanted to tell you that I was wrong, Theodore. Oh gosh." Darla clenched her fists and shook them in front of her in obvious frustration. "I mean *Theo*. Sorry."

He unfolded his arms and stuck his hands into his pockets, a reaction caused by his dwindling confidence. His mother's confession complicated things. Guilt now danced alongside anger, which waltzed along with mistrust. Nothing from his past gave any reassurance that she was on the level. *I can't trust you.* Years of conniving and justifying prevented him from accepting her at face value.

"I don't know what to say to you," he admitted, because it was true. He couldn't think of a single thing to say short of calling her a liar.

"Have you heard of something called PFLAG?" his mother asked.

*Is she kidding?* "Yes." *Where the hell is this headed?*

"There's a local chapter that meets in Duluth. For the last several months, your father and I have been attending their meetings. We've met some wonderful people there."

If hope had an expression, Darla had it aced. "It's okay to still be angry with me. But I need you to know I'm trying. It's me who has to change, Theo. Not you. The church is very important to me, but not as important as you. I understand now that instead of working on our relationship and attempting to understand the struggles you face, I was, in fact, being selfish. It took us being apart so long for me to really accept and understand it's me who has to adjust."

Clobbered by her admission, he absently moved toward the door, causing a flurry of activity outside. He glanced at the tiny window in time to catch Ian and Alex bolt by. How much had they heard? Part of him hoped they'd been close enough to catch every word. *Who's going to believe this?* A myriad of emotions were begging for his attention. It was Darla's typing that finally came to the rescue, bringing his thoughts back to the present.

"Oh my goodness. Is this ever something," she chimed out. "I never imagined the computer could be so fun. Neat."

The door was right there. He could open it and walk out, dismissing his mother's effort to make peace. It would be so easy.

As he contemplated his next move, Harper strolled into view. He was down by the lake carrying a garbage bag. How odd. Harper wasn't on the grounds because he felt the need to tidy up. He was here to support him. Alex and Ian were spying because they cared, and they didn't want him to be hurt again. These guys were his family now. Theo battled the lump that had formed in his throat. *I'm not the victim any longer. She is.* Knowing his family of friends was close by helped restore his confidence. For the very first time in as long as he could remember, the woman seated just a few feet away appeared human—not the monster he remembered. *This could be an evil trick. The bitch is more than capable of it.* Too much hurt and hate prevented him from giving her the benefit of the doubt. *If you have changed, and what you say is the truth, then you are going to have to work harder to earn me back.*

"Keep at it, and it will get easier." He strolled behind the counter and pulled back the plastic tarp separating the remodel from the front office. "Do you have any questions before I start working?" This hefty dose of Darla had occupied all the time he could spare for the moment.

"I don't think so. I'll just continue down this list of names. It looks like there's plenty to keep me busy for a while."

"Flick the light switch next to the phone, and I'll stop up if you need something." *She'd better not be fucking with me. That's all I can say.*

*WELL, IF nothing else is going right in my life, at least the new grass has taken hold.* An invasive weed had strangled an area in the back corner of the yard. Owen chose to dig it out instead of treat it with a chemical. When possible, he always chose the green option.

He guided the rusted push mower—a gift from the previous homeowner—along the cedar fence separating his yard from Gloria and Mitch Kitowske, a retired couple. Skeptical at having a single guy for a neighbor, they had been hard to win over, at first. Artie eventually brought them around. The previous Christmas, they both hand delivered a basket of homemade delights from Gloria's kitchen.

He contemplated taking a break before starting on the front yard. *Lemonade would be good about now.* Darkening clouds to the west forced him to keep going or risk having to finish the next day. There wasn't much to the front. The bulk of his property was behind the house. Ten minutes and he would have it licked. He enjoyed mowing. And it was important to keep up with Mitch, who mowed almost every day. He had little else to do with his retirement other than stare out the kitchen window while Gloria baked.

Beginning with the boulevard, Owen happily pushed along for several minutes—until he spotted a runner turning onto the street and heading in his direction. It took only seconds to identify Brent charging toward him dressed in running shorts and a muscle shirt. Owen experienced a brief bout of light-headedness. It had been several days since he secretly watched the handsome attorney move into Artie's. He had been searching for the right moment to connect, and now without his even having to try, here it was.

"Owen?" Brent asked, huffing and puffing as he jogged up. "No way. Is this where you live?"

"Hey, neighbor." He felt his face warm. An explanation was probably due, but what could he say that wasn't lame or a lie? *Better go with the truth.* "I thought that was you I saw moving in the other day. Did you buy Artie's house? I didn't even know it had gone on the market."

"It's a long story, but no, I didn't buy. I'm renting it from the guy who inherited it from Artie. Great house. Sure beats the shithole apartment I was living in." Brent grabbed his leg from behind and pulled it up toward his butt.

"Artie and I were friends. We used to get together every so often for a drink and some jazz. He had a nice collection of music." Once again the reminder of Artie's passing triggered a moment of melancholy. Artie would have been great to have around during all of this mess with the law.

"Almost everything he had is still in the house. Part of the long story—I'm getting a break in rent to help box his stuff up for a sale later in the summer. Are you interested in his music collection? I'm sure I could work out a very favorable deal." Brent chuckled. With the back of his hand he wiped away the sweat that had accumulated on his forehead.

The first rumblings of thunder made them both look toward the sky.

"I'm keeping you from mowing." Brent smiled. "Why don't we plan on meeting again early next week? I'll have some updates by then. Fern will give you a call to set up the appointment."

Resisting the urge to give Brent the once-over, which he desperately wanted to do, Owen kept his focus on Brent's face. Despite this awkward challenge, he still had to make a move. *Don't let him get away.* "What are you doing a little later? Feel like coming over for dinner?" He had no idea what the policy was in regard to fraternizing with clients. But as his grandfather was so fond of pointing out—*Owen, it takes so little energy to ask.*

"Seriously? Oh man, I would *love* that." Brent's face lit up. "I'll get cleaned up…."

He was interrupted by a loud clap of thunder. The storm was almost upon them.

"Fantastic. I'd better get a move on or I won't have this finished before the rain starts. Give me an hour. You're welcome to come over any time after that," Owen offered eagerly.

"Thanks. See you soon."

Having successfully averted the embarrassment of being caught checking out his hot body, Owen threw caution to the wind and watched with delight as Brent's ass snapped from side to side as he strolled across the street. Fueled more by the prospect of spending an evening with a gorgeous man than by an impending thunderstorm, he stepped up his effort, moving to the patches of lawn that framed the walk to his front steps. He completed the last patch as the first large droplets of water splattered onto his head. By the time he had hauled the mower to the back and placed it in the tiny shed, he was soaked.

Inside, he peeled off his shorts, his T-shirt, and for no reason other than he felt like wearing a fresh pair, his boxers. In the laundry area, he placed them in the dryer and hit the start button. He'd probably end up washing everything before wearing it again, but he didn't want wet clothes in his already damp basement to get funky.

He took a bag of frozen shrimp from the freezer. Kabobs had been on his mind all day. There were enough fresh vegetables from his visit to the local farmer's market earlier in the week to easily feed two. Throw together a batch of rice, and *voilà*—a tasty, casual summer dinner. If it stayed warm after the rain stopped, he would set up the little table in the backyard. His heart raced. He couldn't wait for the opportunity to get to know his attorney in a more relaxed setting. The attraction was potent. Brent's boyish charm, which seemed to ooze out of every pore, was nectar he couldn't resist. He had devoted hours to analyzing and speculating about what made the guy tick.

Thinking about what might happen after dinner had an immediate impact. To ignore the urge to satisfy his growing need, he raced through the mechanics of showering and didn't succumb to temptation. He toweled off, threw on a fresh version of his unofficial summer uniform—baggy shorts and a well-traveled T-shirt—and raced downstairs to organize dinner.

With the meal prep complete and only a few minutes to spare before the guest of honor would arrive, he turned his attention to music. Trusting his instincts, he picked out a well-rounded selection of vinyl and placed it in a neat stack next to his turntable. Off the top, he carefully removed one treasure he had recently snapped up at a yard sale—a John Coltrane import. If Brent was familiar with the exquisite saxophonist, hopefully this disc would impress. Regardless, it was great music and would create what he thought to be the perfect mood—relaxed, with just a pinch of sexy. Back in the kitchen, he grabbed a bottle of white wine out of the refrigerator and then put it back. He'd leave it up to his guest to decide what to drink.

INTENSELY AWARE that first impressions are important, Brent, naked, laid out four pair of underwear on his bed and then, with a frustrated sigh, took a step back. Unless something totally unexpected occurred, Owen would never have the opportunity to evaluate his underwear choice. *So what? I care, and that's still a good reason.*

Starting from the left, he mulled over a navy and green tartan boxer, a black boxer brief, a bright red boxer with a lightning bolt print, and last in the row, his most conservative choice, a classic powder blue boxer. Holding each of them up to his waist, he posed in front of his full-length mirror and presented his "come hither and slather my balls with sloppy kisses" look. He decided on his tried-and-true favorite—the tartan.

"Life isn't fair," Brent whined, hiking the underwear up over his hips. The men he was most attracted to were always either taken or for some other reason off-limits. Any feelings he'd recently had for Owen were ethically prohibited because he was a client. Still, there was something brewing, and as hard as he fought to keep it at bay, it fought a harder battle to surface.

Could he talk it over with his close friend and law partner? Part of him wanted to, but a strong current of guilt quashed this thought every time he examined it. Harper could easily misunderstand it as a covert excuse for his less-than-stellar performance on the case so far. That was the last thing he needed. *Absolutely fucking not!*

Seated on the edge of the bed, he stared into his closet. *Let's see, what am I in the mood for?* Last weekend he had organized his shirts into two groups—casual and dress. Taking it a few steps further, he grouped the collection by color and then arranged everything from light to dark. The challenge now was to keep it organized.

For tonight, his mind was set on wearing a pair of moss green chino shorts. They had a way of clinging to his ass that looked and felt perfect. When he wore them, they made him feel inexplicably sexy. There was nothing wrong with wanting to look your best, regardless of the occasion.

*Yes.* He hopped to his feet and nabbed a peach and white bowling shirt off its hanger. When he had finished dressing, he inspected the look to see if he had hit on the right tone. *You're the man. Casual, playful, and highly... fuckable.* Exasperated, he gave the mirror a piece of his mind. "I can't help it. This is me."

He slipped on a pair of flips, rushed down the stairs, and grabbed a six-pack of beer from the refrigerator. Looking around the room, he wondered if he was forgetting anything. *Music?* Although Owen had mentioned he used to listen to jazz with Artie, he made the decision to leave the music up to his host. He didn't want to bring over a crap choice and have Owen feel obligated to play it. He locked the front door and puddle jumped across the street.

*What a beautiful night.* The early evening sun sparkled on the rain-drenched leaves and grass. Steam rose from the pavement. This would be a great chance to get to know his client better. *Nothing more, shithead.*

Anxious to get the evening rolling, he leapt up the stairs of the stucco house. The front door was slightly ajar, and he could hear music. He decided to knock rather than ring the bell. Seconds later he heard footsteps approach.

"Welcome," Owen greeted as he opened the screen door. "Come on in."

"I still can't believe we live across the street from each other. That's awesome." He presented the six-pack. "I brought a few brews, if you're interested."

"Thanks, but you didn't have to bring anything. I was wondering if you were a beer or a wine kind of guy." Owen read the label out loud. "Speckled Egg Ale. Now that's one I haven't heard of before."

"Beer is my first choice only because I know virtually nothing about wine. I enjoy it, but it intimidates me. Anyway, I have a supply of the 'Egg' to keep me going for a while. But please, don't feel obligated." He was prone to control situations such as this. Something he had vowed to avoid. It was Owen's dinner.

"Follow me. I'd love to try it." Owen led them through the living room, into the kitchen at the back of the house. "I'm afraid I don't have any chilled glasses. Will a warm pilsner do?"

"The bottle is just fine with me." Their brief journey to the kitchen offered a prime opportunity to ogle every inch of his client. *Scrumptious.* Dressed in navy shorts and a faded University of Minnesota T-shirt, Owen was so hot it was tough to look anywhere else. *You're not making this easy for me are you, stud?*

"This is a great house, by the way." Brent had scarcely had a moment to look around but knew from experience, having been invited home so many times for hookups, this was one of the first things the guest needed to say. It was one of the universal icebreakers.

"Oh, Thanks. There's also a bottle of white wine chilling." Owen twisted the cap off a beer and handed it to him. "I'll open it to have with dinner, and you can try a glass if you'd like."

"Perfect." Pesky urges made it impossible for him to stand in one spot. He needed a purposeful destination or he risked looking like a freak, so he walked to the open door leading to the back. "What a great yard," he observed through the screen.

"Thanks." Owen sampled the Egg. "I like this. Interesting flavor." He offered his bottle. "Cheers."

"Cheers." Brent clinked it.

"I think I'm going to let you decide." Owen placed the remainder of the beer in the fridge and removed a tray covered with aluminum foil.

*Let me decide? That's easy. Us naked. The bedroom. And put whatever it is you're serving for dinner on hold.* "Huh?" Brent's face grew warm. He needed to stop this and stop it now. *Think how pissed Harper would be if he knew how close you are to jeopardizing a perfectly innocent attorney-client relationship. Get a fucking grip.*

"It's all easy. You decide. We can either eat on the porch in front, out in the backyard, or in the dining room." Begging to be jumped and ravished, Owen leaned against the red Formica counter and waited with a smile for him to choose.

"Hmm…." Brent had no trouble making up his mind. "It's such a nice night. Let's eat in back." He enjoyed the first sip of his beer—always the best.

"I was hoping you'd say that." Owen grinned. "I love being outside. And if our luck holds out, the mosquitoes will give us a break. So far this season, they haven't been too bad at night."

"Oh, I forgot about those hungry critters. I've been avoiding my yard because it needs work, and I'm not too handy with gardening. Actually I just lied. I hate yard work. There always seems to be something else to do instead. How's that for padding my application for home ownership?"

They both laughed.

Owen sipped and then adjusted his glasses. "I'm in desperate need of a project to take my mind off my troubles. Why don't you let me tool around in Artie's yard? I love gardening and working outside."

If he was offering to help because he felt obligated or wanted to ensure he got the best representation, that wouldn't be right. He searched Owen's face and found nothing suspect. Still, from an ethical standpoint, it probably wasn't a good idea.

"Owen, I can't let you do that. It wouldn't be right." He sipped and shook his head no.

"Why? You would be doing *me* a favor. I'm going crazy. The distraction would be wonderful."

*Maybe it's okay. What's the harm? If Owen would benefit, there was no real reason to say no.* "If you're sure you're not doing this because you feel some sense of obligation for my handling your legal situation, then I would be glad to accept your help."

"Oh my," Owen snickered. "I never even considered that."

There was a brief pause in their conversation. Owen ended it by looking over with concern and stating, "Even though the fees for your legal services through the Center are reduced, I intend to pay full price. Call it a donation. And that's regardless of the outcome."

In a rare flash of clarity, Brent took a moment to think before offering a response. There was an element of pride involved, and he didn't want to take that away from Owen. After reviewing his options, he answered, "That would be entirely up to you, but it certainly isn't necessary."

"Right." Owen smiled. "You know, having you over is exactly what I needed. I feel good about myself right now. That's huge."

"So, what's for dinner?" It was best to move things along. Brent was starting to receive signals from his naughty parts that could quickly escalate out of control.

Owen removed the foil from a tray and revealed four picture-perfect kabobs. "Shrimp kabobs, Jasmine rice, and salad. How's that sound?"

“Wow. This is going to be the best meal I’ve had since moving up here.” Like gardening, he had no interest in cooking, but almost always enjoyed the efforts of those who did.

“Do you like lemon-flavored things?” Owen asked.

“Love lemon. Why?” It seemed everything out of Owen’s mouth carried a sexual subtext. The kitchen had suddenly become very small.

“I picked up a pint of Yvonne’s incredible lemon bar frozen custard yesterday. The only reason there’s any left to share is because I completely forgot I had it.” Owen laughed. “It’s the best.”

“Sounds tasty.” *I’m sweating.* The last several minutes standing in such a confined space with arguably one of the best-looking men he’d ever met was starting to take its toll. Brent needed to move around.

Before he could come up with a plan, Owen said, “I’m ready. Care for another beer?”

“Yes, please.” He gulped down what was left in the bottle and exchanged it when Owen handed him another.

“You have to promise to tell me if you’re getting hungry.” Owen resumed his spot against the counter. “I eat late. During the school year, I’ll come home, grab a snack, and work out. Then, after I’ve relaxed for a while, I’ll eat something, and then either catch some television or head to bed to read. As you can see, Brent, my life is extremely complicated,” he announced with a deprecating smirk.

Operating in a heightened state of awareness, a survival technique to combat the effect Owen’s mere presence was having on him, Brent stumbled upon one of the reasons he thought he was so attracted to Owen—his sincerity. He came off as so pure and honest that it made him all the more desirable. Desperate to flee the intimacy of the tiny kitchen, he suggested, “How about that tour you promised?”

“Right. The tour.” Owen strolled to a doorway just to the right of the back door. “Let’s start with the basement and work our way up. Follow me.”

When they reached the bottom of the stairs, Owen snapped on a light that illuminated the entire space. It was damp and familiar. “This isn’t much different from Artie’s,” Brent noticed.

"Most of the houses on this block were all built in the same style during the same period. I'm lucky. Although it's hard to tell, there hasn't been any serious water damage down here. My neighbors have had to deal with some real messes over the last few years.

"That's fortunate for you." Brent was ready to move on. Except for the essentials in the laundry and furnace room, there wasn't anything else to hold his attention other than Owen.

"This is a space I use for laundry, and that's about it. Let's head back up." Owen gestured for Brent to lead the way.

"So, are you enjoying the Speckled Egg?" Brent asked as they passed through the kitchen.

"I'm not much of a drinker, but yeah, I'm really enjoying it."

He watched Owen take an obligatory sip and wondered if he were just being kind or if he really enjoyed it.

"It's so nice you came over." Owen led the way out of the kitchen and into the dining room.

"Thanks for inviting me. Other than my friends at the Center, I haven't met anyone to hang with." There was more to add, but he couldn't land on a way to express himself that didn't sound like he was hitting on his new client. "This is a real treat," he added, satisfied his response was appropriate.

"My layout is roughly the same as Artie's, except at some point, the previous owners added a small bathroom between the dining and living rooms. I'm sure a good-sized closet was sacrificed. It's nice not to have to climb the stairs every time I have to pee, but I'm really short on storage space. This"—Owen had moved past the bathroom—"is the second bedroom, but I use it as an office slash sunroom. That leaves the upstairs for last."

*Father give me strength.* Brent began the climb to the bedroom. Stepping aside at the top, he waited for Owen to join him.

"On the right is a full bathroom. The built-in drawers"—Owen pointed on the opposite side of the hallway—"are nice, but I could use more closet space to hang stuff.

*That's a yummy scent. It must be his cologne.* Spicy in a manly way, it did nothing to quell Brent's curious dick. *Salmon spread. Dr.*

*Phil.* He tried to flood his mind with undesirable images, hoping to keep the little bastard calm.

The bedroom took up most of the upper floor. "I never expected you'd have so much space up here. Both bedrooms are on the upper floor of my house, and they're tiny. What do you do when you have guests over?" *You really just asked that?*

"I don't have many overnight visitors," Owen confessed. "My parents come a couple times a year, but they prefer to rent one of the resort cabins on the lake. Which is fine by me. On the rare occasion when someone does come to stay, I give them my room and I crash on the daybed in the sunroom."

An awkward silence brought attention to the large four-poster bed. Owen, standing on the opposite side of it, looked over and smiled. Brent made a beeline for the window and wanted to shoot himself when he observed, "Oh, this is great. You have a view of the street."

"Yes, the street. I get a nice breeze blowing through here, and that's important. This bed was my grandparents'. When they passed away a few years ago, I was the lucky recipient."

*You're fucking kidding me. We're back to the bed?* "That's nice. Great bed." Brent's imagination was already one step ahead of him. For a brief second, a naked Owen pulled down the covers—a vision which launched his dick into phase two, tenting the front of his shorts. Desperate times called for desperate measures. "What do you say we head back down?" He was halfway to the stairs before he heard Owen say, "Sounds good."

Equipped with new beers, Owen led them into the backyard.

Cooled at first by the rain, the air had regained much of its warmth. It was a gorgeous summer evening. Owen brought out a few rags and began wiping down the two chairs and table. Needing a moment to regroup, Brent strolled around admiring the flowers along the perimeter of the yard.

Owen joined him a moment later and pointed to a clump of fern. "I'm slowly trying to mix in native perennials with the other flowers. I'm not having the best luck with that. I think at one time the soil was changed out for grass. It doesn't seem to be what you'd naturally find in this area. So, many things I've tried never come back up the next season."

Light-years out of his element, Brent followed Owen around. In an attempt to show interest, he stopped at some weird-looking plant and asked, "What's this one called? The leaves have kind of a…." *You better come up with something intelligent.* "It looks like it came from a jungle." *Nice.*

"That's an autumn sedum. A *succulent*," Owen replied so close to him their shoulders made contact. "Whoops. Missed one." Owen bent over and rummaged in a cluster of some other green stuff. "I just weeded this bed a few days ago."

Operating independent of his mind, Brent cupped the contour of Owen's left ass cheek with his hand.

"Hello!" Owen bolted back up.

"I'm not sure I can explain that," Brent confessed. Mortified, he stepped back. "I clearly have issues with invading other people's personal space."

"Listen, Brent…."

"You have an amazing body and…." *I'm a total loser.*

"I'm flattered," Owen laughed. "I really am. No worries." He rested a hand on Brent's shoulder.

Their eyes locked. *Might as well go for broke.* Weak and wanting so much more, he stepped forward and guided his lips toward his handsome client.

Owen reciprocated by wrapping his arm around Brent's waist, pulling him closer.

Birds chirped their encouragement as they kissed.

A kiss typically meant nothing more than just another obstacle before you got to the prize, or prizes, depending on what he was in the mood for. Something about this kiss was different. Brent hoped it would never end. And when it did, he immediately went back for seconds—and thirds. They kept at it until a dog barking on the opposite side of the fence broke the spell.

"That's Gigi," Owen whispered, his arm still holding Brent tightly in place. "She's a pug. I think she wants in on the action."

He chuckled, and Owen released him. "Let's head inside. We need to talk."

Back in the kitchen, his host asked, "Do you mind if I go first?"

"Sure." Brent leaned against the counter, fighting the urge to paw.

"From our first meeting"—Owen stood only inches away—"I felt a connection to you. At first I thought it was because I was so scared and helpless. You, whether you know it or not, had become my knight in shining armor. But it's more. I feel a strong attraction to you, physically. You're very handsome." Owen coughed and then blushed.

"Thank you." Brent wasn't very good at handling compliments.

"The day you moved in," Owen continued, "I sat on the couch and spied on you and your friends. But every time *you* came into view, my heart kind of flipped. Until tonight, when you made the first move, I never thought I'd be anything more than your client."

This admission melted any apprehension Brent had concerning their sudden bout of passion.

Staring at the floor, Owen added in a whisper, "Perhaps that hasn't changed."

Unable to resist the moment, Brent moved in for another kiss. "You're impossible to resist."

"I love kissing you." Owen reached up and ran his hand tenderly across the side of Brent's face.

"I love kissing you too." Out of habit, Brent began rubbing his rock-hard cock against Owen's thigh. "You're making me crazy," he admitted, void of any remorse.

"I can think of a few things I can do to take care of that." Owen reached down and squeezed him through his shorts. "And I have plenty to work with here."

Enjoying the attention, he rested his head on Owen's shoulder.

"Your hair is so soft," Owen complimented while his fingers explored.

A kiss on the top of his head sent a shiver throughout Brent's body. *I have to say something. I can't… let this happen. At least not right now.*

"I guess it's my turn." Brent stepped back, still searching for the best way to convey what was troubling him. "Owen," he reluctantly began. "I have a history of being a horndog. I love sex."

Owen inched closer. "I like where this is going."

Brent closed his eyes in an attempt to focus. "I'm not sure why I just told you that. I think it was to let you know what happened in the backyard a few minutes ago, what I initiated, had something to do with the fact you make me really horny, and I'm extremely attracted to you too."

Bringing his hand up to his mouth, Owen coughed. "I see. So other than fulfilling a sexual need, you don't see us getting to know each other better? Or starting a relationship?" Wearing a look of defeat, Owen retreated a step.

*Oh fuck. That's only one of the reasons.* "No. I'm doing a piss-poor job right now of communicating." He looked into Owen's eyes and tried again. "It's not that. Nothing could be further from my mind. But it's complicated. I'm your attorney. Although he's never directly commented on it, if my partner Harper found out you and I were in some kind of relationship while I was representing you... well it wouldn't be good for anyone. I just know this about Harper. He would go ballistic."

"Now *that* I can deal with." Owen gave his shoulder a playful jab. "We have conditions, then? Rules?"

"Yes. That's it exactly. And I don't expect you to play by them." He was happy, with considerable help from Owen, to have finally synched his mind up with his mouth. "I want to spend time with you. With only one exception in the past, I've never felt this strong a connection to anyone. And... I'm scared." *God that felt good to say.*

"Scared? How so?" Owen searched his face for the answer.

"This job I have, working with Harper—who by the way is as talented as he is pretty—is a dream come true. So, I have this great conflict going on. I'm very eager to get to know you better, but at the same time, I'm reluctant to do anything that might jeopardize my career. I think I might be getting off track here again."

"It's okay. I'm with you. Keep going."

*Say what you feel.* "Owen, I want to start something with you. Right this very second. I'd be lying if I said anything different. But life for us over the next month could get really tense and awkward, until we get you past this legal issue. I'm not sure I have the ability to be secretive. I've worked my nuts off to get where I am." Brent saw the opportunity and laughed mightily. "I don't want my nuts to be my downfall."

Owen roared. "That's very good."

"I try." Brent raised his bottle. "Cheers."

"Cheers."

*Was that like, the most fucked-up thing you've ever had to communicate to someone, shithead?*

"I'm basically a loner," Owen shared. "I'm so used to being alone… on my own, that I'm very comfortable taking things slow and careful. Honestly, I'm willing to give anything a try. It may or may not work out, and that's okay. It's worth the gamble. If it's any consolation, I know my mom will adore you."

"Moms… they usually don't," he confessed knowingly.

"Another kiss?" Owen wrapped his arms around Brent's neck.

"Absolutely."

Their tongues twirled, licked, and teased until the time was right to take a break. Brent caressed his host's butt. "Your ass is rock hard."

"Yep. A self-proclaimed hardass, here."

To his joy, Brent felt Owen's hand move back down and take a more aggressive approached as it explored. His cock pulsated. "If you don't mind, I'd like to introduce you to someone."

"I'd be honored, I'm sure. There are a few friends I'm hoping you'll enjoy getting to know too. You're very formal, attorney Brent."

"I'm not at all shy in situations like this, though." He slid his hand up inside Owen's T-shirt, grazing each pert nipple as he kissed Owen's neck.

Owen made his own move, unbuttoning Brent's shorts and hauling down the zipper. He worked his hand under the waistband of his boxers.

*I wonder if he'll like my undies?*

"Nice," Owen said softly, sliding down to his knees.

He gasped when Owen slid him into his mouth. Closing his eyes, he savored the warmth of Owen's throat. It had been several months since he had been pleasured by anything other than his hand or a toy. An unwanted record. Nothing could compare to the real thing. It wasn't long before he felt his body signal its surrender.

Reaching down, he grasped Owen by the arm and pulled him to his feet. Their lips met again. He felt his shorts fall to his ankles as the kisses and caresses grew more urgent. Ready for things to go a step further, he lifted Owen's T-shirt over his head and dropped it on the floor. From there, he unbuttoned Owen's shorts and, in one well-rehearsed move, brought them, along with his underwear, down to his knees, allowing gravity to finish the task.

*Holy Anaconda. How did I not know this was coming?* Much larger than expected, Owen's, thick, long dick, like its master, appeared shy until Brent had a moment to stroke and encourage it. He'd been so preoccupied with his backside that he had completely failed to assess what might be waiting up front. *Boy do I have a home for you when the timing's right.*

He fell to his knees and wasted no time busying himself. Cupping both of Owen's asscheeks, he relaxed his throat until he had managed to swallow him to the root. After a moment of adjustment, he employed his expertise on what was truly a prized specimen of manhood.

"Oh my God. Please don't stop," Owen begged, running his hands through Brent's hair. "Your hair is so soft."

He had no intention of stopping. Once he had achieved a steady rhythm, he added creative ass play into the mix, and was rewarded with a series of loud and approving groans. It appeared they shared a common goal. *The sooner I finish up front, the sooner I can have a turn on the opposite end.*

"*Brent*," Owen cried out, slapping his shoulder. "I'm so close. Oh my gosh."

That was the last he heard out of him before Owen shot deep into his throat. Gulping to keep up, he sucked and licked until his victim, who was panting like a rabid dog, collapsed onto his knees.

"Holy smokes," Owen gasped. "That… was amazing."

THIS WAS an angle of his kitchen Owen had never seen before. From his low perspective, he had a clear view under his table. Straddling Brent's face, he admired his toned legs. *He has perfect toes.* Without any discussion, the floor had become their playground. *I could stay down here forever.*

"You have an Olympic speed skater's ass, did you know that?" Brent complimented.

Owen felt a sloppy tongue slather his butt cheeks. "I had no idea, is that a good thing?" he inquired. Based on what he had seen in the showers, he knew his dick was bigger than average. But he had never considered how his ass rated.

"Oh yeah, man," Brent encouraged, playfully slapping and caressing. "I'd give anything to have an ass like this."

"You have nothing to worry about. Your body is so well-proportioned. I'm lovin'—" He was stopped midsentence by Brent's skillful tongue penetrating an area that had seen very little exploration. Except for a rare instance in college when he was coaxed into screwing some dude he hardly knew, he had pretty much ruled anal sex out, for no specific reason other than it seemed like too much trouble for what he was in the market for. Certainly he would never allow himself to be on the receiving end unless it was with someone he was in a serious relationship with. The curiosity was there. The right moment hadn't presented itself.

Eager to return pleasure, he lowered his head and took Brent into his mouth. He tasted of sweet soap, and the aroma was intoxicating. Relaxed and confident, he got creative and massaged the perfect set of balls resting under Brent's cock. The response was ass slaps, grunts, and an increase in tongue assaults. He hunkered down and increased his effort. They operated like a well-tuned machine for several minutes before Brent's body tensed under him.

"Owen, don't stop. I'm almost there."

Brent's hands gripped Owen's waist and pulled Owen's ass tighter into his face, signaling Owen to increase his own efforts. Seconds later powerful jets coated Owen's throat, neck and face.

"Fucking shit, *fuck* that was amazing," Brent announced between near hysterical chortles. "I've seen the promised land."

"I enjoyed it too." Owen leaned against the cupboard and sat his wet ass on the cool hardwood floor. He picked up his T-shirt and wiped off.

Brent sat up and rested his head on Owen's shoulder. "This is going to be trouble, you know."

"Why's that?" Owen couldn't imagine anything like what he had just experienced being a bad thing.

"I'm going to want more." Brent chuckled.

"Me too," he countered.

"We live across the street from each other. I'm not great at rationing, that's all I'm going to say." Brent reached over, extricated Owen's balled-up shirt from his hand, and used it to wipe his face. "I'm not proud."

They sat in silence for several minutes. Every now and then, Brent probed him with his toe, as if to stir up trouble, which made them both laugh.

"You hungry?" Owen eventually asked, standing up and handing Brent's beer down to him.

"I'm super hungry. Can I help?"

Owen pulled on his shorts, leaving his underwear on the floor. "Not really. Have a seat at the table. You can keep me company while I get dinner going."

"Sounds like a deal." Brent dressed. "Can you believe it? It's almost dark."

"I'm so discombobulated, I haven't got a handle on anything. Let's do this. I'll open the wine, and we'll go out back while I grill these babies. Sound good?"

"Yes. It's still a beautiful night."

With only one brief, annoying intrusion by Gigi, who was shushed and hauled back inside when she began barking, the evening was perfect.

"Dinner and you were really tasty," Brent complimented as he came into the kitchen with the last of the dishes.

"Set those on the counter. I'll deal with everything later." He gestured to an area near the sink.

"I'd be more than happy to help clean up."

"And waste valuable time together? No way." He walked up and wrapped Brent in his arms. The evening had been everything he'd hoped and much more. "I feel reborn. I don't know how else to say it."

Cupping Owen's chin in his hand, Brent initiated a kiss. "I'm in uncharted territory here too. You're a special man, Owen. I feel incredibly lucky to have met you."

"I don't want you to leave and break the spell," he said, caressing Brent's back. *Please don't go.*

"Is that my cue to head home?" Brent grinned. "Sometimes I'm slow to pick up on things."

"Any chance you'd consider spending the night, or at least part of it? I could set the alarm and send you off before the sun's up." *You're pushing for too much.*

"I was hoping you would offer. Let's start our stealth-like cover tomorrow."

"Come, then." Taking Brent by the hand, Owen led them up the stairs. *Maybe things aren't so bad, after all. Getting arrested is a hell of a price to pay for romance, but I wouldn't give this up for anything.*

# CHAPTER Seven

BRENT STROLLED into the reception area on the lookout for one of Fern's homemade treats. He tried not to appear disappointed. There wasn't a plate of cookies or gooey chocolate bars in sight.

"Good morning," their assistant chimed over her glasses. "Your notes from yesterday are waiting for you on your desk, and there's a fresh pot of coffee, if you're interested."

Brent had woken up with an outlook on the day, perhaps on his life, that he found exhilarating and that made him want to share the joy with others. Fern's lavender chiffon blouse had caught his eye. "Thank you. By the way, that's a very good color on you."

"I'm not staying late," Fern stated with more than a hint of defiance. "So don't even bother asking."

"Excuse me?" He was clueless to why his compliment would produce such a strong response. "Has Harper asked you to stick around tonight for some reason?"

"Nope. But when a man in his twenties compliments an old lady like me on her blouse… well something's up. I wasn't born yesterday."

He laughed. "I'm serious. That shade of purple looks great on you."

"Someone's in an awfully good mood this morning. If I wasn't such an old prude, I'd ask for details. It's best that I don't. I'm sure it's more than my tired heart could endure."

Stunned, he forced himself to chuckle, even though it took all he had to fight back a scream. *Holy shit. If she detects something, Harper's going to nail me for sure.* "I wish," he lied.

"That's a very interesting case—the young man who was arrested in the woods," Fern opined.

"Yeah. It's hard to believe something like that could happen. The police are supposed to protect us. We'll get to the bottom of it. I'm convinced he's innocent." He wasn't at all beneath campaigning for support. On the way to work, he had decided to chase after Harper once more to see if he could get him to lighten up on their client.

"I probably shouldn't say this, but I think he's a very nice man. And based on the way he acts when he's here, and from your notes, I would have to agree. He's innocent. He's also very lucky to have you in his corner."

*Am I just being weird about this? She seems to be working hard at connecting me to Owen.*

"Thanks, Fern. Is Harper in? The door to his office is closed."

"He was here when I got in this morning. There was a note on my desk asking me not to disturb him." Fern looked up from her screen and frowned. Brent could tell it pained her not to be able to offer more.

"He likes to start early," Brent offered, only partially convincing himself that the reason his partner was in this early had nothing to do with his having sex with their client. Fern's earlier remark had started an avalanche of insecurity that could eventually bury any wonderful memories he might have of his night with Owen. *Relax, shithead, or you'll give yourself away.*

"Send any calls of his my way, for now. I'll be in my office."

"Will do. Brent?"

"Yes?"

"Does this color really look good on me? It's been a long time since anyone has paid me such a nice compliment. I usually avoid lavender."

He fought off an urge to hug her. "Absolutely. I wouldn't say it if it weren't true."

The smile he received in return cleared out, at least for the moment, all the apprehension that had seeped into his perfect morning. *Fern, you don't know how lucky we are to have you. I might have had my reservations earlier, but you've blasted those thoughts to bits.*

On the way back to his desk, he stopped just shy of Harper's office. Leaning as close to the door as possible, not wanting to chance being observed from the crack at the bottom, he listened for any noise that might indicate what his partner was up to. *He must be reading. I can't hear a thing.*

He powered up his PC. Still puzzled over why Harper was in so early, he opened his partner's calendar for some clues. July first contained only a single entry. "Lollie."

*Fuck. It's the anniversary of her death.* He sat back and closed his eyes. *This isn't the day to do battle with him. Table it until tomorrow or risk losing a testicle.*

He nabbed a water from his fridge, logged onto a legal website, and began researching cases similar to Owen's. Ten minutes into the process, he was reminded how difficult it was to separate Owen the client from Owen the potential new boyfriend. Worse, he had to fight off an urge to call Owen, just to chat and laugh and confirm their next date. They had made tentative plans to talk later that night, possibly in person, but for sure by phone. Lost in a pleasant memory, he jumped when his phone rang.

"Brent Burns," he answered.

"It's Harper. We need to talk about your case. Can you stop by, or are you in the middle of something?"

*Shit. The timing really sucks.*

"Sure. Give me a minute to use the can, and I'll be right there."

In the bathroom, he splashed water on his face and peered into the mirror. The image staring back screamed naughty frat boy, which seemed an insurmountable handicap when Harper was the opponent. He toweled off and headed to his partner's office.

On the way, he decided not to bring up Lollie's passing. It might seem strange he had noted the death of Harper's beloved grandmother on his calendar, even though he had a special place in his heart for the kind, generous woman. He had made the trip to Iowa for her funeral. It was a very sad day. It would be best to let

Harper bring it up. Chances are he wouldn't. In matters like this, he was typically silent.

*Be yourself. For all you know, it's a day like any other.*

"Good morning." Harper had opened the office door.

"Hey. How's it going?" Seated behind the big desk, Harper was all smiles. If he was suffering at all, you sure wouldn't know it, Brent thought as he took a seat. "Good. I'm doing… good."

"Great." Harper sat back. "I met with Trout Simmons yesterday, and I thought we should go over my notes so we're both on the same page.

"Right. How did it go?" He forced himself to appear relaxed, and in the process, grew increasingly uneasy as the seconds ticked away. The muscles in his neck were already begging for relief.

"Trout's a good man. Let's start there. And as I mentioned before, he's also a friend. Early on he made it known to Ian and me that if we experienced any trouble, he'd make sure to see it was stopped. That, in and of itself, earned him a shitload of points right out of the gate. So why am I telling you this?"

"It's cool." He found it easy to understand their relationship, but he wished it didn't exist. Not now, not as far as this case was concerned.

"I've spent a good deal of my morning trying to separate Trout the friend from Trout the chief of police and boss of this Daniels guy."

Sounds like they both had some sorting out to do. For Brent's part, it was going to take considerable effort. He drove to work giddy over the fact he now had a new boyfriend.

"I wanted to make sure when we talked that I was coming at this from the right perspective," Harper explained. "It was harder than I thought, but I think I have it worked out. One of the biggest challenges with this process had to do with a personality trait I've grown to trust in Trout… and admire. He calls dem like he sees dem, if you know what I mean. And he'll be the first to tell you, as he did during our meeting, that he can spot a bullshitter a mile away."

Lucky enough to see where this was headed, Brent began to formulate a defense. *There's a first time for everything.* He crossed his leg and smoothed his tie over his lap. "So, you're getting ready to tell me you believe Trout, but not our client?" Feeling more confrontational than he had hoped, he understood that, if he had any chance at all in this fight, he would have to come out of the gate swinging.

"Yes. That is exactly what I'm going to tell you. Thanks for cutting to the chase."

The confident smile Harper flashed challenged Brent to go for broke. "And I would have to counter I think Trout's wrong about this one. There are people who are masters at deception. I think, from what I've heard from Owen…." *Stop using his first name. Stick with our client. It's less personal.* "Our client. This Daniels guy is a monster. He would have to be. It's despicable what he did."

"Okay. I was fairly certain this would be the path you were going to take. However, it could just as easily be said that you're the one that has been bamboozled, not Trout. That would be fair, wouldn't it?"

*You're dead wrong.* He was surprised at how strong a reaction he had to Harper's threatening logic. Of course it was fair. "It might be fair, but it's *wrong.*"

Unable to stay seated while under fire, Brent stood and walked behind his chair, loosening the tie that had begun to strangle. "You've had ten minutes at most with our client. How can you be so sure he's the one lying? That, I *don't* find fair. I find it kind of surprising, in fact."

"I'm terribly sorry," Harper spoke evenly. "But if you recall, I asked you to take the lead on this case. I'm relying on *you* to interpret our client objectively and to uncover any hidden inconsistencies or untruths. We both know from our previous meeting you have work to do in this area, my friend."

Blood rushed to his face. Disgrace boiled up from his core. This meeting was not going in the direction he had hoped. In fact, it was a far worse start than he thought possible. Harper had masterfully directed the conversation away from Trout, which was totally unexpected.

"That's so unfair," he said. "When it comes right down to it, I'm not the lead on this case, you are." Reaching for something more to combat Harper's unjust assault, Brent recklessly continued, "Admit it. And frankly if I were the lead on this case I'd…."

The look on Harper's face stopped him from continuing.

"You'd what?" Harper shot out of his chair. "You'd what, Brent? Grow a pair and finish your sentence," he thundered. "Take off your Sunday school outfit and change into your big-boy clothes. I don't have time for this."

Stunned, Brent could only stare back in disbelief. This was a side of Harper he'd never seen before. Not with anyone.

"If that came out a little too strong…" Harper sat down and began organizing the papers on his desk. "I apologize." Looking up, he gestured for Brent to take a seat. "You're already a very skilled attorney, and you have the makings of a great one. But you have to understand that you get there one case at a time. It's my feeling that you have a learning experience here. Don't waste it by taking a side you can't argue successfully."

Refusing to sit and wounded by Harper's harsh words, Brent had no idea how to extricate himself from this rabid disagreement and still hang on to at least a morsel of dignity. Taking a deep breath, he stared at the bookcase, unable to look his partner in the eye. "Owen," he started in a voice rich with emotion, "was attacked in the woods by a psychopath. You can say all you want about my shortcomings, but his innocence is my gut instinct, and I'm going to fight for him. And here's something else to think about. Daniels… neither of us has had an opportunity to see what we're up against. For fuck's sake, don't you think that's a little unprofessional? Coming to a conclusion without examining all the aspects of the case? Harper?"

Harper sat back in his chair and sucked on his pencil. His eyes, gorgeous and playful when relaxed, bore into Brent like lasers. "What I find unprofessional is your attitude. You came in here with a preset judgment on your client—your *first* client, I'd like to point out—and you've taken issue with me because I happen not to agree with you. Half the role of being an attorney is being persuasive in your argument. Frankly you're acting like a child. You have some kind of a…." Harper paused and sipped his water. "It's like you've developed some kind of a relationship with this client. Fuck him.

He's playing us in hopes we'll overlook the fact he's accused a cop of serious misconduct—a cop who, I've been told, is the very model of professionalism."

Shaking from head to toe, Brent could no longer formulate any type of response he could trust. Faced with the prospect of digging an even deeper hole, he chose the path of least resistance and walked out on his friend, his mentor, and the senior partner of Burns and Callahan, LLP.

GIDDY, OWEN didn't know what to do with himself. *Did last night really happen?* Giggling, he walked back into the kitchen and stared at the sheet of paper towel on the counter.

> *Good morning, Owen. I'm sorry I left without waking you, but you looked so peaceful and handsome and hot and inviting, I knew, if I did wake you, I'd never leave. I have no regrets about last night. It was fantastic from start to finish. I hope you feel the same way, because I already know I want you and me, even though it's tricky now, to become "us" as fast as possible. Think about this, and let's talk tonight. Have a great day! Of course, I'll be thinking of you. How could I think about anything else?*
>
> *Hugs (and tons of smooches) Brent*

Carefully folding the note, he placed it in his pocket. "I want you and me to become *us* as fast as possible," he shouted at the top of his lungs and then realized the kitchen windows were open. "Whoops." He laughed at his own indiscretion. "Bake some cookies, Gloria," he mouthed toward his neighbors. "Mow the lawn, Mitch. Poop away, Gigi. I'm in love."

A warm breeze caressed his cheek as he stood, eyes closed, relishing the memory of what it had been like to explore Brent's toned physique. His calves, his chest, his biceps, that amazing ass, even his toes had definition. Owen felt his body react as images of their time together danced joyfully through his mind. He found it easy to conjure up each playful kiss and marveled at how such tentative beginnings had paved the way for more intimate exploration. Skillful, attentive, and impossibly naughty, Brent had, for at least one night, managed to blast away the doom and gloom that recently had become Owen's life. Falling asleep in Brent's arms was the perfect finish to a wonderful evening. *Shoo, you meanie.* A noisy blackbird brought him out of his daydream.

Pocketing his phone, he headed down the front steps and crossed the street. As promised, Brent had left the side gate unlocked. He entered the backyard and glanced around to assess the degree of neglect since Artie's passing. Clumps of mulch and leaves remained where they had been placed last fall. He'd start with those, and after the gardens were finished, he'd move on to the more cosmetic elements like cutting the grass and washing the patio. It wasn't as bad as he had envisioned. A few days of work would make a huge difference.

*Shit.* It occurred to him he had forgotten to ask Brent to unlock the side door of the garage. Artie had every garden tool imaginable. Not having to run back and forth between houses would make the job much more enjoyable. But he was surprised to find the door unlocked. He stepped inside the dark, damp space, and the absence of his friend's truck, totaled in the accident, gave him pause. It felt strange being there, like he was trespassing. Then it dawned on him how happy Artie would be that his yard was getting a little TLC, and that made everything seem right. *I've got your back, my friend.*

He spent a good hour carefully uncovering a bed of lilies. He had just fluffed up the soil around a cluster of peony bushes when his cell phone vibrated in his pocket.

*Brent.*

His body tensed when he saw it was Deena Phelps instead. *Why is she calling? This can only be bad news.*

For a moment he thought about not answering but then decided against it. Whatever she wanted, it was best to know now, or he would beat himself up speculating. "This is Owen."

"Owen, good morning. It's Deena."

"Hello." Biting his lip, he waited.

"I'm sorry to bother you, but I thought it important to let you know the school board has scheduled a special meeting next Wednesday night to discuss you and… your situation."

The normally upbeat lilt in her voice sounded forced. He didn't need to see her face to understand she was concerned. He felt sick to his stomach.

"I haven't gone to court yet. Do they know this?" Surprised at his spontaneous reaction, he quickly added, "I mean, don't they want to know the facts before they get into this?"

"Please believe that was the first thing out of my mouth. From what I can gather, Jerome Peebles, who personally I find more challenging than words can express, has got a few other members all worked up over this. I'm doing what I can, Owen, but I would be lying if I didn't voice my concern."

"I see," he answered softly.

"Don't take it personally. Any news is big news to some of these people. Right or wrong, it's a rare opportunity in a relatively docile community to show they have our students' best interests at heart. Take from that what you will. Any updates you can provide before I go up against Jerry Peebles would be a big help."

"Let me talk to my attorney, and I'll get back to you. Thanks for the heads-up, Deena.

"I'm in your corner, Owen. I'll do what I can to save your job, but this is very serious. They don't need an outcome in court to make their decision."

Kneeling down on the grass, Owen fought to keep the emotion out of his voice. "I appreciate your support."

"Good teachers are hard to come by. Great teachers, like you, are one in a million. Don't lose hope. I've gone up against these dinosaurs before, and I've won. Do what you can to help me out. Call me on my cell anytime. I'm here for you."

The maternal inflection in her voice almost broke him. "Thanks again, Deena."

He fell back on the grass and stared up to a sky so blue, it looked fake. An eagle soaring into view, majestic and free, reminded him of how trapped he felt. Tears streamed down his face. The joy of having begun something with Brent was wiped away. Life was about to get really shitty. And there was nothing he or Brent or Deena or anyone could do to stop it. Fraught with anxiety, he forced himself to keep going. What he really needed was to be held by Brent until the bad melted away.

BRENT WALKED down the hall toward the reception area—a wrong turn. His intention was to take refuge inside his office until he could properly evaluate the situation. He understood that shutting down their argument was a mistake he couldn't reverse, and he pounded his forehead in frustration. They had never argued before. Not even raised a voice in all the years they had known each other. A strong sense of sadness slowed him by the time he reached Fern.

"What was that all about? It sounded a little heated." Fern, after finishing a flurry of tapping on her keyboard, looked up and frowned.

He walked to the couch and collapsed. "We disagree. Strongly disagree."

"I gathered that." Fern pushed her glasses up the bridge of her nose. "There's nothing wrong with a healthy disagreement now and then. Crap. My husband and I would have killed one or the other by now if we didn't let the you-know-what fly from time to time. Cleanses the soul and helps with digestion."

Fern's playful wink did little to boost his spirits. "I'm not very proud of what happened back there. Instead of holding my ground and battling it out, I turned my back and walked out." He stared at the ceiling, wishing he could rewind the last fifteen minutes.

"That happens. Especially if you're taken by surprise. Sometimes it's better to clam up tight rather than risk making a mountain out of a molehill."

Fern resumed her typing. *Oh sure, I get that.* But this was Owen everyone was weighing in on. His Owen. He knew what he had to do. He stood and forced a smile. "I think it would be in my benefit to wander back into the lion's den." This was going to be tough, but it was the right thing to do.

Resting her elbows on the desk, Fern leaned forward and asked, "Do you mind if I speak candidly with you?"

"Of course not." It appeared to be open hunting on shitheads. *Please don't scold me. I'll cry.*

"I was hired to work at Burns and Callahan. You're a partner in this enterprise, Brent Burns. Never lose track of that. I'm sure Harper wasn't looking for a *yes*-man when you two teamed up. Hold your ground and fight for what you think is right. There's merit in that, regardless if you win or lose."

"Thanks, Fern." *I love you.*

He threw back his shoulders. *I can do this.* He set course back to Harper's office. When he reached the door, he stopped to collect himself. What happened next was anyone's guess. Sucking in a deep breath he knocked on the door jam.

"Yes. He's back." Pushing his notepad away, Harper motioned for him to come in. "Take a seat."

"Harper, I'm—"

"Please don't tell me you're sorry," Harper said. "This is an important case for us, and I'm pleased to see your passion. That quality, once fine-tuned, will be a wonderful asset. It's what's missing in so many young… missing in so many attorneys these days."

Unable to fully accept his partner's compliment, Brent shook his head and admitted, "I hate that I walked out on you. It was a defeatist move, even though I still know I'm right."

"I know you do, and that's fine," Harper assured him. "I think I'm right too. But if you ever walk out on me again, don't be surprised if I'm not as forgiving. It's me here, Brent. You know better. Anyway I'm over it, and you should be too."

He shifted his weight from left to right. Truthfully he would have been surprised if Harper had made a big deal out of his lapse in judgment. Still, it was a relief to see his partner had moved on. This allowed him to say what was foremost on his mind. "We need face time with Daniels."

"Yes. I agree. Your point was well taken. Have Fern shell up a deposition notice, and we'll serve it after I've had a chance to give Trout a heads-up."

"Thanks."

"Because you got all pissy"—Harper turned away to heap on the drama—"with *me*, I wasn't able to communicate to you I've already alerted Trout there might be a need for Daniels' deposition."

"Pissy?" Brent couldn't help but laugh.

"You were. Little-Lord-Fauntleroy pissy. You're a natural." Harper flashed his megawatt smile so there would be no mistaking his playful intent.

"Whatever." Brent was relieved by the humor. "Do you want to depose him here or at the station?"

"We'll need to do it at the district attorney's office. Fern can set this up for you. The more relaxed the subject, the better chance he'll slip up and fuck himself. Which, from what I've gathered, might not be a bad thing to watch."

"Got it." Brent turned to leave.

"Wait."

He turned back and was surprised to see Harper had gotten out of his chair. "Are we good?"

"Oh yeah," Brent assured him. "I'm more than ready to move on. Being at odds with you sucks."

"I'm sure it won't be the last time. We're both strong-minded." Sitting back down, Harper dismissed him with a wave of the hand. "Leave me now. I have to review case law so I can rid myself of this fucking workers' comp case before it brings down the entire firm."

"Later." Brent stopped at Fern's desk on his way back to his office. "Thanks for the encouragement earlier. I wanted you to know all is well."

"Thank you. I knew you men would find a way to reconcile your differences. You're both too smart and talented to waste time bickering." Fern winked.

"I'm not staying late, so don't even ask me, Fern."

HIS MIND detached from work, Owen moved around Brent's yard like a zombie. It was impossible to keep Deena's short call from wreaking havoc on what he had thought would be a relaxing day of gardening. At his darkest, he mourned the potential opportunity to head up a marching band, a wishful thought that had grown with each passing day. He was born to have this experience.

Until then he had refused to believe he would ever be removed from Jefferson High. His innocence would be validated in court, and everything would soon get back to how it was before his arrest. The call from his boss destroyed his confidence and unleashed a flood of worry.

*If I can't teach, what will I do? Sell the house? Move somewhere where they haven't heard of me and start over?*

These were not new concerns. In the past few weeks, he had shed buckets of tears over the possibility of losing his job. What would he tell his parents? His friends? Sure, they would all be sympathetic, but would they really believe his innocence? Every time he looked into their faces, would he see doubt?

By late afternoon he had all his work done. Nature would have to step in and do its part to finish the job. Artie's yard would be beautiful once the perennials kicked in and began blooming. He would pick up some accent plants from Hansen's Garden Center and decorate the patio. But not today. His heart wasn't in it.

He showered, forced himself to eat a sandwich, and stretched out on the couch. When his phone woke him up, the sun had already set.

"Hello," he answered, his mouth dry from sleep.

"Owen, hey. It's Brent. I just got home. Have you eaten?"

"I must have drifted off." He got up, walked into the kitchen, and poured a glass of water.

"No doubt. I peeked in the back to see if you had been over, and I about shit my pants. The yard looks amazing. I can't wait to sit out there and enjoy it."

"Thanks. It was nothing." The cool water refreshed his parched mouth and throat.

"Can I bring you dinner? I thought I'd swing by the A&W and pick up burgers. If you have something going on, I'll understand. Am I catching you at a bad time?"

*Yes and no.* "I need to see you, Brent."

"Is something wrong? You sound down."

"I'm okay. I'll tell you about it when you get here. I got a call today from Deena Phelps." He waited to see if and how the name would register.

"Yikes. Okay. We can talk everything over. No worries. What can I pick up for you?" Brent asked.

"I'm not fussy. Just a burger, I guess." He wasn't hungry.

"You got it. I'll see you in a few minutes. Leave your front door unlocked so I can slip in without being noticed. We need to step up our game."

"We can meet at your house if it's easier," Owen offered.

"Well," Brent said, laughing, "it's not just my backyard that's a mess. You're a good reason to get off my butt and catch up on some housework. I just haven't had the chance. You'd take one look and run screaming."

"Okay. I'll see you in a few," Owen answered.

Owen moved through the house turning on lights. He'd been asleep for almost four hours. *Great. I'll probably be up all night now.* A splash of water on his face helped get him going. He walked out of the bathroom at the same time Brent arrived, carrying a sack of food and drinks. "Hey, neighbor."

"Here. Let me help you." Owen grabbed the drinks and led the way into the kitchen. "Did you get root beers?"

"Absolutely. How can you go to A&W and not?" Brent laughed. "I just about squealed when I moved up here and saw you guys still had one open. Almost all of them have closed in the Twin Cities."

"That sucks." He grabbed plates and napkins and brought them over to the table. "I wasn't hungry, but I knew the minute I smelled food I'd rally."

"I'm fucking starving. Worked through lunch." Brent emptied the bag onto plates and unwrapped his burger. "I ordered them with the works. I figured you could scrape off what you didn't want. I had to get french fries and onion rings, because I always want both. Brent dived into his dinner and then came up for air. "So, tell me about the call with Phelps."

"This looks so good." Owen took a bite and then sipped his soda. "The school board is meeting next week to decide my fate. They aren't waiting until the legal process runs its course."

"Honestly, that doesn't surprise me. Don't take this the wrong way, Owen. Children are involved." Brent paused.

"I understand," he said, nodding.

"No doubt you're the talk of the town. We expected that, right?"

"None of this is a surprise. It's intense to see it all unfold for real."

"What else did she say?" Brent stuffed his mouth with a combination of fries and a ring after slathering them with ketchup.

"Apparently there's a guy on the board, Jerry Peebles, who is spearheading this whole thing. Deena called Peebles and his peers dinosaurs, if that tells you anything." The excitement over seeing Brent and sharing dinner was starting to wane. Dread was strong-arming into their time together, despite his efforts to keep it away.

"Look at me, Owen. Don't let this eat you up inside."

"I'm sorry. My job means so much to me." He didn't have the strength to conquer his fear. "I'm so fucking scared." He stared at his plate.

"I know you are." Brent took another bite and wiped his hands on a napkin. "I need to discuss this with Harper. My first thought is they have the power to suspend you, probably with pay, but not to fire you. Once the case has settled in your favor, which might be before the school year starts, you should be reinstated and on your way to getting your life back."

"That's what I was hoping you'd say."

"I don't have all the answers, Owen. The legal process is about strategy. We may lose some ground, gain some ground. It's a battle until someone is proclaimed the victor." Brent held up his finger to buy time while he sipped his drink. Then he continued. "I want you to reach out to me when you get scared. Together we'll talk through the steps, so as many of the surprises can be eliminated as possible. Some of this is new territory for me, so you'll have to be patient and wait while I go hunting for the best solution possible. That might not sound too reassuring, but I'm a good little researcher. I'm confident I'll succeed. Plus there's the Harper factor. He's brilliant. The best there is. So…."

Owen smiled when Brent reached for his hand.

"What I need you to do is keep the faith. Don't give up hope. You're a good man. Daniels is a snake. We're going to prove that in court."

Owen picked at his dinner while Brent inhaled his. "Something has changed," Brent offered as he stuffed all the wrappers back into the bag. "With me, that is." Brent picked up the plates, brought them to the sink, and ran water over them.

"What do you mean?" Owen asked, loading the dishwasher.

"Come here." Brent opened his arms. "Remember last night, when I told you I was a horndog?"

"Yeah. I thought you were just in this for the sex." He stepped forward, allowing Brent to hug him tight.

"That's right." Brent kissed his neck tenderly. "I don't want to go home to an empty house."

Owen wanted to be needed. He wanted to assure Brent that his door was always open.

"Before, with other guys, once the sex was over, I couldn't get out of there fast enough," Brent offered. "I loved being independent, and I was very careful and protective of that. I felt in control that way. It's the opposite with you. I could hold you all night. I don't think I need or want to feel like I'm in control."

Owen traced his hand across Brent's chin. "I think we need each other. Let's move into the living room." He took Brent by the hand and walked to the couch. "I'm good right now without television or music. How about you?"

"I just want you." Brent sat and motioned for Owen to back up to him. "Today, when I thought about you a whole bunch of times…." He chuckled. "I also thought about the future. I projected us months, years down the road. It happened several times before I became conscious of it. That means something."

"Nice. I like that." Owen pulled Brent's strong arms tighter across his chest. "Sometimes we're ready for things, and we don't even know it. I wasn't looking for a relationship either, but something inside me sent a signal that I shouldn't let you get away."

Several minutes passed without a word spoken.

"I'm thirsty." Owen arched his head back and kissed Brent's chin. "There's a few Speckled Eggs left over from last night, if you're interested."

"There are? Oh that's right. We had wine when we finally got around to dinner. Sure. I'll take one."

"Wait right there."

Owen returned with their beers, resumed his position, and eased back into Brent's arms. "Can I ask you something?"

"Sure."

"Last night—" He sipped and then placed his bottle on the table. "—you mentioned there was another person you once had feelings for. You don't have to talk about this if you don't want to, but I'm curious."

"No. It's fine. The minute that came out of my mouth, I figured you might want to know more." Brent repositioned Owen in his arms and continued. "He lives here actually. His name is Alex."

"He lives here?" This took him by complete surprise.

"It gets even stranger. He's Harper's son… now." Brent laughed.

"Huh?"

"This could get to be a pretty long story, but I think I can condense it enough so you won't fall asleep on me."

Owen felt a kiss behind his ear. "I want to hear this."

"I met Harper when I was assigned to be his assistant at a big firm in the Twin Cities. Gosh, so much happened during that period. Harper met his husband, Ian. Harper was shot outside the courthouse by the psychopath wife of one of our clients."

"Are you shitting me?" Owen broke free and sat up on the couch.

"Nope. We were coming out of the courthouse after our client was convicted of masterminding a Ponzi scheme, and as we headed down the steps, the wife came up and shot him. It was one of those moments in your life when everything kind of stops. I held him in my arms until the paramedics arrived."

"That's like something on television. Holy shit." He was amazed to learn this.

"Isn't it? Obviously he survived. After a long recovery, he and Ian decided to say good-bye to city life and do something else with their lives. That brought them to the North Shore and the Palisade Beach Resort. Is this boring you?" Brent asked after taking a swig.

"Are you kidding? I'm enthralled." *I can't believe this. What a story.* "Go on."

"Well the great thing for me—by that time I wasn't Harper's assistant any longer. I was his friend. So, moving this along, the resort was still in pretty rough shape that first winter. So they hired this local kid, fresh out of high school, to spend the winter on the property in the apartment behind the resort office. That was Alex."

"Ahhh." Owen still couldn't figure out how this was all going to come together.

"I know. I can tell by the look on your face you're not sure how this all ends." Brent leaned forward and initiated a kiss. "Damn, you're handsome, Owen."

"Keep going." He was hooked.

"Right. There's roughly a ten-year age difference between Alex and Harper. Alex tragically lost his father that first year, and Ian and Harper took him under their wing. Alex eventually moved into the new home the guys built that following spring. It was during this period that I got to know Alex. He's a few years younger, but there was something about him I found so refreshing. One night while I was visiting the boys, we had a few beers, and after Harper and Ian went up to bed, we started fooling around. Turns out we were a good match sexually, so from there, we started planning time together. I'd come up here when I could, and Alex would come down and camp out at my apartment for the weekend. It was great."

"It *was great*?" Owen reached for his beer. *I sure hope I'm not opening any wounds here.*

"We sort of limped along like this for a year or more, and then Alex met Theo, and they fell in love." Brent shrugged as if to say, what could I do?

"I'm sorry." He felt a pang of guilt for encouraging Brent to revisit this part of his life.

"Don't be. I'm here now with you, Owen." Brent scooted up closer and took him back into his arms. "By that time I was well on my way to getting my law degree. Harper and Alex opened up the Center, and once that was up and running, Harper completed the project by opening up the law firm. I got a call from him, asking if I'd be interested in relocating. Because of my grades, I had been courted by several of the firms in town, but none of that mattered when I was offered the chance to work alongside someone who I believe to be an extraordinary legal talent. The surprise was, he was asking me to partner with him. Can you imagine? Fresh out of law school?"

"It doesn't surprise me." Being with Brent made him feel special. Whatever good fortune Brent had been blessed with was moving in his direction, despite his legal predicament.

"To wrap this up, I've gotten to know Theo. He's great. Alex is very happy. So my loss is easier to deal with. Bottom line, we're all pretty close. Like a family. The bond between Ian, Harper, and Alex is so strong that a few weeks ago, they legally adopted him. And by the way, they're going to adore you. You're good people, Owen, and you'll fit right in. I told you it was going to be a long story. Come here."

They shared soft, easy kisses until the urge for more prompted Brent to push Owen back into the corner of the couch. He eagerly complied and hauled Brent up between his legs. Deep, sensual kisses kept them busy for a very long time. Owen could feel Brent's hard cock against his thigh. Like before, he reached down and stroked it.

"No." Brent sat up and brushed away his hand.

"No?" Owen was stunned. *Did I do something wrong?*

"I want things to start out differently with you, Owen. I need to break away from my usual MO, which is a ton of sex without ever getting to know the person. You deserve more restraint—more respect."

"I do?" He wasn't so sure. He had become wet. All systems were a go.

"I have this guilt thing going with sex that I have to come to terms with. Is there any way in hell you understood what I just said?" Brent brushed his finger across Owen's lips.

"It's the horndog thing again, isn't it?"

"Yeah, it is. Once we get some miles behind us, I'll be fine. And trust me, if you need things to move faster than they are, I'll make that adjustment so fast your balls will ring."

Brent's comment made them both laugh.

"I'll be fine. Spending time with you is the most important thing." Owen leaned over and planted a wet sloppy on Brent's cheek. "I learned more about you tonight. That was wonderful."

"That's good. Hey, you just reminded me. I have news pertaining to your case." Brent sat up.

"Okay." The segue wasn't as smooth for him as it had been for Brent. Just the mention of his case caused his body to tense.

"I hate that this fucking Daniels asshole has you so fucked over. We are going to kick his ass so hard he's going to wish he was never born. I'm hoping there will come a time soon when you start trusting this." Brent patted his knee. "Damn, I'm not saying you're doing anything wrong. I would be traumatized in the same way, I'm sure. Maybe as you start to see the legal process progress, you'll gain confidence, and that will start to make the bad go away."

"I'm not there yet. But I have a feeling I'll get there. That's more than I could say a week ago. I'm hopeful. Now what were you going to tell me?" He braced himself.

"We're going to serve Daniels with a deposition notice in the next few days. We'll depose him at the district attorney's office. I'm looking forward to it. Harper will be there, which is huge. He has this ability to see through people when others can't. I'm confident that, once we are seated across from this piece of shit, the plaster will start to crack."

"You just made me think of something." Owen could finally explain something that had been bothering him from the first day he set foot in the firm.

"What's that? Wait, hold that thought. I have to piss super bad." Brent dashed into the bathroom.

Harper. He finally had an explanation for why he was so uncomfortable around him. Granted, their time together had been very short, but the first impression he got from Brent and his senior partner were like night and day.

The toilet flushing signaled Brent's return. "Sorry about that. What were you going to tell me?"

"This is sort of out there, because I don't have much to go on. We spent so little time together. I felt so uncomfortable with Harper in our first meeting. I was relieved when he had to leave."

"You did?" Brent asked.

"Yes. Anyway, when you were telling me about the deposition, I got to thinking maybe Daniels will feel the same way. I felt threatened, maybe he will too. I think Harper has this way of looking at you that makes you want to crawl into a corner."

Brent threw his head back and roared. "You nailed it. He does. Fuck. I'm sorry you got a taste of that the way you did, but yeah, he's intimidating as hell. Nicest guy in the whole world if he's on your side, but if he's not… you're totally fucked."

"I'm feeling better." Owen laughed. "What kind of things will you ask Daniels?"

"We'll question him in detail about that day in the woods. Have him go into his background. What will be different from our initial questions with you—he's not going to get the benefit of the doubt at all. Any weakness or inconsistencies we uncover will get shoved under the microscope and then mercilessly attacked. The goal is to catch him lying and have it documented. Honestly, he doesn't stand a chance. Not with Harper in the room."

"Wow. I guess I never really knew how that sort of thing worked." An image of Daniels seated in front of bright lights, breaking out in a sweat, flooded his mind. It was a glorious vision he would frequently call up in the days to come, he was sure.

Brent glanced at his watch. "Well…." He smiled.

It was one of those smiles that oozed subtext. He had a response. "Time for bed?" Owen asked.

"Time for bed? I was thinking I'd better get going."

"I was thinking about you and me lying in our own beds, separated by a narrow band of asphalt, and how unnecessary that was." He didn't want to be alone if there was anything he could do about it.

"You're good. Really good." Brent laughed. "I need to do some work before I crash. I'd love to stay, but tonight isn't good. How about tomorrow night?" Brent collected his bottle and stood.

"Okay." Owen wasn't surprised at how disappointed he felt. "I'm bummed. But I understand. I'm also feeling needy, and that sucks." He took Brent's bottle out of his hand. "Go off into the night. And thanks. You're leaving me in much better shape."

"Thanks for understanding. Harper is an early bird, and that puts pressure on me to fall into step. We're going to prep for Daniels' deposition together. I want to walk into his office in the morning with some quality work." Brent took Owen into his arms and hugged hard. "Let's talk tomorrow. What do you have going on?"

"I'm going biking. I just decided that. It will be the first time since my arrest. Something shifted tonight. I can feel my fear turning to anger. I'm not about to let this prick fuck my life up any more than he already has. You made this happen, Brent." Owen hugged back. "Thank you."

"I could tuck you in?" Brent offered and planted a kiss on his lips.

"One last thing before you go." Owen kissed him back. "Summers are vacation for a teacher. You're working. Don't compromise for me. I might whine and pout, but I understand. You're worth being patient for. Good night."

"I'll call tomorrow. Enjoy your biking."

Owen found it hard to leave the doorway. It was as if lingering there would keep their night from coming to an end. When he started to feel foolish, he finished cleaning up and marched up the stairs to bed.

*It's okay to look.* He crossed the dark bedroom, parted the curtain, and felt a tremor charge through his body at the sight of Brent seated under the light at his dining room table with his laptop open next to a stack of documents. *Give him some breathing room, Owen. He's everything you've been waiting for.*

He stepped away from the window, undressed, and climbed into bed. His last thought before falling asleep was that maybe the narrow strip of asphalt separating them wasn't the barrier he had first thought. "Good night, Brent," he whispered.

# CHAPTER Eight

SEATED ON a bleacher between Harper and Theo, Brent sipped his beer and watched Earl Henderson step to the plate. It was a warm, glorious Fourth of July evening at Lake County Fairgrounds. The Taconknights trailed the Beavertown Otters by one run in the top of the ninth, with two outs.

"They're so close. Tear it up, Earl," Harper shouted at the top of his lungs.

"Out of the park, Earl buddy," Theo shouted, cupping his hands around his mouth to maximize projection.

Brent stole a glance at his watch, placed his beer between his feet, and whistled through his fingers—an attempt to show support, even though spiritually he was a million miles away. Everything about the night rocked, except for one nagging problem—Owen Grady. Because their relationship was on the down low, it was impossible to take in the game together. For Brent to miss this game wasn't even a consideration. There would be no believable way to explain his absence. The compromise—once the game was over, he would excuse himself from the gang and head back home to hook up with Owen. They would enjoy the fireworks from Brent's porch roof, without the hassle of parking and dealing with the crowds. It sounded like the perfect solution.

The batter, Earl Swenson, accepted the pitch and answered with a smoking line drive inside first, advancing Skip Taylor to third and catcher Bobby Cornish onto second. That brought Ian to the plate.

"Here we go!" Alex, who had been quiet for most of the game, snapped to life. "Go, Mommy," he hollered as Ian, devastatingly handsome in his navy and blue uniform, sauntered up to the base.

"*Daddy's* going to march your ass out to the car, if you don't cut that shit out, princess," Harper cautioned Alex, sending everyone into hysterics.

Brent held his breath as he watched Ian rack up one ball and two strikes and then connect with a slow pitch he sent deep into the outfield. Otter nearly caught it, allowing Skip and Bobby to make it home and giving the Taconknights a one-run lead.

This brought a majority of the crowd to their feet.

"Hey." Harper poked Brent when things quieted down. "Look over there, by the dugout. Could that be our Officer Daniels?"

It didn't take long for him to spot Harper's target. The buff officer dressed in a khaki uniform, complete with gun holster and cuffs, was engaged in a lively chat with several women in the first row. Even from where they were seated, it would be impossible to imagine anyone else physically matching Owen's description. Daniels' flirtatious expressions managed to survive the distance as well. Brent experienced a chill as Daniels effortlessly played to the women, eliciting smiles and bursts of laughter.

"Mighty popular with the ladies, it looks like." Harper sipped his beer and brought his attention back to the game. "Come on T-Knights, make it one more!"

Ian, stranded on second, cautiously inched toward third. Bert Macklemore, arguably the weak link in the batting lineup, rarely came through in the pinch. He lived up to his reputation by striking out on the third of only three pitches.

"Fuck he sucks," Theo whined. He added, "Off to piss. Be right back."

Brent watched Theo bound down the bleachers, right past Daniels, to the bank of portable bathrooms. To his amazement, he observed Daniels momentarily break contact with his captivated audience and watch Theo until he was inside the can.

"Did you see that?" he asked Harper. "Theo had an audience on his way to the bathroom. It was very obvious."

"I missed it," Harper admitted.

Phil Style, the T-Knight's seasoned pitcher, gave up only one ball and retired the Otter's first batter.

"Watch this." Brent nudged Harper and pointed down to Daniels. As expected, Theo again captured the officer's attention as he innocently strolled by. Another chill raced through Brent as Daniels held his focus on Theo until their friend sat back down next to Alex.

"Interesting." This time Harper held his gaze until the action in the game resumed. "Very interesting."

Style continued his strong performance at the plate by eliminating a second batter. One more to go and the Taconknights would have a much-needed win.

"Hang in there, Phil," Theo yelled.

"End the game with some *style*, Phil," Alex added and then laughed when he realized everyone within earshot was looking up at him and snickering. "What'd I do?"

Theo grabbed Alex around the shoulders and administered a spirited noogie—to everyone's delight.

Falling prey to a curve ball, the Otters lost the game, and the home crowd went crazy.

"Thank heaven," Harper chimed. "That was a close one."

By the time they all reached the bottom of the bleachers, Daniels had moved on. They waited near the dugout for Ian, who arrived minutes later to hugs and congratulations.

With darkness setting in, Brent needed to make his move. The rest of the gang was going to walk out past the outfield to watch the fireworks. They had all parked their vehicles on the far side of the fairground to easily remove coolers and lawn chairs for the event. He had purposely parked near the ball field to aid his escape. "I'm parked over here," he said with a frown. "I'm going to move my car now, so I can get out of here easier when it's all over. I'll catch up with you guys in a minute."

"Hurry. We don't have long." Ian patted him on the back. "It should be a good display this year. A very popular resort known for its innovative landscaping kicked in big bucks."

"That's right. I wouldn't miss it." *Shithead.* "See you guys later."

Brent separated from his pals and bolted toward the parking lot. Rounding the concession stand, he passed within a foot of

Daniels and nearly screamed in surprise. The scent of cheap cologne stuck with him all the way to the car. *Snake oil.*

His plan appeared to be working. There were a ton of cars heading to the other side of the park, causing a massive traffic jam. He would later tell everyone he got stuck in traffic and ended up having to watch the fireworks from his car, which he was forced to pull over to the side. Hopefully they would all think he was an idiot and not read anymore into it.

Heading away from the fairgrounds, he made it home in minutes. He turned into the alley, passed two garages, and came to a stop behind his own. Procrastination had prevented him from installing an automatic garage door. His laziness kept the car outside night after night.

*Got to get around to that door one of these days.*

He entered the yard through the back gate and was surprised to find Owen already seated at the patio table.

"Owen." He walked into his new boyfriend's arms. "Sorry I'm late. The game was a close one, and I ended up having to stay until the end."

"No worries." Owen hugged him tight. "It's such a gorgeous night. I've been enjoying the quiet. Every now and then, I could hear cheers from the park. How did our team—the Taconknights, right? How did they do?"

"They won. Ian had a few nice hits. Are you getting bit up out here?" he asked, leading them to the house.

"Just a few nibbles. I'll take a cold Speckled Egg, if you have one handy."

"You bet. I was thinking the same thing." Inside, Brent flipped on lights and fetched a few beers. "You know what?"

"What?" Owen asked, giving him a pinch on the rear.

"More and harder," Brent joked. "Let's do this." He reached into the cupboard, took out a bowl, and filled it with more bottles. "This way," he added, emptying ice from a bag in the freezer. "We won't have to climb off the roof for a refill."

"Sounds great. Hopefully I won't fall off." Owen planted a kiss on his cheek.

"Onward and upward." Brent headed up the stairs.

The window onto the roof that faced the park was right at the top of the stairs. “Wait here a minute. I’m going to grab a sleeping bag from my closet for us to sit on.”

“Okay. But I’m fine.”

“Not me. I’ve been sitting on wooden bleachers for the last three hours. My butt needs some cushion. Plus somebody keeps pinching it.” Brent winked.

“I’d be happy to massage it later. Just say the word.” Owen winked back.

For a brief moment, he entertained the idea of watching the fireworks naked, but then thought better of it. “That’s an offer I might have to take you up on.”

He returned with the sleeping bag and climbed out the window. Once he had his bearings, Owen handed everything out and then joined him.

“We’d better close the window. You don’t want any bats or other critters to get in,” Owen advised.

“Fuck, no.” He agreed. “I hate fucking bats.”

Sitting side by side, Owen, with his long legs stretched out in front, placed his arm around Brent’s waist. “I’ve been waiting all day for this.”

“Oh, me too.” He snuggled his head into Owen’s neck. “The last hour of the game was agonizing. I love watching Ian play, but man, I wanted to get back here. Back to you.”

Almost a week had passed since their romp on Owen’s kitchen floor. Brent’s resolve to slow down the sexual aspect of their relationship seemed a good idea at the time, but now it seemed ridiculous. On the drive home he had decided to invite Owen to spend the night. He planned to blame it on his lack of restraint, which was neither a stretch of the truth nor a lie.

“What did you tell everyone?” Owen asked and planted a series of kisses on his ear.

“I think I pulled this one off without anyone suspecting otherwise.” He outlined his escape.

“Genius,” Owen chuckled. “I actually had that happen to me the first year I was up here. People come from everywhere to celebrate—”

The first rocket exploded overhead. "Oh great. They're starting."

Brent leaned over and planted a kiss on Owen's cheek. "Artie wasn't kidding. The view is great.

"It is. I'm loving this." Owen placed his hand on Brent's crotch.

Brent reciprocated with a similar move, and they enjoyed the finale of the fireworks while they fondled each other.

The night still held most of its warmth, rare for the North Shore. And so far they had managed to evade the mosquitoes. Starving for sex, Brent opened Owen's shorts and brought down the zipper.

"What's mine is yours," Owen offered, nearly breathless.

"I was hoping you'd say that." He stroked and petted Owen until he had achieved the result he was looking for. "I think it's dark enough to enjoy a little more of the night up here, undetected. What do you think?"

"I don't think I could move right now if I wanted to." Owen leaned against the house and sighed. "I wasn't expecting this tonight. Did you have a change of heart?" he asked as Brent snuggled in closer.

"I was a fool. How could I possibly pass up… this?" By then, Owen was nearly bursting out of the cotton restraint of his boxers. Brent moved his hand up Owen's stomach to his chest. "You have to promise to let me know if the sex part of us is getting out of hand, though. Is that a deal?"

"I promise. I'm not anticipating that being a problem." Owen removed Brent's hand and sat up. "I have an idea. Lean forward… but *please* be careful. Falling off the roof right now would really suck."

As instructed, Brent leaned forward while Owen stretched his legs out on the sleeping bag. When he had completed the maneuver, he took Brent by the arm and guided him onto his body. Their lips connected as Brent felt Owen slide his hands down the back of his shorts and cup his naked buttcheeks.

"That was a pretty smooth move, Mr. Grady," he confessed, kissing Owen on the forehead.

"You inspire me. Well, that, and I've dreamed about your ass lately so much it would scare you."

Owen kneaded and soothed his sore rear. "I love having my butt played with. It drives me crazy," Brent said.

"Your ass is amazing. You probably know how I feel about it by now," Owen snickered.

Brent responded to the compliment by pulling Owen's throbbing cock out of its confines. Then, lifting his body up, Owen pulled his shorts and boxers down to his knees. Brent rubbed his body against Owen's.

"Oh fuck, that feels good," Owen confessed, pulling him tighter. "I'm thinking I could, you know, go all the way like this."

"Stranger things have happened. I'm so happy with you, Owen. I can't wait until we're free and clear to do whatever it is we—" To his disappointment, a car pulled up and stopped directly in front of the house. "Don't move."

"The lights are on," a voice said from inside the car.

"He must be home then. I wonder why he didn't answer his cell?"

"Fuck! It's Harper and Ian," Brent said as softly as he could. Conscious that his lily white ass was exposed, he slid off Owen with as little movement as possible and stuffed his deflating dick back into his shorts. Owen, still flat on his back, followed his lead.

"We'd better check it out, just to make sure he's okay. You never know. Wait here."

A car door opened, and Ian, barely recognizable, got out and walked up the short flight of stairs to the front door, directly beneath them. Brent held his breath. He could feel Owen breathing slowly. A bell clanged from inside the house. This happened several times before Ian gave up and walked back to the car. "He's not answering. What do you think?"

A brief discussion ensued. Brent could hear only Ian clearly. Whatever Harper was saying sounded jumbled. Eventually Ian turned from the car and walked across the grass to the gate on the side of the house.

*Fuck. Did I lock the back door?* He wasn't sure how far Ian would go. Usually he locked the door, but with the excitement of seeing Owen, it was entirely possible he hadn't. Several agonizing minutes passed, and then, to his horror, he heard Ian call out from inside the house, “Brent? You home, buddy?”

“What do we do now?” Owen asked noticeably freaked.

“We stay put.” He felt nauseous. His worst fear was precariously close to becoming a reality. Harper would find out about them.

“Brent, you here?”

Ian was either heading up the stairs, or already on the second floor. His voice was strong, even through the closed window.

What seemed like hours passed until they heard the side gate open. Brent held his breath and watched Ian move across the lawn, back to the car.

“His cell phone is on the kitchen counter. I thought maybe he might be in the shower, but I went upstairs to check it out, and he wasn’t there. What now?”

More mumbled discussion.

“He runs at night?” They heard Ian ask. “That probably explains it. Do you want to wait around to make sure everything is okay?”

*You don’t need to stick around. It’s late. Go home. Fuck. Please go home!*

Ian got back in the car and, to his relief, they drove off.

“That was….”

“Fucking insane,” he finished for Owen.

Owen responded with a snort, which blossomed into a giggle that exploded into a series of guffaws. Everything deteriorated fast from there. Soon Brent was in hysterics. Eventually Owen got himself under control enough to suggest, “We’d better head back in.”

Laughing, they both stumbled through the window and onto the hallway floor.

“Why didn’t I figure in the cell phone?” Brent wondered. “That was what fucked us over. I’d better call them before they send out the National Guard.”

He raced downstairs, dialed Harper, and raced back up to Owen. “Hey, it’s me. Sorry I didn’t call to let you know what happened to me.” He hit speaker so Owen could listen in.

"Where the hell were you?" Harper asked, sounding mildly annoyed.

"I couldn't get close to you guys. Traffic was a bitch. I ended up watching from the side of the road."

"That's what we figured."

Brent smiled, acknowledging his plan's success. Holding his finger in the air so Owen would pay particular attention to the skill involved, he implemented the back end of the ruse.

"Got home and decided to go for a run."

"Ian walked right into your house looking for you. Lock your doors. He could have left with anything he wanted."

"Sorry. I'm usually careful about that." It was time to wind this up. "Well, I'm going to hit the shower and then go to bed. What time are you getting into the office tomorrow?" Brent held back any mention of the deposition prep they had planned. With the Officer Daniels sighting and Harper's history of distrusting Owen, the chances were good that Harper could say something offensive.

"I have a few things I need to do at the resort," Harper reported. "Expect me in around noon."

"Great. Thanks for looking in on me. Sorry to worry you." He couldn't mask his delight. He had successfully averted a close call and compromised nothing.

"Fuck." He fell back against the wall after Harper dropped off the call. "The sad thing is," he shared with Owen,. "I don't think we'll ever be able to share this with anyone. And that's a shame, because it's an awesome story."

Owen stood, reached outside, hauled in the bucket of beers and the sleeping bag, and handed them inside to Brent. "Want a beer?" He pulled one out of the ice and passed it over.

Brent accepted it and slid down to the floor. Exhausted from the ordeal, he was content to stay there for a while. "You're a trooper, Owen. Thanks for hanging in there."

"I'm a grown man, and I was scared shitless," Owen confessed.

It was time to initiate part three of his plan. "How do you feel about spending the night?" Brent asked.

NAKED, OWEN waited on the bed for Brent to return from the bathroom. There was something highly erotic about being in another man's bed for the first time.

"I'm not going through that again, I can tell you that." Naked too, except for his watch, which Owen had come to understand never left his wrist, Brent crawled in beside him. "That took years off my life."

"Don't go there," he begged. "My face hurts from laughing." He couldn't remember laughing that hard in his entire life.

"Are you tired?" Brent asked, snuggling into Owen's chest.

"Not really. I feel exhilarated. Fear can really get my juices flowing. What's on your mind?" he asked, sensing the question had been posed for a reason and not just to be conversational.

"A bunch of stuff." Brent drew a circle on Owen's chest with a finger. "For starters, how wonderful it feels to be here with you."

"It's nice." Owen intentionally kept his response short. Something else was on his new lover's mind, and he needed to nurture it out of him.

They petted and stroked each other lazily until Brent propped his head up with his hand.

"I'm not sure how to ask this, so I'll just fling it out there." Brent chuckled. "Do you have much experience sexually?"

*I think I know where this is headed.* "Are you by any chance asking me what I'm comfortable with? Where I'm willing to go with another man?" If he was on the right track, he'd soon find out.

"That's exactly what I was asking. Thanks for making it easier."

"Is there something specific you're wondering about?" Owen asked.

Brent laughed and a sheepish smile took over his impossibly handsome face. "Yes," he answered. "I can't wait to feel you deep inside. I love… well, getting fucked. I know it's not for everyone."

"I was prepared for something more out there. Like bondage, hot wax, or fisting." Planting a kiss on Brent's cheek Owen was proud to report, "I've taken another man before. It was fine. It wasn't someone I cared that much about. And I think alcohol was involved too. It was in college."

"When it feels right, I'd like you to take me." Brent snuggled in tighter. "No rush. It was on my mind, and I wanted you to know."

Running his fingers through Brent's hair, one of his new favorite pastimes, he contemplated the request. Did they need to put something like this on hold? Not really. He wasn't one of those people who felt he had to save something for a special time. That certainly wasn't the case back in college. His feelings for Brent were already strong. "Is there any protection nearby?" He studied Brent's face, lying next to his. Being safe was his only real concern. "If you'd like, we could give it a go now. I mean, I've got a ton of pent-up energy from earlier. I'm thinking what you propose might just be the ticket to relaxation and a decent night's sleep."

"You're sure I'm not talking you into something?" Brent asked, running his finger over Owen's lower lip. "Please be honest. I don't want to do that to you."

"Not at all." Owen hoped to reassure and visualized the mechanics involved. "You might have to give me a few pointers," he snickered.

"Hang on." Brent made a trip into the bathroom and returned seconds later with a familiar-looking foil packet. "Let's start and see how it goes. If it isn't working for you, I'll completely understand. Wait."

"What?" Owen sat up against the headboard.

"I obviously enjoy this, but it's not a showstopper. I mean, it's certainly something I can live without. I wanted you to know that, so you wouldn't feel pressured."

He thought that the best response was to get the ball rolling and give it a go. Owen removed the packet from Brent's hand, opened it, and placed the wrapper on the table next to the bed. "Remember. It's up to *you* to let me know how this is supposed to go."

"Here. Let me get this party started." Brent kissed the tip of Owen's penis and then licked the entire shaft from top to bottom.

Owen responded instantly to Brent's tongue and just when he thought he could tolerate the tease no longer, Brent placed the condom on the tip of his cock and rolled it down until it could go no farther.

“Whoops. I forgot the second most important thing,” Brent announced abruptly.

Owen was left in an awkward state of readiness, wondering what it could be.

“And with you, Owen, that would be a serious mistake.” Brent returned with a tube in his hand. “There’s many ways to do this, but I think for now, this might be the best.” Straddling Owen, he squirted from the tube into the palm of his hand.

Fascinated, Owen watched as Brent liberally coated his latex sheathed cock from top to bottom. Once this step was completed, Brent squirted another dollop into his hand and leaned forward. With their heads only inches apart, he pulled Brent in for a long, sensuous kiss. When they parted, Brent reached back and carefully guided Owen into place.

“You’re big… which is great. Trust me, I’m not complaining. But we need to go slow.” Brent leaned forward for another kiss.

Gradually, Owen felt Brent relax and open for him. How different this was compared to his earlier experience. Not rushed. Gentle and tender—two bodies in the process of becoming one. Their eyes remained locked the entire time it took for Brent to finally accept him completely.

“Mission accomplished,” Brent whispered. “How are you?”

“It feels… awesome. So warm and so intimate.” His cock pulsated with anticipation.

Brent began to slowly move his body up and down, barely perceivably. Taking this as a cue, he reached under his adventurous partner and cupped both of his buttcheeks with his hands. He lifted and released, until a natural rhythm was established.

As Owen thrust in and out, Brent squeezed and hugged, caressed and licked at every spot within reach. Thinking he owed Brent’s cock some attention, Owen removed one hand from his pert bottom and began to stroke.

“Not this time,” Brent grinned, removing the hand. “I’m already enjoying every inch of you.”

Gaining confidence, he put more muscle into the effort, his large hands holding his lover off him while pumping into him from side to side, which seemed to bring about the most satisfied reaction. Brent's face was a perfect barometer to gauge his performance.

"Yes." Brent threw his head back and bounced up and down. "You're driving me wild."

Owen had started to sweat. Brent's body was already glistening. Small and unassuming at first, Owen soon identified a familiar sensation building in intensity. He was getting close. Seconds later he was there. "I'm coming," Owen announced as his body bucked violently into his new lover, who by now was leaning forward on his hands and knees as Owen continued to pummel him.

The orgasm, when it finally hit, was one for the record books. It was all consuming. The intensity stole everything from Owen but the happiness he felt at providing something Brent so obviously enjoyed. Exhausted but unwilling to have it end, he hugged Brent tight. "I'd be up for that again. Say the word." Owen brushed Brent's hair, now soaked and matted, away from his eyes.

"I've never had better," Brent confessed. "Damn. I forgot to turn off the bathroom light." Before he had a chance to get up, the light went off on its own. "Wow. How's that for timing?"

"Not bad. Maybe it was Artie."

"Artie… that's another story. Remind me to tell you sometime. I'm so ready to sleep." Brent rested his head on the pillow beside him. "Night, hon."

"Pleasant dreams, handsome."

"OUR CLIENT detected what he thought was a California accent." Seated in the conference room preparing for the deposition, Brent hoped they would find this detail useful.

"A California accent? I'm not sure I know what that means. Is that all you have on this?" Harper asked.

"I've searched on several of that state's databases to see if I could come up with a link to his name, but struck out. It's probably nothing."

"No, it's not," Harper cautioned. "Little seeds like this can sometimes blossom right before your eyes. If, at any point during the deposition, you see a way where this can be used to our advantage, either initiate it yourself, or signal for us to take a break to discuss. I've got it underlined in my notes."

That was the first sign things were starting to turn. The second came out of the blue.

"We haven't talked about the Fourth of July yet." Harper cracked his knuckles. "What are your thoughts?"

Before he could answer, the phone on the conference table buzzed. Fern picked it up from her desk.

"You expecting any calls?" Harper threw his arms into the air and stretched.

"No. This is the only thing I have going on right now. How about you?" He looked down at the phone console to see the light blink off, signaling the call had ended.

"Hang on." Harper pressed the intercom. "Fern?"

"Hello, Harper."

"Who was that?"

"It was a woman inquiring about the Owen Grady case. She asked if we were representing him."

Harper frowned. "What did you tell her?"

"I asked her to identify herself, but she wouldn't, so I told her it wasn't our policy to give out the names of clients."

"Perfect. If that happens again, put them on hold and grab onc of us."

"Will do. You guys need anything?"

"I don't. Brent you need anything? A white wine spritzer? Your loafers sanitized?" Harper winked.

Fern laughed. "It will be a cold day in you-know-where before I ask you fellas that again."

"I don't blame you." Harper chuckled after Fern was gone. "So, what do you make of that call?"

"I guess, given the nature of the case, I'm sort of surprised we haven't received more calls. You know… from concerned parents. The school board meeting is tomorrow night. There's probably a spirited campaign on both sides heating up." Brent flipped a page over in his notes.

"Good point. If it were something legitimate, they would have given their name and stated their intent. You're attending the meeting, right?" Harper asked.

*Say what?* Brent felt his face warm and then ignite. He had fucked up. He tried to minimize the blunder by explaining, "I assumed it was a closed meeting. We haven't been invited." *Oh, well, then it's fine. Totally understandable.* "I should have pursued the meeting. I realize that now." He waited for the shit to hit the fan.

"Even if it were a closed meeting and you weren't given an engraved invitation, it would be prudent to attempt to gain admittance." Harper dropped his pen. "Grady is our client. They're more than likely going to say some nasty things about him at this meeting and make some accusations that, at this point, haven't been proven. Even if they tell you to go home, it shows everyone there his defense cares about what's being discussed. I'll go if you can't."

He was embarrassed and knew Harper could see it. *Getting Owen off doesn't mean throwing your feet up over his shoulders. You're a warrior in a fight here, shithead. Fucking get it together.* For one brief second, he thought about coming clean with Harper. Maybe even taking it a step further and asking for advice on how to deal with a relationship you've developed with your client while understanding it to be wrong. The look on Harper's face made it clear nothing would be gained by that. "I can go," he answered, unable to mask disappointment in his lapse of judgment. "If the deposition hasn't finished in time for me to get there, I'll leave early." *You'll leave early?* Flustered, he quickly tried to gain ground by asking, "What do you advise?"

"The deposition starts at one. We'll be out of there by four, if not sooner."

The curt response was appropriate. "I have to use the can. I'll be right back." Brent stood and walked to the door. Even though he couldn't piss if his life depended on it, he needed to get the hell out of there for a minute.

"Let's take a ten-minute break. I need to give Ian a call." Harper followed him out.

Brent walked into restroom, closed the door, lowered the lid on the stool and sat. He rested his head in his hand. It was beginning to ache. A few more slipups like that and he would surely risk losing Harper's confidence for good. And who could blame him? That oversight was inexcusable. It hadn't even entered his mind to attend the meeting. He stood and walked to the window, his nerves getting the best of him. *Why did Harper want a break?* Was he having serious reservations about his junior partner's ability to deliver the goods? *Do you fucking blame him?*

This could be the last mistake he would be allowed before there were serious consequences. There was no room for mistakes in lawyering. It was a true and simple fact. Lawyers who make mistakes don't last. He had seen it many times. They had agreed to represent Owen. That meant they would do whatever it took to win. Friendships aside, if Harper thought he had gone from an asset to a liability, he would eliminate the risk and move forward without him.

It was time to go back. When he walked into the conference room, Harper was already seated.

"So, what did you make of Daniels at the game the other night?" Harper asked. "The wandering eyes were pretty obvious, if you ask me."

If a decision had been made regarding his usefulness on the case, it wasn't noticeable. Harper appeared to have recovered.

"I think it's worth considering." Because his confidence was at an all-time low, Brent kept his answer short.

"So do I." Harper pushed his chair back and crossed his leg. "Theo's a damned good-looking man, and in my opinion, Daniels gave him much more than a casual once-over. I saw serious interest."

Brent could feel the balance returning. "The expression on his face—it was intense—like a stalker."

"He's either so confident in who he is that he can appreciate an attractive member of the same sex, or he's a nancy pancy, like me."

That was funny. Harper was one of the most masculine men, gay or straight, that Brent had ever met. Ian too. "How can we use this?" Brent asked.

"Let's introduce a line of questioning that attempts to find out what, if any, experience Daniels has with us gay folk." Harper jotted down a note. "Of course there will be alternative motives involved, but hopefully he won't pick up on them. We need to find out how it came about that Daniels thought he was being cruised by Grady in the first place. My guess is he's going to grow uncomfortable having to detail the exchange between them. Hopefully how he responds to this will let us pursue the idea that our client was somehow led on. Coerced."

"Right." Brent was drained. Up until a few minutes before, he had felt confident he could do a good job deposing Daniels. Now he thought he wasn't the man for this job. A tricky deponent like Daniels required a skilled questioner, which he wasn't. It would be a disservice to Owen if he were in the lead. It was time to address the elephant in the room. "Harper?"

"What's up?" Harper continued writing.

"I don't have the skills yet to do the best job for our client. You need to take the lead on this deposition." He hoped there would be some honor in admitting his defeat.

"Close the door." Harper still hadn't looked up.

He got out of his chair, closed the door, and then sat back down. In the short time that took, he had begun to perspire. There was a familiar tone to his partner's voice, but in the state he was in, Brent couldn't place it. One thing he knew without a doubt—he was about to be officially talked to.

"How long have we known each other?" Harper finally looked across the table.

"Five years?" He had neither the energy nor the cleverness to be strategic.

"At least." Harper tapped his hand gently on the table. "Something is wrong. Ever since this case came into the firm, you've been different. If something's going on, you need to let me know what it is. I'm starting to worry."

Brent stared at the wall, unable to maintain eye contact. If there was a way out of this, he was blind to it.

"So there is something."

The lights, the vent into the room, they all had a specific noise. For the first time, Brent was able to pick up on them all. He had painted himself into a corner. He needed time but didn't have it. In response to an unexpected wave of emotion, he brought his hand up to mask the quivering of his lip. He was close to breaking.

"Let me go at this from another angle." Harper leaned forward. "I'm very close to getting pissed off in a way that wouldn't be beneficial to either of us. I'm already disappointed. You're making mistakes that are elementary, and I'm not sure why that is. If you're holding back telling me something because I'm a perceived threat to you… well then we have a serious problem. Perhaps one we won't be able to recover from."

The tone of his partner's words hit so hard, all he could do was stare helplessly across the table.

"I'm not kidding. What is it?" Harper wasn't going to let him off.

Out of options, he answered, "There is something." Terrified of the reaction the truth would unleash, he got up from his chair and walked to the door. "I've made a huge mistake. It happened so fast, I didn't even see it coming. I've fallen for Owen. We've started something." He waited for the explosion.

"I see." Harper crossed his arms across his chest and sat back.

There was more to tell, and despite serious reluctance to make a fucked situation even worse, he forged ahead. "At first I thought it was just me, you know, being a horndog. So I told myself how wrong it was—what a huge mistake I was making, given he was our client. I envisioned how angry and disappointed you would be. And as much as I respect you and look up to you, that wasn't enough. It wasn't fucking…." Consumed with remorse he cried out, "It wasn't fucking enough, and I gave in. I was willing to jeopardize everything that…." He turned and punched the door, which hurt like fucking hell. Rubbing the pain out of his hand, he admitted, "I was willing to risk everything for Owen."

There was no immediate relief in finally getting it all out. Unable to see Harper's face to gauge his reaction, he leaned against the door and prayed for mercy.

"I have a happy-sad kinda thing going on right now," Harper finally commented after a huge, painful-sounding sigh.

Certain there was more to follow, Brent braced himself and waited.

"Unless, unbeknownst to any of us, Meryl Streep is your mother and John Boehner is your father, I'm going to bet the ranch you were sincerely worried about my reaction to this. That makes me happy in a strange way. Conversely, your lack of self-control and professionalism makes me sad. Very sad indeed."

The energy in the room had dissipated. The air had cooled. Feeling stupid, Brent returned to his seat at the table.

"I'll handle the deposition tomorrow. It's unfortunate you've blown this opportunity to get one of these under your belt. There's nothing more to be said about it. You can either attend as my assistant, or stay back. I will ask, however, that you make every attempt to attend the school board meeting tomorrow night and take notes, if you can figure a way to get in. Is that doable?"

Devastated by the damage his behavior had caused, he simply replied, "Yes."

"We all make mistakes, Brent. Some of them will be big, some small, and some… well… frankly are inexcusable. Had you come to me when you were first experiencing this conflict of interest, I would have been more than happy to help you maneuver around it. I would have worked with you. But you chose not to come to me, and that's significant."

Harper got out of his chair and walked to the door. "I wish I could end this happily ever after, but I can't. I'm not only angry. I'm hurt. I need time to sort this out."

Shamed to silence, Brent fought hard to keep from crying.

"Do the best you can to get yourself together, and for Christ's sake, table whatever you have going on with Grady from this moment on, or let's just shake and wish each other the best."

"I'll end it with Owen," Brent pledged softly. "I'm sorry."

Harper opened the door. "I'm going home."

When enough time had lapsed for the senior partner to either be back in his office or out to his car, Brent stood, walked over to the wastebasket and emptied his stomach.

PARKED ON the remote end of the Budget Saver parking lot, Owen took a minute to muster the courage to go in. Fearing he might be confronted by either a student or a parent, he had made it a habit to shop very early or well past the dinner hour. It was time he knocked off that nonsense and took one more step toward taking back his life. Having Brent around made him realize how foolish he was being. The only thing he was guilty of was falling in love—a crime of the heart he was more than willing to plead guilty to. Understanding Brent neither had the time nor the interest in cooking, he decided to slide into the role of chief cook and bottle washer. He enjoyed being in the kitchen and knew Brent would appreciate not having the responsibility.

The store wasn't nearly as busy as he had anticipated. Grabbing a cart, he strolled to the produce section and began working down his list. The list was important because it allowed him to move efficiently from one area to the next without having to backtrack, cutting down on the time he was actually in the store and reducing the risk of an uncomfortable situation.

Another beautiful night was in the forecast, and he planned on throwing steaks on the grill. Catching the attention of the lady behind the meat counter, he selected a couple of well-marbled rib eyes and then headed to the bakery and the checkout.

"Hey, Mr. Grady."

Owen turned in a panic but then relaxed. Walking down the aisle toward him was one of his favorite students, Liam Pearson.

"Oh hi, Liam. How's your summer going?" It was nice to run into a friendly soul. Liam was his star percussionist. There had been talk of possibly establishing a few weeks of individual lessons during the summer for those who were interested. Once all this crap was over and done with, he would approach Deena with a plan and see if they could get it set up for the following year. Liam was one student who had showed interest in additional lessons.

"Good. Mom was talking about you the other day on the phone. Were you sick or something?"

"Sick?" *Oh God.* "No, I wasn't sick. I'm feeling great."

"We're going to Mount Rushmore tomorrow."

Liam was pumped. It reminded Owen of the trips he used to take with his family, growing up. Mount Rushmore had been one of them too.

"I got to go there when I was about your age. You're going to love it." Liam had a great enthusiasm for life. It was an endearing characteristic that made spending time with him a real pleasure.

"We're doin' some other stuff too, but I'm not sure what."

Liam wasn't doing a very good job of hiding his interest in what Owen had in his cart. Maybe the boy thought teachers ate differently than regular people.

"I'm going to grill steaks tonight," he shared. "Should be a nice night for it."

"I like steak. Dad grilled hamburgers…."

"Liam. Get over here. Now." June, Liam's mother, called out sternly from the end of the aisle. She had always been very friendly.

"Hi, Mrs. Pearson." He waved. "Have a great trip, Liam, and enjoy your summer." *She didn't even wave back.*

"Now, Liam."

"Bye, Mr. Grady."

He looked on as June Pearson gestured frantically for her son to hurry.

*Better try and get used to this. There's bound to be more.* He was surprised at how little the incident affected him. His encounter with Liam seemed to have broken the ice. Standing at the checkout, he felt stronger than he had walking into the store. *Bring it on. Say whatever the hell you want about me, but you're going to be really sorry once the truth comes out.*

Back home, he put the groceries away and tidied the kitchen. Next year he would think about a remodel. Since the day he moved in, it had been a dream to extend the kitchen a few feet into the back. It would be nice to do away with the traditional door and replace it with a sliding glass one. He also wanted a small deck between the house and the patio.

He headed out to water. Unless he was really rushed, he preferred to do everything with a nozzle instead of attaching a sprinkler. It cut down on his water bill and gave him an opportunity to see how everything was faring. Another week or so, and he would be able to start cutting little bouquets to spread around the house. He had just uncoiled the hose when his phone went off in his pocket.

*Awesome. It's Brent.*

"Hey there." He dropped the hose, walked to the patio, and sat. "What's up?"

"Are you busy with something right now?"

"Naw. Just putzing around in the backyard. Why?" If Brent had a late-afternoon romp on his mind, Owen was in.

"Would it be possible for you to come over to the office?"

"Sure." Something was off. Owen missed the usual zip in Brent's voice. "Has something bad happened with the case?" With the school board meeting on for the next evening, and given the way Mrs. Pearson had acted in the store, anything was possible.

"I need to talk something over with you."

That didn't sound good at all. "I'm in shorts. Do I need to change for any reason?" Owen asked.

"No."

"I'll be there in a few minutes." He started into the house.

"Fern will know I'm expecting you. I'll be in my office."

"Okay."

The drive to the Center was agony. It had to be something connected to the case. Maybe a nasty letter or a threat.

His stomach ached as he entered the firm.

"Good afternoon, Owen." Fern smiled.

*She doesn't seem any different. Relax.*

Brent's expecting you. May I bring you something to drink before you head back?"

Nerves on the way over had left him parched. "I could use a water, if it's not too much trouble."

"Not at all. I'll be right back."

He waited by the window until the receptionist returned. "There you are."

"Thank you."

He heard music from somewhere down the hall. As he got closer, it was clear it was originating from Brent's office. "Hey there," he greeted as he walked in.

"Hey." Barely looking at him, Brent shut down the tunes, stood, walked to the door, and shut it. "Take a seat."

The change in body language and the serious look on Brent's face was alarming. Something significant had happened. They both sat down at the same time.

"Just tell me. I know the news is bad." He couldn't stand the suspense.

"I can't be sure, but I may have lost my job. At the very least, I'm in deep shit with Harper." Brent pulled off his tie and wrapped it around his fist.

"Seriously?" He couldn't believe it. "Is it because of me?"

"It's because of us." Brent sat back in his chair and unleashed a massive sigh.

"I'm confused. How did Harper find out about us?" Was it possible they were spotted on the roof from his car?

"I told him," Brent admitted.

"You what?" He couldn't hide his surprise.

"I know. Trust me. I had no intention of ever saying a word until after the trial." Brent shifted in his chair, visibly uncomfortable.

"Yeah, okay." Owen was at a loss for words, but he knew he had to say something.

"I'm fucking up your case, big time. I'm unfocused, missing obvious shit that someone in my position shouldn't miss. I'm jeopardizing the firm's reputation, and it all came to the surface this afternoon in a meeting with Harper."

"Is he still here?" It pained Owen to see Brent take the fall for actions they were both guilty of. "Would it help if I talked to him? I mean, this is as much my fault as it is yours."

"I appreciate that, but it's different for me. You're our client, and up until today, I was given the privilege of taking the lead on your case." Brent shook his head in disgust. "I let us get in the way. Don't you see?"

They had both understood the risk from the very beginning. Owen always assumed that, if they were found out, Brent would get hollered at, slapped on the wrist, and they would be forced to lay low until Owen was cleared of the charges. Brent and Harper were good friends, after all. "I get the part about Harper being angry, but maybe I'm missing something here. I'm struggling to see how you've jeopardized my case. That's the part that isn't making sense."

Brent stood and stepped away from his chair. "I guess the school board meeting tomorrow night is the best example I can give you. Not once, not for a single minute, did I think about attending that meeting. That's a huge mistake, Owen."

"It is? I'm pretty sure, even if you had thought about it, you wouldn't be allowed access. There are public meetings where people are allowed to vent, and then there are private meetings, where matters like mine are discussed behind a closed door." *Seriously? That's a huge mistake?* The only thing going through his mind was what a huge fucking dick this Harper guy was.

"That's fair, but it's not how things work in this business. Success has everything to do with being thorough and getting as much out of every opportunity handed you. This is something you're taught from day one. In some instances, you need to create opportunity. It's all about strategy. I think I mentioned this to you once already. In that department, I failed miserably. There's more, but you probably wouldn't understand why it's a big deal." Brent leaned into the wall and folded his arms across his chest. "Harper has lost confidence in my ability as an attorney."

"I can hire whomever the hell I want. I want you." Anger was setting in, and there was nothing he could do about it. None of what he had heard seemed fair. "I mean, has Harper ever heard of a learning curve?"

Brent managed a smile, but it didn't last long. "It's more complicated than I'm able to communicate to you." He sat down. "If there's a chance for me to salvage my partnership, I'm not going to risk losing that opportunity for anything."

It was impossible to miss the intention of Brent's last statement. He sat quietly in his chair and tried not to feel hurt. It sounded like his career meant more to Brent than their future together. To actually hear this come out his mouth stunned Owen because, even in the short time they had spent together, he knew he would risk anything for Brent. If he was being true to himself—and he was pretty sure he was—this was where he stood. Brent was that important. "I don't know what to say." He got up from his chair and wandered to the door. "I think the best thing for me to do right now is to leave."

"Owen, please don't go. Whatever it is you're thinking.... Well, I'm pretty sure you have it wrong." Brent was over to him in a second. "Sit back down, and let's talk about this."

Brent took him by the arm, attempting to move him away from the door, but he held his ground.

"Please," Brent begged, not giving up.

It was the desperate look on Brent's face that changed Owen's mind. *Hear him out.*

He sat down and Brent followed. "I've wanted to be a lawyer for as long as I can remember. I never really thought about being anything else. So to get this far, only to have it all yanked away... well, I hope you can imagine how devastating that would be. It wouldn't matter what else I had going on in my life. I would be different. Changed. That's what I was trying to say earlier."

So far, Brent hadn't said anything to make him feel like he mattered. "Trust me. I understand that part." He was getting angrier.

"I understand now why you're reacting the way you are. I wanted to make a point, and it went too far."

Brent grabbed Owen's hand and clasped it tight before he could claim it back. "I don't want to lose you, Owen. I should have said that first. Are you kidding me? You matter to me. You're important. I just can't risk my career right now for you."

"I don't need you to risk your career for me." He tried to remove his hand, but Brent wouldn't let go.

"What you and I have going on is ethically something that could have bigger ramifications. I could be disbarred. The firm would be hurt in the press. A lawyer gone bad is something people love to hear about. Unfortunately because we have some real assholes in our ranks—too many—we're the scum of the earth."

Owen understood that. He thought Brent trusted him to be discreet.

"We need to shut us down until your matter is resolved." The expression on Brent's face was so pained it prevented Owen from responding.

"Completely stop," Brent continued, his voice shaking with emotion, "any non-case-related contact… because you're consuming me."

Owen felt completely betrayed. "How is this all my fault?"

"That was bad too." Brent slapped the side of his chair in defeat. "It's good, Owen. I'm trying to tell you, you're the one. From my perspective, we have a great future. I'm falling for you hard. But I'm not capable of managing both my career and you at the same time, and nobody knows that better than Harper. Unfortunately I've done a fantastic job of proving just that."

As hurt as he was, Owen was starting to see what Brent was wrestling with. He wasn't getting the rug yanked from under him, after all. There were two important things in Brent's life, and it sounded like he was one of them.

"My initial reaction to what you said," Owen confessed, "speaks more than any words I can come up with. You matter to me too. I've allowed myself to fall in love and to project us into the future." He turned to the side and faced Brent. "This is the first time that's happened to me with another person. It wasn't planned. It just seemed right, so I gave in. I thought you were giving me up for your job—permanently. I see now you're not."

"I'm not."

It wasn't easy, but Owen forced a smile. They would get past this. "Say whatever it is you need to make things right with Harper. That's as important as anything, right now."

"That's part of the reason I had you come by. I plan on telling him in the morning that we've talked. Fern can back me up that you were here. I wanted him to know how serious I am about turning this around." Brent tightened his grip. "Please don't toss me away because my job just got difficult."

Owen took a moment to collect his thoughts and responded, "I have no apologies for how we started out, and even given the shit that just happened, I'm sorry, but I wouldn't take any of it back even if I could. You gave me hope. I still have that. I just don't have you physically to reinforce it." He leaned over and took Brent's other hand. "Go be a lawyer. I'll be waiting when you get back. I promise."

"Thank you, Owen."

Grinning at the thought, he asked, "How did Harper react when he found out we were living across the street from each other?"

"He doesn't know that yet. I'm not sure I can bring myself to tell him." Brent visibly trembled. "Fuck. Do you think I should?"

"I don't think there's anything, at least for now, to be gained by telling him. Would he go so far as to ask you to move? That would really suck, down the road. It's your call, but I wouldn't go there. Not unless you have to." Owen stood. The tension made him restless.

"It's possible that, in one of our meetings with you, Harper could bring us up." Brent stood and walked to the window. "How do you feel about that?"

"I'm not sure. He's not registering very high with me on the likability meter, right now. I'm not sure I could tolerate a lecture of any kind."

"If the tables were turned, I don't think I'd do well in that situation." Brent walked over and wrapped his arms around him. "I guess, just try and understand where he's coming from."

"I'll give it my best shot." Owen wrapped his arms around Brent's shoulders. "The last thing I want you to do is worry about how I'm feeling."

"I don't know how I'll be able to not do that." Brent brushed his lips across Owen's nose.

"Stay focused. We have each other to come home to when the time is right." He brought his lips to Brent's. "I'm here for you if you need me."

"That means so much."

This would likely be the last physical contact they would have for a long time. It was an important kiss, and he made the best of it. They swayed in each other's arms until, feeling his emotions on the rise, Owen voluntarily broke out of the embrace. "I'll call the office if I need anything." He took a step toward the door.

"Call here whenever you need to. Harper would want that." Brent's voice was filled with assurance.

The lump in Owen's throat was threatening to make itself known, and that would only prolong this difficult moment. He opened the door, turned back, and waved his hand. That's all he could risk.

He managed to drive for several blocks before the lump had figured a way out. Not giving a shit who saw, he pulled over, leaned into the steering wheel, and wailed. It wasn't that he doubted Brent's sincerity. He didn't. It sucked to have the one thing in his life that was helping to balance the bad taken away. If possible, he hurt worse now than after his arrest. *Keep me in your heart, Brent.*

# CHAPTER Nine

"GOOD MORNING, slugger." Harper, dressed for the day in a charcoal suit, the jacket of which he carried in his hand along with his tie, entered the kitchen and smiled. Ian gave his tail a seductive shake from Command Post One, the stove. Over the years, he had become Mr. Breakfast.

"What time did you come to bed? Was it late?" Ian handed over a cup of coffee. "I hit the pillow, and bingo bamboo, *à la crème brûlée*, I was out. You could have shoved a pineapple up my ass, and I wouldn't have known."

"I'm not sure that statement works in your favor." He kissed his husband on the neck and pinched his khaki-clad butt at the same time. Besides being the better cook, Ian could rock a pair of khaki shorts and a golf shirt like no one else on the planet.

"Love-pinch abuse. That's how it all starts." Ian emptied the frying pan onto two plates. "Grab the toast. Everything else is on the table."

Harper did as he was told and sat down.

"You feeling okay, hon?" Ian asked, pouring them both orange juice. "You seem down."

"I'm fine. Got a lot on my mind." He wasn't ready to talk about Brent or any part of yesterday's meeting. It was hard to say whether or not Ian would let him get away with such a lazy response.

"A string quartet is playing down by the lake in front of cabin four tonight, from seven to eight thirty. Any chance you'll be home to take it in with me?" Ian dived into his breakfast.

"Oh, that's tonight?" He would only miss it if Brent were unable to attend the school board meeting. He was understandably shaken, but Harper fully expected him to stay engaged. "I should be able to be there. If the forecast holds true, they should have a great night."

"So far the weather this summer has been incredible. Hope it lasts."

When he had finished eating, Ian brought his plate to the sink and began cleaning up. "Hey. Walk part of the grounds with me before you head into the Center. The gardens are looking mighty fine, if I say so myself, and we can stop in and see how Theo's doing on the office remodel."

Harper checked his watch. "Okay. But we have to get a move on."

"I'm waiting on you, counselor. I'll clean up later."

Gulping down the last of his juice, Harper brought what he could carry back to the counter. "I'm following you."

Ian started down the trail leading from their residence to the edge of the resort grounds. The path was marked private, but occasionally they would have a visitor who was either nosey or not paying attention make their way to the house. Occasionally they had to chase unexpected guests.

"This is the first year a majority of the perennials are mature. It makes such a difference in the overall look. I'm really pleased." Ian stopped at the end of the path so they could take in the view.

The vista was impressive. He could see several of the cabins, the lakeshore between the pines, and the majestic palisade rising up in back. As beautiful as it was, all he could think about was Brent. *How the fuck am I going to deal with that?*

"Come and see the new bed I put in this spring." Ian marched down toward the lake. "The color and texture of the plants play really well together."

Harper followed. Like everything else Ian touched, the new addition looked lush and professional. Perfect.

"Well?" Ian turned for a reaction.

"Yeah. I like it." Wishing he had begged off on the tour, Harper struggled to stay focused.

"Ah, fuck it, Harp. Go back to the house. I'm sorry to waste your time." Ian waved him off and started toward the office.

Startled at first by the angry reproach, Harper quickly moved to make amends. "Ian, stop." He caught up and grabbed him by the arm.

"You're a million miles away. You won't tell me what's on your mind, and I'm busy as hell too. Go do your lawyer thing." Ian broke free and resumed his course.

"Can I talk to you?" Harper begged, trailing behind like a puppy. "Please?"

"What?" Turning, his hands thrust deep in his pockets, Ian waited for an explanation.

"I'm sorry for being such an asshole." He reached over and gently rubbed the back of his hubby's neck. "I've got a real fucking mess going on with Brent, and I'm not sure how to handle it."

Ian grabbed him by the arm and hauled him to a bench positioned to give its occupants a postcard view of the lake. "Sit."

Harper brushed off the surface and sat.

"What's going on with Brent?" Bringing his knee up onto the bench, Ian faced him, waiting.

"Where to start…." He did a quick inventory of his top concerns, organized them for the best presentation, and started with, "Ever since we took on this sexual-misconduct case, he's been a different person." Harper went on to outline some of his mistakes so Ian would have a better idea of what was troubling him.

"That sure doesn't sound like Brent." Ian brushed a fly from his lap. "What does he have to say about all of it?"

"Are you ready for this?" Although rhetorical, it felt right to ask the question as a warning for Ian to be prepared for what he was about to hear. "He's established a fucking relationship with the client."

"The sexual-misconduct client?" Ian asked. "A *fucking* relationship?"

"Yes."

"That's like a huge no-no, right?" Ian sounded genuinely surprised.

"You have no idea how disappointed I am in him." Staring out at the water, he added, "I feel betrayed, lied to, you name it. I don't know if I can overcome this."

"Did you tell him to knock it off?"

Impatient, he responded with his best what-do-you-think look.

"Sorry," Ian apologized. "Of course you did."

"This thing they have going on explains away some of his mood swings and oversights, but it sure as hell doesn't dismiss them. This is our business. It's my reputation he's fucking with." He threw his hands up in the air. "This was a huge step up the ladder I handed him by making him a partner, and he's pissing on me."

They sat in silence for several minutes, fixated on a hawk skimming the surface of the lake for his next meal.

"That's going a little too far. You're a god to Brent, and you know it. I would bet he's not doing any of this intentionally," Ian cautioned. "He's an overachieving, bright little sex-crazed kid who has lost his way."

Ian was mostly right—as hard as it was to admit.

"You know," Ian continued. "Here's something else to think about. Looking back on us, and how we came together. I remember my friends being very upset at me for moving on you so fast. They were convinced I was making a mistake. I knew I wasn't, and despite the tough time they gave me, I didn't give in. I didn't care who thought what. I was falling in love with you and would have risked everything for you."

"Interesting. I don't recall people having doubts about me. Everyone loved me from day one, I thought." Harper needed a minute to noodle Ian's theory.

"Oh they did, Binky. They just didn't know it at the time." Ian smiled the way he always smiled when he knew he had just scored a victory.

"I'm considering giving him his walking papers." This was only a thought. He wanted to punch Brent, but the need to be violent was hard to communicate.

"That would be a huge mistake."

Anger permitted him to say things that normally he would filter, even with Ian. "So what should I do?"

"I think you already know, but I'll play along." Ian stretched his legs out and clicked his work boots together as if they were made of rubies. "Put the fear of God in him, which knowing you the way I do, you've already done. Make sure he understands you're monitoring his performance going forward, and keep the door open for him to come to you when he's confused or overwhelmed. On paper, he might be a partner, but he's also inexperienced and in need of leadership, whether he knows it or not."

"I knew there was a reason why I married you other than your landscaping talents." Harper reached over and tweaked Ian's clean-shaven cheek. "The grounds look sensational by the way. You should be so proud."

"The real reason you married me is going to be up your unlubed ass in a minute if you don't get over this hissy fit you're having with the Brentster. He probably feels worse than you do."

"You've called it right. He's devastated. It's not in his game plan to be thought of as something other than top-of-the-class brilliant."

Ian laughed and stood up. "The other problem here—you two are so much alike, but you're the last to get the memo on that, I bet."

Harper sprang off the bench feeling a whole lot better. "Are not."

"Are too." Ian swatted his mate hard on the ass.

"Ouch." He rubbed the sting out of his left buttcheek.

"Let's take a quick look at the office, and then I have to get to work."

It had been over a week since he'd stopped by. Stepping into the office, he was blown away by what he saw. "This is looking really fantastic."

"Good morning." Darla Engdahl, dressed in a burgundy pantsuit, stood smiling behind the reservation desk.

"Hello, Darla. How's it going? Starting to feel like home?" He hadn't had as much interaction with their new office manager as the rest of the gang, and probably wouldn't, now that the firm was up and running.

"Oh yes. I'm really enjoying it here. There's always plenty to keep me busy. We had a last-minute cancellation, and I filled it in less than an hour," she shared proudly. "This place sure is popular."

"Hey." Theo poked his head out from around the corner. "I thought I heard a familiar voice."

"It's inspection time, Theo. I brought Mr. Picky along for his blessing." Ian slapped Harper on the back.

"Mr. Picky?" He feigned being hurt by the remark and then added, "If you're over budget, I'll have to take you out back and shoot you."

"Over my dead body," Darla interjected, causing them all to laugh.

Ian had done a great job reteaming mother and son. By all accounts, it was a huge success. Theo appeared to enjoy having her on the premises, and to everyone's delight, Darla seemed to have taken to the job better than anyone could have hoped.

"Mind if I have a look?" Harper stepped around the counter.

Ian stayed in the front, discussing a procedural question with Darla, while Harper followed Theo into the back. "Holy shit. You're really cruising along here."

Theo walked him through the changes and challenges of the remodel. "I'm heading down to the Twin Cities over the weekend to look for display fixtures. What I can't find, I'll probably end up building."

"How's your mom?" Harper asked. He wasn't shy about raising the topic. Mostly he wanted Theo to know he was interested.

"Believe it or not, she's doing great. I was totally skeptical when she started, but as much as I hate to say it, she's changed. God must have visited her and given her the what for," Theo whispered. "Thanks for giving her a chance. I never would have considered it."

"You're worth making the change for, Theo. Don't lose track of that."

Theo responded with his characteristic lopsided smile. "So, you like what you see so far?"

"Yes. Very much. You're doing a wonderful job." He reached over and gave Theo a pat on the back.

"Thanks."

He made his exit from the office, which included planting a loud kiss on Ian's lips just to test Darla's progress. Then he jogged back to the house, nabbed his computer bag, and took off for the office. There would be time, provided he was in, for a talk with Brent before they headed to the deposition. He was relieved to see his partner's car parked in the Center's lot. It would have sucked to go through the day wondering about him.

BRENT BRACED himself when he heard what he was sure was Harper entering the back door.

"Hey, buddy," Harper said stopping briefly at Brent's door. "Can we talk?"

"Sure." Brent stood as he answered.

"Great. Give me a few minutes to check in with Fern and then stop by."

"Will do." Harper seemed much his old self, at least that was the impression Brent got from their brief exchange. He listened intently for more clues in the hope he could avoid being blindsided.

"Fern. Speak to me," Harper boomed.

"Crap, you scared the daylights out of me." Fern frowned, patting her chest.

"Sorry. I'm in fifth gear this morning. Anything I need to know before I head over to the deposition?" Harper asked.

Brent frowned. Did this mean he was being left behind? His heart sank.

"No. It's been relatively quiet this morning."

"Good. Brent and I are going to meet for a few minutes. Please hold our calls until we're done."

"Got it."

Again the sound of footsteps made Brent's heart race and his palms break out with sweat.

"Hey." Harper strolled in and took a seat across from him. "How'd you sleep?"

"Harper…."

"Me either," Harper laughed. "Look, yesterday was one of the worst days I've had in a very long time. I suspect you could make the same claim."

Brent nodded. He wished he could blink and make this moment magically disappear.

"Your status here hasn't changed, and I don't expect it to change—provided we move on with a solid understanding in place. I believe in your talents as an attorney and I cherish your friendship. More than anything, I don't want to lose that."

Any relief Brent might have felt regarding his job was slow to show itself. Cautious, he responded with another nod.

"Let's discuss the client first." Harper folded his hands on his lap. "Ian reminded me this morning about the power of love. You can't control where or when it hits. I know you understand the implications of romancing a client, and I know you didn't deliberately set out to break the rules. I struggled with all this yesterday and last night, but I think—thanks again to Ian—I have a better perspective."

Playing it safe, Brent continued to nod to indicate he was following.

"So, if this Owen Grady is, in fact, the right man for you, he'll understand when you set him aside until his case has settled and he ceases to be our client. Do we agree on this?"

"Absolutely." Brent sat up in his chair. "I called Owen into the office after you left yesterday and spelled the whole thing out to him. He understands and will not challenge me on this. I can guarantee it."

"I can't imagine that was an easy thing to do, but I'm happy to hear you took care of it already. Now, regarding some of the judgment calls of late." Harper gripped the sides of his chair. "It appears you understand the gravity of the situation. You need to know that I blame myself as much as I blame you for the mistakes in this case. In a way, it happened because you're so damned smart and you're so good already, I'd forgotten you were just starting out. That was unfair to you."

Brent was uncomfortable. He wanted to express his sadness over the events being discussed, but words continued to escape him. Thankfully, Harper had more to cover.

"In the future, for as long as we both agree it's a benefit and not a waste of valuable time, we're going to discuss every aspect of a case and make sure all of our i's are dotted and our t's are crossed. It was a huge mistake to let you run with this. If I were you, I'd be pissed." Leaning forward he asked, "How does that sound?"

"It's a huge relief to hear you suggest that," Brent confessed. "And don't get me wrong, it's not because it felt awkward coming to you with a question or a problem. That's never been the case. My feelings for Owen are strong. They're the real thing, Harper. I thought I might have to make a choice between him and my career." Brent felt his confidence start to come back. Harper was cutting him more slack than he could have ever hoped for.

Harper nodded and smiled. "So, do we know any more about the school board meeting?"

"Yes. I spoke with Owen's boss, Deena Phelps, this morning," Brent reported, easing into his chair. "It's a closed meeting, but she has agreed to let me wait in her office and has volunteered to bring me up to speed on what was discussed as soon as the meeting has ended."

"Did you get any read on where she stands? Is she in our client's court?" Harper asked.

"I believe she is. Owen supports that as well."

"That's very good news. Let's clear our schedules and dive right into issues concerning the board meeting tomorrow morning. What did you decide about the deposition?"

*What did I decide about the deposition?* Brent was astounded at his good fortune. "I wouldn't miss it for the world. Should I drive separately?"

"What time is the meeting?" Harper asked.

"Seven thirty."

"Naw. Let's ride together." Harper glanced at his watch. "We have roughly half an hour before we have to leave. I'm going to review a few notes, and then I'll stop by and pick you up."

"Do you want me to run for a sandwich?" Brent stood.

"I'm good. Get one for yourself, if you want. There's time."

"I hope you feel at least half as good as I do right now." Brent waited for Harper to respond.

"I do. And Brent?"

"Yeah?"

"I owe you an apology."

*Oh no you don't.* "For what?"

"You're right. It's taken considerable thought to get here, but I concur with what you thought right out the gate. Grady is innocent.

Your belief in our client is impossible to ignore. That, and Daniels' wandering eye. He likes the boys, there's no doubt about that."

BY THE time Brent climbed into Harper's car, the tension from earlier had dissipated. Something had changed, but not in the bad way he had anticipated. The relationship they shared seemed to have jumped to another level, with most of the components he valued still intact.

"Have you met this Hansen guy before?" Brent glanced at the business card he had attached to his notes.

"Nope. What's his first name?" Harper asked, pulling out of the parking lot.

"Todd. Todd Hansen, District Attorney, Lake County," he read aloud. "I'm thinking midthirties, married to a grade-school teacher. They have two kids, both nerds, and he has a deer stand out in the woods he tries to get to every weekend in the fall."

"You're taking to this area like flies to a doughnut. Nice job." Harper eased around a garbage truck. "Here's what sucks about us being the new kids on the block. If we were handling this case from the big bad firm in the Cities, the chances would be good someone there would have experience or even a professional relationship with the DA. That can be huge to your case. It can open the door for negotiations, and in many instances, your client never even sets foot in court. A bargain is struck, and usually it's because the attorney knows, going in, what the DA will agree to and what might be asking too much. DUI cases use this bartering approach all the time. If they didn't, there would be a backlog so heaped you'd wait years for your day in court."

Located on the opposite end of town from the Center, the courthouse took less than five minutes to get to. Built in 1905, the majestic brick and stone structure was one of the architectural treasures along the North Shore. Harper admitted to being in the building only twice—once for his marriage certificate and another time to renew tags on his car. Brent walked up the stone steps of the main entrance. *How long will it be before I know this place like the back of my hand?*

"It's a little early, but I think we should check in. I'd like to get a feel for the room before the deposition starts." Harper approached the information desk. "Can you point me in the direction of the District Attorney's office?"

"It's in the east wing on the second floor," a security guard not long out of high school cheerfully directed. "Elevators are located to the left of the stairs."

"Thank you." Harper led the way. "You ready for this?" he asked, when they reached the top.

"I'm a little edgy," Brent admitted. "But mostly I'm curious about Daniels. I can't wait to spend some quality time with him."

"My goal is to make him cry." They laughed and walked up to the receptionist. Leaning farther over the desk than appropriate, Harper announced, "We're here for a deposition. I think Todd's expecting us."

*Todd?* Brent smirked.

"Burns and Callahan?" The thirtysomething woman asked with the early stages of a snarl. From his lofty vantage, Brent peered at a day planner that showcased its owner's penchant for using multicolored highlighters. It sat next to a lipstick-stained "I (heart) Maple Syrup" coffee mug.

"That'd be us. Direct from our sold-out engagement at the Flamingo."

Witness to a multitude of inappropriate Harper quips over the years, Brent couldn't quite hang on. His spontaneous snort caught everyone within earshot by surprise. "Excuse me," he offered, only marginally embarrassed.

"Straight down the hall on the left. It's the *only* conference room we have."

"Perfect." Turning away from the desk, Harper commented loud enough to matter, "Someone's having a bad day. Follow me, Burnsy."

"What the fuck was that all about?" Brent chuckled, barely keeping up with Harper, who barreled down the hallway.

"I don't want to go into this thing tense. That helped."

The door to the glass-walled conference room stood open. Inside, two men were already seated at the end of a long table, huddled around their notes. One of them was Daniels. The other man was either Todd, or someone's grandfather, or both. A woman—the court reporter—had set up at the opposite end, leaving the middle of the table up for grabs.

"Uncanny how you nailed Todd," Harper teased and entered the room extending his hand. "Harper Callahan. This is my partner, Brent Burns."

"Todd Hansen." Borderline feeble, the man stood. He was almost swallowed up by an ill-fitting, black pinstriped suit. "This is my client, Officer Luke Daniels."

They exchanged handshakes, and after a moment to scope out the terrain, Harper sat directly across from Daniels and gestured for Brent to take the seat next to him.

"Would you like a few minutes of privacy before we get underway?" Todd asked, still standing.

Brent shrugged when Harper looked over.

"We're ready to roll, Todd." Harper reached into his computer bag, hauled out a small spiral-ring binder, and opened it to the first page. Brent was impressed. If nothing else, it indicated to the other side that they were prepared.

The deposition began as they typically do, with everyone identifying themselves, and for the benefit of the reporter, spelling out their names. Once through this formality, Harper took the lead. "Good morning, Mr. Daniels. Thank you for agreeing to spend some time with us today."

"I'm happy to assist."

If he was nervous, Daniels was hiding it well. He was all smiles.

"Very good. That should make what we need to accomplish today an easier task."

Surprised by Harper's casual approach, Brent wondered if the two men seated across from them had any idea how quickly that could change. His partner thrived in difficult situations.

As planned, Harper opened with a series of questions intended to highlight Daniels' background prior to joining the force. The first hint of a possible lie occurred when he asked for specifics regarding the officer's educational history.

"I'm your classic example of an army brat. We moved so many times, there're probably locations we lived that have completely escaped my memory."

*Nice try.*

Observing Daniels' seemingly effortless responses to the questioning, it struck Brent that this asshole was like a cheap knockoff of Harper. The penetrating eyes, the winning smile, the abundant charm—it was all there. But with Daniels, those traits rang false. He found them frightening.

*You're the devil's son.*

"What year did your family move to Minnesota?"

"I believe it was 2008."

"And you moved here from…?" Harper flipped back a page in his notes as if this were information they had already obtained.

*Smooth move.*

"That would be Alameda. Alameda, California." Daniels sat up in his chair. The change in posture was interesting. Did it signal a lie?

"I've never been. Where exactly is Alameda, California located?" Harper asked.

"It's close to Oakland."

Bringing his pen up to his lip Harper asked, "Which is very close to San Francisco, correct?"

"Correct."

"I've been to San Francisco on several occasions. There's a marvelous Indian restaurant in the Castro. Anyway, it's a stretch to assume you're familiar with the Castro."

Harper had just planted a huge seed of insecurity without any effort at all. Just because you lived in the vicinity of San Francisco didn't mean you had knowledge of the Castro, its reputation as a gay mecca, or specifically, an Indian restaurant. That is, unless you actually were gay, albeit stuck in the closet. Little spit bombs like this could change the entire dynamic if the deponent was lying. He marveled at the Harper touch.

Flipping over another page in his notes, Harper continued. "Okay, so your family moved to Minnesota from Alameda in 2008. What year in school were you?"

Daniels shot his attorney a look that Brent interpreted as a call for the aged DA to put an end to Harper's quest for backstory.

"I have to object to your line of questioning," Hansen interjected. "I see no relevance pertaining to the events leading to *your* client's arrest."

"If I could just have an idea of where the officer was in school in the year 2008, I'll move on to more current events."

Hansen reluctantly nodded for Daniels to answer the question.

"It was the summer before my senior year in high school."

"Were you eyeing any colleges at the time?"

When Daniels responded with a shrug, Harper reminded, "Please remember to answer my questions with at least a yes or a no. The lady at the end of the table is creating a transcript."

"No."

"Okay. Just one more question, and I promise to move on. What school did you attend that senior year, the year you graduated?"

Another shift in his chair, coupled with what could have been a momentary bout of panic—definitely discomfort— signaled to Brent that Daniels was about to start running from the big bad wolf. *Let the lying begin.*

"Or, perhaps you obtained your GED that year?"

Harper had it. Brent was sure of it. Daniels dropped out of school before graduating.

"It was a year later I earned my GED." The officer was embarrassed to admit this. It was written all over his face.

"Which would be 2009? You received your GED in 2009?"

Harper was pushing, and Daniels had apparently had enough. Responding to another one of Daniels' looks, Hansen said, "You can subpoena records if needed, but my client will not answer any more questions regarding his educational history today."

"I thought it was an easy enough question to answer, but okay. Let's move on to your criminal-justice career."

They spent the next fifteen minutes mining information from Daniels about his law-enforcement training. Gone was the easy, relaxed manner the officer had exhibited earlier. His answers now were terse, offering nothing more than the minimum required. *You getting a little hot under the collar, buddy? What are you going to do with all that anger bubbling around inside?* This was exactly the behavior Brent had hoped for. He wondered if Harper was picking up the same vibe.

"Okay," Harper forged ahead. "So you got your GED, and then you attended the Patterson Police Academy in Minneapolis from 2011 to 2012. Is that right?"

"Yes," Daniels answered in a borderline hiss.

"Did you graduate?" Harper gave the sword one more twist.

"Yes." Whether or not he was conscious of it, Daniels had begun to push his chair away from the table.

"And it was sometime shortly before your graduation that you responded to an advertisement on the bulletin board at Patterson Police Academy seeking an officer in Two Harbors?" Harper flipped to a new page.

"Yes."

*Someone's not having any fun.*

"I hope I'm not wasting your time today," Harper commented, obviously responding to the officer's pithy responses. "I'm one of those complete-picture kind of guys." Chuckling to the others in the room, he added, "I hope you'll continue to bear with me."

It was a joy to watch Harper needle and pry into his prey. The condescending lilt, just enough to agitate, but not enough to be called out, was a masterful blend, skillfully deployed.

For the next several minutes, Harper had Daniels walk through his duties as officer. Eventually Harper asked, "And so, if I understand this correctly, you made random stops out at Connor's Point to monitor the area specifically for underage drinking? Is that correct?"

"Yes."

Perhaps feeling relieved to finally have the deposition focused on the events leading to Owen's arrest, Daniels appeared to relax. This was probably the area of questioning they had rehearsed.

"Is there one specific area where this violation regularly occurred?" Leaning over, Harper pointed to a spot in his notes. Brent canvassed the page as fast and as best he could, but failed to make a connection. Then it dawned on him. Harper was fucking with Daniels—making it appear he had information when he didn't. Potentially provoking another lie.

"It's a few hundred feet to the right of the parking lot."

"That's where you've encountered remnants of drinking parties on prior visits?"

"Yes, that's correct." As if to show he was back in control, Daniels looked at his attorney and nodded.

"Interesting. So on June fourth, you headed farther into the woods, well past the point where the drinking parties historically were held, to what, enjoy the surroundings? Maybe do a little hiking on your own?" Harper cocked his head and waited.

"I'm going to advise my client not to answer that question." Hansen reached over and placed his hand on Daniels' arm.

"That's fine, but according to *my* client, Mr. Grady had traveled a considerable distance from the parking lot before he was aware your client was following him."

"I wasn't following him," Daniels shot back.

Pleased with the result, Harper folded his hands on his notes. "I'd like a moment to use the restroom, if you don't mind."

"How am I doing?" he asked when they had walked a few paces down the hallway.

"Great." Brent waited while Harper sipped from the water fountain. "You established a California connection. You made him feel like a dumbass for not finishing high school. That was a highlight. And he hates you."

Harper laughed. "That's not going to improve, I'll tell you that. Let's get back and wind this thing up."

"I can't wait to do some hunting on the Internet," Brent shared.

Back in the conference room, they took their seats but couldn't start because Daniels was out of the room. He must have slipped out in the opposite direction.

"How long have you been in the district attorney's office?" Harper asked Todd.

"Thirty-seven years." Hansen appeared to use his time of service as a caution. It was one of those "don't you dare fuck with me you sniveling punk" moments.

If Harper had hoped to initiate a conversation with this opener, he tossed the notion aside.

Several minutes passed and there was still no sign of Daniels. Feeling the need to contribute in some way, Brent looked at the court reporter and smiled. "Are you based out of Two Harbors?"

"Yes."

It appeared Harper had pissed her off too.

"Would you be so kind as to check up on your client?" Harper consulted his watch and confirmed he had waited long enough.

"I thought he was headed to the restroom." Hansen left the room and then walked right back in with Daniels.

Either by accident or on purpose, the officer sat in the seat his attorney had occupied. This flustered Hansen, but instead of pointing out the mistake to his client, he scooped up his notes and sat across from Harper.

Undaunted, Harper got up and moved over so he was again seated directly across from Daniels. "It's me again." Signaling to the reporter he was ready to begin, he asked, "Can you recall what Mr. Grady was doing when you first spotted him that day?"

"When I came around the corner he was standing on the trail looking in my direction."

"How far away from you was he?" Harper jotted down a note.

"Maybe a hundred feet separated us."

Anxious for this next series of questions, Brent leaned forward until he felt the edge of the table pinch into his stomach.

"What was it that prompted you to approach Mr. Grady?"

"I didn't approach him. I was ready to turn around and head back to my vehicle. He approached me."

"He approached you? You're sure about that?" Harper looked at Brent as if to ask, "does this make any sense?"

"That's right."

Brent caught it, and he wondered if Harper did too. To add credibility to his statement, Daniels clenched his jaw and stuck his chin out as if he was daring them to doubt.

"What happened from there?" Knowing this was the spot where Daniels was going to really start lying his ass off, Harper looked at Brent and smiled.

"I remember he waved. I had no idea who he was, so I ignored it. I would have continued to ignore him, but he started massaging himself as he walked toward me."

"Massaging himself?" Harper made another note. "Can you be more specific?"

"He was rubbing and squeezing his crotch."

"You mean like an itch? Or like that guy thing we all do when we think we're not being watched?" Harper looked at the court reporter and smiled.

"It was more than that," Daniels stated flatly, again with the aid of his jaw.

"Have you ever knowingly been pursued by a gay man before?" Harper sat back and petted his tie.

"No, sir."

"I thought most men, especially attractive men like you, Mr. Daniels, would have suspected at least once or twice, another man's interest. But you haven't?"

"I said no. The ladies—" Daniels puffed out his chest. "—are another story all together."

"You get cruised by women often?"

"All the time. I don't mean to brag, but that's my biggest problem, the ladies. If guys are doing it… well I haven't ever noticed. But the ladies? It happens all the time."

Harper dismissed the officer's bravado by displaying a look that could only be described as "go figure." Brent bit his lip. Was Daniels trying to overcompensate for the fact that it wasn't the ladies he was interested in? There was just a little too much detail in his response.

Allowing the last exchange to float around the room for a few beats, Harper came back with, "What other kinds of experiences have you had with homosexuals?"

"Your question is highly inappropriate," Hansen fumed. "Don't answer that."

"Fair enough." Harper gestured with a wave of his hand for Hansen to settle down. "Back to this rubbing thing Mr. Grady was supposedly doing. That's what signaled to you he was trying to engage you in a sexual act?"

"Not entirely." Daniels shot a quick side glance to his attorney and then added, "he removed his cock from his shorts and wiggled it in his hand."

"I see. Do you recall noticing whether or not Mr. Grady was circumcised?"

Surprised as anyone in the room by Harper's question, Brent gripped the sides of his chair.

"I'm going to advise my client not to answer. Again, your line of questioning is disrespectful and unnecessary." It was clear by the look on his face that Hansen was miles outside his comfort zone. Brent fought the urge to laugh. This was one DA they wouldn't be forming a special bond with.

"Forgive me. I'm not trying to be perverse in any way," Harper explained. "But merely trying to establish to what extent my client was advertising his intent. I'm assuming there wasn't much distance now separating Mr. Grady from where the officer was stationed."

Although it pained him, Hansen gestured for Daniels to answer the question.

"I was too stunned to notice."

*I'll bet you were. I had a similar experience the first time I saw it.* Shocked that he had allowed his thought to go the distance, Brent sat up in his chair and tightened his tie. *Knock that shit off.*

"Is it safe to assume that, up until now, no words had been exchanged between you and Mr. Grady?" Harper asked.

"Yes."

"Were words ever exchanged, and if so, can you tell me what was said, please?"

"After he motioned for me to follow him off the path, I identified myself as law enforcement, and that's when he took off running."

Undeterred by the menacing jaw jutting in his direction, Harper asked for clarification. "Did Mr. Grady motion for you to follow with his hand, or did he motion with his…?"

"That's quite enough. Quite enough, indeed." For a brief moment, it appeared the top of Hansen's head might blow off.

"Counselor, what I'm having a hard time with here is understanding precisely what it was that signaled to your client that my client was shopping around for an assignation in the middle of the woods. I want that crystal clear, and if that takes answers you find inappropriate, well, then too bad for you."

Having crossed the line so many times in his questioning, Brent marveled at the extent to which Harper was able to justify his unconventional approach. Hansen was so obviously uncomfortable with all things homosexual, it was impossible to tell what he would allow and what he would object to.

Waving for his attorney to back off, Daniels decided on his own to answer. "I had no trouble interpreting Mr. Grady's intent. He was becoming aroused."

"Thank you." Harper threw his hands in the air. Shaking his head in exasperation, he jotted down a note and then looked up and asked, "After identifying yourself as law enforcement, you claim my client fled, is that right?"

"Yes. That's correct."

"What direction was he headed? Away from the parking lot? Can you help me visualize this?"

"He took off running down the trail, away from the parking area. I started after him, and it was at this point he left the trail and started off into the woods."

"Did you call out to him? Was anything else said at the time?"

"I hollered he was evading arrest and that he should stop running."

"And that's when he stopped running?" Harper sat back and folded his arms across his chest.

"Not exactly. He tripped over a branch and crashed headfirst into the side of a tree."

"Oh right. That's how he came about a black eye and other substantial injuries to his face and neck." Harper stared across the table at Daniels. This was, of course, a flat-out lie, and Brent understood by pausing here, Harper was making sure that Daniels understood he wasn't buying it. The tension in the room was palpable, and the officer responded to it by extending his jaw farther than any of the previous times. The extension impressed Brent.

"What happened next?" Harper asked without breaking eye contact.

"I helped him to his feet and then slapped on cuffs."

*You low-life, lying piece of shit.* Brent fought the urge to spring across the table and knock Daniels' fucking jaw into the next room.

The deposition came to an end after Daniels described how he walked Owen to the place where Owen had stashed his bike and gave a brief description of the booking process and his release on bail. There were no handshakes. Packed up and standing at the door, Harper had one final comment before they were on their way. "We'll see you in court."

"That was fucking unbelievable," Brent gushed as they walked to the car.

"He's slippery to be sure."

On the way back to the firm, Harper explained, "I want both Daniels and this Hansen to understand that just because Owen Grady is gay, it doesn't mean he's preordained to solicit sex in the woods. That isn't part of the gay gene."

"I hope the jury understands that. Hansen was disgusted." As exciting as it was to watch Harper drill Daniels, Brent had concerns. "His story makes sense. Plays out logically."

It does on the surface, but we both know there were an abundance of lies flung at us. We'll have some fun with those," Harper winked. "Listen, thank you for being there today. It helped to have your support. We have an event at the resort in a few hours. Ian is requesting I attend. I'm going to head out."

"Oh. Okay. I'm all set to hit the meeting tonight." He undid his seat belt and opened the door.

"Great. I'll be back here bright and early. We'll roll up our sleeves and dig right in." Harper gave him a salute.

"Sounds good. Say hi to Ian."

"Will do."

Back at his desk, Brent stared at his phone. He was desperate to give Owen a call and share with him the details of the deposition.

Instead, he placed it in his pocket and began a detailed documentation of the deposition. *Un-fucking-believable.*

THE RADIO, barely audible, was tuned to some oldies station. Brent was seated in Deena Phelps's office, waiting for the meeting to break. He had made his second trip to the bathroom, not because he had to go, but because he was starving for something to eat away at the clock. He sat and waited.

Deena had met him at the entrance to the school and ushered him to her office. They had only a few minutes to chat, but it was enough to pick up on what a fan she was of her music teacher. He felt a little better than he had on the drive over. He was nervous—nervous for Owen. It was likely, and the principal had confirmed, that Owen would be suspended with pay until he could be cleared of the charges. It was one thing to anticipate this, but another to have it happen. Owen would be devastated, and Brent would be helpless to provide him comfort, other than what could be achieved over the phone. They could meet and discuss it at the office, but that was as far as his support could go.

As he contemplated a third trip to the can, he heard voices in the hallway and hoped it signaled the meeting had ended. In agony, he waited for what seemed like an hour before Deena finally entered her office.

"There are people on this earth who add value, and then there's Jerome Peebles." With a huff, she plopped on her chair. "That man is going to be the death of me."

Brent forced a smile and waited for her to continue. He wanted to know more—and yet he didn't.

"Where to start…." Deena took off her glasses and placed them on the desk. "Suspension with pay until the matter is decided in court."

"No surprises there, right?" It must have been the discussion leading up to the decision that had taken its toll on her. "This is going to upset Owen, but we'll get him through it," he assured her.

"All I could think about, picture in my mind, was Owen's face when I call to give him the news. By the way, I don't care if you get to him first, but officially I will have to make that call."

"I understand." *What else was said?*

"Owen has this wonderful quality about him that, on more than one occasion, has rescued me from a very bad day." Deena smiled. "You've probably observed this too. You see it when he's walking the hall, talking to a student, or standing in front of a classroom of kids eager to make a whole bunch of noise. It's the most unselfish look I think I've ever seen. He's here for them. It's all about the kids." She tagged on, "I wish I could bottle that."

"What seemed to be the biggest concern?" Brent was eager to move things along. He was starting to fade, and his stomach had begun to rumble.

"How long have you lived in the area?"

"Just a few months." He wished he had more history, but that was that.

"This is what worries me." Deena put her glasses back on. "About five years ago, in a park on the outskirts of Duluth, people in the area began complaining about an increase in single men walking the paths. Of course, without saying it, everyone knew what was going on. There were some nasty accusations made in the local papers, and eventually the police were asked to step in."

"You'd be surprised at how many communities have experienced similar issues." He felt compelled to enlighten her, perhaps as a way to take the burden off Owen. "Gay people, particularly gay men, faced with a shortage of places to hook up, found those woodland settings worked well." Wary of being perceived as an advocate, he added, "It's a sad commentary on how far someone will go when they're faced with no other options. Acceptance wasn't what it is today." *I wonder if she knows about the hanky code?*

"Understood. That's why places like the Men's Center are so important."

"Exactly."

"Once the police were brought in and a few arrests were made, the men stopped coming. But as time went on and the police relaxed their efforts, they came back. Early one spring morning, a local teenager was sighted off the path by a jogger. He had been strangled and, at some point, violated sexually."

"And this came up tonight in the discussion regarding Owen?" Brent looked over in disbelief.

"Jerome Peebles was kind enough to link the two." The sad look on the principal's face said it all. "It gets worse," she confessed. "No arrests were ever made in the case. The murderer is still at large."

It didn't take a rocket scientist to see where this was headed. "Did someone speculate that Owen could possibly be responsible for that… that horrible crime?"

"Just short of that. But I'm sure it was the intent." Deena shook her head in disgust. "I don't know about you, but I'm certainly not going to be sharing that with Owen. My God, can you imagine?"

"You're right. He doesn't need to know that. At least not right now. *Hopefully not ever.* It's a hateful hypothesis, even if it wasn't directly implied," he said.

"Mr. Burns, here's my concern. False accusations like this can easily be used to cause even more damage. The safety of the student is paramount in any educator's mind. There might be enough misinformation out there to permanently harm Owen. I've seen this happen before. A careless discussion point gets whipped into a frenzy, and before long, Owen loses his job out of an overabundance of caution. Peebles will certainly have a few supporters on his side."

If he felt disgusted before, nothing could describe how he felt after she voiced her worry.

"You look how I feel," Deena observed.

"Something like this can destroy a person." He felt sick to his stomach. The threat to Owen's future was tangible. A victory in court might not be enough to exonerate him in the eyes of the school board, or worse, the parents and students. Owen's teaching days at Jefferson High could certainly be over for good. *What a fucking shame.*

He thanked Deena and drove home. It had been a very long day, and he couldn't wait for a warm shower and a bite to eat. He walked through the dark living room to the front window. Only Owen's bedroom light was on. *You knew this would be hard. Stay focused.*

Brent relaxed in the shower, slid a frozen pizza into the oven, and began reviewing his notes. There was no way he was going to sleep until he had a detailed to-do list. Thinking it could wait until morning, he decided against calling Harper. It was already after nine and it would be only hours before they met at the firm. With a cold beer and a plate of barely edible pizza, he sat down and worked until he was interrupted by his phone.

"Sorry to call so late," Harper opened. "I'm curious about how the meeting went off. How did it go?"

"Owen's suspended with pay until after the trial. It's what we expected." Brent sat back and noticed the light was still on at Owen's. *I wonder if Deena's called him?*

"How was the principal? Is she on our side?"

"Oh yeah. She's great. We talked after the meeting in her office." He recounted their conversation as best he could.

"Oh for fuck's sake, are you kidding?" Harper seemed equally annoyed by the careless association made between their client and the unsolved murder. "That must have happened around the same time Ian and I moved up here. The prudent thing to do, I guess, would be to find out as much detail about the homicide as possible so we can systematically untangle our client. I can't believe this shit. Anything else?"

"No. Deena was going to call Owen to let him know how it went down. She wasn't going to mention the murder piece to him."

"At this point, I don't know what good it would do to share that with him. Could drive him over the edge, and we need to prevent that from happening."

"The suspension is going to hit hard enough as it is." Brent worried his comment might be interpreted as a request to connect with Owen outside the office. As much as he wanted to contact him, he didn't want Harper to spend a minute worrying that this might lead to an infringement of the rules. "He'll be fine. Should we bring him into the office tomorrow?"

"I'd like you to call him. I'd do it myself, but you'll offer more comfort to him than I ever could."

"I'll do that first thing when I get to the office. Are you thinking we'll meet with him in the afternoon?" Although he didn't expect to be completely prohibited from contact, he was surprised by Harper's request.

"Call him tonight, Brent. It's important he knows you're working hard for him. See what his plans are tomorrow, and if he hasn't anything going on, let him know the possibility exists for a meeting. I can't make that decision right now."

Brent sat back in shock.

"Are you thinking that's a bad idea?" Harper asked, most likely in response to his silence.

"No. Not at all. I think he would appreciate the call." *Thank you, Harper.*

"I'll see you in the morning."

"THANKS FOR the call, Deena. I really appreciate it." Owen sat motionless on the edge of his bed, his mind racing to process the update. A sliver of optimism had just been defeated, once and for all. Secretly, despite the predictions, he had hoped for a miracle. Despair was a familiar friend by now, but it didn't lessen the night's bad news. He set the phone on the bedside table, turned off the light, climbed in, and pulled the covers up to his neck. Knowing sleep was impossible, he reached for the remote and turned on the television. As if part of a cruel plan, he watched helpless as Professor Harold Hill marched down Main Street with a band of fresh-faced students close behind, all dressed in handsome new uniforms, blasting out the musical's iconic "Seventy-Six Trombones." He fumbled for the remote and managed to shut off the television, but not in time. The damage had been done. He was never going to be Harold Hill, and there was a real possibility his career at Jefferson High was history.

As he contemplated his existence, he was startled when his phone rang for the second time that evening.

"Brent?" he answered, caught off guard by the call.

"Hey, Owen. I hope I didn't wake you up."

"No. Not at all." He sat up, and the blankets fell off his chest.

"Did you receive a call from Deena Phelps tonight?"

"Yes. Sounds like things went down as we had thought. I'm cool." He wasn't cool. He was destroyed, but it seemed pointless to confess that over the phone, given the circumstances.

"I wish they'd waited until after the trial, but it wasn't meant to be."

Closing his eyes, he pictured Brent on the phone—his lips, his boyishly handsome face, his ruddy cheeks.

*Wait.*

Kicking his feet out from under the covers, he darted to the window. It was a hunch, but it paid off. Like the other night, his lover was seated at the dining-room table. It felt strange to spy. He contemplated a confession but decided against it. Even this distanced connection was better than nothing. He knelt, sat back on his haunches, and said, "Deena mentioned you met in her office after the meeting. What did you think of her?"

"She's great. Totally in your corner."

At once Brent was animated, gesturing with his free hand as he talked. "I got the feeling that, if there had been any way possible for her to delay the suspension, she would have done that. Apparently there's a guy on the board that's nothing short of an asshole."

"Jerome Peebles." It was impossible for Owen to contain his dislike.

"Yep. That's him. Sounds like your garden-variety homophobe. Nobody likes a bully. We'll shut the bastard down. No worries, Owen."

Immediately following this comment, Owen observed his attorney propping his head up with his hand. Was he tired? Probably. It had been a long day. But still, the body language didn't seem to match his confidence.

"How did the deposition go?" he asked, both interested and not wanting to let the call come to an end.

"Harper was in rare form. Daniels lied his ass off. Sometimes effectively, and other times, not so much. He gave us some stuff to work with. Wow. I feel like it was yesterday." Brent sat up. "The DA is a real prude. He was clearly uncomfortable with the whole sex-in-the-woods scenario."

"Is that a good or a bad thing?" He tried to remember back to his arraignment, but it was all such a blur, he didn't remember much. He didn't recall what the district attorney looked like.

"I think it will work in our favor. He's probably not going to get into specifics in front of the jury. Harper will take advantage of that."

The forehead returned to its nesting spot in Brent's hand.

"You sound tired." Owen rested his elbows on the windowsill. It pained him to watch the typically energetic Brent so downcast.

"I guess I am."

Unsure of where to go with their conversation, Owen sat and watched in silence.

"I miss you, Owen. That's most of it. I really miss you." Brent's voice was barely above a whisper.

"I miss you too." Leaning forward, he kissed the window. "Please don't worry about me. Get some sleep, okay?"

"I will. Pleasant dreams, lover."

"Pleasant dreams, lover," he repeated softly.

When the call ended, Owen watched Brent place his phone on the table and then bury his entire face in his hands. Feeling guilty for spying on Brent, he stood, walked to the bed, crawled in, and pulled the covers back up to his neck. *Be strong for Brent.*

# CHAPTER Ten

SEATED ON a rock, Owen peeled the wrapper from his PB&J and started biting off the crusted border, saving the rich, gooey center of his sandwich for last. Staring into the infinite shades of green, he breathed a contented sigh. It felt really good to be in the woods. It always had. A pang of anger tried valiantly to ruin his mood, but he stomped it into tiny bits before it could do any real damage. It was unfortunate he had wasted so many beautiful summer days at home, but he was out again, enjoying the splendor, and that's what mattered most.

It had been a snap decision to go on this outing. Fully expecting to be called into the law firm for a meeting, he was surprised when he received Brent's voicemail informing him he was cleared for the day. The upbeat tone in his lover's voice was a good sign, and a visit by a handsome Rose-breasted Grosbeak stopping off to chew a seed on the neighbor's fence had sealed the deal. He wasn't sure when he would feel comfortable accessing the park from Connor's Point again, so rather than confront his fear, he used the much-nearer town entrance instead.

When he finished with lunch, he packed up and stepped back onto the main trail. If his memory served him right, up around the next bend was a side trail leading to a small stream. The year before, he had spotted a Great Horned Owl nestled deep in the pines with two babies perched at its side. Thrilled by the reminiscence, he quickened his pace until he rounded the curve. He found the path right off the bat.

*Are you alone?*

Owen was seized with an acute need to ensure he wasn't being watched. A prolonged glance in both directions quelled his concern.

He entered the secluded world of the forest and laughed. *I can't believe how much I've missed you.* Binoculars in hand, he moved quietly, his eye and trained ear focused on his surroundings. He reached the stream—barely a trickle now that the spring rains had stopped. He plopped down on a fallen tree and waited patiently for nature to grow accustomed to his presence and come out of hiding.

Minutes passed with only a pair of feisty chickadees vying for his attention. He stared up into the trees for signs of a nest or a series of holes indicating the presence of woodpeckers. He was sure he was in the same location where he had sighted the owls. He continued to search the canopy until he felt the hairs on the back of his neck bristle.

He eased onto his feet and his heart raced. Looking up the stream, he could find nothing to explain his anxiety. He cautiously took a step forward, peered down the trail he had just walked, and listened intently. Still nothing. The feeling of being watched intensified. If he wasn't able to identify the source of his discomfort, panic would set in. With fear already nipping away his confidence, he turned his body so he could view the area directly behind where he had been seated.

Beginning with the bank on the other side, he peered down the stream until, with a rush of relief, he spotted a gray wolf watching him from the water's edge. *You devil. You scared me half to death.*

The woods had always been a source of enormous interest. He felt as comfortable there as he did anywhere. His encounter with Daniels had left him fearful. It saddened him that the evil emanating from that man was so far-reaching.

For the next hour, he hiked back and forth along the stream, but his mood had changed. Angry at having such a sacred part of his life altered, possibly forever, he called it quits and started back toward the main trail. He had only walked a short distance when he heard, "You know you want it. How *bad* do you want it? Bad enough to come and get it?"

The voice, instantly recognizable, brought him to an immediate halt. Daniels was close but he couldn't tell how close. Panicked, Owen searched through the branches to identify where the monster was hiding. Were the questions directed at him? Feeling every muscle in his body tighten, he stepped into the undergrowth and waited. His heart pounded. He had begun to tremble. Unsure of his next move, he knelt down on one knee, poised to spring up at any second, if needed. The sound of footsteps crunching through the brush did little to prepare him when the frightening image of Luke Daniels crept into his view. The officer, thankfully, was looking in the opposite direction. Owen held his breath. Seconds later another man entered his frame of vision.

"You nervous?" Daniels asked with a snicker.

"Yeah. A little," the man answered.

"Don't be. It's just you, me, and *this*."

Partially blocked by leaves, he could see enough to understand what was going on. Daniels had lured another victim into his den of terror.

"I hope you're hungry." Daniels placed a hand on the guy's shoulder.

The man reacted by sinking down on his knees. In the process, Owen caught a glimpse of his face. It wasn't anyone he recognized, but for a brief moment, he felt compelled to holler at the top of his lungs so the unsuspecting man could flee before something bad happened. Profound fear kept him right quiet.

"That's right. Take it all," Daniels encouraged. "And *relax*, dude. We're in no rush. Take your time and enjoy."

Dizzy with fear, Owen fought off nausea. If only this guy knew who he was dealing with. He shivered at the thought of someone having their mouth on this freak show's dick. The contents of his stomach soured even more when he remembered how close he had come to being in the same situation.

"Oh yeah. Nice and easy. Where have you been all my life?"

Avoiding a cramp in his leg, Owen shifted the weight of his body from one knee to the other. When he looked up, he had a clearer view of both men.

"Grab my nuts. Go on. Squeeze 'em hard. Oh yeah. That's how I like it."

If only there were a way to capture what was going on. It would exonerate him and expose Daniels as a closeted sexual predator. Too disgusted to watch, Owen rested his elbow on his thigh and came in contact with his phone.

*There's a good shot from here. You have to try.*

In order to remove his phone, Owen was forced to shift his body again. He had to sit back on his heel and extend his foot. In the process, he must have gotten too close to a mouse or a baby rabbit. Whatever it was, it sprang noisily from the safety of its hideout and scurried away.

He froze, barely able to breathe. If he could see Daniels, it was possible that the officer could see him. He waited motionless, praying he was still undetected.

"Don't stop now. Fuck. Do not stop now."

Daniels was obviously caught up in the moment. Relieved at not being discovered, Owen revisited the idea of taking a picture. He slid his hand into his pocket and pulled out his phone. Initiating the camera, he positioned it so it faced his subjects. His hands trembled from nerves. To avoid having a blurred result, he used his knee to stop the shaking. With a quick adjustment to the zoom, he was satisfied he had the best shot possible, and using every ounce of concentration he could muster, brought his finger up to the shutter button.

*Da da da daaa…. Da da da daaa….* Beethoven's Fifth blared from his hand like a car horn.

BRENT STEPPED behind Fern's desk, cut off his third wedge of cake, and slid it onto his plate. Earlier Harper had opened a letter he received from the attorney representing Ms. Dingman's former employer. He offered a substantial financial settlement and the opportunity for the wing nut to resume her employment with no penalty, if she wanted. It was their first victory at Burns and Callahan. More importantly the letter brought closure to a supremely unsatisfying case that had cast a dark cloud over the firm from the day they agreed to take it on. The impromptu celebration was a welcome break from sorting through recent developments in the Grady matter.

"This was a hard-learned lesson, and I can pledge to you both"—Harper pointed his plastic fork first at Fern, and then his partner—"it will never, *ever* happen again. No matter how hungry we are, we will screen every client carefully before taking on their case. No exceptions."

"Not so fast," Fern cautioned. "I'll still be learning your lesson well into next week, if I know anything at all."

Certain of where Fern was headed, Brent was already laughing when she added, "It will take at least a half dozen phone conversations with her before she'll understand the settlement. And the questions she'll ask…." Fern pushed her glasses back up her nose. "Crap. I don't even want to go there."

"That's true." Harper chuckled. "But we're very close to being rid of her. I'll draft a letter later today outlining in the simplest of language what it all means. Who the hell knows? If it eliminates one call, it's worth it, right?"

"That's right." Fern jotted down a note. "I'll frame up the letter and e-mail it to you."

"Perfect." Harper tossed his plate into the waste bin. "What do you say, my friend? Are you ready to get back at it?"

"Yep. Thanks for picking up the tasty treat, Fern." He dropped his plate on top of Harper's and started toward the conference room where they were reviewing documents."

"My pleasure. I'll leave it here in case you get the urge for another piece."

"Did you have time to research the park homicide?" Harper asked as they walked down the hall.

"I think there's enough on the Internet to suit our needs." He sat in what was quickly becoming his seat in the conference room.

"Run down what you have." Harper made a move to close the door but then stopped. "Let's leave it open. It's kind of stuffy in here." He joined Brent at the table.

"You know what I find strange in all this?" Brent shuffled his notes.

"What's that?" Harper asked.

"How weird it is that more wasn't made of this homicide when it happened. And then it dawned on me. Maybe the reason it wasn't a bigger news story had to do with the fact it was perceived by the public as a gay crime. You know, one that doesn't really count because it involves gay folk doing bad things to other gay folk who are viewed as expendable." He sat back waiting for Harper to weigh in on his theory.

"Now there's a cheery thought." Harper shook his head. "That could very well be the reason. You want not to think that. But hey, both you and I know worse is out there, if you take a good look." Harper sat forward. "Let me ask this. Did you come across anything about that crime that could be linked to our client, other than the location—men in the woods doing what men in the woods sometimes do?"

"Not really." Brent considered burdening Harper with a darker idea—inking Daniels to the murder. But considering what they already had to contend with, he decided to save it for later. Hoping to avoid another instance where his judgment fell into question, he added, "What I found interesting, to the point where it was hard to read on, were all the reader comments following the reports. Many people in the area were repulsed by the notion that men would become so desperate for sex that they would take to the woods to find it. Maybe it's growing up in the city, but after reading one comment after another, I thought, really? This is *that* surprising?"

"I wish you could have been around for some of the discussions we had with locals when the Center was just starting to take shape. You would have been amazed at the naiveté." Harper laughed. "Shit. A few times I went home feeling kind of dirty because I knew all this gay stuff like the back of my hand and the others involved didn't. I felt slutty in a bad way."

Brent laughed. Harper, of all people, having these insecurities. It seemed impossible.

"This is a good point to focus on, though." Harper tapped his pen on his notepad. "I think consistency is going to be our friend. From start to finish, we have to present our client as… well, what he really is—wholesome and naive. Didn't you say Owen was surprised to be propositioned? That it never dawned on him something like that might happen?"

"Exactly," he concurred. "Please don't chide me for saying this, given my recent indiscretions, but our client will project this image without even knowing he's doing it. To me, he naturally comes off as wholesome and innocent. I think he'll present to others the same way. All we have to do is avoid going down the dark alley." He sat back and smiled. He was where he needed to be. In his mind, Owen had switched back from lover to client. He and Harper were operating as a team.

"And when others head down that alley," Harper quipped, "we have to make damn sure they don't take our client along."

"I'm sorry to disturb you." Fern's voice filled the room from the phone console in the middle of the table. "Brent, there's a Ms. Hennessy here to see you."

He looked to Harper and shrugged. "I have no idea who that is."

"Did she say she had an appointment?" Harper asked.

"To my knowledge she—"

"What happened? We lost Fern." Harper looked over quizzically.

"I'm not sure." He got up and started for the door. "I'd better go see what's up. She sounded funny.

"Funny?" Harper sipped his water.

"Bad funny," Brent clarified, tucking in his shirt.

"Promise me you'll never say 'bad funny' again? Will you do that, please?"

"Fern." Startled by her presence at the door, Brent stepped back into the room, allowing her to enter. "I was just headed your way."

"I thought I'd better come down here and give you a heads-up." Not only did she sound funny, but she looked funny too.

Harper turned around in his chair and asked, "What's up, Fern? You look… well, you look *Fern*klempt. Ha. Ten-pointer regardless of what anyone else thinks."

Delighted by his own cleverness, Harper chuckled until Fern crushed his enjoyment by pursing her lips in a way that whipped his smartass into silence and said, "I think she might be…."

Brent held his breath. This could go so many ways, and although he was starting to get to know her fairly well, her expression was new and offered no hint. Her next clue came without prompting in the form of a raised eyebrow—the left if you were facing her. So arresting was this complex look that he was unable to avert his gaze.

"She might be what?" Harper seemed equally perplexed.

"A hooker," Fern blurted out through clenched teeth.

"A hooker? And she asked for me?" Brent wanted to make sure she wasn't just picking on him because he was the junior partner.

"Yes, sir. She did."

"Wish me luck." He sucked air deep into his lungs and gestured for Fern to lead the way.

Brent stepped into the reception area, took one glance at the couch, and was at once in total agreement with Fern's assessment. Dressed in a hot pink short skirt, matching skintight top, and an excessive array of gaudy accessories, Ms. Hennessy looked like a cheap call girl.

"Are you Brent Burns?" She stood and smiled.

*Damn she's tall,* he realized after she had reached her cruising altitude. "Yes. Ms. Hennessy, is it?" He extended his hand, hoping she would allow him to have it back.

"Celine Hennessy," she answered with a vigorous shake. "Hennessy, fancy like the cognac, I like to tell people," she added with a wink and a giggle. "I'm sorry to stop by unannounced, but I think I have some information that might be of value to you regarding Mr. Grady's arrest."

By now Brent had had an opportunity to evaluate her entire ensemble, in all its pink glory. Adding to her height, her big hair had been teased mercilessly into tufts spearing out in every direction. High heels easily added a couple of inches to her naturally elongated frame. It was a calculated look that he surmised played well, somewhere. "I have time now, if you'd like to chat." The sooner he could find out what this was all about, the better for everyone. Fern, back at her post, was doing a poor job of pretending not to pay attention.

"Thank you. I appreciate your time."

Knowing the conference room was a mess, Brent was about to lead Celine to his office when Harper came around the corner. "Fern, are there any messages for me?"

Of course there weren't. Fern, per instruction from Harper, made sure she communicated messages in real time. It was clear that curiosity had gotten the best of his partner too. "This is my partner, Harper Callahan. We're both working on the Grady matter. Harper, Ms. Hennessy has information she feels might be beneficial to our case. Would you like to join us?"

"Pleased to meet you, Ms. Hennessy." Turning back to Fern as if time were an issue, Harper confirmed, "I'm sure I can find a few spare minutes. Should we meet in my office?"

"Would you care for something to drink?" Harper asked as they all took seats facing his desk.

*If she asks for a whiskey sour, I'm going to shit my pants.* Brent braced himself.

"Thank you. I'm good." Celine crossed her long legs and tugged on her skirt.

"I'm good too." Brent quashed an urge to mimic her by crossing his legs and tugging on his pants, but thought better of it.

"Ms. Hennessy, I'm curious to hear what you have for us." Harper folded his hands on his desk.

"I got a call this morning from a friend who knew about a special meeting up at the school last night. She mentioned Mr. Grady had been suspended."

"We heard about that too but have no official documentation supporting it." Not unexpectedly, Harper was being cautious.

"Well, I think that just sucks." Their surprise visitor apparently had strong convictions.

"Unfortunately, we have no control over what the school does."

Did this woman come all the way down to tell them something they already knew? If she didn't cough up a substantive nugget of new information, Harper would surely give her the boot. Hoping for more, Brent asked, "Is there something other than the school board meeting you'd like to share with us?"

Uncrossing her right leg and then crossing her left, she leaned over to him and rested her hand on his arm. "I used to date Officer Luke Daniels."

Harper sat up in his chair and banged his knee loudly on the desk. "Recently?" he asked, not caring who watched as he tried to rub away the pain.

"Up until two weeks ago, on and off for almost a year."

Harper sat back in his chair and scratched his chin. "Interesting."

This was too good to be true. Brent could barely stay seated. "Would you pass me a notepad?" Taking notes would have to replace pacing for the time being.

Harper handed over a yellow legal pad. "How much do you know about Mr. Grady's case?" By the demure way he was acting, Brent could tell his partner had gone from mildly amused to genuinely optimistic.

"I know Mr. Grady was out in the woods by Connor's Point and that he supposedly made a pass at Luke."

"That works, for now." Harper stood and walked to his fridge. "Are you sure I can't offer you something to drink?" he asked, nabbing a bottled water.

"I had two pots of coffee this morning. I'm fine."

"Brent?"

"Water please."

"Do you have any information in opposition to Daniels' claim?" Harper slid his beverage over. "If you do, it could be very helpful to us."

"I'm a widow," Celine began. "My husband was killed in the line of duty three years ago this August."

"I'm very sorry."

Reaching into her purse, she pulled out a picture and placed it on the desk. "This is my husband, Brian."

Harper gave a good look before passing it over to Brent.

Dressed in army fatigues, Brian was hot by every definition. With an approving nod, because he felt the need to react in some way, he handed back the picture.

"Not bad?" Celine's smile had more to say than words.

"Not bad." He felt his face warm. Celine had his ticket.

"Shortly after Brian was killed in Afghanistan, my son Carter crawled into a big old shell and stayed. I credit Mr. Grady for bringing him out of that shell."

"Carter is one of his students?" He wanted to make sure he was tracking.

"Yes, sir. That boy's taken to the bassoon like... well, the kid loves his music. And I have to tell you, until someone starts to really get the hang of that damned instrument, it can put a cloud over your world like nothin' else. I know Carter wouldn't mind me saying this now, because he's gotten so good, but for a while it sounded like he was slaughtering a herd of cattle when he practiced. I thought I was going to lose my mind. But that's another thing I credit Mr. Grady with. Darlin'? Maybe I will take water if it's not too much trouble." Harper was on his feet and delivered her water within seconds.

Pausing long enough to take a sip, she twisted the cap back on and continued, "Mr. Grady had my boy playing real music in no time. I can listen to Carter play that thing for hours on end now."

"I love a good bassoon," Harper interjected, his face coloring a second later.

Incapable of maintaining eye contact with anyone, Brent drew a doodle that resembled nothing.

"Mr. Grady is the best thing that ever happened to that school, if you ask me. I'm here to do whatever, and I hope you heard me right, fellas, *whatever* it takes to make sure we don't lose him because of a bunch of fucking hayseeds who haven't crawled out of their own asses long enough to know which end is up. Excuse my French."

Celine's last remark floated about the room like a lazy dust particle with plenty of landing options. To save his soul, Brent couldn't come up with a response. Apparently neither could Harper. After his reckless bassoon comment, he nodded his reply, sporting a smile as wide as the gorge separating Celine's blue-ribbon knockers.

"How did you meet Luke Daniels?" Harper asked.

"I first came in contact with him last spring at a barbeque my best friend, Charlene, threw for her husband's birthday. Ted works for the city, and that's how Luke got invited. They know each other."

"I might ask you a question you won't feel comfortable answering. Please let me know if this happens, and I'll just move on."

Harper held her gaze to make sure she understood he was being sincere. What Celine didn't need to know, Brent thought, was how resourceful his partner could be at revisiting the same question from a different angle and, without offending, receive a different result.

"I'm not introverted." She pointed to herself and added, "I mean look at me."

"Okay." Harper chuckled, honoring her deprecatory admission. "Who approached who first?"

"Luke expressed interest in me through Ted, who told Charlene, who then asked me if I would consider going out with him. For a long time after Brian's death, I had no interest in seeing anyone. But I was lonely, and I also had Carter on my mind. He's a teenager, and it was an important time for him to have a man in his life."

"Sure. I understand." Harper took a swig and asked, "So you started dating?"

"We started seeing each other. I never thought there was a difference, but now I do."

"I'm not sure I understand," Harper admitted. "Is there a difference?"

"There is with Luke. Excuse me." She removed a tissue from her purse and blew her nose. "You have to understand," she continued. "I'm used to men being aggressive with me. I mean, I'm used to men wanting to put their hand in the cookie jar before they find out what kind of cookie is in there, if you know what I'm saying?"

Laughing at the analogy, Harper answered, "I do. That was a wonderful way of explaining that, by the way."

"Well, that's how Luke was different from the other men I've been with. He wanted to show me off plenty—movies, dinner, all the ways you spend time with someone at first. He was doing all of this, but as we moved along in our relationship, he never seemed to want to take it further. And trust me, by then I was ready for some lovin'."

"You're telling us—" Harper sat back in his chair. "—that Mr. Daniels didn't appear to be sexually interested in you."

Like an exotic bird, Celine sat tall in her chair and puffed out her chest for the world to see. "Take a look at me, fellas. Now I *know* you're battin' for the other team, and that's just fine and all.

But honestly, do either of you think I've had much problem stimulatin' interest in the bedroom?"

"No, ma'am." As if rehearsed, they answered in unison.

"And that's my point, exactly." Celine relaxed her pose.

For the second time in their short meeting, Brent was at a loss for words.

"Here comes one of those difficult questions I mentioned earlier." Harper forged ahead. "Did you and Daniels ever share a sexual experience?"

"Twice," Celine answered without missing a beat. "Both times initiated by me. Both times a complete disappointment. I mean, it was so bad it made me angry, and I have a huge heart when a guy gets nervous. It wasn't that. He didn't want me for sex. To this day, I'm not sure what he wanted me for, but it wasn't sex."

Celine was truly a gift. Hopefully Harper would have a clear idea of how her testimony could be used to maximum effect. Brent asked, "Do you suspect Officer Daniels might be homosexual?"

"He's conflicted, I think, but I don't know how in the world to prove it." Celine crossed her legs and then wiped a wisp of hair from her eye. "We laughed about it the first time. You know, over how he ran out of steam before he even got going. But I could tell he felt bad. He was embarrassed by his poor performance. I did everything I could to make him understand it was okay. But the second time was different."

"How so?" Harper leaned forward and rested his elbows on the desk.

"We had been out drinking. Not drunk, but definitely not feeling any pain, if you know what I mean. All night at the bar, Luke was touchy feely. So on the way home, I asked him if he'd like to spend the night. I'm very careful not to do anything that would make Carter uncomfortable. I want you to know that. But by this time, I could tell my boy was fond of Luke, so I felt okay about inviting him to come home with me."

Confused, Brent asked, "The first time you attempted sex was at Daniels' residence?"

"Yes, honey." Celine patted her hand on his. "I should have made myself more clear."

"You're doing just fine," Harper piped in.

"We go into the bedroom, and I close the door and then turn on the light on the bedside table." Celine followed this with a "no big deal" gesture. "Turn that off!" she barked in a voice significantly lower than her own. "I don't like it when the light is on."

Shaking her finger in Harper's direction, she went on. "And this is interesting to me now, because at Luke's house, we had the lights on. Maybe he thought that was the reason things didn't work out, that time. I'm not sure."

"Right. Could be anything," Harper speculated.

Brent shared a look with his partner and suppressed a grin. *Here comes the good part.*

"Thinking I'm probably the more experienced one in the bedroom. I take the lead and start undressing him. You know, all playful and the like. I thought a little seduction might help for a better outcome down the road, if you catch my drift."

"I'm with you," Brent encouraged but then wished he had kept his mouth shut.

"Oh God, I'm so sorry." Celine wore the look of someone who might have offended.

"Why?" Harper asked, surprised

"I don't need to go into such detail." Flustered, she recovered with, "The bottom line is, it wasn't good. And what makes this time different from the first, when he climbed off me after several attempts to get going—he started to cry. I mean bawl, like a little baby."

*Pathetic.* The image of Daniels crying repulsed Brent. "Did he give you any indication, other than performance issues, that he was troubled?"

"I'd like to expand on what Brent just asked." Harper straightened his tie. "Anything concrete, like an admission to being attracted to men over women, would be of great use."

"He said he didn't know what was wrong with him."

"Okay." Understanding they had hit the wall, Harper moved on. "Is there anything he might have said that, maybe not at the time, but now, seems odd or out of place?"

Celine appeared to give this question serious thought. Perhaps to buy time, she took another long sip of her water before answering. “I don’t know if this is what you’re looking for, but there was one thing he said on several occasions that I found strange. It happened when we were out with other people, you know, socializing, and he was having a good time. He’d look over to me and either kiss or squeeze my hand and say, ‘The guys at Birchwood would sure be proud if they could see me now.’”

“Birchwood?” Harper looked at Brent to see if that registered.

Brent shook his head no. “Did you ask what it meant?”

“Yes. And he always brushed it off by saying something like ‘oh never mind.’ I finally gave up. It’s probably something silly, but you asked.”

“Is there anything else you’d like us to know? A question we didn’t ask but should have?” Harper, all charm, was bringing the meeting to a close.

“I’ve probably told you both more than you ever wanted to know. I care deeply about Mr. Grady. He’s important to Carter, and that makes him important to me.”

Harper stood and came around from his desk. “Thank you so much for stopping in today.”

Celine rose out of her chair, shouldered her purse, and smiled. “If I can help you in any way, please let me know.”

“Thank you.” Harper placed a hand on her shoulder and guided her out of the office. “If you think of anything, night or day, give us a call.”

“Thank you very much,” Brent added. “We appreciate your time.”

Following her to the reception area, Harper thought to ask, “Can we have a contact number for you?”

Celine fired off a number, and Fern jotted it down.

Brent, with Harper at his side, watched Celine climb into an orange Kia station wagon and drive off like a loved one heading out to sea.

“Holy shit,” Harper announced when he turned to face Fern. “That was amazing.”

“Hooker?” Fern asked with a grimace.

“Not even close,” Harper answered. “The details will be in Brent’s notes. You’re going to love it. I need a break. How about you?” he asked, giving Brent’s shoulder a flick of his finger.

"I need a drink," Brent confessed.

"It's almost three. Let's meet back in the conference room at three thirty," Harper proposed. "Does that give you enough time to catch your breath?"

"Sure."

Brent sat at his desk, fired up his laptop, opened a new document, and typed in bold at the top, "Celine Hennessy (fancy like the cognac)."

PETRIFIED, OWEN ran as fast as he could back to the stream. He crossed it, dove into a patch of tall ferns, and, panting like a crazed man, waited to see if Daniels had pursued him. He hoped he had moved quickly enough to prevent detection, but he couldn't be certain. If Daniels had managed to recognize him, he could be in real danger. Who knew what the guy was capable of? Owen was still shaking when he pulled his phone out of his pocket. *Wouldn't you know?* The caller was his mother. "Nice timing," he mumbled. "You could have gotten me killed."

A painful hour passed before he felt safe enough to make his move. Inching up above the top of the green fronds, he peered across the water to the opposite bank. Birds, a trustworthy barometer, if you knew how to interpret their activity, flitted noisily from branch to branch, indicating they were unaware of a threat. He stepped into the clearing, untied his boots, slung them over his shoulder, and waded down the stream toward home. When he reached the parking lot, he climbed into his car and sped away.

Once he had safely parked in his tiny garage, he raced up the stairs, jammed his key into the lock, opened the back entrance to his house, and stumbled inside. Fighting to catch his breath, he backed up against the door and locked it. *Thank God I'm home.*

He poured a glass of tap water, gulped it down, and sat at the table. Closing his eyes, he replayed the unexpected encounter. He was sure he had sprung to his feet instantly. Daniels had his pants around his knees. It would have taken him a few seconds to get to the point where he could pursue. Was there a chance the officer had caught enough of a glimpse to determine who he was? Possibly, but not likely. At least that's what he had told himself all the way home. What would Brent think?

*Call him. He'll want to know about this.*

Owen scrolled through his list of contacts and found the number but stopped shy of pressing the call button. The last thing he wanted was to get Brent into more trouble than he was in already.

*Call the firm directly.*

That was it. He'd call and ask to speak to Brent. He leafed through a mountain of papers he had stockpiled on the table and located the agreement he had signed with the firm's telephone number listed in the header.

"Burns and Callahan," their receptionist answered cheerfully. "This is Fern. How may I help you?"

"Oh hi, Fern. This is Owen Grady. Is Brent available?" He felt his pulse race. He was excited to communicate his news.

"Hello, Owen. Can you hold for a minute while I check?"

"Sure. Thanks."

"I'm going to transfer you," Fern informed after a brief moment.

"Thanks."

"Owen. It's Brent. What's up?"

Hearing Brent's voice was like the comforting rush he felt when he stepped through his own front door. "Something happened to me today I think you should know about."

*Keep calm.*

"I'm meeting with Harper. Do you mind if I put you on speakerphone?"

Did he mind? Was there anything he could do if he did? He needed to believe Harper wasn't a big, bad meanie looking to make their lives hell. Maybe this call would help smooth over the edges. "Sure."

"Hello, Owen."

Although he hadn't heard it since their first meeting, Callahan's voice was as he remembered—deeper than Brent's and more deliberate.

"Am I disturbing you?" Owen asked, hoping he didn't come off as a pest.

"Not at all," Callahan assured. "We've been going over notes on your case. What can we do for you?"

"When I found out you guys didn't need me today, I decided to head out to do some birding," he began, conscious of keeping the emotion out of his delivery. "On the way back to my car, I… ran into Luke Daniels."

"Wow."

It was Callahan who reacted first when he finished his story. "I think you would have mentioned this, but I have to ask—did you get the picture?"

"I have a shot, but it must have happened at the same time the phone rang. It's a total blur." He was embarrassed he wasn't able to pull it off, knowing how important it could have been to his case.

As if sensing his disappointment, Callahan was quick to reassure. "Hey. Don't worry about it. You're right to assume. Had you been caught, there could have been a serious altercation. The guy is missing a few spokes. Who the hell knows how he might have reacted. You're safe. That's what counts."

"How much distance do you think separated you from Daniels?" Brent asked.

"Not much. Maybe thirty-five feet?" He could visualize it as if he were still crouched down, watching.

"And it wasn't an open area? I mean," Brent clarified, "in addition to the blind you were behind, there was more brush, more visual obstacles separating you?"

"Yes. It's hard to explain, but when I first spotted them and stepped off the trail, I didn't really have any view to speak of. When I moved a few feet farther in, I had a better view. Later, I shifted my body to avoid a cramp, and then Daniels must have moved too. That's when I found myself with a fairly unobstructed view." He laughed nervously. "I wish, instead of snooping, I would have gotten myself out of there sooner. I guess I was just compelled to watch, given what I'd been through."

"There isn't anyone who could fault you for watching. Don't waste a moment on that. And truthfully," Harper reminded, "had your picture been a success, it would have been worth everything to your case."

"I'm so disappointed it didn't turn out." He wished he had something other than fear to take away from the experience, which reminded him to ask, "Do you guys think I have anything to worry about?"

"Meaning?" Callahan apparently didn't understand what he was asking.

"I don't think there's any way Daniels could have known it was me who was watching. That's what I want to believe anyway."

"Given your description of the encounter, I don't think he had a chance to do much looking around. It takes a few moves to extricate your penis from someone's mouth. That would have been *my* first order of business. And then wouldn't your next move be to pull up your pants?" Harper laughed. "By the time all that was accomplished, you were already a vapor trail speeding down the path."

"I think you're safe too," Brent concurred. "You don't have anything to worry about."

"Okay." Having them both weigh in helped him relax.

"Keep an eye out, though," Harper cautioned. "I think it would be prudent for you to always be aware of your environment and who's sharing it with you. And report to us any suspicious behavior. We'll understand your concern and never think poorly of you for letting us know."

"Thanks. I'm feeling much better, talking this over. Listen. I know you're busy, so I don't want to keep you."

"Anytime," Harper answered. "Thanks again for giving us a call."

"Hang in there, Owen," Brent added, and they ended the call.

Owen sat back and exhaled a ton of worry. Almost as good as the relief he experienced in sharing his story was the connection he felt he made with Callahan, who never once sounded anything other than supportive. He was starting to understand the complexity of Brent's relationship with his partner. *I'm in good hands.*

"ENJOY." BRENT handed a cold beer to Harper and then sat at his desk.

"Cheers." Unbuttoning the top of his shirt, Harper stretched out his feet. "It's been quite the day."

It was the classic understatement, Brent thought. And for now, it would have to do. So much had happened in the past twenty-four hours, it was hard to keep track. Minutes ticked by before either spoke.

"What's on your mind?" Harper asked with a grin.

"I was thinking about Owen," he admitted. "How scared he must have been. And I know he feels like shit for not getting a clear picture we could use. I'm glad you said what you did. It will help, but he'll still beat himself up over it."

"My first reaction was to laugh. The timing was something right out of a movie. What are the odds that would happen at the precise moment you're about to take the shot of a lifetime?"

Brent reacted to Harper's observation by spewing beer out of his mouth and onto the carpet, triggering a colossal laughing fit that consumed them both. It continued until, out of frustration and respect for Owen, he was able to rein it in.

Harper had a few rogue bursts of hilarity before he pulled it together. "Shit, I needed that." Harper wiped his eyes.

"Me too. What are we going to do with all of this random information? It supports our case, but how the hell can we share it in court? Make it work for us?"

"Right now, I haven't a clue," Harper admitted.

"Put Celine on the stand?" he opined.

"I'm more inclined to think that would work against us." Harper looked frustrated. "Not that she wouldn't do a great job. And she'll do whatever we need her to do. I just think it's a weak defense. A jury could very likely react to her the same way Fern did. And that would be disastrous."

*True*. As much as he loved Celine's personality, others could equally be threatened by it. "What about that reference to Birchwood?" he asked paging through his notes. "What do you think that was all about?"

"Now, see." Harper sat up in his chair. "That, my friend, could very well be the diamond in the rough. It's significant. First, Daniels would not have said it repeatedly to her, and second, she would not have thought it worth mentioning to us, if it weren't important. I say we go after it and see where it gets us."

"Birchwood," Brent mumbled. "It sounds industrial. Was it somewhere he worked?"

"Could be." Harper scratched his stubbly cheek. It was after four o'clock, and the famed shadow darkened his complexion. "What went along with it? Something about 'the guys would be proud?' Do you have that in your notes?"

"The guys at Birchwood would sure be proud, if they could see me now," Brent read from his notes. "And then I have 'social settings' and 'having a good time.'"

"Does that mean Daniels was proud in some way? It's bragging, to be sure. Was he proud he'd scored a big-titted babe like Celine? I mean no disrespect to her, but you know what I'm getting at." Harper sipped and stared into space.

"I'm not sure." Brent had the beginnings of an observation, and after circling around it a few times, thought enough of it to share. "The guy considers himself a ladies' man. He brags about that. His deposition supports it. So, instead of him bragging he was the lucky guy, wouldn't she be the lucky gal instead?"

"Interesting." Harper stood. "I have to piss. Be right back."

While Harper was away, Brent initiated a search on Birchwood. The results were staggering—everything from an outdoor movie theater to churches, schools, industry, and even a floor wax. *This is going to be impossible.*

"What did I miss?" Harper plopped back in his seat.

"For shits and giggles, I just did a search on Birchwood. It's going to be a bitch to make a connection, I think. Too many choices." He pushed his laptop away.

"I figured as much."

"Should we grab dinner and then come back and work?" Brent asked in response to a rumbling stomach.

"I want to sleep on all of this," Harper confessed. "I need to spend some time on my own with this new information. Let's start fresh in the morning."

"Sounds good." Brent powered down his computer and stashed it in his bag with his notes. That night he would review everything and begin to organize it, an exercise that always proved worth the time investment. Besides, sleep would be difficult. "Anything else before we call it a day?"

"Even prisoners get conjugal visits," Harper stated without a hint as to what he meant.

"Excuse me?" Brent stood, gathered up their empties, and tossed them into the trash can under his desk.

"Ian's started calling me the warden at home. It's really getting under my skin."

"Are you keeping him prisoner? Wait, you're withholding sex for some reason? Punishing him?" He searched Harper's face but still couldn't solve the riddle.

"It's not about me, it's about you."

"Me?" he asked, surprised.

"He's making me feel guilty for keeping you and Owen apart." Harper broke his gaze and tapped the sides of his chair with his hands. "It's working."

"Ian…." Brent smiled. "Harper, I'm fine. Owen…. We're fine. It's for the best. No hard feelings or anything else like that."

"Officially I'm looking the other way, provided you guys continue to be discreet. Ian's right. It's cruel to stand in the way of love. And truthfully, ethics aside, I'm not sure I'd obey the ordinance either. I felt like an asshole listening to you guys on the phone today. Even though you've both been model citizens of late, the strain was palpable."

"Seriously, this is making me feel awkward. I would never ask you to do this or expect it." Brent was surprised at how adamantly he was arguing in favor of Harper's decree. Maybe it was their working relationship doing the talking. Whatever it was, he had resigned himself to abide by the law until their case had been tried.

"Be extremely cautious." Harper stood and walked to the door. "He needs you, Brent. That's a very scary thing he went through today. You can help chase those fears away by being there for him. In that dirty way I know you're already considering."

He had to laugh. "Dirty way."

"This was a good day for our client. I'm not sure just how good, but we'll figure that out soon, I hope. Good night."

“Harper.” Brent moved into the center of the room. “I appreciate this, and I know Owen will too. No worries, okay?”

“No worries. “What I don’t know won’t hurt me. What I do know, will hurt you. Understood?”

“Yes, sir.”

Brent glanced around to make sure he had everything, turned off the light in his office, and walked to the reception area. Fern had already gone for the day, leaving the rest of the cake, as promised—raspberry lemon with cream-cheese frosting. It was addicting. He grabbed the box and slid it under his arm. Then he headed to his car. The night was his, and if there was one thing he knew for sure, he wanted to spend it with Owen. As Harper had pointed out, Owen might need him, and that was a good reason to hook up. Staying apart had been a fucking bitch.

“I THINK I’d like to meet this Ian guy,” Owen chuckled as they relaxed in the tub after sex. “Maybe send him roses.”

After everything that had happened that day, the last thing he expected was to have his new man resting against his chest in a tub full of warm water, with candles, soft music, and wine.

“I can’t wait for you to meet the rest of the guys. They’re like a big family. You’re going to fit in so well.”

“I’m looking forward to getting to know everyone.” Owen kissed the nape of Brent’s neck. The skin was warm against his lips—moist, and fragrant from the bath salts. The flickering light from the candles, one on the sink and the other next to them on the floor, produced an infinite array of dancing images on the walls of the tiny bathroom. At least for the time being, all the nastiness the world had thrown his way had vanished. Wrapping his arm around Brent’s chest, Owen hugged him tight to his body. He never wanted this moment together to end.

“This is paradise,” Brent cooed. “I can feel all of the pent-up tension from the last few days melting away.”

“Me too.”

"So," Brent said, reaching down to the floor and hauling up a plate of cake they'd been sharing, "I've been meaning to ask you this all night."

Owen waited for Brent to pass a forkful back. "This is really awesome cake. You already know how much I love lemon."

"You don't want to know how much of this I've eaten today. I can't help myself." Brent chuckled, spearing another bite-sized hunk.

He giggled while chewing. "It feels funny when you're up against me and you laugh. Sorry. What were you going to ask?"

"I met someone you know today." Brent took a bite and put the plate down. "Celine Hennessy."

"Fancy like the cognac?" This time they both laughed, causing the water in the tub to splash about.

"Exactly. She said that today." Brent snorted.

"What an amazing woman. I have a soft spot in my heart for her." Owen nestled his nose behind Brent's ear. "Of all the parents I've met, Celine really made an impression on me. And not in the way one would typically think, given her flamboyant fashion sense. She's a solid parent who places her child's needs above her own. That isn't as common as one would think. How did you come to meet her?"

"She showed up at the office today."

"What's that? Is she in trouble? Wait. Client privilege. Strike that last question." He was happy to have caught the mistake before Brent had to respond. "I hope she's okay. That woman deserves a break."

"She came for you. Word got back to someone she knows about the school board meeting last night—the suspension. Celine came in swinging for you. She thinks you're the best."

"Well how about that?" Not sure what to make of it, Owen revisited Brent's nipple with his finger.

"Carter is her son?"

"Carter Hennessy," Owen confirmed. "He's my first big success as a teacher. That kid was a mess when I started working with him. Shy, awkward, and very sad, Carter was broken in so many places." He hadn't thought about it for a while. It wasn't a good memory. "Not sure if you know this, but his daddy was killed in Afghanistan."

"That was mentioned."

"What else did you guys talk about?" Owen began fingering the other nipple. Without too much effort, he could turn it rock hard. Brent's body was a variable playground of delights.

"There're aspects regarding today's meeting I don't feel comfortable sharing right now. Nothing that's harmful to you, in any way. The main reason she stopped by was to offer her support to you. It's too early to tell if we'll use her in the case. Both Harper and I came away from the meeting liking her. That look she has going on is a real doozy though. This can't leave here, but our assistant, Fern, thought for sure she was a hooker."

"That's exactly what I thought too," Owen chuckled. "I understand about you not wanting to talk about everything." It was clear from how Brent responded there were other things discussed at the meeting. He fought off the urge to needle. It wasn't hard, he was starting to fade. Unable to contain a large yawn, he asked, "What do you think? Waterlogged?"

"I'm wiped out." Brent scooted his body forward in the tub and stood. The water cascading off his body matted the hairs on his legs in a way Owen found irresistible. He thought about initiating a second round of sex. They could both use a good sleep. If Brent wanted, Owen would gladly rise to the occasion. But for now he was content to cradle Brent in his arms all night long.

A rumbling shook the house just as he stepped out of the tub and reached for a towel. "Was that thunder?" Before Brent could answer, a much louder clap confirmed the approach of a storm.

"Yikes. I'm kind of skittish about being in water during a storm. Even if it's a bathtub," Brent confessed. "Looks like we got out just in time."

"Can you get electrocuted inside a house from lightning?" He'd never given it a thought.

"I don't know, but I sure as hell never want to find out." Brent carried a candle into the bedroom. "My mother won't talk on the telephone during a storm. The Burns family is held captive to a myriad of old wives' tales and superstitions."

Rain pelted the roof as Owen walked to the window opposite the bed. Before he could close it, he observed a squad car slowly passing by. Fear bubbled up when it stopped directly in front of his house. A flash of light from the storm illuminated the interior of the vehicle. *Fuck. It's Daniels.* Owen stepped away from the window and watched until it continued down the block. How many times had he spotted a cop in his neighborhood since he'd been living there? Not many.

"What are you doing, Owen? Get in here," Brent called out, already safely tucked in.

"I'm coming."

As he crossed the room, a bolt of lightning hit and the booming thunder was instantaneous. "Holy shit," he squealed, diving under the covers. Brent's body was already warm. Owen spooned him tight.

"Good night, Owen," Brent purred.

"Good night."

Minutes later, Brent's soft snoring filled the room. Owen stared at the ceiling and prepared for a night of worry. *Daniels knows it was me.*

# CHAPTER Eleven

"DID YOU have a chance to type up Brent's notes from yesterday?" Harper asked while leafing through the mail. "Sorry." He realized his mistake and set the pile down. Fern became noticeably irritated if he or Brent got to the morning's delivery before she had a chance to sort, date stamp case-related documents, and place it all in bundles on each of their desks. He had a great appreciation for the workings of the front office and a huge respect for Fern. She had more than met his expectations, and he felt very lucky to have her on the team. Her happiness was never far from his thoughts. The mail could wait.

"Oh my gosh, yes," she answered as she refilled her stapler. "And I thought family law was a soap opera."

"Any ideas how we can wrap it all up into a pretty package for the jury?" he asked. He sat across from her on the sofa with his "Dads Rule" coffee mug—a recent gift from his new son, Alex.

"Have you guys considered hiring someone to dig around for you?" Perhaps feeling pressured by his presence, Fern retrieved the mail and began to sort it.

"I haven't," he confessed. "I don't know much about that sort of thing, to be honest. I guess I could have Brent call around for a recommendation. Do you know someone who might be willing to help us out? We don't have much time before the trial next week."

"It just so happens that I do." She shoved the mail aside, reached under her desk, and hauled up an enormous black bag. After a flurry of digging, she produced a business card and held it out. "He's an ambitious young man who has a strong work ethic. I highly recommend him."

"Really?" Harper got up to retrieve the card. "Michael S. Smuckler, Private Investigator. Fern?" He laughed when he read the name. "Who is this?"

"My youngest," she admitted with a prideful air.

"I guess that explains the strong work ethic." He winked. "And he's in the Twin Cities?"

"Michael graduated from the University of Minnesota with a degree in criminology last spring. He works out of his apartment." Fern returned to the mail. "You know how it is just starting out."

"Excellent." The idea of hiring someone else to dig around into Daniels' background was appealing. But to involve another individual at this point with so little time—was it worth it? "Would he have the time right now to make our case a priority?" he wondered out loud. Then, thinking it had the potential to offend, added, "I'll be honest with you. I'm concerned about spending what little time we have bringing someone else up to speed on the facts. With the trial next week, it might be better to just own this responsibility ourselves and hope for the best."

"He's got the time." Fern looked up from under her glasses. "I just spoke to him this morning."

"Let me know when Brent comes in, if I don't see him first. I'd like to run this past him before making a decision."

"Will do." She handed over a small stack of mail. "Nothing but junk this morning."

"Thanks." Harper started for his office.

"I know what you're thinking."

"You do?" He turned back.

"It's the fear of hiring a friend or a relative, only to find out it was a big mistake." Fern smirked.

"Guilty." He chuckled. "I can't help it. It's the way I think."

"Not even Michael can guarantee the results you're hoping for. It's the nature of the business. But I will tell you—and yes, this is a very proud mother speaking—he's detail orientated and a very hard worker. The child has been that way his entire life."

"I'm sorry to make you have to hard sell your own son."

"You wouldn't be good at your job if you didn't have those concerns." She sat back and smiled. "If you decide to give him a call and you still have reservations, I'll completely understand. If he can help in any way, all the better."

"Thank you for that."

Back at his desk, Harper read through Brent's notes from their meeting with Celine. Then he sat back, folded his hands behind his head, and stared at the ceiling. "Holy shit. We're in bad shape."

Because they were such a trusted force in the community, juries tended to believe law enforcement. So far, they had nothing substantial to combat that bias. The reference to Birchwood held the greatest potential, but because it was vague, it offered very little hope. *Call in the artillery.* Birchwood was so random, anyone might crack the code. All they needed was a sliver to go after. By the end of the day, Harper planned to touch base with Alex, Theo, Ian—the whole gang—and ask them to search for a connection.

"Good morning." Brent walked into the office with his computer bag slung over his shoulder. "I had an idea driving in. We should reach out to the boys and ask them to help research this Birchwood thing. That will free us up to work with the information we already have."

"Great idea," Harper said. "I've got something else for us to mull over. Let's meet in the conference room in ten minutes."

"Works for me."

The old Brent was back. Despite their difficulties, it had been a real joy working with him. The partnership was working the way Harper had always envisioned it. It was time to reward Brent for turning things around.

"I DON'T think Fern would have brought him to our attention if she didn't have confidence in his abilities. She's too professional to risk her reputation." Brent stared at the business card in his hand. "Why would we not give this a shot?"

"Exactly. Beggars can't be choosers, now can they?" Harper's face was as telling as anything. They had a long way to go and short time to get there.

"Should we jam on a list of questions for this guy, or do we wing it?" Brent was unsure of how to work with an investigator.

"Wing it," Harper shot back. "That is, unless you have a strong conviction not to."

"I was hoping for more from you," he joked. "Do you want to call him now?"

Rising out of his seat to close the door, Harper asked, "Will you drive the call? Given what we have on our plates, you should own this piece of the pie."

"Me?" Brent was surprised by the request and wished he had responded with more confidence. "Sorry. I wasn't expecting that," he confessed. "Yes. I can drive this."

"Good. I think it would be prudent to start working differently. My thought? You could focus on the hunt for new evidence while I work at crafting our argument using what we already know. I hate to say it, but we might not have much more going into the trial than what we have now."

"That sounds good." Brent understood he was more valuable at conducting research than preparing for trial. He felt both a sense of relief and an eagerness to prove his worth.

"Ready when you are, Ace." Harper cracked his knuckles, folded his arms across his chest, and grinned.

"Here goes nothin'." Brent dialed.

"He works out of his apartment," Harper whispered.

After the second ring, an earnest voice said, "This is Michael."

"Michael, my name is Brent Burns. I'm calling from the law offices of Burns and Callahan in Two Harbors. I work with your mother."

"Oh sure. She's mentioned you."

"I'm here with my partner, Harper Callahan. I'd like to put you on speakerphone, if you don't mind."

"That's fine."

Brent punched a button and asked, "Can you hear me okay?"

"Yes. What can I do for you?"

"Hi, Michael. This is Harper."

Using his notes as a guide, Brent proceeded to detail, as succinctly as he could, the gist of their case. "So, do you think you might be able to help us out? We know there's not much time."

Harper slid over a note with "nice job" written on it.

"Yeah. I mean I'll do what I can. You never know, with this stuff, how fast it'll break."

"We're working on our end to identify leads. But for now, you know as much as we do." Brent was relieved to hear Michael sounded game to give it a try, given the little there was to work with. He also appreciated that he made sure they understood the realities of the process.

"A photograph would be really helpful. Either recent or dated, preferably both, if you can manage it."

Panicked, Brent covered the mouthpiece and looked to Harper for direction.

"Tell him we should have one soon," Harper prompted.

"We should be able to get something to you soon," Brent answered, his confidence shaken by the unexpected request. "I'll e-mail it to you as soon as I can."

Harper leaned forward and asked, "Michael, let's talk cost, for a minute. What are your rates?"

"I bill out at $125 an hour, but because of your connection with my mother, that's flexible. You would have to assume any additional expenses, like travel."

"I think $125 seems like a fair rate," Harper answered. "However, let's cap it at $2,000, for now. Does that sound agreeable?

"I'm comfortable with that."

Gesturing for Brent to take control, Harper eased away from the table.

"Do you have set hours? How does that work?" Who the hell knew when something useful might surface? Brent was sure Harper would agree that the sooner a lead could be communicated, the better.

"Seriously, call anytime, given your time constraints. If I don't pick up, leave a message, and I'll get back to you as soon as I can," the young investigator offered.

"Check later today for an e-mail from us," Brent advised. "I'll scan what we have and send it off for you to look over."

"Will do."

"Great. Harper, do you have anything else?" Brent wiggled his eyebrows, pleased at how the call had gone.

"I'm good. Thanks for taking this on, Michael. We appreciate anything you can do for us." Relieved this guy wasn't an idiot, Brent relaxed in his chair.

"Thank you. And say hi to Mom. I know she's enjoying working with you guys."

"We love her," Brent confessed.

"She keeps us in line. Take care and thanks again." Harper ended the call.

"I'm cautiously optimistic." Harper stood and stretched his arms in the air.

"We need asshole's photo," Brent reminded.

"I feel a plan coming on." Harper opened the door. "Come visit me in a few minutes."

"ARE YOU sure he's on patrol and not just heading somewhere for lunch?" Aware they had one chance to get it right, Theo pressed Alex for more detail.

"I've been trailing him for the last ten minutes, Theo," Alex reported with a noticeable lack of patience in his voice. "He's just driving around looking at shit."

"Alex says it's a go," Theo reported back to Ian and his mother who were waiting patiently for their part of the scheme to kick in.

"Great," Ian said, holding his camera in the air. "We've got this dickhead for sure. Sorry, Mrs. E."

"That's okay. I've heard worse," Darla Engdahl assured with a forced smile.

"Stay with him until after we make the call," Theo advised and hung up. He sucked in a deep breath and asked, "Okay, Mom. Are you sure you want to do this?"

Darla, sitting poised on the end of her seat, looked ready to jump into action. "Yes. I'll be fine. It makes more sense for an old lady like me to get flustered than it does for a young man. It's more believable, I think."

"I don't see an old lady anywhere in *this* office. How about you, Theo?" Ian asked with a wink.

Darla had transformed since she assumed the responsibilities of office manager. Theo had never seen her happier, and everyone was thrilled with the job she was doing. “Okay. You’re up. Place the call.”

Nerves made Theo’s palms start to sweat. He wiped them on his jeans and paced in front of the resort desk wishing the whole mission was over. Ian took a seat at the small table near the window.

“Hello. I need to report a robbery.” Nodding in response to the voice on the other end of the line, Darla closed her eyes, probably to minimize distraction as she concentrated on the script Theo had rehearsed with her. “Yes. I’m calling from the Palisade Beach Resort. That’s correct.”

*You’ve got the perfect amount of worry in your voice. Hang in there, Mom, you’re doing great.* He was pleased.

“When I got into the office this morning, I discovered our weekly deposit was missing. I don’t know what I’m going to do. This is just terrible.”

Ian waved Theo over. “Make sure she insists someone come out to check for a break-in.”

“Hang on.” Theo walked behind the desk, grabbed a piece a paper, wrote, *Make sure they come out and look for a break-in*, and handed it to her.

Darla nodded. “Not that I can tell. I don’t even know what I’d be looking for. Please send someone out. It was a lot of money.” Looking up from her desk, both Theo and Ian rewarded her with smiles and enthusiastic thumbs-up.

“Oh, thank you so much. Yes. My name is Darla Engdahl, and I’m the manager. I’ll be in the resort office. It’s the first building you see when you drive in. Thank you.” Placing the phone in its holder, Darla flashed the biggest smile he had ever seen on her. “They’re sending someone right out.”

“Nice job, Ms. E.” Ian jumped out of his chair and gave her a high five.

“That was great, Mom,” Theo echoed, thrilled by her performance.

“Get back to Alex and let him know all is well here.” Ian walked to the door. “I’m going to take up my post.”

"Good luck." Theo walked behind the desk and gave his mother a loving pat on the shoulder. "You did great."

"Thank you." If his mother was put out by having to tell a lie, she wasn't showing it. But he could tell she was relieved to have it over.

"Hey. Supposedly they're sending someone right out," he reported to Alex.

"I know. Douche bag is on his way," Alex confirmed. "I just watched him turn onto the highway. No flashing lights, though."

"Fuck." Theo looked over in horror when he realized he had just released the F-bomb in front of his mother. It was too late now. Ian and Alex had potty mouths that could put most people to shame. Chances were good she had already been exposed to much worse.

"What?" Alex asked.

"I forgot to put the Closed for Maintenance sign on the office door. We don't want any guests wandering in here until he's gone." Theo opened a drawer behind the counter and found the sign.

"That's a good idea. I don't think it matters much, though. Is Ian ready?" Alex asked.

Theo hung the sign on the door, stepped back inside, and reported, "Ian's hiding somewhere with his camera."

"Great. I'm going back to the Center. One of you should e-mail the pictures, and I'll walk them over to Harper and Brent."

"Got it. Bye." Just as Theo pocketed his phone, a squad car pulled into the parking lot. "He's here, Mom. You ready?"

"Lord, give me strength. Yes, son. I'm ready." Darla stood up with her hands at her sides.

"Good." He joined her behind the desk. "Start counting the money like you normally would." Knowing this piece of the ruse was his, Theo ran through his lines as the sound of someone approaching the office door grew louder.

Pretending to focus on sorting the cash, checks, and credit card receipts, they both looked up as the screen door opened.

"Hello," Daniels said, stepping into the office. "Did somebody here report a robbery?"

"Yes. I called," Darla confessed, her face coloring on cue, adding authenticity to the moment.

With a smile that both charmed and alarmed, Daniels crossed the room and placed his clipboard in front of them on the reception desk. “Why don’t you start from the beginning—when you first discovered there’d been a theft.”

*You’re up.*

“That won’t be necessary, officer. It was miscommunication on my part. The money is all here. I removed the deposit from the safe earlier, without letting anyone else know.” Wearing what he hoped was a believable look of guilt, for the first time in his life, Theo welcomed the sensation of his own face coloring.

“Who are you?” Daniels asked, turning his full attention to Theo.

A bad case of the creeps threatened Theo’s performance. The little he knew about this freak was enough to make his skin crawl. *It’s the eyes.* Deep and penetrating, they bore right through you.

“I’m Theo Engdahl. This is my mother. She called into the station before I got back to the office.”

“Were you at the Taconknights Fourth of July game last week?” Daniels held Theo’s gaze while he waited for an answer.

Stunned, Theo struggled to stay composed. *What the fuck? There were a ton of people there. Why me?* “Yeah. I was there, I guess.” Flustered, he wanted to kick himself for such a stupid response.

“You guess?” Daniels snorted. “Your son seems to be having communication issues today.” When Darla failed to respond, he added, “I’m sure I saw you there. Great game, wasn’t it?”

“Yeah.” He shared a look with his mother that he hoped communicated his relief that she had stayed out of the conversation. Their part was finished. The sooner they could get him out of the office, the better.

“You like baseball?” Daniels asked.

“Nope,” he shot back.

An eternity seemed to pass before Daniels picked up his clipboard and no longer smiling, replied, “I don’t suppose you would.” Turning his back to them, he gave the office a once-over. “Well, I’m glad to hear we don’t have a robbery to investigate.”

Theo felt his stomach knot when Daniels turned, looked directly at him, and asked, “Is there… anything else I can do for you?”

"Sorry for the inconvenience, officer." Darla came sweeping around from behind the desk. "We'll do a better job of communicating in the future."

"No worries. If I can be of assistance in the future, just give me a call." Flashing a smile that chilled Theo to the bone, Daniels turned and left.

Neither of them spoke until he had gotten back in his car and pulled out of the parking lot.

"Glad that's over with," he shared as he grabbed the sign off the door and returned it to its place in the drawer. "He's creepy."

"Honey, did you talk to him at the game and not remember?" Darla inquired, taking her seat behind the desk.

"I've never seen him before in my life."

"Well, you must have made some sort of impression."

His mother's innocent comment added to his repulsion. *Was he stalking me?*

"We did it," Ian cheered as he bounded through the door. "Nice job, you guys."

"I can't remember when I've been this naughty." Darla giggled. "It feels kind of good. Not a word of this to your father," she ordered, shaking her finger at Theo.

"I got a good shot of him when he first got out of the car and then some even better shots of him coming out of the office. The boys at the firm should be happy with the results."

"Oh good." Darla clapped her hands.

"Did you ask your mom about Birchwood?" Ian filled a Styrofoam cup with complimentary coffee from the pot at the end of the counter.

"Not yet. Mom, Harper wants us all to think about the name *Birchwood*. What do you think of when you hear it? Anything come to mind?"

"Well that's easy," Darla answered. "Birchwood was the name of a supper club down the highway near the Palisade. Unfortunately it burned to the ground before you were born. Gosh, I miss that place. Best food on the North Shore. Your dad and I used to set money aside so we could have a night out there. What wonderful memories I have."

"Interesting." Ian removed his camera from around his neck. "That's a piece of local history I haven't heard before."

Perhaps sensing her answer wasn't what they hoped for, Darla offered, "I'll give it some more thought. My mind is in a million different places right now. When I get home tonight, I'll ask your father. He's much better at remembering than I am."

"That would be great. Thanks." Still freaked out about his encounter with Daniels, Theo followed Ian to the door. "What are you up to now?"

"Huh? Oh, I'm going to load these pictures onto my laptop. Maybe fire up Photoshop, if they need work. Honestly I think they're going to be fine. I'll e-mail them to Alex. He's waiting for them, right?"

"Right. You mind if I tag along?"

"Not at all." Ian turned back and saluted. "Thanks again for your help today, Mrs. E."

"Mom, I'm going up to the house with Ian. I'll be back in a few minutes if anyone is looking for me."

"Sounds good. See you boys later."

When they had gotten a safe distance from the office, Theo stopped and shared, "Something really weird happened when Daniels was here."

"Doesn't surprise me. From what Harper's told me, he's one sick critter. What happened?"

"He asked me if I was at your game on the Fourth."

"Maybe he was just making small talk. That doesn't sound too weird."

"It was the way he asked, 'Didn't I see you at the game?' He knew I was there. It gave me the creeps."

"Okay. That's different. And you don't remember seeing him or talking to him?" Ian asked.

"I've never seen him before. Not even out patrolling."

"That is fucked up." Ian led the way up the trail to the house.

"Between you and me, I think the asshole was checking me out." It felt strange to admit, but he wanted Ian to understand why he was so troubled.

"You're such a dog too. Makes no sense." Ian continued up the path.

"Fuck off."

"Make sure to tell Brent or Harper about this," Ian advised as they approached the house. "You never know if something like that will be important to them."

"Okay. I sure hope they expose this guy for what he is—a bona fide sicko." Theo followed Ian up the steps.

"TONIGHT WE should probably be on our own. From now until the trial is over, it's going to be late nights and early mornings. We'll have to see how it goes." Brent wanted to make sure Owen understood it was only work that limited the amount of time they spent together. This relationship thing was tricky. In the early stages, it was important to overcommunicate to avoid damaging misinterpretations. It was a piece of advice he couldn't claim to have discovered on his own, but one he'd heard from friends over time. He didn't know shit about relationships. He never gave a moment's thought about how the other guy felt, because aside from the sex, there really wasn't anything else that interested him. The pieces of wisdom were invaluable now that he actually cared for someone enough to worry about their feelings.

"I understand. And," Owen added before Brent had an opportunity to move on, "even if we sleep and nothing more, I'm okay with that too."

"You're so easy."

"I am not," Owen argued. "The plan is to trap you in a web before you're even aware you're my next meal."

"That's grisly in a way that makes me hard," Brent joked. Then realized their discussion was already making him hard. "Bye, sexy."

"Bye, sweetie. Keep in touch."

It was true. Owen was easy in ways that made it impossible not to want to be around him. Even if he had turned out to be a challenge, Brent wasn't sure it would matter. His attraction was like nothing he had experienced before. It wasn't a conquest, or a challenge. It was love. What he felt for Owen was very similar to what he had felt with Alex. But by the time he realized how strong his feelings were for Alex, it was too late. The sting from that relationship smarted, even though it hadn't ever been defined, and he had vowed to never again let someone who mattered get away. How lucky was it for lightning to strike in the same place twice? Owen wasn't going to slip through the cracks if there was anything Brent could do to prevent it.

Michael Smuckler was the next call on his list, but he didn't hold out much hope. Daniels had given them so little to work with. Or they hadn't done a very good job of looking in the right places. Regardless, the sands of time were rapidly running out.

*Please have some good news for us.*

"Hey, Michael. It's Brent Burns. I had a note to give you a call this morning to see if there were any developments or to answer questions you might have." That was as good a lead-in as he could come up with, given that the arrangement was for Michael to call them if *he* had news.

"Nothing concrete to report. I have feelers out to a few sources I'm waiting to hear back from. I've provided them with the photos you sent. One of my classmates lives in the San Fran area. He's checking the Alameda connection for me. There's a real 'you pat my back I'll pat yours' way we go about obtaining facts in this business. Hopefully he'll uncover something soon."

"I'll let Harper know." Brent trusted Michael's commitment. "Nothing new here," Brent was sad to report. "We're doing everything we can to dig something up."

"From experience, I can tell you the way this works. When you least expect it, something of interest drops in your lap. I know it's getting close, but we still have time. Try not to let the process get the best of you."

Investigation was a lot like love, Brent mused. Love certainly had struck when he least expected it to.

"Who you talking to?" Harper rushed into his office noticeably excited.

"Smuckler." Brent pressed mute.

"Get him back on." Harper sat in the chair across and scooted it right up to the edge of his desk.

"Michael, Harper just came into the office." Brent pointed to the phone console. Whatever the urgency, it had Harper worked up like he had never seen him before.

"Hey, Harper."

"I think we might have a breakthrough with Birchwood. There's a sexual-conversion clinic outside of the Twin Cities—nationally known because the guy who runs it is the husband of Veronica Talbot, the whacked senator from the third district. Any guess what it's named?"

Brent squealed. "Of course. I've heard all about it, but I'd forgotten what it was called. We always referred to it as 'Talbot's pray-away-the-gay prison.'"

Harper leaned in. "Michael, do you know what we're talking about?"

"Sure. You think Luke Daniels might have undergone therapy there?"

"It's sure as hell a possibility. Daniels is a walking, talking example of how well that brainwashing shit really works." Harper sat back.

"I'll get right on this." Michael picked up on Harper's enthusiasm. "This could potentially be the piece of the puzzle you guys were hoping for."

"It's our fucking meal ticket if we can make the connection," Harper said.

"Do you guys have anything else for me? I need to make some calls and get the ball rolling on this."

"Brent, did you have anything?" Harper asked.

"Nope." He forced himself to breathe. They might have a very promising piece of information.

"I have one more thing," Michael shot out. "Have you guys ever considered Luke Daniels might be an alias?"

Locking eyes with Harper, Brent shrugged. The thought had never occurred to him.

"Oh no." Harper's shoulders sagged. "Why do you ask?"

"It's odd I haven't pulled up any hits on a Luke Daniels, other than a few records I've been able to pull from Patterson Police Academy. Sometimes the lack of hits is a red flag that maybe the individual we're after has an alias. Or two, or many, in some cases. Anyway, give it a thought."

"We'll do that." The look on Harper's face was hard to take. Brent ended the call. "Thanks, Michael."

"You know what this means, don't you?" Harper asked, slapping the side of his chair.

"Maybe not completely," Brent admitted. "But I have a feeling it's not good."

"Let's say Daniels is an alias. And let's say the first time he used it was at Patterson."

"Fuck." The pieces were starting to fall into place. Brent placed his head in his hands.

"If this turns out to be true, then it also means we don't have a fucking link to any history before Patterson. Most likely, he's used a bogus ID all along the way, but how the hell are we going to prove it? What a kick in the nuts. Especially given the time frame we have to work with, here."

Their elation over finding a meaningful connection with Birchwood had gone right into the shitter before they'd even had a chance to enjoy it. He wanted to cry. Suddenly the uphill climb appeared insurmountable. "How did you come upon the association of Birchwood to the Talbot clinic?" Brent asked, totally defeated.

"Theo's dad," Harper answered, crestfallen.

Brent fought the urge to laugh. He hadn't met Theo's father, but the image of him going through conversion therapy was more than he could take, given the fragile condition he was in.

"I know why you have that amused look on your face." Harper pointed a finger. "To my knowledge, Theo's father is confidently heterosexual and has never had reason to call that into question. Theo's fucking lucky he wasn't shanghaied into a program like Birchwood, given how his parents reacted over his sexuality when he met our little Alex."

"I'm sorry. I know Theo had a rough time." He had always hated how his mind took him in the opposite direction of what he expected. For a long time, he had hoped it would someday become an asset, in a "think outside the box" kind of way. To date, it had been nothing more than a pain in the ass. "How did Theo's father make the connection?"

"This is pretty remarkable." Harper was beginning to recover from the alias blow. "Apparently during one of their PFLAG meetings, the Engdahls heard an ex-employee from Birchwood speak about the dangers of—holy shit." Harper jumped out of his chair. "The guy from the PFLAG meeting. Maybe he could ID Daniels from our photos."

"How can I help?" Brent was on his feet. The energy in the room had gone up and down like a rollercoaster. A few minutes before, they had been faced with a case going nowhere fast. Then along came another reason to remain optimistic.

"I don't know yet." It was rare to see Harper pacing. "We have to find out where or how we can get to this guy. Wait." Harper came around the back of his chair and leaned into it. "We need to contact whoever it is that organizes the PFLAG meetings for the Duluth area. They should be able to provide contact information for this guy. I would be shocked if he refused to help us out."

"Let me take that piece," Brent begged. "I've got enough now to run with it."

"It's yours." Harper was out the door.

BRENT SPREAD the map out on the dashboard, and traced his finger along County Road C, hoping to locate his turnoff. It was starting to get dark. Either he had missed it, or he hadn't gone far enough.

*Where the fuck is it?*

Little did he know the easy part of his adventure had been obtaining the contact information for Oliver Morton, the guy from Birchwood who had spoken at PFLAG. Morton offered to meet up the following afternoon at his residence—a cabin on Lake Miller, located twenty miles Northwest of Duluth. Brent was looking for a wooden mailbox with Morton's name painted on the side and a yellow fire marker numbered twenty-three.

*You haven't gone far enough.*

Moving the map to the passenger seat, he turned his lights on bright and continued down the dirt road. To his relief, he rounded a curve and spotted the turnoff to Morton's cabin. He parked behind a white pickup, grabbed his computer bag, and walked to the door. He didn't have to knock. The door opened before he reached it.

"Saw the lights from your car. I'm Ollie."

Ollie was much older than Brent had anticipated. On the phone, his voice sounded more youthful. He was dressed in jeans and a faded Minnesota Twins sweatshirt.

"Hey, Ollie. I'm Brent. Pleased to meet you." It was clear from the moment he walked in the door that Ollie lived a simple life.

He led them to a screened porch that supposedly faced the lake. It was too dark to see much farther than a few feet into the trees.

"Thank you so much for agreeing to meet with me." Brent took the seat he was offered at the kitchen-style table nestled in the corner. He felt a strong urge to shove Daniels's picture in the man's face and not waste any more time. Instead he decided to open up with a bit of small talk. "Do you mind if I ask how you came to work at Birchwood?" Maybe the guy didn't get many visitors. Brent didn't want to be rude.

"Nobody has ever thought to ask that before. There's not much to tell really. Say, before we get started, can I offer you something to drink? A beer, maybe a soda? You came a long way."

"If you'll have one with me, I'll gladly take a beer." *Or two.*

"Coming right up." Ollie returned with two bottles of Grain Belt Premium.

"Cheers." Ollie sat. "I was a janitor at Birchwood for five years before moving here. Oh, excuse me. I was their *custodian.* That was my official title, but it's just a more complicated way of saying janitor, if you ask me." He chuckled.

"So, there was no specific reason you took a job there?" Brent asked.

"Not exactly." Ollie shifted in his seat. "I have a grandson who's homosexual. Timothy. When I first found that out, I about flipped a switch."

"I understand." He smiled.

"I'm a little ahead of myself. The job I had previous to Birchwood came to an end when the company went out of business. I needed to start working right away or face digging into my retirement. This—" Ollie waved his hand in a grand gesture. "—is my retirement, by the way."

"Must be nice." Brent didn't actually think so, but he knew it was the right response.

"It is. I'm the only cabin on the lake, which is why it's such a bitch to find me. Did you have any trouble?"

"No. Your directions were great," he lied again.

"I kind of got interested in the whole program at Birchwood because of Tim. At that point, I was hoping to help him, if I could. That is, I thought maybe there was something I could do to make him see life differently than the path he was on." Ollie sipped. With a broad smile, he continued, "If I knew then what I know now. But isn't that so many people's story?"

"I can sign up for that." Brent was happy to agree.

"Birchwood. It's a horrible place. It took me a while being there to notice it, but there's nothing good about the outfit. What those people do there, all in the name of God, is criminal."

"That's what I believe too." Brent hoisted his bottle and drank.

"Long story short, I worked there until I was sixty-five and could retire."

"How did you end up speaking at a PFLAG meeting?"

"Don't get me wrong. I love the solitude out here, but in the winter, you can go crazy. If I'm not fishing or hunting… well, then I need contact with the outside world. That brings us back to Tim. He's met someone now and has been in a relationship for several years. Thankfully us ignoramuses didn't work him over too badly. This kid he met, though, apparently his parents gave him a pretty hard time. That is, until they got themselves fixed up with PFLAG. I located a chapter in Duluth, and to get out of the house, started attending their meetings. I've sure learned a lot from those."

"I'm happy to hear things have worked out for your grandson. It can be a terrible struggle for some kids when they don't have support from family." *I'm such a lucky shithead for having the parents I did.*

"Right. Well, one night this husband and wife showed up at the meeting and asked if anyone had any experience with conversion therapy. I sat quiet as mouse to see if anyone would respond.

Nobody did. So I raised my hand, and in my usual fashion, told it the way I saw it. Wouldn't it be funny if those folks were the parents of your friend?"

*Not only funny, but highly probable.* "I wouldn't be surprised at all."

"You had some pictures you wanted me to look at?"

Captivated by Ollie's story, Brent had momentarily forgotten why he was there. "Yes." He reached into his bag and pulled out a folder. "This is the individual I mentioned to you on the phone." He removed two eight-by-ten photos and slid them across the table. "These pictures are very recent. If you can, try and picture someone who looks about five years younger. That's about the time he would have been there. About five years ago."

Ollie adjusted his glasses and studied the pictures. "Just a minute," he said, getting up from his chair. "The light is so poor out here. I'm going to head into the house where it's better."

Brent followed Ollie into the kitchen and the light from an overhead florescent fixture.

"Five years, you say?" Ollie asked.

"Probably," Brent answered, hoping his voice remained steady. The suspense was killing him. It meant so much to their case for Ollie to have a positive response.

"He looks familiar." His host switched back and forth between photos. "I seem to remember a young guy who could very well be the same as this one here."

Brent needed a little stronger conviction. "So you think the guy might have been a resident at Birchwood?" he asked.

"I do. Yes."

"Do you recall his name?" He hoped with all his might Ollie could pull it up.

"Offhand? I don't. Maybe if I heard it."

"Luke. His first name might have been Luke." Brent took a long pull from his bottle and waited.

"Luke. I've got to be honest with you. My memory isn't good to begin with. That doesn't ring a bell." Ollie handed back the photos. "On a scale of one to ten, I'd say the chances of this guy being the one I remember is a solid seven."

For a minute, Brent thought he had hit a bull's-eye. *A solid seven? Shit.* He struggled to not appear disappointed. "I'll take a seven." He hoped Ollie didn't pick up on his frustration. It sure wasn't his fault. Five years was a long time for anyone's memory.

"You helped. Really helped. Thank you so much for agreeing to meet." He placed his empty bottle on the counter. "I should get going."

Back on the county road, Brent placed a call to Harper. "Hey. I'm on my way home."

"How did it go?"

"We got a seven out of ten." Brent said.

"Great. See you in the morning."

"You don't even know what that means." He laughed at Harper's response.

"Yes I do."

"It sounds like you're trying to get rid of me. Did I call at a bad… I mean, a bad-good time?" Brent pried.

"This guy you met up with gives the certainty Daniels was at Birchwood a rating of seven out of a possible ten. How did I do?"

"I have to go now. Love you." Sometimes it pissed Brent off that Harper could be so keen.

It was Harper's turn to laugh. "Are you bummed about the rating?"

"Yeah. I am." It had also been a very long day. And the next day would be a very long day, and so would the next. Such was the life of an attorney preparing for trial.

"I'm not, at all. The guy sounds like he was just being honest. He could have lied and said a ten. Or worse, Daniels could have scored a zero. I say, nice work, counselor."

"Thanks. That's the better way to look at this." Harper's reasoning did make him feel more confident.

"Drive safely and get some sleep. I'll see you in the morning."

"Sounds good."

By the time he passed through Duluth, Brent had made up his mind. He dialed Owen.

"Hey, hon," he answered in a sleepy voice.

"Did I wake you?"

"It's okay. I'm still downstairs. I must have fallen asleep on the couch listening to music." Owen yawned.

Brent yawned in return. "I had a meeting with someone tonight. I'm finally on my way home."

"You had a long day."

It would be so nice to crawl into a bed with a warm Owen. *Stick to the plan.* "I'm ready to drop. I think it would be best if I stayed at my own place."

"Get a good night's sleep and call me tomorrow."

"I will." The urge was there to say more, but Brent couldn't come up with anything that felt right. *How do you communicate feelings for someone when you can't voice them yourself?*

# CHAPTER Twelve

"I AM here to prove to you that my client, Owen Nathaniel Grady, had no intention of committing a crime." Understanding the power of a pause, Harper waited a few beats before continuing. "He was simply there to enjoy the beauty of the park and to partake in one of his favorite hobbies, bird-watching." Taking a few steps back from the makeshift podium, he asked, "How was that?"

"I like the simplicity of the end, and it works better now that you've taken your voice down a few notches. The section before that, where you summarize Owen's attributes? It still needs something. It needs to be stronger," Brent advised.

Standing at the opposite end of the conference room, Brent's job was to critique the opening statement. Harper insisted he be brutally honest and had encouraged him to suggest ways to make it more effective. He didn't care how they got there. It had to be pitch-perfect, and he knew from experience, you didn't get to that place if you were hindered by pride of ownership.

"Is it too saccharine?" It didn't feel right. It was not a closing argument. He didn't want to alienate anyone, and certainly not before he had a chance to present their entire case. It was imperative they win over members of the jury as soon as possible.

"Just the opposite," Brent advised. "I would slow down here too. Milk each of these attributes so the jury has the time to consider them individually. Right now it sounds like a package, and personally I think it loses impact that way. Does that make sense?"

This was good stuff. Brent was invested, and that's exactly what he needed. "It makes complete sense." Flipping back several pages, Harper added slashes with a highlighter to indicate where the breaks should go. Then, he grabbed his pen and wrote, "Slow down here." The script would be his guide, but he would memorize it.

"One of my law school professors did an excellent job of breaking down an opening statement," Brent recalled. "One comment, in particular, really stuck with me. He said that at this stage of the game, you're planting seeds with the jury. These seeds will grow and blossom into a favorable result for your client if you allow them to have the time they need to germinate." Brent laughed. "I'm easily impressed, maybe."

"There are a million books and papers written on opening statements. But honestly, I've never heard that piece explained so effectively." *Go Brent.* "That gives me an idea."

"What's that?"

"Piggybacking on your professor's theory, what if I presented our client's strengths in a way that removed all argument?" Pointing his finger in the air, he completed his thought before sharing, "I'd like to convince the jury, by being more deliberate in this section, that it's impossible to argue with who our client is. Owen is wholesome, stable, and well regarded in his profession. How could you ever believe he's possible of these crimes?"

"Okay. I'm catching on." Brent paced along the wall. "Yes. Absolutely do that if you can achieve results without sounding pompous."

"I certainly don't want *that.*" It was a fine line. "I'm warning the jury not to be influenced by how the prosecution has portrayed Owen."

"I really like that, Harper." Brent pulled out a chair and collapsed. "This is going to be a strong opening. I'm feeling so much better. How about you?"

"Let's take a short break, and then, if you don't mind, I'd like to go through it one more time."

"I'll keep at this as long as you want." Brent checked his phone for messages.

Earlier in the day, Brent had appeared withdrawn and sullen. Harper thought about bringing it up, but then decided it might be better to just let him be. It had to be hard. Brent's heart was invested. Time was down to the wire, and so far they didn't have a strong hand to play against their opponent. Once they'd rolled up their sleeves and begun picking apart the opening, his mood had changed.

Fortified with a fresh mug of coffee, Harper stepped up to the podium. “Clock this one.” During the break, he had decided it was time to throw everything he had into the delivery—as he would do when the actual jury was his audience. The material, foreign and rough when he started working it, was now familiar and smooth. The areas highlighted for special emphasis added both texture and a touch of the dramatic. Owen’s defense was serious business.

The phone on the table buzzed. Fern was already gone for the day.

“Fuck.” Harper slapped his script down.

Brent answered the call. “Brent Burns.”

“Hey, Brent. It’s Michael Smuckler.”

“Oh hi, Michael. Harper’s here. We’re working on trial prep. What’s up?”

“Hello, Michael.” If Harper was going to be interrupted by anyone, this was the guy. *Please let this be good news.*

“I just got off the phone with my guy in California. Tonight a few people canvassed bars in the Castro with the pictures of Daniels. We have a positive identification on the photo. Actually two men in two separate clubs said they had seen him before. Both men remembered him as a regular in the area during the time frame we’re targeting, and one guy thought his first name was something like Derrick, but he couldn’t remember for sure.

“Fantastic.” Harper sat on the edge of the table and waited for more detail.

“Way to go,” Brent piped in.

“Derrick.” Harper rubbed his chin. “That’s much better than John or Michael.”

“Right. It’s a more distinctive first name, to be sure. And the guy who thinks his name was Derrick remembers a New Year’s Eve party your guy attended. It was memorable because of a fight Daniels was involved in at the apartment where the party was taking place. Sounds like your guy might have anger issues.”

Thrusting his fist in the air, Brent shouted, “Yes. That fits with our suspicions perfectly.”

"I thought you'd like that part," Michael concurred. "It's good stuff."

"And trial starts tomorrow morning at nine." Harper got up and walked back to the podium. It wasn't any fun raining on the parade. "Where does that leave us, Michael?"

"The last thing I want to do is offer false hope. Have you discussed asking for a continuance?"

Back on his side of the room, Brent leaned into the corner, a deflated look on his face.

"It's an impossible calculation, I know, but how much time do you need to work this?" Harper asked.

"As much time as you can get. My buddy on the west coast is fired up, and I can guarantee you I won't be getting any sleep tonight."

"I need to discuss this further with Brent. The political climate here is complicated." He tilted his head back and sighed.

"If you get a continuance or you don't, it doesn't make much difference to me right now. I've got a lead, which to me is like a fresh log on the fire. I'll work it until I hit a dead end."

"One of us will call you in the morning for an update." He looked at Brent. A less-than-enthusiastic nod was all he got in response.

"I'll have my cell nearby all night. Don't hesitate to call if you need to," Brent offered, appearing to come out of his slump.

"That sounds good. I wish I had more for you guys, but at least it's something."

"Thanks again, Michael." Leaning across the table, Harper released the call.

"Between a rock and a hard place," Brent said. "What are you thinking?"

What was he thinking? "A day late and a dollar short. Your turn." Harper grabbed his mug, carried it to Brent's end of the table, and took a seat. "When you think about it, it's not much, is it?"

"No. But it's more than we had before the call. I keep trying to stay positive. How am I doing?" Brent appeared on the verge of complete despair but had somehow found a smile to share.

Asking for a continuance was a risk. If they got one, they had to make it count. Particularly when the odds were stacked against them. "I'm leaning toward asking for a continuance," Harper announced, more for himself than Brent. "It's a risk, but it's one I guess I'm willing to take."

Brent put his elbow on the table and rested his head in his hands. "I was hoping you would say that."

"Let's make the final call in the morning. Maybe we'll have heard from Smuckler again." Glancing at his watch—it was after seven—he wondered if it would do any good to run through the opening again. Did he have the energy to give it his all? "How did the last run-through sound?"

"Spot on." Brent sat up in his chair. "Seriously, I thought it was all working."

Harper was relieved. "Well, that's good, because this old man is running out of steam, and tomorrow is going to be one hell of a day."

"How should we work tomorrow?" Tapping his pen on the table, Brent seemed just as relieved to have his day winding down.

"Let's meet here at seven. I want to run through the opening at least one more time before we head over to the courthouse." *What else?* He ran through a checklist he had somewhere in the back of his mind. "I saw the trial binders on Fern's desk. We should go through them and make sure they're in order. I think we can tackle both of those tasks in an hour and a half without too much strain, don't you? I want to leave for the courthouse at eight thirty."

"That's plenty of time. What about Owen?" Brent asked.

"Owen. Owen who?" He couldn't resist the tease. "I'll leave that up to you. Either ask him to come with you at seven, or make sure he's here before we leave at eight thirty. I'll say a few things to him in the car on the way over. And make sure he wears a jacket and tie."

"Fuck. I'm glad you mentioned that." Brent laughed. "Seriously, I hadn't even thought about it."

"I bet he cleans up really nice," Harper opined.

"Glasses or contacts?" Brent asked with a grin.

"You're talking about Owen who?"

"Yes."

Harper stood and began gathering his notes. "You pick." Brent obviously had a reason for asking, and frankly he didn't care.

"He looks more scholarly in glasses. That's my vote." Brent stood by the door.

"Works for me." Harper stopped. "Hang in there, pal."

"I'm good. Your opening is killer. Owen's innocent. We're living life large." Brent patted Harper on the shoulder and headed to his office.

"That we are, my friend."

Back at his desk, Harper called home. "Hey, pumpkin."

"Hi, Binky. Late night?" Ian asked.

Harper could hear water running. Ian was most likely in the kitchen. There were times when just a voice was all he needed. It triggered a pool of unexpected energy. "Nope. I'm just leaving. Do you want me to pick up something for dinner?"

"You can if you're in a fussy mood and can't sign up for BLT's and tomato-basil soup. I wanted to make something you could eat whenever you got your ass home. Sound okay?"

"That sounds so good." He stashed most of the contents of his desk into his shoulder bag. "What's for desert?"

"Pecker cream pie if you remember to wash your hands before dinner."

"Ha." Harper shut off the light and walked down the hall. "See you in a few."

"Drive safe, Bink."

Stopping at Brent's door, Harper asked, "Is there something I can help you with so you can get the hell out of here?"

"I'm organizing for tomorrow. I'll be gone in five minutes." It appeared Brent had also found some untapped energy after their working session.

"Good night, partner. Be safe."

"Good night, Harper."

"Pecker cream pie," he chuckled getting into the car. *How did I get so lucky to have such an awesome husband?*

"WHAT AN unexpected treat." Naked, Owen stretched out on the beach towel Brent had placed on top of his bedding. "I've never had a massage like this, but I'm pretty sure I'm going to like it."

"I've been told I have magic fingers," Brent shared while he inventoried a cluster of supplies he had gathered from the bathroom.

"That doesn't surprise me in the least."

Before he left the office, Brent had called to say he was done for the evening. They decided he would stop on his way home and pick up dinner from the Lip Smacker. Due to the early call the next morning, they would hang out at his place and play the rest of the evening by ear.

"There. That's everything I need. Brent unbuttoned his shirt and let it drop to the floor. Pants, underwear, and socks followed. "I love giving massages." He squeezed oil into his hands and vigorously rubbed them together. "Nice and warm."

Owen was caught by surprise when Brent moved to the end of the bed and cradled his foot in his lap. With considerable force he began working the oil into and around each of his toes. "People don't always remember to spend time on the feet. I like to start here and work my way up."

"I'm a little ticklish," Owen confessed with a giggle. That was true, but most of his delight came from the highly professional air his masseur had assumed.

"I'll try not to tickle." Brent moved on to the ball of his foot and used his knuckles to knead the area so hard that Owen yelped. "Relax," Brent encouraged. "You'll get used to it."

Or maybe not. Owen buried his head into the pillow and longed for a less-challenging time. *Damn he's wound up.*

When Brent had worked his way up to the ankle, he placed one foot on the bed, took up the other, and put it through an identical torment. "You'll really notice a difference when you walk after this."

*I don't doubt that for a minute.*

Brent switched focus from Owen's feet to his calves. Years of biking had made the lower portion of his legs hard with muscle. Perhaps sensing a stronger touch was needed, Brent upped his game and attacked the area with a vengeance, using an elaborate combination of both knuckles and fingers. "God I love your calves," he admired, his voice strained and labored from his efforts.

"I do too," Owen responded with a grunt and gripped the side of the bed, fearful of what was to come. There had been signs of trouble the minute Brent walked into the backyard with dinner. Maybe nerves were affecting Brent's ability to relax. It was easy to see the toll the case was taking on his handsome lover. But tonight was entirely different. Brent was antsy and struggled to stay focused in a conversation, as if his mind were involved in a heated game of ping-pong. When Brent suggested they head upstairs, Owen was all for it. Spirited sex had a great way of calming. But he was discovering the massage was a big mistake. If anything, it encouraged his chaotic behavior.

"I like to use different oils on each part of the body." Brent was back at the bedside table reloading his palms. "This one has a tiny bit of grit. Very stimulating."

Brent moved back to the end of the bed, shoved a hand up under Owen's torso, and yanked his junk out from under him.

"Stop," Owen commanded and jumped off of the bed. "Holy shit. I can hardly walk." His feet ached and his legs felt like spaghetti.

"What's wrong?" Brent stepped back. "I thought you were enjoying it."

Sensing action might be more effective, Owen nabbed Brent by the arm and pulled him facedown onto the bed. He followed this lightning-quick maneuver by using his entire body to pin Brent down. "I'm sorry, honey," Owen whispered, inches from Brent's ear. "We need to find a different way of releasing this aggression you brought home. I can't take it."

"I'm sorry," a tiny, smothered voice eeked back.

He rode Brent until finally, after several minutes had passed while Brent panted like a mad man, Owen felt his body begin to calm. "There, that's better." He kissed Brent's neck, rolled over on his side, and enveloped Brent in his arms. "There, baby. Just relax."

"I didn't mean to hurt you."

"Shush. I'm not hurt." *I can't wait for tomorrow to be over.* "I want you to listen to me," he requested softly. "You have to trust that no matter what happens tomorrow, we will still have each other. And to me, that's more important than anything else. I know you're working hard for me, and I'm glad you are, but regardless of the outcome, we've won. You have to believe that."

Chilled by an evening breeze wafting through the room, Owen got up and pulled the covers from under Brent. He climbed back into bed, took Brent back into his arms, and pulled the bedding up around them both. “There’s nothing you can do tonight. Let it all go. Tomorrow we’ll wake up, and then we’ll head off and slay the big, old dragon.”

“Owen?”

“Yes”

“I hope this doesn’t scare you, but I have to say it. Now feels right.”

“Say what, hon?”

“I love you,” Brent purred.

“And I love you, my fierce warrior.” Owen kissed the top of Brent’s head. “Sleep tight.”

WORD HAD obviously gotten around that Owen’s trial began today. The courtroom—usually empty, with the exception of the attorneys, court staff, and jury—was packed. Brent fought off nerves as he stood and watched the Honorable Henry Tompkins enter and take his seat.

Not unexpectedly there had been no further word from Michael Smuckler. As if to counter the disappointment, Harper had flawlessly run through his opening. They were as ready as they could possibly be.

As agreed, the only witness would be Daniels. Dressed in a crisp uniform, he was seated across the room next to the district attorney, Todd Hansen, who represented him at the deposition. They both appeared far more relaxed than Brent would have liked.

Owen, dressed in a gray suit, white shirt, powder blue tie, and his glasses, sat between his attorneys.

After several minutes of organizing, Tompkins gave a nod to the court deputy, who announced, “The State of Minnesota versus Owen Nathaniel Grady.”

“Good morning,” Tompkins greeted the room in a “business as usual” manner. “Counsel, are you ready to proceed?”

“We are, Your Honor,” the district attorney stood and replied.

Harper rose. “Your Honor, may I approach the bench?”

“I see it’s going to be one of those mornings,” Tompkins commented flatly, peering over his glasses. “You may.”

Dressed impeccably in a tailored navy blue suit, Harper stepped around the table and walked up to the judge, who placed his hand over his microphone to prevent the rest of the courtroom from hearing the exchange. Brent didn’t need to hear their conversation. Harper would reveal recent developments to support his request for a continuance.

“You’ve had how many weeks to prepare for this trial?” Tompkins asked loudly enough to carry deep into the room.

It was clear the judge was reluctant to grant the extension. Brent gripped his knees under the table and waited for Harper to respond.

“Within the last twenty-four hours,” Harper argued, apparently unconcerned his voice too could be heard past the bench, “I have received new information I think the court will ultimately find substantive, once I’ve had an opportunity to corroborate its authenticity. It is not without great consideration that I come before you with this request.”

“Todd, would you approach the bench please?”

*Great. The judge is on a first-name basis with the prosecution.* Brent wanted to scream. Owen stared ahead with a blank look, his hands folded on the table. Brent spied several members of the jury spending a good deal of time observing him. To anyone paying attention, he was projecting the image they wanted—calm and collected.

“Officer Daniels is extremely busy,” Hansen complained. “Schedules were rearranged to allow for his time here today. I would encourage Your Honor to refuse this request.”

The DA wasn’t at all happy about the possibility of a delay. From experience, he probably knew it would damage his case. Something unexpected had developed that was significant enough to have an impact on the verdict.

Harper and Brent had discussed the risk of requesting a continuance. It could be perceived as stalling. Brent hoped the jury would see it as an honest move in the quest for the truth.

"I certainly hope this isn't a waste of our time, counselor," Tompkins warned. "I'll give you twenty-four hours and not a minute more."

"Thank you, Your Honor."

*Are you fucking kidding me?* Brent was stunned. He had secretly hoped for a couple of weeks, or at the very least, one week. Twenty-four hours was almost counterproductive, given the damage it may have already wreaked on their ability to win over the jury.

Banging his gavel, Tompkins barked, "Court is adjourned. This case will resume tomorrow morning at 9:00 a.m. sharp."

"WHAT A fucking crock of shit." Brent pouted, not caring how stupid he looked. "Twenty-four hours is a slap in the face."

"It's twenty-four hours we didn't have. I'm disappointed too, but I'm not all that surprised." Harper took another bite of the chopped salad he had been playing with for five minutes. "It's the middle of the week. They probably have a loaded docket. At least we got something."

Pushing his partially eaten chicken salad sandwich away because his appetite had vanished, Brent sipped his ice tea in disgust.

"Let's see, it's just noon here, so that makes it 10:00 a.m. on the West Coast. Michael might have something in the works we don't know about. Let's give him a call, and at the very least, let him know we have another day to work with." Harper flicked a crumb off his chin.

Brent leaned over the table and punched in the number. The phone rang four times, and then the greeting kicked in, "Hello. You have reached the Michael Smuckler Agency. I'm currently away from my phone. Please leave a detailed message, and I will get back to you as soon as I can."

"Michael, it's Brent. I'm here with Harper. We won a twenty-four hour continuance. Give us a call when you can to strategize."

"He could be asleep," Harper speculated. "Who knows how late he worked."

"We're not paying him to sleep," Brent shot back only half-serious, surprised to have voiced his inner thoughts without filtering.

"Listen to you." Harper chuckled. "It's okay. I feel the same way. How did you think Owen handled today?" he asked, changing the subject.

"I think he's doing better than I am, actually."

"He's a nice guy, Brent. I'm enjoying getting to know him better. You guys seem like a good fit." Harper loaded his fork with selective pieces of salad, shoved it in his mouth, and chewed.

"Thanks." Brent thought about elaborating, but his thoughts were interrupted by an incoming call.

"Hey, guys, Michael Smuckler is on the line," Fern reported without any hint she was referring to her son.

"Hi, Michael," Brent answered.

"Hi Michael," Harper echoed.

"Hey, guys. Sorry I missed your call. I was in the shower."

"We thought you might have been sleeping." Harper displayed a mischievous grin.

"Hell no," the investigator answered with a laugh. "There's no time for sleep. Especially when you only have twenty-four hours to pull a rabbit out of a hat."

Smuckler sounded punchy. Brent felt a pang of guilt for his earlier comment.

"About that rabbit…," Harper responded with a wink. "Do you have anything new for us?"

"We're still trying to nail down the name. I'm confident once we have that, the doors will open for us. I'm doing everything in my power to make that happen."

"I know you are," Harper sympathized. "I'm assuming you have contact information for the guys who recognized him from the photo."

"We do. Well, it would be sloppy work on our part if we didn't. I'm assuming we do and I'll confirm that once we are off the phone."

*Why did Harper ask that?* Something must have hatched he hadn't had the chance to share.

"Brent and I are going to work this afternoon on tailoring our defense based on these guys identifying Daniels. As a precaution, I'm going to fax you affidavits for their signature. At least to the jury, that might make it look like we have something more substantive than we do."

"Do you think the judge might issue a second continuance when he sees those?" Michael asked.

Brent smiled. He and Michael had the same question on their minds.

"I guess it's possible," Harper speculated. "But not likely. It seems the judge might be in bed with the DA on this one. Like friends with benefits, they appear to have history."

Michael laughed. "Okay. I get the picture."

"Brent?" Harper asked. "Do you have anything else for Michael before we let him crawl back into bed?"

"Easy," the investigator cried out in defense.

"I don't. Thanks for all you're doing, Michael."

"Let's plan on talking sometime around the dinner hour," Harper proposed.

"I'll be here. Later."

"So, when did the affidavit thingy surface?" Brent asked.

"I'm fluid. Always on the rebound." Shoving the remainder of his salad back in the bag, Harper tossed it into the wastebasket on the other side of the table. "He scores!"

"That did not just happen." Brent shook his head. "I'll head back to my desk and throw together the affidavits for you to review."

"Let's hand that one off to Fern. I need you here to bounce ideas around on our new and improved defense." Harper turned on the intercom. "Fern? You there?"

"I'm here."

"Can you stop by for a minute?"

"Be right there."

"WHEN'S THE last time you checked for a fax?" Harper asked through a yawn. It was after 10:00 p.m. "California has had almost eight hours to get signatures on the affidavits. I don't like how this feels," he shared and then wished he hadn't. It was up to the leader to remain positive.

"Five minutes ago, when I got up to pee." Slumped in his chair, Brent was exhibiting signs of defeat.

It was late. Harper thought the best thing to do was to touch base with Michael to make sure they had the latest greatest. If there weren't any new developments, it was time to go home and try to sleep. "Let's give him a call." He gestured to the phone. "Waiting any longer is ridiculous."

"This is Michael," he answered after a long series of rings. He sounded groggy.

"Guess who?" Exhausted, Harper was unable to do much more than spew words toward the phone.

"Hey. You woke me up," Michael admitted. "I was sneaking in a few winks."

"No worries. We're just about to call it a day here too. Any news?" he asked.

"I spoke to California about an hour ago. For whatever reason, the guys who identified Daniels aren't returning calls. It's like they're spooked or something. We'll keep trying, but honestly, it doesn't look good."

"Fuck." Frustrated, Harper tossed his notepad against the wall. "Spooked?"

Several seconds ticked by without a response from their investigator. *That's it. I'm pulling the plug on this.* "Michael, I don't know what more you can do between now and court tomorrow. Get some sleep, and we'll talk later in the week. I guess we shouldn't rule out an appeal, if it comes to that. I sure hope to fuck it doesn't." Looking at Brent, who appeared near tears, he mouthed, "What else can we do?"

"What time are you guys back in tomorrow? Or are you heading right over to the courthouse?"

"We'll probably gather here a good hour before leaving. Certainly I'll be here by eight, if not sooner." He couldn't bring himself to sign Brent up for more than what was needed.

"Okay. Well, I'm sorry we're ending the day like this. I'll call if I hear anything. You can count on that," Michael pledged.

"Thanks again." Stiff from spending hours in his chair, Harper stood up. "You okay?"

"I'll be fine. Just disappointed." The color had drained from Brent's face. He was running on fumes, both physically and emotionally.

"Are you hooking up with Owen tonight?" Harper walked to the door and waited for Brent to follow.

"No. I called him around eight, and we decided it was best to be on our own."

"Will you take responsibility for making sure he's at court on time? Not that I worry, but one of us should be watching out for him." Harper shut off the light.

"I will do that."

"Our case isn't the best, and it isn't the worst. It's workable. Don't lose hope, my friend. Okay?" He patted Brent affectionately on the shoulder.

"I'm trying to be adult about this." Brent plodded down the hall. *Okay, Mr. Harper Callahan. You better argue your fucking ass off tomorrow. There's some serious shit at stake here.*

BRENT FELT like he had never left the courthouse. Nerves and lack of sleep made the events of the past two days a blur. The condescending tone of the district attorney was starting to piss him off. *Wrap it up, you fucking right-wing dickhead.*

"Many of you may recall the tragedy that occurred in Duluth a few years back. A young man lost his life participating in the same type of deviant behavior as Mr. Grady. It's important for you, the jury, as representatives of this community, to send a clear message to Mr. Grady, as well as others, that this behavior is not tolerated now, nor will it ever be tolerated, and those who break the rules will be punished to the full extent of the law. I know you will give this matter careful consideration. You'll no doubt be offered many excuses and explanations by the defense in their attempt to prove their client's innocence. That's what they are paid to do."

Referencing his notes as he had several times, the stodgy DA flipped over a page in his tattered legal pad and continued. “As an investment in the safety of our children, don’t allow fancy talk to cloud the truth. What Mr. Grady did in our beautiful forest is unacceptable and unforgivable. Thank you.”

Infuriated by the prosecution’s opening statement, Brent summoned every ounce of restraint he could muster and stared forward, careful not to show any sign of anger. Linking Owen to an event that took place five years ago was a cheap ploy. That, and the fact Michael was unable to come up with any further leads, made their job even tougher. Seated on the opposite side of their client, he wondered what was running through Harper’s mind. And what was Owen thinking? It had to be horrible being associated with such a despicable event. Thankfully Harper had prepared Owen on the ride to the courthouse that the DA might take the low road.

Like the day before, the courtroom was filled with curious locals.

Judge Tompkins jotted something down, then looked up and asked, “Mr. Callahan, are you ready?”

“Yes, Your Honor. I am.”

Dressed in a gray pinstripe suit, Harper approached the jury without his notes.

“Good morning, ladies and gentlemen.” Resting his hand on the rail separating the jury box from the main area of the courtroom, Harper glanced at his nemesis and smiled. He turned back to the jury, without the smile, and spoke with a clear and even voice. “A lot of assumptions were made by Mr. Hansen a minute ago.”

In an earnest and conversational way, Harper went off script and systematically discredited the prosecution’s accusations. The entire time he spoke he moved along the railing, ensuring he made a connection to each and every juror. It was masterful to watch how he played to them. They rewarded his easy style with looks of compassion and consideration. Harper was delivering the goods.

With a flawless segue, Harper worked back to his planned opening. He excelled when he described Owen’s admirable qualities and achievements, spending just the right amount of time on each component.

The contrast in skill between the two attorneys could not have been more striking. Brent stifled a grin and, with a sigh of relief, relaxed in his chair as Harper launched into the final segment.

"I am here to prove to you that my client, Owen Nathaniel Grady, had no intention of exposing himself to anyone." And just as they had rehearsed, he paused before ending with, "He was simply there to enjoy the beauty of the forest and to partake in one of his favorite hobbies—bird-watching. Thank you."

Harper returned to his seat without any indication he was pleased with his performance.

"In light of yesterday's delay," Judge Tompkins stated with a perceivable hint of annoyance, "I'm going to ask that we move right along. Mr. Hansen, are you ready to call your witness to the stand?"

*Fuck off.* Brent dreaded the day he would have to argue in front of this judge.

"I am, Your Honor. The state calls Officer Luke Daniels to the stand."

Brent watched the jury intently as Daniels sauntered up and took his seat to the left of Tompkins. There were no smiles or any outward indications of allegiance. When would they be given the opportunity to question his legitimacy? Would the arrogance they witnessed in the deposition leak out to tarnish his credibility? It was definitely the officer's game to lose. *Lie your ass off, asshole. Harper will annihilate you.*

"Officer Daniels, can you tell us where you were on the morning of June fourth?" Hansen asked.

"Yes, sir. On my way into the station, I made a stop at Connor's Point."

"Connor's Point in the Superior National Forest?"

"Yes, sir."

The DA took a minute to check over his notes and then asked, "Why did you stop there?"

"Connor's Point has a history of being the location where underage drinking takes place. We, I mean the department, makes it a point to keep an eye on it."

"I see. So you were there officially, and not for your own personal recreation. Is that correct?"

"Yes, sir."

"Were you dressed in uniform?"

"I was not. In the summer, I usually change when I get to the station."

"Sure." Hansen nodded as if this were the most logical thing in the world. "I think we all understand you were, in fact, killing two birds with one stone. By that I mean you were knocking off a scheduled duty while on your way into work."

"Exactly."

"What did you find when you got to Connor's Point?"

"Not much. There was a little action earlier in the spring, before graduation. But at least then, it wasn't being used for any illegal purposes that I could tell."

Hansen again referred to his notes. An excruciating amount of time passed before he appeared ready to continue. A few members of the jury began to fidget, and there were multiple bursts of coughing. To Brent's dismay, the only positive thing the prosecution had was Daniels. The officer was presenting in a believable way, which helped make up for the DA's inability to keep track of his questions.

"Okay. So let me ask—what did you do after your inspection of Connor's Point?"

*Let the games begin.*

"It was a beautiful morning, so I thought I'd head a little farther down the trail to see if there were any visible signs of drinking or partying beyond Connor's Point."

"Had you come into contact with the defendant at this point?"

"No, sir."

"When did you first encounter Mr. Grady?"

Interest in Daniels' testimony had silenced the room. Hansen was getting into the specifics everyone was waiting for. This would be a difficult stretch for Owen to sit through without becoming upset. He hoped they had adequately prepared him for what was coming.

"There's a curve in the trail. It's the first one after Connor's Point. When I rounded it, Mr. Grady was standing a couple hundred feet ahead of me. Maybe a little more."

To Brent's delight, Hansen broke his momentum again by having to reference notes. *Alzheimer's?* It was painfully delicious to watch.

"Sorry, I wanted to make sure I didn't miss anything." Hansen smiled at the jury and then asked, "What was the defendant doing when you first spotted him?"

"He was standing in the middle of the trail looking in my direction, like he was waiting for me."

"Waiting," the DA repeated. "Could you elaborate, please?"

"His hands were in his pockets, and he was smiling. He wasn't watching birds."

"At this point did you suspect any inappropriate behavior?"

"Your Honor," Harper said, rising from his chair, "I object. This is entirely speculative and without evidentiary support."

"Overruled. I don't think there is any harm asking the question." Gesturing to Daniels, Tompkins instructed, "Answer the question."

"In law enforcement we're taught to listen to our instincts. Sometimes they can save you, or someone else. Instinctively I had certain suspicions."

"How did you choose to act on these suspicions?"

"I advanced toward him."

Daniels, as if asking approval, looked at the jury. It was an odd move, ripe for misinterpretation. Whether the glance was a conscious or unconscious decision, Brent was certain it worked against Daniels.

"So, up to this point, you were acting on instinct. When did the defendant display inappropriate or offensive behavior that supported this instinct?"

"Almost immediately. As I got closer, he reached down with his hand and started touching himself."

Harper was back on his feet. "Your Honor, I object. This is wildly speculative and begs for misinterpretation."

Peering over his glasses, Tompkins evaluated the request and then asked, "Mr. Hansen, can you rephrase your question?"

"Yes, Your Honor." After shuffling his papers, Hansen asked, "At what point did you know for certain the defendant was behaving inappropriately?" Daniels took a moment to think the question over. "When I got to within fifty feet of Mr. Grady, he placed his hand on the crotch of his shorts and began massaging that area while looking directly at me with a smile on his face."

"And how did you react?"

"I was shocked. The gesture was so suggestive it allowed for only one interpretation."

"And that would be?"

Shuffling in his chair, Daniels stole another glance at the jury and then answered with what Brent was sure was a calculated, planned sign of discomfort. "He was making a pass at me."

Harper shot up out of his chair. "I object."

Before he had the chance to finish, the door in the back of the courtroom banged open. Brent turned and watched Fern charge down the aisle.

"Fern Smuckler," Judge Tompkins said in surprise. "What are you doing in my courtroom?"

"Good morning, Your Honor." Fern walked behind the defense's table and presented a folder to Harper. "The top sheet summarizes the contents," she pointed out under her breath.

"To what do we owe the honor? You're not connected with this bunch are you?" Tompkins asked with a wink.

"I'm going to sit down in back, if you need me," Fern informed, ignoring the judge.

"Perfect. Thank you." Harper unclipped the top page of the folder and leaned across Owen to hand it to Brent. "There is a Santa Claus," Harper whispered.

"I hate to interfere with your lunch order," Tompkins commented dryly, "but I believe we have a trial going on here."

"Your Honor?" Harper stood. "May I approach the bench?"

"Make it quick."

Brent was reading Fern's synopsis and paid no attention to the exchange between Harper and the judge. It appeared Michael had come through for them in a very big way.

Harper presented the folder to the judge and waited while he looked it over. A conversation ensued and then the judge said, "We're going to take a short recess. Counselors, please meet in my chambers. Ladies and gentlemen, we will resume shortly. I'm thinking no more than fifteen minutes."

Harper signaled for Fern to join them at the table. "Owen," he whispered. "Fern is going to stay with you until we get back from chambers. I can't take the time to go into it now, but we received some incredibly damaging evidence on Daniels."

Unable to contain himself, Brent reached over and gave Owen's arm a squeeze. "It's the fucking best."

Daniels had left the stand and was engaged in what appeared to be an intense discussion with his attorney. Brent tapped Harper on the shoulder so he would have an opportunity to observe the exchange.

"I wonder if our buddy there has any idea what we stumbled upon," Brent asked with a chuckle he couldn't suppress.

"Let's hope not. It will add to the drama down the road." Harper winked and then turned back to Fern.

"First," Harper said, reaching for Fern's hand. "Thank you so much for taking the initiative to get this to us. Buckets of gold stars for you."

"My pleasure." She beamed.

"Stay here with Owen until we get back. I have no idea how Tompkins is going to react to this."

"His bark is much worse than his bite," Fern said with a giggle. "I actually like him."

"That's one person on the planet. Do we have another?" Harper signaled to Brent. "We need to fly."

Tompkins' chamber was an odd mix of office space and library. It contained two desks, one massive, his own, and another much smaller, most likely for his clerk.

The judge's first question was directed at the DA. "Were you aware of any of this?"

"I'm not sure what you have." Hansen looked as if he were about to shit his pants.

"It appears Officer Daniels hasn't been entirely truthful. With anyone," the judge tacked on with a snort. "Merrick Jon Reynolds. According to these documents, he's the son of California senator

Mitch Reynolds. The picture is pretty conclusive, if you ask me. Is this high school?" Tompkins looked to Harper for clarification.

*This is too good to be true.* Brent's heart was racing. *Mitch Reynolds is one of the most conservative, right-wing senators in the country. He's the pig who led the battle against Proposition 8.*

"No, sir," Harper clarified. "It's from a small publication distributed in the Castro. The accompanying article I mentioned to you is attached. The date is on the header."

While they waited for the judge to finish reading, the ancient cuckoo clock on the wall behind his desk rang once, signaling the half hour.

"These are serious charges," Tompkins said, handing the fax to Hansen. "There should be court documents supporting these charges."

"I would think so," Harper agreed. "At the very least, it brings up questions regarding the application he submitted for employment with the county. Who knows how many false identities this guy has been operating with. The fact he's connected with the beating of a gay man that was so severe it nearly killed him, indicates to me this guy has serious issues."

"I can't disagree. In all my years, I've never seen anything like this. I can't imagine how Trout Simmons is going to react." The judge motioned for the DA to hand back the fax.

"Your Honor, what do we do with my client?" Harper asked.

That was the million-dollar question. As good as the information was for Owen's defense, it might be premature to ask that his charges be dropped. After all, the folder only contained faxed copies, not originals.

"I'll take care of that from the bench," the judge advised.

"THANKS, FERN," Harper said. "You might want to hang around for the next couple of minutes. It should get interesting."

"All rise," the court officer announced as Tompkins entered the courtroom. People got to their feet.

Unable to resist, Harper glanced at the prosecution. Hansen was seated at the table with a worried look. The chair next to his was empty.

"Brent," Harper whispered across Owen. "Look who's a no-show."

"Excellent," Brent whispered back. "Maybe something got caught in his zipper during recess."

Owen, the pinnacle of good behavior until then, began to giggle. Harper couldn't help laughing either. Something was up, and it wasn't long before Tompkins picked up on it. "Mr. Hansen, I'm assuming your client is on his way back?"

"I'm not sure where he's gone to," the DA admitted sheepishly.

The judge signaled for the court deputy to approach the bench and spoke briefly with him. The officer then communicated something into a mobile device and ran out of the courtroom.

Several agonizing minutes passed and still no sign of Officer Daniels. The judge, visibly angered, looked at his watch, surveyed the room one last time, and then leaning in to his desk. "I think enough time has been wasted today. Ladies and gentlemen," the judge announced, looking at the jury and then the entire courtroom. "There have been developments in this matter I find impossible to ignore. Therefore, the case of the State of Minnesota versus Owen Nathaniel Grady is hereby dismissed."

The courtroom erupted in a flurry of speculation. The judge immediately quelled it with his gavel. "What's important for all of you to remember as we leave here today is a simple but fundamental aspect of our legal system. The charges that were brought against Mr. Grady have all been dropped. I would caution anyone who disputes this unexpected development to remember each and every one of us is innocent until proven otherwise. That's the law."

"I'm a police officer, you motherfuckers," Daniels bellowed from a side entrance. Seconds later, he was hauled into the courtroom by two court officers and deposited in front of the judge.

Harper could see by the demented expression on Daniel's face he was unraveling. The spectators who showed up for today's trial weren't going to leave disappointed. Justice was going to be served in a way none of them could have predicted. This was going to be memorable. One of those career moments—a standout.

"Officer Daniels, does the name Merrick Jon Reynolds mean anything to you?" the judge asked.

"This can all be explained," Daniels hissed while attempting to shake off the court officers who held him firmly by each arm. Sweat had broken out on his forehead. His struggle to free himself only added to his desperate, failed attempt to maintain a sense of dignity. The animal has been captured, Harper thought as he watched with delight.

"You know," Tompkins responded, looking out over the room. "I don't think it can. For starters"—the judge redirected his focus to Daniels—"it's almost a certainty you've lied on your county employment application." Body posture enthralled Harper. As if someone had poked a hole in him, Daniels began to deflate. His shoulders, once high and defiant, slumped visibly.

"There's also the matter of a prior out-of-state arrest. Oh wait. I bet that's something that can be explained too." Judge Tompkins, it appeared, wasn't going to make the same mistake twice. Justice had almost been circumvented on his watch, and it seemed to infuriate him. "You should be ashamed of yourself," he scolded. "Please do your best to understand that whatever charges I can possibly apply to punish you for your masquerade, I will. And before you even have a chance to entertain the idea, let it be said that no amount of money will benefit you in this court. The weight of the law is on your shoulders, and if I were you, I'd be very fearful of the consequences. Take him away."

Stunned to silence, everyone watched as Daniels was led out of the room in disgrace.

"I think that's plenty for one day," Tompkins opined, shaking his head. "Court is adjourned."

"I didn't see that one coming," Brent shared as they walked to the car.

"Caught me by surprise too," Harper agreed with a relieved sigh. "Owen, you've been pretty quiet. You okay, buddy?"

"I'm numb," Owen replied with a grin that filled his entire face. "Thank you both for everything you've done."

Harper found it impossible to hide his delight. The day's events would be the talk of the region for a long time. And the little firm that could, did. He couldn't have asked for a better way to introduce Burns and Callahan to the community. *And we're off.*

# CHAPTER Thirteen

"WHAT SOUNDS good for Sunday night?" Owen pushed the shopping cart down the aisle and stopped in front of the spaghetti sauce section. Had he been shopping only for himself, he would already be home and unpacking. In the days following the trial, he and Brent had settled into a routine of sorts, spending the majority of the time at his house. It made more sense, given it was still summer and he wasn't working. Brent had yet to identify basic housekeeping as one of the essentials. They had different strengths and weaknesses. It would take time to mesh their lives together, regardless of the signals they received from their hearts.

"It's Friday, Owen. How the hell would I know?" Brent laughed. "Menu planning is an entirely new concept for me."

"I'm trying to flush out some of your favorite foods. The list has to be longer than pizza, pizza rolls, cheeseburgers, brats, and frozen waffles." He gave Brent a playful shove and steered the cart in the direction of the meat department. "I really like to cook. Don't hold back."

"Hmm…." Brent strolled through the selection. "I love pork chops, but whenever I've tried to fry them up, they always come out dry and shitty."

"Perfect." Owen selected a package containing two bone-in center cuts. "Sunday, it's chops. If the weather stays nice, we'll toss them on the grill with a little Cajun seasoning. I have pretty good luck with these."

"Sounds awesome." Brent crossed the aisle to the chicken. "My mom makes this fantastic fried chicken. She wrote the recipe down for me, but after I read through it, I thought, fuck this. It's too hard. I'll just stick with KFC. It's not as good as—" He was interrupted by his phone. "This is Brent."

Whole cut-up chickens were on sale. Owen picked through them, selected one that he thought had good color, and placed it in the cart. *I'll see if I can get ahold of his mother's recipe and give it a shot.*

"We're at the grocery store. Why?"

Owen crossed back to the meats and rummaged through various cuts of steak. Meat prices had gone through the roof recently. If it wasn't marked down or on sale, he avoided it.

"It's Alex," Brent mouthed. Though he and Alex had once been casual lovers, Owen had no reason to think Alex was anything more now than a really good friend. "Wow. That's so cool. I'll let him know. Thanks for giving us a heads-up. Later."

Brent peered into the cart and asked, "How're we doing? Almost done?"

"Yeah. I've got the next few days covered." Was he or was he not the subject matter of the call? Owen felt the urge to ask but decided to hold back. It was only curiosity, not concern. If Brent felt like sharing, he would.

"Good. Let's get going." Brent took command of the cart and started toward checkout. "Deena Phelps invited me to wait in her office tonight while the school board meets." Glancing at his watch he confirmed, "It's almost five and the meeting is at six thirty."

Owen knew that. "Right." Brent had already planned to attend the meeting.

"Alex suggested we drive by the school on the way home." Waiting for the person in front of them to check out, Brent began unloading their cart. "It's a surprise, so don't ask."

It was the consensus among Deena, Harper, and Brent, given the results of the trial, that Owen would be reinstated without any further dispute. Deena thought Jerome Peebles would probably be a little prickly. He wasn't one to take defeat easily. But other than a manageable stink from Jerome, there would probably be no rumbling. What was so important they had to drive by the school? Brent had promised it was something good. Beating back nerves, he sat in silence as they pulled out of the supermarket lot.

Owen gasped when the school came into view. There were protesters. Not just a few, but dozens. "Brent—"

"It's not what you think, Owen. It's all good." Brent turned into the parking lot and pulled up to a bank of cars near the entrance.

"It's my students, and my students' parents," Owen exclaimed in amazement.

"Alex spotted them on his way home from the Center. You have supporters."

He was shocked. "Who do you suppose—?"

"Come on, let's get out and see what's up." Brent opened his door. "Don't be shy. These people obviously care about you, or they wouldn't have gone to this trouble."

Never comfortable being the center of attention, Owen reluctantly opened his door and got out. "I'm just blown away by this."

Before Owen knew what was happening, he and Brent were swarmed with affectionate admirers.

"We're here to make sure the board does what's right," Regina Walters exclaimed. Her daughter, Felicity, showing off a mouthful of shiny new braces, stood smiling at her side.

"You're number one in our book, Mr. Grady," Clyde Baxter, of Baxter Ford, the area's largest car dealership, announced as he shook his hand. "Eric's at camp, or he would be here too."

Eric Baxter, popular because of his gymnastic prowess, had absolutely no musical sense that Owen had been able to identify. Eric's interest in band compensated for his lack of talent. After several false starts, Owen made a home for him in the percussion section. With practice, he had learned to keep a sure and consistent rhythm on the bass drum.

"Hey, Mr. Grady. Hello, Brent," Celine Hennessy called as she sauntered to the front of the crowd carrying an "Owen Grady—Teacher of the Year!" sign rendered with hot pink glitter on a bright yellow background. Carter followed close behind with his own sign, which simply read, "Mr. Grady Rules!" Although he too had chosen glitter as his medium, Carter had used Jefferson High's official colors—red and black.

"Ms. Hennessy," Brent said, raising his eyebrow, "did you have anything to do with organizing this?"

"Maybe a little," Celine answered coyly. "I made a few calls to the girls, is all."

"Thank you, Ms. Hennessy. Thank you, everyone," Owen called out to his supporters. "This means a great deal to me."

"Is it true Jefferson might have a marching band next year?" someone asked from the back.

"Wouldn't that be great?" Owen answered. "I know it's being talked about, but that's as much as I know. I'm sure game."

Like well-wishers at a wedding, everyone filed by to pledge their support, not only for him, but for the program. When the first school board member arrived, the pack hounded her all the way up to the door. Celine and Carter stayed back.

"You don't have to answer this. I'll understand." Celine aimed her question directly at Brent. "What do you think is going to happen to Luke? I can't bring myself to call him by that other name."

"He's being held without bail pending the results of the county's investigation," Brent informed. "I'm not a part of the investigation, so I probably don't know much more than you do."

"I felt a terrible chill run through me when I read in the paper they were going to exhume the body of that young man who was murdered in Duluth a few years back. It's a terrible feeling to be close…." Celine stopped.

"I can imagine," Brent sympathized. "That's a terrible spot for anyone to be in. We can't thank you enough for coming forward when you did.

Because of his exalted political position, Senator Reynolds was able to conceal his son's attack on a gay man in San Francisco. And he sent his son to Birchwood. Again because of political connections, it was the logical choice. Owen still had trouble comprehending it.

"Oh my gosh, yes. I knew those places were a bunch of bunk. Anyway, I was happy they caught him before he had a chance to slip away. With the money his family has, who knows where he could have escaped to." Celine appeared to shudder at the thought.

Despite Celine's good intentions, Owen sensed Brent needed an out. "Oh look. There's, Deena."

"What time is it?" Brent asked.

“I’ll let you fellas go.” Celine squeezed Owen’s arm. “I’m so happy for you.”

“Thank you.” He followed Brent to the car. “Do you want to stay, and I’ll pick you up?”

“Naw. We have time to head back, if we hurry. I don’t expect this meeting will go as late as the last one, but who knows. You can kick back and relax. Maybe plan next week’s menu.”

Brent was starting to tease on a regular basis. Another sign they were growing closer. “Or create a ‘how to’ manual for cleaning a bathroom,” Owen shot back.

“Touché.” Brent chuckled.

“That was unbelievable.” Owen turned back for one last glimpse of his supporters as they drove off.

“Wasn’t that the coolest fucking thing, *ever*?” Brent reached over and gave Owen’s neck a hearty rub.

“Do I need to worry about tonight’s meeting?” Owen was suddenly stricken with a wave of anxiety. The past few months had taken a serious toll on his confidence. He was still fragile.

“Put it this way.” Brent got out of the car and opened the back hatch. “I’m thinking it would be suicidal on Peebles’ part to make much more than maybe a little stink as the scumbag tries to save face. It’s one of those situations where even the stupidest person in the room gets it.”

“You’re right.” Owen had to agree. The nightmare was rapidly coming to an end. He needed to trust time, and more significantly, Brent, to heal his wounds.

BRENT GAVE Owen a tour of the resort grounds and the new office remodel. As they approached the house, he explained, “Believe it or not this is a prefab home Ian and Harper had trucked in. Of course, there were a few adjustments made. So act surprised if they share with you it’s a prefab. They’re really proud of how it turned out and love how shocked everyone is when they find out that detail.” He walked up the steps, opened the door, and hollered, “Knock, knock. Is anyone home?”

“We’re in the kitchen,” Harper yelled back.

"You go in alone. I forgot something in the car." Brent turned back toward the door and saw Owen's frightened expression. He burst into laughter, wrapped his arms around him, and reassured, "I'm fucking kidding. Come on."

"That was really, really mean."

Brent grabbed Owen by the hand and led him down the hall and into the kitchen. Ian and Harper were huddled over the stove. Alex was nowhere in sight, and Theo, wearing an oven mitt, sat at a stool on the great room side of the kitchen, emptying muffin tins onto a plate.

"Hey, guys." Brent let go of Owen's hand. Brotherly love would take it from here.

"You must be Owen." Wiping his hands on his apron, Ian walked up and took Owen into his arms and gave him a hearty pat on the back. "I'm Ian."

"Nice to meet you."

*I should have warned him about all the touchy-feely. Hope he doesn't have personal space issues. If he does, he's fucked.*

"I'm Theo." Coming around the counter, Theo extended his hand, which, true to form, was more his style. "It's great to finally meet you, Owen."

"Thanks. You too."

"Where's snotty?" Brent asked.

"He's in the powder room pooping," Ian shared as casually as if Alex were bringing in wood from the garage.

"Hey, Owen," Harper greeted while stirring a pot. "Nice to see you again."

"You too, Harper."

"Motherfucker," Brent yelped, and the entire room froze. Alex had snuck up from behind and pinched his ass.

"Sorry, old chum. I couldn't resist." Alex, like Ian, took Owen into his arms for a hug. "Hey, Owen. I've seen you at the Center, but I don't think we've had a chance to meet. I'm Alex."

"Paybacks are a bitch," Brent promised. "Alex oversees the Men's Center. Hey. Can we help with anything?"

"Grab something to drink." Harper added a few dashes out of a bottle into the pot. "There's beer and wine in the fridge and a bottle of red wine open on the counter over by Theo. Dinner is about ten minutes away."

"Smells really good," Brent said with a sniff. "What would you like to drink?"

"I'll have what you're having," Owen replied.

"Nope. You have to tell me what you want," Brent insisted.

"White wine. I'll loosen up, starting now."

There was just enough time to give Owen a quick tour of the house. Starting at the bottom, they worked their way to the upper level. "This is my favorite," Brent shared, stepping into the large master suite. "I could live up here."

"I want this too." Owen was impressed. "I still can't believe this is a prefab. Some really good planning went into this house."

Back downstairs, the effort to get dinner on the table had moved into its final stages. The room was filled with the aroma of BBQ.

"Sit wherever you want," Harper instructed, carrying a plate of corn on the cob into the dining area.

"You guys outdid yourselves," Brent complimented, pointing to a large platter of steaming ribs in the center of the table. Scattered about were salads, a potato dish, and a basket containing what Brent hoped were cornbread muffins, one of his very favorites.

"Pass this down to Owen." Harper handed over a bottle of wine to Alex. "There. Anyone need anything before I sit down? Is there butter on the table?"

"It's right here," Ian pointed. "Sit, oh handsome husband of mine."

"I'm super starved," Alex confessed, eyeing his options.

"Harp? Will you say grace?" Ian asked, holding his hands out for someone to clasp.

"Absolutely I won't," Harper shot back, spooning a hefty amount of coleslaw onto his plate.

"Wait." Ian slapped his hand on the table. "What the hell is Alex doing with real utensils?" Looking around the table, astonished, he said, "Remember last time?"

Before anyone, including Alex, had an opportunity to shut him down, Ian waved his hand across the table. "Theo. Stand up and pull down your pants. Show Owen the scar you have on your left buttock from fondue night." And then to Owen, in a whisper everyone could hear, he tagged on, "Alex gets super mean after a few Mountain Dews, so be on top of your game at all times."

"What the hell is this?" Alex asked to the entire table in disgust. "Dinner or amateur night at the Improv?"

The banter stayed lively throughout dinner. Brent felt the love of the group as he watched each of them go out of their way to engage Owen in conversation. For his part, Owen seemed to be enjoying himself. It was already a great night.

"Who's responsible for these ribs?" Brent asked, taking his third helping without the slightest bit of shame.

"Me, me, and me," Ian stated proudly. "Not bad, huh?"

"They're the best." Wiping a glob of sauce off his chin, Brent marveled at how easily the meat fell off the bone. "Did you do these on the grill?"

"In my new smoker," Ian reported. "It was a Father's Day gift from Alex and Theo."

"Next year you're getting socks," Alex threatened with a menacing look.

"Owen, what's the status of the marching band I've been hearing about?" Harper asked.

"Oh, you know about that?" Owen seemed surprised and then looked to Brent with a smile.

"Guilty," Brent confessed with a laugh. "I think I want the marching band to happen more than Owen."

"I just found out the program is slated to begin after the first of the year. We'll have to do a lot of fund-raising for uniforms, which are very expensive. And there are other costs, like additional instruments and music. Somehow we'll make it happen," Owen reported with confidence. "There seems to be a lot of support in the community."

"And it's not just Jefferson High or Two Harbors involved?" Harper asked. "It's two other communities joining forces?"

"Right," Owen confirmed, sipping his wine. "High schools in Tilden Woods and Comstock will participate. Jefferson has the most extensive music program of the schools, so that's partially why I've been asked to take the lead on this. Hopefully we'll end up with a decent-sized band."

"You were a member of the University of Minnesota marching band," Brent added proudly. "That's a great feather in your cap."

"Well, it was an experience I'll never forget. Mostly for good reasons," Owen joked.

"That sounds great. I *love* marching bands." Ian stood and began collecting plates. "I hope you guys saved room for dessert."

"Are you serious?" Owen patted his stomach.

"Oh yeah, I should have warned you." Brent stood to help clear. "It's the full-meal deal when you're over here for dinner."

"He's such a friendly guy," Ian offered when he and Brent stepped away from the table. "I like him. A lot."

"Good. He's a little overwhelmed right now. Once he relaxes around you guys, you'll enjoy his sense of humor. It's on the dry side, like Harper's."

"Oh great," Ian joked. "Just what we need. Another smartass. Here." He handed Brent a pie from the fridge. "Take this bad boy in to the savages. I'll bring the plates."

"Is that what I think it is?" Alex sat up in his seat all smiles as Brent approached the table.

"Maybe." Ian handed out plates.

"You get over to the Lip Smacker much, Owen?" Alex asked.

"Yeah. I like that place. Good food."

"Audrey," Alex enthused, "the owner, makes the most incredible banana cream pie you'll ever taste."

Brent sat back in his chair and roared. "Dude. You should see your face when you even talk about it. It's like—"

"You and Denzel?" Alex apparently wasn't about to be the subject of another joke without putting up a fight.

"Easy," Brent cautioned, fearful Alex might take them all to the dark place. Owen hadn't had the pleasure of meeting his hard rubber playmate. There was a strong possibility it might never happen, given Owen's more than adequate performance in the same role.

"I used to wait tables at the Smacker when I was in high school," Alex moved on. "I'd be motivated for an entire shift knowing at the end of it, I could sit down to a scrumptious piece of Audrey's pie."

"Banana cream is one of my favorites too," Owen admitted.

After they managed to devour every morsel off the tin, Harper began clearing the table.

"You want us to stick around and help clean up?" Theo offered.

"Just set everything down on the counter. I'll work on it later tonight and in the morning." Harper collected empty beer and wine bottles from the table.

"Alex and I are going to head out, then. I promised to help my dad with a project tomorrow morning. It was nice to meet you, Owen." To Brent's surprise, Theo hugged the newest member of the gang. As Theo was the least outwardly affectionate of the group, this was a good sign, indeed.

"Good to meet you," Alex echoed, as he exchanged places with Theo.

"Drive safe, you two. We'll plan something soon." Brent gave Alex a playful punch.

"Like maybe a baseball game?" Ian interjected. "We have another good one coming up next week—the Browerville Hornets."

"We're there," Theo pledged, marching Alex toward the door.

"Are you sure we can't stick around and help?" Owen asked.

"It looks worse than it is," Ian said, smiling. "There are a few ribs left. You guys want to take them home?"

"Sure." Brent was never one to refuse food.

"Hang on." Ian grabbed a baggie out of a drawer and loaded the last of the platter into it. "Just nuke these babies on low, and they should come back perfectly." He handed Brent the bag and then took Owen into his arms. "Owen, you're welcome here anytime. It was a pleasure getting to know you."

"Thanks, Ian. I really enjoyed myself. You guys outdid yourselves."

"We try," Harper piped in, returning to the kitchen from who knows where. "This is for you." He handed an envelope to Owen. "Open it when you get back home."

"Don't look at me." Brent shook his head in response to a quizzical look from Owen. "I have no idea what it is."

"I'M IN shock. Do you realize this tiny piece of paper in my hand is the very beginning of something truly important?" Overwhelmed by the generosity, Owen had brought the manila envelope he received from Harper to bed with him. He held in his hand a check from Palisade Beach Resort, Inc. made out to Jefferson High School in the amount of five thousand dollars. Attached to it was a simple Post-it with the message, "One small step toward the dream," written, Brent confirmed, in Harper's writing.

Brent stepped out of the bathroom clad only in his boxers and wristwatch, his toothbrush dangling out the left side of his mouth, and mumbled, "When I see you and the kids marching down the street for the first time, I'm going to cry. It's going to be so cool."

Included in the packet with the check were two catalogs from companies who supplied band uniforms. "Harper's had this in the works for a while. I wonder how he knew the board would approve the program. I just found that out."

"He's visionary, for lack of a better word."

Owen walked to his side of the bed—he had chosen the right after a few steady weeks of sleeping together. —He watched Brent pull down his underwear and then bend over to take them off.

"Oh man." He stared at Brent's bare ass in horror. "You should see the raspberry on your butt. It's huge."

"From where Alex pinched me?" Brent stretched around to try and get a look and then moved to the full-length mirror across the room to get a better view. "Son of a bitch. I'm going to have a bruise there for a week at least."

"He got you good." Owen slid the check back into the folder. "Come here, sweetie."

"Little bitch." Brent took one final look and then padded back to the bed.

"Turn around so I can get a closer look."

Brent did as he was told, and when the bruise was within reach, Owen stretched across and gave it kiss. "There. Tomorrow it will be all gone."

"My ass it will," Brent joked, climbing into bed. "I'll have to think of a good way to get him back."

"It was so funny watching you guys together. You're right." He slipped his hand under Brent's shoulder and brought him closer. "You're like a big family. Brothers and sisters."

"Sisters?" Brent cocked an eye prompting Owen to clarify.

"I don't mean literally. As I watched how easily you all interacted with each other, I was reminded of a large family of brothers and sisters. Don't worry. You were one of the brothers," he assured with a chuckle and gave Brent's nose a tweak. "And everyone was so huggy. I love all the affection you show one another. It's wonderful. Made me feel like I was hanging with someone special. Which of course you are."

"Was anyone different than you thought they'd be?" Brent snuggled into his embrace.

"Let me think about that for a minute. Was anyone different than I thought they would be…."

Brent had done a good job with stories and other bits of information he shared over the course of their time together, so Owen could piece together their personalities without too much trouble. "I guess." He thought about each character. "Ian was the one going into the dinner I knew the least about. He's a supercool guy. I don't know how else to express the vibe I got from him. Everyone was cool, but I came away from meeting Ian wanting to spend more time with him."

"Years ago, when Ian and Harper first got together, I was so jealous of him." Brent confessed. "I had the worst crush on Harper back then. I remember being miserable when I found out Harper was dating him. Harper innocently asked me to pick up a piece of jewelry, a bracelet he wanted for Ian. It was terrible. I started to cry in the car on the way over to the mall. But you know—" Brent turned and smiled. "—Ian was so loveable, right from the start, he won me over, and I haven't given it much thought since."

"It's okay if you don't answer this, or better yet, you answer it from the heart. Either way, I'll understand." He ran his hand through Brent's hair. "I understand your past feelings for Alex, but do you still have some of those same feelings for Harper?"

"Nope. I don't at all. What I have now has morphed into respect. I love him for many different reasons, none of them romantic. It's weird to think of him that way. Makes me uncomfortable." Brent turned to make eye contact. "You don't have to worry about that at all."

Feeling guilty for even asking, Owen was quick to assure Brent it wasn't an issue. "I'm not worried. I'm not sure why I asked. It was dumb."

"Not dumb." Brent pulled his hand tighter across Owen's chest. "What do you have planned tomorrow?"

"Maybe a little gardening. Touring the resort grounds today was inspirational. Why?"

"As long as you're okay with it, I think the timing is right to move in with you." Brent turned on his side. "It seems kind of silly bouncing back and forth when we already know that neither of us wants to sleep a night apart from the other."

"I'm so cool with that, babe." Leaning forward, Owen planted a kiss on his lover's forehead. "If we move your stuff over in small batches, it won't be such a big deal."

"I was thinking of telling Harper I would continue to pay rent here, at least for the next few months."

"That seems like a waste of money." Afraid that there might be an issue, Owen asked, "Are you concerned about something not working out between us?"

When Brent didn't answer immediately, Owen pressed him. "This is important, Brent. You must have a reason for wanting to maintain your own place and not sleep there."

"I'm scared you might get tired of having me around. It's me playing it safe."

*Seriously? How is it possible you could even think that?* The words he needed came easily. "I'm basically a realist. At least, I think I am. After living on my own for so long, I'm prepared to make changes, though, at the moment, none come to mind. I'm ready to make changes is probably a better way to put it. There will be some bumps in the road, no doubt. But that's life. Do you think it was always smooth going for Harper and Ian?" Owen asked. "I bet not."

"I've never told this to anyone." Brent dragged his hand across Owen's chest. "My nickname for myself is shithead."

"Shithead?" Owen laughed. "That's… I don't know what that is."

"Shithead seemed like a good fit. I've worked hard for what I have, but I've also been lucky, and I know for a fact I haven't always been the nicest guy on the planet. I'm a shithead."

"You are not." He couldn't fathom how someone so caring could be so hard on themselves. "You can think that, but I never will."

"It's not as brutal as I'm making it out to be. But it is why I haven't been involved in many relationships. I didn't trust they would last once they discovered I was a shithead."

"Hmm. Let's table that one for tonight." Owen made a mental pledge to go out of his way to make sure he was being forthright and honest. Over time, that would do the best job of creating trust. "We'll work on that one, okay?"

"Okay." Brent punched his pillow and sat up. "Can I look at one of those catalogs?"

"Sure." Owen handed one over. "Uniforms are kind of strange, when you think about it. They're really not much different than a costume. Let me know if you see something you really like."

"This one is hot." Brent pointed to a uniform closely resembling a palace guard. "Sort of looks like a Beefeater. Maybe we could order one of these for you to wear, you know, on special occasions here at home. My treat."

"Would you like that?" Owen looked to see if Brent was joking. "I could get into it. I think."

"Really?"

"Let's go to sleep and dream about the palace guard and his prince. We can fine-tune the scenario as we go along. Here." He handed Brent the envelope. "Put this on the table, please."

"The palace guard and the prince—that's fucking funny." Giggling, Brent reached up and turned off the bedside lamp. Seconds later, the light in the bathroom flickered on and off.

"It's Artie," Owen whispered. "He's trying to tell us something."

"Really? Do you think Artie's spirit is still in the house?" Brent pushed his butt into Owen to spoon.

"I guess it's possible. Should we ask a question and see if he answers?"

"Go for it," Brent said through a big yawn.

"Hey, Artie, do you think the palace guard and the prince is a hot idea?"

After several seconds of nothing, Owen, struggling to stay awake, kissed Brent on the back of the neck and explained, "He must be working late at the engine shop…."

*Snap! Whap! Whap! Whap!*

Without warning, the shade on the bedroom window recoiled with a ferociously loud snap and then noisily flapped around on its rod several times.

"Fuck," Brent whimpered. Several agonizing seconds of silent terror passed.

Astonished and equally freaked out, Owen attempted an explanation. "I think Artie just gave the Beefeater outfit a green light."

Minutes passed before Owen felt Brent's body relax in his arms. Soon he heard him snoring peacefully. Grateful beyond words, Owen allowed the darkness to lure him to sleep. An owl, perched somewhere close by, hooted into the night. *I'm glad you approve, Artie. Sleep tight.*

# *Beneath the Palisade: Reliance*

A Beneath the Palisade Book

By Joel Skelton

Rising star attorney Harper Callahan hires Ian Burke to landscape his backyard, but it's his heart that gets the real makeover. Cautious at first, Ian is soon won over by Harper's good looks and charm, and before they know it they're on the fast track to romance.

Then a brush with death makes Harper and Ian reassess their plans for the future… and offers them an opportunity for adventure. What starts out as a casual fantasy of owning and operating a B&B on Lake Superior soon explodes into reality as Harper and Ian realize that when they rely on each other, they can accomplish great things.

http://www.dreamspinnerpress.com

*Beneath the Palisade: Courage*

A Beneath the Palisade Book

By Joel Skelton

Theodore Engdahl's sexual identity crisis clashes with his faith. Raised to believe homosexuality is a sin, Theo finds himself on the ropes with his girlfriend as well as his straight coworker, whom he can't stop staring at. Luckily, before he can panic too much, Theo discovers the support system provided by the Men's Center.

At the center, he meets Alex, and the two hit it off. Unlike Theo, Alex wears his sexuality like a favorite shirt. Alex is also easy on the eyes, but for Theo, following his example is anything but uncomplicated.

With a little help from Alex and his mentors, Ian and Harper, Theo realizes that living well requires courage. While he struggles to take the next step with Alex and to come out to his conservative parents, life beneath the palisade goes on. But when Alex and his boat disappear during a terrible storm, Theo must find the strength to hope.

JOEL SKELTON lives in the thriving Minnesota arts community commonly referred to as the Twin Cities. Writing is the latest destination in the author's tour of the arts, having previously dabbled in music (alto saxophone), and the theater.

Website: http://www.joelskelton.com

# *Dress Up*

By Joel Skelton

Broadway director Wyatt Stark's smash hit, *Dress Up*, a free-spirited, spaghetti strap of a tale set during New York's legendary fashion week, has played at full capacity for almost two years. Wyatt is taking his wildly successful musical to Hollywood with the help of his business partner, Murphy. But Wyatt is on the edge, overworked by the industry and overwrought by a terrible breakup, and so he agrees to spend the summer before production starts recuperating at Murphy's secluded beach house in Maine.

It's there that Wyatt meets and falls for Ryan Taylor—but Ryan isn't who he portrays himself to be. Distressed and desperately in love, Ryan weaves a web of lies in an effort to secure Wyatt's heart, hoping and praying that their romance can survive the deception. When Wyatt discovers the truth, will their love be there to stay, or will it be, like a worn-out fashion trend, yesterday's news?

http://www.dreamspinnerpress.com

WORKPLACE ENCOUNTERS
SERENA YATES
THE CHAUFFEUR

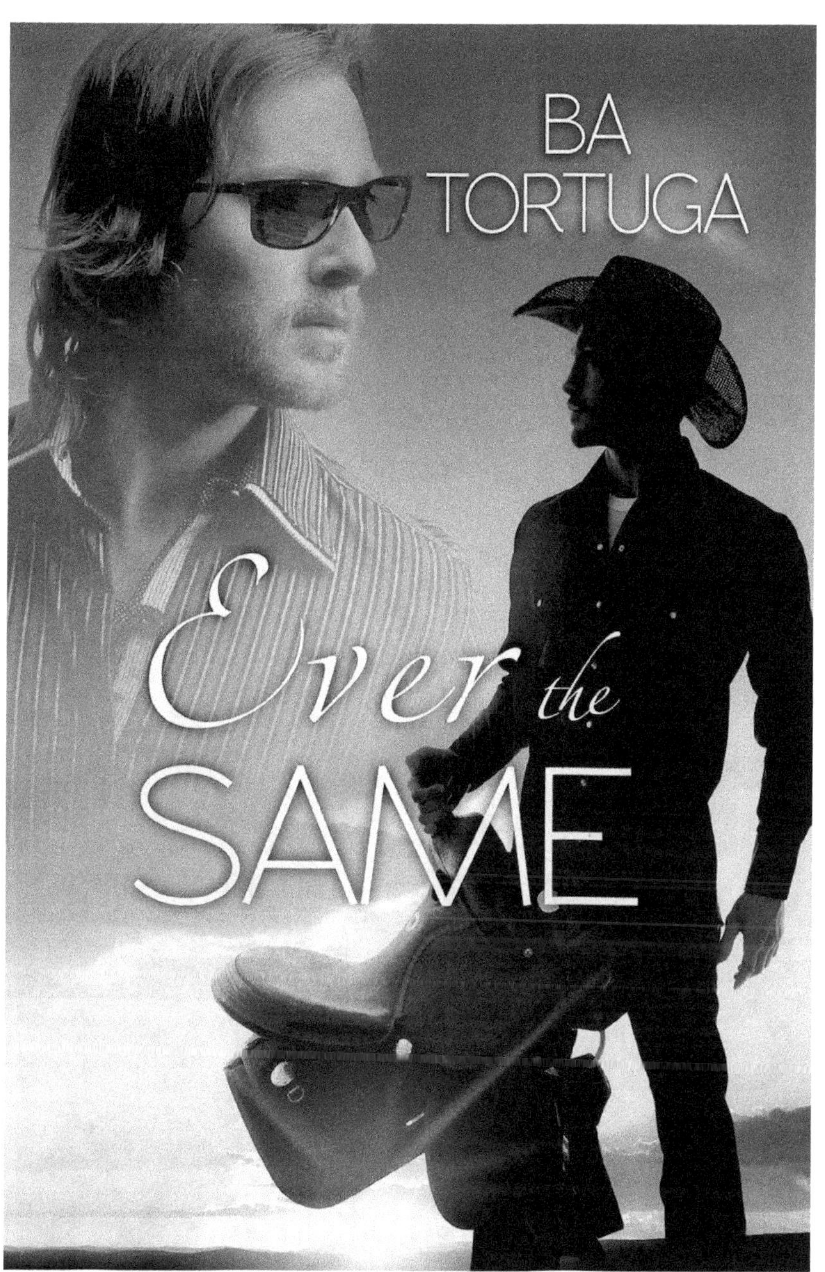
BA
TORTUGA
Ever the
SAME

www.ingramcontent.com/pod-product-compliance
Lightning Source LLC
LaVergne TN
LVHW020538100826
845148LV00010B/1517

* 9 7 8 1 6 3 2 1 6 8 4 3 6 *